Mystery of the Moonfire

Volume Two of the Joel Suzuki Series

Brian Tashima

Prism Valley Press logo by Purnima Prasad

ISBN: 0998775525
ISBN-13: 978-0998775524

To T & M

CONTENTS

ACKNOWLEDGMENTS

Mahalo to: Karen & John at Autism Empowerment, Susan at Indigo Editing, my fellow authors from NIWA and SCBWI, and all the fans and supporters of Book One.

CHAPTER 1: HOW TO TALK TO GIRLS

Joel shot a glance at the trio of zombie werewolves that were staring at him from the other end of the room.

"Hey—Suzuki," the tallest one called out.

Ugh, Joel thought as he quickly averted his eyes. *Shouldn't have looked over there.*

"What're you reading?" the tallest one asked in a tone of voice that didn't sound particularly friendly.

Joel clenched his teeth as he took a deep breath in through his nose. He sank a little lower into his couch seat and hid his face behind his brand-new tablet computer.

"Hey—I'm talking to you," the zombie werewolf continued as he took a few steps in Joel's direction. "You have Asperger's, right? Does that make you deaf or something?"

"No," Joel replied, not looking up.

"Then answer me. What are you reading? You seem pretty into it—must be interesting."

"Just—um, just some random sci-fi book."

Be confident, the words on the screen said.

"Lemme see that," the zombie werewolf grunted, reaching out and grabbing the tablet from Joel's hands.

"Hey!" Joel protested. He lunged for the tablet but seized only air as the zombie werewolf jerked it away. "C'mon, give it back."

The zombie werewolf inspected the tablet's screen for a couple of seconds before he burst into laughter. "*How to Talk to Girls*? Oh man, that's hilarious. Dudes," he chortled, turning to the other werewolves, "he's reading an article about how to talk to girls."

"What a loser," Werewolf #2 scoffed.

Joel pursed his lips as his face grew hot.

"Seriously, that's pretty sad," Tall Werewolf said, tossing the tablet onto the empty space on the couch next to Joel. "Some rock star you are."

"Yeah, I can't believe you even got a record deal in the first place," Werewolf #3 spat as he strapped on a five-string Music Man bass.

"I can't believe that we have to open for you guys," Werewolf #2 said scornfully, playing a sweeping arpeggio on his Washburn Flying V guitar. "Joel Suzuki and the Aspies."

"Um, that's Wavemakers," Joel said. "Joel Suzuki and the Wavemakers."

"Pfft, I know, I'm not stupid."

I didn't say you were stupid, I was just correcting you is what Joel wanted to say, but instead, he closed his eyes and took another deep breath.

"Anyway," Tall Werewolf said as he picked up a drumstick and twirled it between his hairy fingers, "after tonight, people will know who the real rock stars are."

"And they won't be wearing lame wolf costumes," Felicity remarked as she trotted down the stairs into the club's green room, which was really just a basement storage area dressed up with tattered couches and old carpet that smelled like vomit.

"Hey, these costumes are awesome," Tall Werewolf retorted. "I don't even know what you poseurs are supposed to be."

"Houseplants?" Werewolf #2 said, to the laughter of his bandmates.

"Just get your set over with," Felicity shot back, rolling her eyes.

Joel allowed himself a small smile as he inspected his tablet to make sure it wasn't damaged. Only he and Felicity knew that they were dressed up as Spectraland natives, with their sleeveless vests, light-green body paint, and the little fake leaves that were attached to their arms and legs. As an added touch, Felicity had dyed her grown-out blond hair a dark shade of green and woven it into multiple long braids, making it appear as if vines were sprouting out of her head.

"These guys giving you trouble?" Trevor smirked as he emerged from the stairway. He sauntered up next to Felicity and placed an arm around her shoulder.

"That's an original line," she replied, sounding annoyed but not making any attempt to escape from the physical contact.

Joel's smile faded.

"Gross. Let's go before they start making out or something," Tall Werewolf grumbled as he pushed past Felicity and Trevor toward the stairs. The rest of his pack followed.

Trevor took his arm off of Felicity and aimed a high-five gesture at Joel's face. "Joel, my man! Ready to rock this joint?"

Joel raised his hand and squinted, as if warding off the sun's rays. "Uh, yeah, I guess."

"You guess? Dude, this is so cool!" Trevor raved, completing the high five with such fervor that Joel was knocked backward in his seat.

"Settle down there, tiger," Felicity muttered as she took her white Gibson SG guitar out of its case.

"I've always wanted to play here," Trevor chuckled, looking around at the flyer-covered walls. "Man, I'm so glad I joined your band."

Joel wasn't sure if the feeling was mutual. Trevor was a talented bassist, to be sure, but his relentless energy and over-the-top mannerisms could be very tiring and intimidating at times. And then, there was the other problem...

"Better not get too comfortable," Felicity said with a half smile. "One day we might realize you're not good-looking enough to keep around."

"Babe, I'm hotter than Brad Pitt, and you know it," Trevor declared.

Joel's brow furrowed. *Is this considered flirting?*

"Brad Pitt?" Felicity scoffed. "He's, like, ancient. And don't call me babe."

"You know you love it."

Joel stood up and placed his tablet on the couch as he tried to ignore Trevor and Felicity's ongoing banter. He'd thought about firing Trevor, but after their original bassist left during the summer, the ensuing search for a replacement had been so grueling that he really dreaded the prospect of going through that process again.

"Hi, honey!" a voice called from the stairway. Alison, his mother, was there, along with his kid sister Taylor and Art, his former boss at the music store—and current drummer.

"Oh—hi, Mom," Joel said.

"Good luck with your show tonight," she said, hugging him.

"Um, okay."

"Hey, kiddo!" Trevor called to Taylor. "Ooh, sweet Zelda costume. Where's Link?"

"I dunno." Taylor shrugged.

"I'm taking her trick-or-treating," Alison explained to Joel. "We'll see you at home. Don't stay out too late, okay? You still have school tomorrow."

Joel nodded.

"He'll be fine, right?" Alison said quietly to Art.

"Of course," Art replied.

"Thanks," she said before planting a light kiss on Art's lips.

Joel cringed. It had been over three months now, but he still wasn't used to the idea of his mom and Art...*dating*.

"'Bye, everyone!" Alison waved before she headed up the stairs with Taylor in tow.

"'Bye, Joel's mom! See ya, Zelda! Watch out for Ganondorf!" Trevor called after them.

"Later," Felicity said without looking up from her guitar tuner.

The sounds of the werewolf band's opening song came crashing down the stairs.

"Hey, babe, let's go check them out!" Trevor said to Felicity.

"Hello? Still tuning here," Felicity objected, nodding at her guitar.

"Tuning is overrated," Trevor sniffed before turning his attention to Art. "Dude, I have this great idea. You should, like, make a naked drummer video, like in that Rainn Wilson movie."

Art laughed. "Because I'm old?"

Trevor's eyes widened. "Yeah! And Joel's sister can post it online, and we'll get all super famous and stuff! We're just like the band in that movie—isn't that weird? It's, like, a sign or something."

"I have to admit, it is pretty uncanny," Art said with a smile.

"Anyway," Trevor continued, turning back to Felicity, "c'mon, let's go. Those guys actually sound pretty decent."

"Fine," Felicity sighed as she laid her guitar down on the couch. "Joel, can you finish tuning this thing for me?"

"Um, sure," Joel said dispiritedly.

Art took a seat on the couch across from Joel as Trevor and Felicity darted up the stairs. "I can do it for her, bud."

"No, it's okay. I'll do it," Joel replied.

"You sure?"

"Yeah."

"Okay. Want to go check out that band after you're done?"

Joel shook his head. "No."

A piercing guitar solo wailed from the stage above.

"You all right?" Art asked.

"Yeah, I'm fine."

Art stood up and walked past Joel toward the disassembled drum kit in the corner, placing a reassuring hand on Joel's shoulder as he did so. Joel picked up Felicity's guitar and plucked each string in quick succession. Every one of them was already perfectly in tune.

"Art?"

"Yeah, bud?"

"What do you think love is?"

"Wow," Art laughed. "Are you sure you want to ask me that? This could take hours."

Joel inspected the white guitar in his hands. A barely visible three-inch hairline fracture ran down the side of the instrument's body. He assumed it was from the time Felicity threw the guitar across the stage at their summer-tour stop in San Francisco one hundred and ten days ago, the day after his birthday.

"Well," Art continued as he unpacked his cymbal bag, "love comes in many different forms. You care deeply about your family and want the best for them—that's love. You lose yourself in a great song or a great book—that's love too."

Joel blinked. The werewolf band's first song ended, to raucous applause.

"Love is attachment, and letting go," Art said, assembling his hi-hat cymbal. "Love is affection...attraction...forgiveness, even. Or, like Mr. Rogers said, to love someone is to accept that person exactly the way they are, right here and now."

"Who's Mr. Rogers?"

"A wise man who had a long-running show on TV." Art smiled.

"Okay, this is pretty confusing."

"Believe me," Art chuckled, "you're not the only one who feels that way."

Joel took a deep breath. "Do...do you love my mom?"

A sympathetic expression spread across Art's face. "I do—very much. I hope you're okay with that."

"I guess."

The werewolf band launched into a cover of a song by the multiplatinum band Biledriver. Instantly, Joel was reliving the incredible events he'd experienced a little over six months ago: near the end of a particularly bad day, Marshall Byle, the supposedly dead lead singer of Biledriver (who also happened to be Joel's idol at the time), showed up out of nowhere and invited Joel to a place called Spectraland—a tropical island on some alternate, alien world where music had magical effects. Marshall said that learning how to create musical magic in Spectraland was the key to his success on Earth, and that if Joel and Felicity (who had been invited separately) followed his teachings, then they too would unlock the secrets of hit songwriting and become rock stars, just like him.

Unfortunately, it all turned out to be an elaborate ruse designed to trick Joel and Felicity into helping Marshall retrieve a powerful artifact known as the Songshell, which he intended to use for malicious purposes back here on Earth. In the end, however, with the help of a Spectraland native named Fireflower, they were able to confront and defeat Marshall, who ended up exploding with the Songshell in a blinding shower of light.

Despite his anger at Marshall's betrayal, Joel felt a twinge of guilt about that. *He got what he deserved*, he reminded himself.

"I'll never replace your dad," Art was saying, "but just know that your mother and I make each other happy and I care a lot about you and Taylor—like I always have. In a way, it almost feels like we were all meant to be together."

"You can replace my dad, that's fine," Joel stated matter-of-factly, shifting his negative thoughts about Marshall to the other adult male in his life that he resented. "He was the one who left us. Stupid jerk." There were some other words that Joel thought about using, but swearing in general made him feel uncomfortable.

"I'm sure there were a lot of complicated reasons for what happened," Art replied in a gentle tone. "Has your mom ever talked to you about it?"

"Not really. She just said that they grew apart, or something like that."

Art stroked his goatee. "Well, regardless of what really happened, you should probably try to forgive him. I know it's hard to do—I still struggle with forgiveness myself—but if you can do it, it makes your own life that much brighter."

"Okay," Joel said, not really wanting to continue with the current topic.

Art changed the subject, apparently picking up on Joel's discomfort. "By the way, I really dig these costumes. We're plant people, like Poison Ivy, right?"

"Um, yeah, right," Joel responded. Being on the autism spectrum, he still wasn't really sure how so-called "neurotypical" people—people not on the spectrum—were able to do what Art had just done. It was like some kind of magical mind-reading ability. Although Joel knew he was smart and had come to accept that being neurologically different from most of his peers was part of what made him unique, he still had to deal with a lot of challenges, particularly when it came to reading body language, staying focused, and communicating with others. In school he had a social communication class where he practiced skills like making small talk and advocating for himself. Although he had improved over the years, it never felt natural—like it seemed to be for most of his classmates, his mom, his sister, and Art. It's like they were using different operating systems. He was a Mac and they were PCs.

"Cool. You and Felicity did a great job putting these together," Art said, wiggling one of his arm-leaves.

"Do you think she likes him?" Joel blurted out.

"What? Who?"

"You know...Felicity and Trevor."

"Oh—well, I don't know, to be honest. He's a pretty friendly guy—he seems to get along with everyone."

"Yeah," Joel said, absently strumming an open G chord on Felicity's guitar. "I mean, I can't really tell for sure, but they seem to act like the people in movies do before they end up becoming a couple...you know, like in *The Empire Strikes Back*, when Han and Leia were arguing and stuff. I dunno—does that make any sense?"

Art nodded and gave Joel an understanding smile. "I know what you mean. But hey—I wouldn't worry about it. You're an awesome guy, and the two of you seem to have a lot in common. Just relax, be yourself, and things will work out the way they were meant to."

"What are you talking about?"

"I think you know," Art replied as he carried his kick drum over to the base of the stairs.

Joel frowned. If things were working out the way they were meant to, then apparently they were meant to be kind of lousy, at least as far as his "relationship" with Felicity was concerned. When the two of them were in Spectraland, they had slowly developed what he thought was some kind of a connection as they discovered that they were not only both musicians, they were both on the autism spectrum as well. Ever since they got back, though, her attitude toward him seemed...*different*, somehow, as if some kind of switch had flipped in her head. Joel couldn't quite put a finger on it. They were still friends and bandmates, but that was the extent of it, and he had no idea what to say or do to change the situation. All the books and articles that he read about the subject—even the ones that supposedly broke things down into steps—were not very helpful. There were simply too many different directions in which a particular situation or conversation could go, and, like when he had tried to ask Suzi Lee to the prom in April, things never turned out quite the way he expected them to. If regular everyday conversation was like algebra, then this whole talking-to-girls thing was like quantum physics. Only more complicated.

"Sounds like that band is having some technical difficulties," Art noted. The music had stopped, and Joel could hear unintelligible shouting and the rumblings of general crowd discontent.

Just as Joel was walking over to Art, Trevor and Felicity came hustling down. "Oh man," Trevor laughed. "Those guys are *ticked off*. It's hilarious."

"What happened?" Art asked.

"Mister real-rock-star-drummer-singer-dude doesn't like the sound in his monitors," Felicity scoffed.

"Yeah, I guess the sound guy tried to fix it after the first song, but he still wasn't happy," Trevor added.

"Oop, here they come," Felicity warned.

Tall Zombie Werewolf stormed into the green room and flung his drumsticks at the wall. "Nope, the show is over!" he shouted.

"C'mon, man," Werewolf #2 pleaded. "Let's just finish up. This is the biggest crowd we've ever played to."

"And you want to sound terrible in front of them? I don't."

"Sounded okay to me," Trevor opined.

"The sound was fine. The songs...meh," Felicity said, making the so-so gesture.

"Shut up, Aspie Chick," Tall Werewolf snapped.

"Wow, nice comeback," Felicity replied.

Joel noted the devilish grin on her face. *Ah—sarcasm.*

"What's going on here?" a short, stocky man yelled as he came running down the stairway. It was Julio, the representative from the record label that had signed Joel's band. "Why did you guys leave the stage?"

"The sound sucks," Tall Werewolf spat. "I couldn't hear anything in my wedge."

"So?" Julio spat back. "You guys are loud enough as it is. Get back up there. The crowd is getting mad!"

As if on cue, the sound of boos started to rain down from above.

"Yeah, let's go," Werewolf #2 said, grabbing Tall Werewolf's arm and casting an anxious glance in Julio's direction.

"No way!"

"Look, we don't have time for you guys to argue." Julio waved his index finger at the various wolves. "Either get back up there, or I'm sending the other band out."

"Sure, let those poseurs go on," Tall Werewolf said, turning and heading for the door that led to the street outside. "See how *they* like not being able to hear themselves."

"Dude—you know that's the guy from the record label, right?" Werewolf #3 hissed as he and Werewolf #2 followed their bandleader out.

"Morons," Julio sighed, shaking his head. "Think they're rock stars already. So—Art, can you guys set up real quick and start your set? And maybe play a few extra songs?"

Art glanced around at each of his fellow band members. Trevor nodded. Felicity shrugged.

Joel stood there in silence as everyone turned to face him. "Oh—um, yeah, that's cool," he said after a two-second delay, realizing that they were waiting for his consent.

"Great," Julio said as he leaned into Joel. "Listen, promise me that you guys will play a longer set. If we don't fill the time and people ask for refunds, it's not gonna be pretty."

"Uh...what's not gonna be pretty?"

Julio leaned in closer. His breath smelled like beer and cigarette smoke. "I mean, we're going to lose money. And if we lose money, the booking agent will get mad. And if the booking agent gets mad, we won't get any more shows. And if we don't get any more shows, the label might just drop all of us—including me. Understand?"

"Um, sure." Joel gulped.

Julio exhaled. "Okay, get up there. I'll tell the sound guy what's happening." He vanished up the stairs.

"Wait, do we even *know* a few extra songs?" Felicity asked no one in particular.

"C'mon, we'll just improvise, babe!" Trevor smirked.

Joel felt a knot form in his stomach. *Ugh*, he thought. *I hate improvising*.

CHAPTER 2: A FAMILIAR SOUND

A few hasty minutes later, Joel found himself standing in front of a costumed crowd of over three hundred people, easily the largest audience he had played to so far. He went through his usual pre-show routine of closing his eyes and reciting a random list in his head in order to calm himself; this time, it was band names that started with the letter *Q*.

"Hey, Seattle, how's it going?" Trevor shouted into his microphone. The crowd cheered. That was one thing Joel liked about Trevor—he handled all of the onstage banter, which was something that Joel never quite got used to doing.

Q and Not U. Quarterflash. Quasi.

Art started up the beat of their first song.

Queen. Queens of the Stone Age. Queensryche.

Joel grabbed the neck of his black Les Paul guitar. His fingers formed the opening chord. He opened his eyes and inhaled, ready to sing the first line.

WEEEoooWEEEoooWEEEooo

What the—

Thrown off by the high-pitched warbling sound and the accompanying jolt of pain that shot through his head,

Joel was half a beat late with his entrance. He peered out into the crowd. Everyone was cheering and jumping up and down. A few people started up a mosh pit. Joel glanced over to his right at Felicity and saw that she was looking back at him with an alarmed expression on her face.

I wonder if...

Joel continued the song. Out of the corner of his left eye, he saw Trevor whirling around like a tornado topped off with a mop of brown hair. If Trevor had heard the warbling noise, he certainly didn't seem affected by it.

During an instrumental break, Joel turned around to face Art. Art tilted his head at his monitor and gave Joel an affirmative nod, which Joel interpreted as meaning *the monitor sounds fine.*

The song ended. The crowd clapped and hollered.

"Thanks, you guys are awesome!" Trevor said into his mic.

Felicity rushed up to Joel. "Did you hear that?"

"The sound?"

"No, the—" she started in a sarcastic tone before catching herself. "Yes, the sound. Do you think it's...?"

"I dunno," Joel said. "It can't be. Can it?"

"Joel!" Trevor called. "Start the next song, dude!"

"Oh—right."

Joel played the introductory riff to their second song.

WEEEoooWEEEoooWEEEooo

Joel whipped his head around. Felicity flashed him a grimace as she started playing the countermelody. The warbling noise was definitely the same one that he had heard when Marshall was trying to locate him over six months ago.

But Marshall is gone. Could someone else in Spectraland be trying to find us?

Joel closed his eyes as he sang the verse. Even though he was now accustomed to performing in front of people, the reoccurrence of the warbling noise had shaken his composure, and he fought to get his nerves back under control.

Relax, he told himself before going into the chorus.

The audience started to sing along. Joel opened his eyes and looked out. A small figure covered from head to toe in a large green shawl stood in the middle of the mosh pit, peering back at him.

Fireflower...?

Joel blinked. The last time he had seen Fireflower was when she had sent him and Felicity back to Earth. Although the figure in the crowd appeared quite a bit older, she had the same stern and piercing gaze as the teenage Spectraland native who had helped him defeat Marshall earlier that year.

Could that really be her?

The small figure raised her arm to ward off a slam-dancing vampire who nearly fell backward into her. As she did so, Joel caught a glimpse of something shiny, black, and guitar-like hidden within the folds of her shawl.

It's her, all right, he thought, recognizing the distinct musical instrument known in Spectraland as a wavebow. *What is she doing here?*

Fireflower reached into her shawl and pulled out a piece of parchment. Facing the stage, she unrolled it and held it up over her head with both hands.

Joel squinted at the parchment and saw nothing but lines and dots on it. He strained to get a better look. As he did so, the lines and dots lit up.

They're music notes, he realized. *It's like sheet music. It looks familiar...what song is that?*

Even as he continued playing his own song, in his head he hummed the notes that were scrawled on Fireflower's parchment.

Cool—it's the outro to that old Police song, where Sting just repeats that S.O.S. *line over and over again. Why would she be showing me that? S.O.S....S.O.S.? Oh...*

Joel and his band finished up their song. Then Felicity came up to him again. "What are you looking at?" she asked as the crowd cheered. "Is someone out there? Is it Marshall?"

"No." Joel shook his head. "It's Fireflower."

Felicity's eyes grew wide. As Art counted off the next song, she took another step closer to Joel. "Are you sure?" she shouted in his ear. "What does she want?"

Joel took a second to process the two-part question. "Yes, I'm sure," he replied, turning to face Felicity while he strummed the chords to the third song, "and—and I think she needs help."

Turning his head back to begin singing, Joel accidentally smacked his mouth against the microphone. A squeal of feedback burst through the P.A. system. The mosh pit swirled faster as the tempo of the song increased.

Wincing, Joel licked his lip and tasted blood. He scanned the crowd for Fireflower. She was nowhere to be seen within the vortex of large, costumed bodies.

Oh no, I hope she's all right.

A minute and a half later, the song reached the guitar solo. Joel got through the first two measures of it before he saw a green beach ball being passed around by the raised arms of the audience.

Wait, that's not a ball, that's—

"That's her!" he mouthed to Felicity while still playing the solo.

"What?"

Joel nodded in the direction of the green shape. Fireflower had unfolded from the fetal position and was now rolling atop the crowd like a convenience store hot dog.

"What should we do?" Felicity yelled.

Joel gave her a sheepish shrug. He had seen bootleg videos of bands halting their shows midsong when the crowd got out of hand, but he didn't feel bold enough to try something like that at the moment. He finished up the song and stepped to the microphone. As he did so, he saw Fireflower, who had been passed all the way to the other end of the room, disappear within the folds of the throng.

"Um, thanks, you guys," he said, feeling Trevor's and Felicity's eyes on him. "Hey, uh, if you could try to take it a little easy out there, it's an all-ages show and, um, we have kids who—"

Trevor cut him off with the bass line intro to the next song.

That's it, he's fired, Joel groused to himself.

Two more songs went by as Joel searched for Fireflower. Finally, he spotted a tiny figure, covered in green, standing all the way over by the front door of the venue.

Ah, there she is.

At that moment, a tall zombie werewolf also entered into Joel's field of vision, towering over the little green figure. The werewolf was carrying a small-scale stringed instrument that strongly resembled a...

Oh geez, he has her wavebow!

Joel continued playing as he observed Fireflower and Tall Werewolf engaging in what seemed to be, based on their hand gestures, some sort of an argument.

I need to help her. But I can't tell Art and Trevor about her—can I?

The argument seemed to be getting worse. Tall Werewolf offered the wavebow to Fireflower, only to yank it away a second later.

Worrying is a waste of time, Joel reminded himself, over and over, until finally, his growing panic was replaced by an idea that suddenly formed in his head.

He turned to Trevor after their sixth song was over. "We—um, me and Felicity, I mean—we need to take a little break."

"What? Now?"

"Yeah, you know...sensory overload, and stuff. Super-big crowd—not used to it. Can you do a bass solo until we come back?"

Trevor paused, his face forming an expression that Joel couldn't decipher. "Okay, yeah, I guess."

"Cool," Joel said, taking his guitar off. He laid the instrument on the drum riser and turned to face Art. "Felicity and I need a short break. Trevor is gonna play a bass solo. Can you play with him?"

Art gave Joel a confused look as murmurs started to rise up from the audience. "Well—sure, but are you all right? Your lip—"

"I'm fine," Joel replied. Giving Felicity an urgent *let's go* nod, he hopped off the stage and out of the crowd's view. As he descended the stairs leading to the green room, he felt a hand on his shoulder. He stopped and turned around.

"What are you doing?" Felicity asked, pulling her hand away. "Do you know where she is?"

"Yeah, she's by the front door," Joel answered as the low drone of Trevor's bass echoed through the club. "The guy from the other band has her wavebow."

"Oh geez," Felicity said with an eye roll.

"Hey, that was my reaction too! When I saw that, the first thing I thought was—"

"Just go!" Felicity shouted, nearly pushing Joel down the rest of the stairs.

They rushed out the back door and around the perimeter of the club. Turning the corner, Joel saw that Fireflower and Tall Werewolf had taken their argument outside. As Joel approached them, his stomach suddenly turned cold at the thought of a confrontation.

Seriously? he chastised himself. *C'mon, Suzuki, you took on a bunch of vagabond natives, tons of crazy hybrid monsters, and even Marshall Byle himself. You can handle one lousy Earth bully, right?*

During Joel's internal pep talk, Felicity had stepped around him and walked up to Tall Werewolf. "All right, what's going on here?" she snapped.

"Oh, hey poseurs," Tall Werewolf said with a casual turn of his head. In his hairy left hand, he held a shiny black wavebow by its neck. "Told you the sound onstage sucks, huh?"

"That belongs to our friend." Felicity ignored Tall Werewolf's statement as she pointed to the wavebow. "So you better give it back to her."

"Um, yeah," Joel added, not wanting to seem like he was letting Felicity do all of the work.

"You mean this mandolin thing?" Tall Werewolf snorted, holding up the instrument. "Yeah, right. Like I told your little groupie here, I found it on the floor during your show. It's mine now."

"Well, she dropped it," Joel explained. "Probably while she was crowd surfing."

"Then that's her fault," Tall Werewolf said. "Not sure what a miniature houseplant was doing in the mosh pit to begin with."

"I don't think she had a choice," Joel argued.

"Please," Fireflower implored Tall Werewolf as a light rain started to fall, "you have no idea how important this is." Her mouth movements didn't match her words; a result, Joel knew, of the sound-wave manipulation effect used to translate English into the Spectraland language and vice versa.

"I have no idea how you talk like that," Tall Werewolf said to Fireflower, shaking his head. "Pretty cool trick. It's like one of those old kung fu movies."

Marshall said the same thing, Joel thought. *Guess all jerks think alike.*

Fireflower looked at Joel. "I only have a few minutes before the Rift closes," she said in a hushed tone.

Joel grimaced. *Why'd she have to tell me that? I hate time pressure.*

The growling sound of a heavily effected bass guitar, along with scattered catcalls, filtered out through the club's half-open front door. *Oh man, and we have to finish the show too,* Joel fretted, his internal panic meter rising once again. "Give it back now," he blurted out. "Or we're gonna—I mean, I'll, uh—"

"You're gonna what?" Tall Werewolf chortled.

"I—um, I—"

"Thought so." Tall Werewolf sniffed. "All right, I'm outta here." He brusquely pushed his way between Joel and Felicity, nearly knocking Joel over in the process.

"Hey!" Joel shouted as he grabbed the werewolf's arm in an attempt to regain his balance. The rainfall suddenly turned heavy, sending most of the people on the street scrambling for cover.

"Don't touch me, you little punk," Tall Werewolf snapped as he wrenched one arm away from Joel and raised the other in a threatening manner.

Joel flinched and threw his hands up in front of his face. Through his fingers, he saw Felicity grab the hairy, raised arm and twist it behind the werewolf's back.

"Ow! What the—"

"Yeah, don't even think about it," Felicity said. "Now c'mon, give us the wavebow."

"The what?"

"The—the mandolin." Felicity shook her head. "Whatever."

Tall Werewolf squirmed in an effort to break loose, still clutching the wavebow in his free hand. "No way! You stupid poseurs owe us for messing with our sound. The promoter wouldn't even pay us 'cause—"

Joel felt a small hand grab his arm. He turned and saw Fireflower with her eyes closed, her fingers wrapped around his wrist. A sharp chill ran through his body. At that moment, the strings on the wavebow lit up with a dark-red glow. A single, short note sounded (Joel recognized the pitch as a low D, typical of a stunning wavecast) and Tall Werewolf suddenly slumped to the ground. The wavebow clattered out of his grasp.

"Nice," Felicity chuckled, letting go of Tall Werewolf's now-limp arm.

"Whoa—that was cool," Joel exclaimed. He looked at his wrist. "But how—what did you do?"

"I had to borrow some of your energy," Fireflower replied with urgency in her voice as she picked up her instrument. "But never mind that right now. I need your help—both of you. You must come back with me to Spectraland."

"What? Why—what's going on?" Joel asked, echoing Fireflower's urgent tone.

"It is complicated to explain, but I promise, it will not take very long."

"Oh—good, 'cause, like, we still have to finish this show, and my mom wants me home early tonight, and—"

"Can you send us back to this same point in time?" Felicity interrupted, wiping rain out of her eyes.

"I believe so. At the most, we may be gone for ten of your minutes or so."

Ten minutes? Joel thought uneasily. *Will people stick around for ten more minutes of Trevor's bass solo? I really want to help, but we promised Julio...*

"Will you come? Please?" Fireflower said with a beseeching expression on her face.

Joel glanced at Felicity. His mind flashed back to the end of their last adventure in Spectraland, when it seemed that perhaps, just maybe, she was starting to—what was the expression? Oh yeah—"have feelings" for him. Could going back to Spectraland be his chance to rekindle whatever feelings those might have been? There was only one way to find out...

"Okay, I'm in," he said, a bit more decisively than he had intended.

Felicity returned Joel's glance. "Yeah—yeah, sure, me too."

"Wonderful—thank you." Fireflower smiled with relief as she began to strum her instrument.

"Wait," Felicity interrupted, looking around, "we shouldn't do this out here, right? I mean, if people see us vanishing into thin air, there's gonna be a few questions when we get back."

"Yeah," Joel agreed. "Let's, uh, let's go back to the green room."

"The Rift will close soon—we need to hurry," Fireflower said.

"Just like old times." Felicity smirked as she knelt down and hoisted one of Tall Werewolf's arms over her shoulders. "Joel, give me a hand with this, will you?"

"Oh—right," Joel said, lifting up Tall Werewolf's other arm.

As they carried Tall Werewolf's unconscious form around the corner, a person in an astronaut suit walked by and gave them a quizzical look. "Hey, is he all right?"

"Too much candy," Felicity replied. Fireflower opened the club's back door, and they hustled inside.

"Okay, we should be good now," Joel said, setting Tall Werewolf down on the couch.

Fireflower managed to play only a single chord before Julio abruptly appeared in the stairwell.

"There you are!" the record label rep exclaimed. "When I said to play a few extra songs, I didn't mean a boring bass solo that—" He paused, his gaze bouncing between Fireflower and the unconscious werewolf on the carpet. "Okay, what's going on here? Who is this? And what happened to that guy?"

"Uh, well, we—" Joel stammered.

"Yeah, we were just trying to take a short break when wolf-boy here showed up and started pushing Joel's poor kid sister around," Felicity broke in, putting an arm around Fireflower. "You remember Taylor, right? We made her this matching costume. Cute, huh?"

"What? Why—" Julio sputtered.

"So when Joel tried to defend her, Wolfie smacked him in the mouth," Felicity continued as she brushed Joel's lip with her index finger.

Joel jerked his head back. "Hey—what are you—"

"See? Poor guy's bleeding," Felicity held her finger up in front of Julio's face. "So, anyway, Joel fought back and accidentally knocked the dude out. He's got some serious karate skills."

"I do?"

"I think they both need some medical attention now," Felicity said quickly. "Does this place have, like, a first aid kit or something?"

"He—you—ugh, all right." Julio sighed, running his hand through his hair. "I think there's one in the office—I'll look for it. You guys just get back on stage!"

"We will!" Felicity chirped, patting Julio on the back as he turned and headed up the stairs.

"That was awesome." Joel smiled.

"Yeah, yeah," Felicity said, wiping her finger on Joel's vest. "I'm winning, you know."

"Hey!" Joel protested, gaping at the bloodstain on his costume. "Will this wash out? You didn't have to—wait, winning? Winning what?"

"I'll tell you later. I thought we had to hurry?"

Fireflower had already resumed playing. With his vision starting to blur and a queasy feeling hitting the pit of his stomach, Joel knew that they were on their way back to Spectraland. Just then, however, he remembered something.

"Wait! My tablet—I forgot to shut it down," he said, battling the increasing dizziness. *I don't want anyone to see what I was reading...*

"What?" Felicity shouted through the growing din in Joel's head.

"My tablet," he repeated as he started to head for the couch.

"No!" Fireflower cried. "Joel, do not—"

Just as Joel reached out for the tablet, tiny colored streams of light danced before his eyes and everything went dark.

CHAPTER 3: REGENERATION

Joel opened his eyes. Greeted by blinding sunlight, he quickly squeezed them shut again. A sharp ache pulsed in his head. Realizing that he was lying on a hard surface, he tried to sit up, but a wave of vertigo overcame him, and he slumped back down on the ground.

"Joel! Are you all right?" Fireflower said from seemingly very far away.

Joel opened his eyes once more, slowly this time, allowing his eyesight to adjust to the brightness of his surroundings. Familiar wisps of Aura—the visible field of electrical particles that flowed through Spectraland's air—drifted past his face. "Yeah, I think so," he said. Fireflower appeared above him as the blurriness in his vision cleared up.

"Oh, gross," Felicity's voice sounded from off to the side. "Look—he's bleeding."

"Did—did my lip get worse?" Joel asked.

"Uh...it's not your lip," Felicity said.

"What? What do you mean?" Joel asked, moving his right hand to his mouth.

"No, do not—" Fireflower started to say.

Globs of thick, warm liquid fell on Joel's face. He wondered what it was for a moment before he realized that it was blood, dripping out from his fingers—or, more accurately, the stumps of his fingers. He screamed in horror.

"Stay calm," Fireflower said. She played a short progression of lush, complex chords on her wavebow, and Joel's fingers began to give off a bright golden glow. A couple of seconds later, the bleeding stopped. His headache also went away.

"Wow—um, thanks," he said with a sigh of relief. He sat up and inspected his hand. What remained of his fingers had healed over neatly, but they were still merely stumps, cut off well below the middle knuckle. "But...can you, like, bring my fingers back?"

"I am afraid not," Fireflower replied.

Joel's heart dropped into his stomach. "Wait—what?"

"I can heal bites, burns, and broken bones, but I am unable to regenerate whole body parts, unfortunately."

"Regenerate? But—can't we just reattach them or something? What happened to them?"

"I believe they were cut off during the transfer, when you were reaching for your device. They are lost now."

"Lost?" Joel exclaimed, feeling frantic. "But then—I—how—"

"You will be fine," Fireflower reassured him with a faint smile. "While I cannot regrow body parts, I know someone who can."

"Guess it's your lucky day," Felicity said drily.

"You know someone? Who?" Joel asked, trying to contain his hysteria as he got to his feet.

"A fellow Wavemaker, who we will be seeing soon. Do not worry."

Worrying is a waste of time, Joel reminded himself once more. "Fellow Wavemaker—you mean, there are more of you now?"

"Yes. I pledged to rebuild our order, and I have done so."

"Oh," Joel said as he looked around. Recognizing the patches of grass and dirt scattered around him, he realized that they were on top of the islet called Crownrock, the site of the gateway between Earth and Spectraland known as the Rift. The islet itself was surrounded by a sphere of golden Aura energy, through which he could see the nearby shore, the surrounding ocean, and a bright, late-afternoon sky.

"Dude, I dunno why you were going for your tablet in the first place," Felicity said. "It shuts itself down after a while."

"I know. I hate it when it does that, so I disabled that option."

"Whatever," she sighed.

"I apologize for the abruptness of our reunion," Fireflower said. "It is very good to see you both again."

"Right, so what did you need us to do?" Felicity asked.

"I will explain after we arrive at the Wavemaker Temple," Fireflower answered. "We should get Joel's fingers taken care of first. There might be a limit as to how much time we have to get them regrown."

Joel felt his stress level rise back up. "What? A limit? How long?"

"It depends, but I would say about an hour or so," Fireflower replied as she began to play a soft tune on her instrument.

"Um, but...doesn't it take way longer than that to get from here to the temple on slimeback?" Joel asked, referencing the camel-frog creatures that Spectraland's people used as mounts.

"We will not be traveling by slimeback," Fireflower replied.

"Then how are we gonna get there?" Felicity asked.

As if in response, the tune that Fireflower was playing crescendoed into a soaring, dramatic melody that made Joel's skin prickle. A stream of dark-green Aura flowed out from her instrument and wrapped itself around him, covering his entire body in a sheath of brilliant, pulsating light. After a second, he noticed that both Felicity and Fireflower were also encased in a similar fashion.

Fireflower smiled. "I believe you called this...flying."

Joel gasped as his feet abruptly left the ground. After rising several feet in the air, his body assumed a prone position as he flailed his arms and legs.

"Cool!" Felicity exclaimed, also hovering in place. "You figured out how to do this!"

"I was inspired by our experience," Fireflower said. "It took me awhile, but I have finally perfected the ability. Thank you, Joel, for introducing us to this wonderful phenomenon."

"Um, you're welcome," Joel mumbled, still trying to get used to his lack of footing. During his previous visit to Spectraland, he had learned that—for some reason probably related to gravity, air pressure, and the Aura—nothing on the island could fly. There were no birds, no winged insects, no dragons, and no magic carpets. At a critical juncture, however, Joel had been able to impart his knowledge about the laws of aerodynamics (one of his special interests from a few years ago) to a powerful entity that then gave him, Felicity, and Fireflower the temporary ability to soar through the air like superheroes.

"Are you all right?" Fireflower asked.

"Uh—yeah, sure," Joel replied. Apparently, despite his previous experience, six months of being groundbound back on Earth had restored his fear of heights.

"Just relax. I am taking care of it," Fireflower said. "Trust me."

Joel took a deep breath and closed his eyes. He gasped again as he felt his body suddenly surge forward through the golden Aura sphere and up into the air.

"Woo!" Felicity shouted.

Quicksand. Quietdrive. Quiet Riot. Hmm, there aren't that many bands with names that start with the letter Q.

Feeling a bit calmer (despite the short list of band names), Joel opened his eyes. He saw that he and his companions were about a hundred feet off the ground now and traveling at the speed of the average bird, or perhaps a little faster. He recognized the dense expanse of trees below him known as the Jungle of Darkness, as well as the mountain range called Dragonspine that stretched from one end of the island to the other. Within a matter of minutes—just as he was starting to enjoy the ride—they began to descend, and an incredible sight came into view.

"Whoa," Joel whispered to himself.

They were approaching the clearing where the Wavemaker Temple stood, but the impressive structure that he saw bore only a passing resemblance to the broken-down wreckage that he had visited before. The cloud of dark-purple Aura that had hung over the area was gone, replaced by a shimmering, golden layer of energy—similar to the one surrounding Crownrock—that covered the entire clearing like a dome.

The temple itself had been repaired and enlarged. The original base resembled a seed from which multiple stems had sprouted, as a number of thick, spiraling vines supporting lily pad-like platforms and small spherical tree houses reached up toward the sky. The only features of the temple that appeared unchanged were the four stone statues of Spectraland denizens, each over twenty feet tall, that surrounded the structure.

Making a quick, steep descent, they pierced the golden Aura veil and landed near the base of the temple's front steps. A pair of natives—one tall, one short—came down to greet them.

"Fireflower—welcome back," the taller native said, his voice deep and resonant. Joel estimated the native's height at nearly five foot eleven—uncommon for adult Spectraland inhabitants, who usually stood between four and five and a half feet. The native wore a black sleeveless Spectraland vest over his athletic frame, and his light gray leggings were held up by something that resembled a primitive utility belt. A small, diamond-shaped yellow pendant hung from a brown band around his neck, and a thin chinstrap beard framed his rugged facial features.

"Is everything all right?" the shorter one, a female, asked in a high, soft voice. Joel did a double take; aside from her light-green skin and standard beige-toned Spectraland tunic, this particular native bore an uncanny resemblance to Suzi Lee, his former crush—right down to her deep brown eyes and silky black tresses. "We became concerned when we did not hear from you."

"Yes, everything is fine," Fireflower responded. "Ran into a few delays and had to use up more energy than I would have liked. That other world is...interesting, to say the least. What about here? Any news on Redstem?"

"Still nothing, I am afraid," the tall male said, shaking his head.

"Hmm." Fireflower frowned. "What about the ceremony—how are the preparations coming?"

"Quite well, for the most part. Windblade is out fetching the last of the ingredients that Yellowpetal requested."

"Good." Fireflower nodded.

"So, are these...the ones?" the Suzi Lee look-alike asked with a trace of awe in her voice, her eyes flitting in Joel and Felicity's general direction.

"They are," Fireflower said, stepping aside. "Thornleaf and Auravine, meet Joel and Felicity."

"Forgive me for not recognizing you," the tall male named Thornleaf said with a nod and a hint of a smirk. "You seem more like common villagers than otherworldly saviors."

"Thornleaf, show some respect," Fireflower scolded.

"I was merely referring to their physical appearances," Thornleaf said, unruffled.

Joel looked down at himself. "Oh—um, these are Halloween costumes," he explained. "Halloween is this annual event where people dress up and—"

"So, who are you, the butler?" Felicity sneered as she looked Thornleaf up and down.

"I am a Wavemaker," Thornleaf replied, drawing himself up to his full height. "Fireflower's second-in-command."

Joel glanced at Thornleaf. *Oh, cool—maybe he's the one who can regrow my fingers.*

Fireflower gestured in the direction of the Suzi Lee look-alike. "Auravine here is a Wavemaker as well. A very talented one, I might add."

"I am so happy to finally meet you," Auravine said as she looked at the ground in front of Joel. "Fireflower has told us many wonderful things."

"Um, okay," Joel replied, suddenly feeling nervous for some reason.

"The story about how you retrieved the Songshell and defeated Chief Byle is simply amazing," Auravine continued.

Ugh—"Chief Byle," Joel grumbled silently. *I hate how he called himself that. And got everyone else to call him that too. What a lying phony.*

"I hope that one day I will get a chance to do something just as important and heroic as—oh no, your fingers!" Auravine exclaimed.

"What?" Joel said, momentarily alarmed.

Auravine grabbed Joel's hand and inspected it. "I will take care of this for you. Come, let us head inside—with your permission, Fireflower."

"Of course." Fireflower smiled, placing a hand on Joel's shoulder. "Joel, this is who I was telling you about. She will be able to help you."

Joel's relief was displaced by lightheaded anxiety as Auravine took him by the hand. "Oh—uh, cool," he mumbled. Auravine's palm felt soft and warm in his as she led him up the wooden stairway to the temple's main entrance.

"Wow, just a few minutes ago you were all, like, 'oh no, my fingers!'" Felicity said with mock alarm as she followed them up the stairs along with Thornleaf and Fireflower. "Now it's 'yeah, okay, whatever.'"

Thornleaf chuckled. "So, the tales about your spirited demeanor are true."

"Hey, man, I just tell it like it is," Felicity said.

Once they reached the top, Joel observed that the entryway, unobstructed during their last visit, was now sealed by an imposing set of double doors. Etched into the doors was a symbol similar to the one he remembered from the entrance to Stonelight Tunnel—a shortcut through the Jungle of Darkness that only a select few had access to.

"Hope you didn't lock yourselves out," Felicity said to Thornleaf.

Thornleaf merely smiled and pressed his right forearm to the doors, which, after a faint *whoomp* sound, swung slowly inward.

Once inside, Joel took a few seconds to stand and gawk. Within the expanse of the high-ceilinged hall, thick Aura waves of all colors wove their way around like giant floating serpents. Detailed carvings in the pillars that lined the sides of the room gave off a warm silver glow that slowly faded in and out, while a steady hum that sounded like monks chanting a low B note resonated throughout the air. At the far end of the room stood a dais, in front of which hung a sparkling curtain of golden Aura. On the dais rested a circular stone basin from which all of the Aura waves appeared to originate.

"Different from what you recall, I assume." Fireflower smiled.

"Yeah, just a little," Felicity said, looking around.

"This is what a proper Wavemaker Temple should look like," Thornleaf announced with pride in his voice. "An extraordinary appearance to match our extraordinary talents."

"Modest, aren't we?" Felicity remarked.

"I merely...what was your expression? Tell it like it is," Thornleaf said with a grin.

"This is the main hall," Fireflower said. "Here, we pool our energies and meditate, to gain additional connection with the Aura."

That's exactly what Marshall said the last time we were here, Joel thought. *Marshall...ugh. Need to stop thinking about that jerk.*

Auravine released Joel's hand. "I will prepare the restorative and rejoin you shortly," she said before disappearing through a doorway to the right of the dais.

"So, are we gonna get the grand tour or what?" Felicity asked.

"To explore the entire temple would take some time." Thornleaf smiled. "There are quite a number of amazing sights."

"Not like we've got anything better to do at the moment," Felicity muttered, shooting a side-eyed glance at Joel's right hand.

"While we wait for Auravine," Fireflower said, "you could meet some old friends."

"Old friends? Do you mean Sammy? And Destiny?" Joel asked, recalling the two animals—Sammy, a squirrel-like creature known as a silvertail, and Destiny, his faithful slimeback—who had played such a big role in their quest to find the Songshell.

"The slimebacks are currently asleep in the stable," Thornleaf said. "They usually sleep throughout the day, since they are older and we do not require their services much anymore." He paused and turned in the direction of an open doorway to the left of the dais. "But your other former companion is through here."

Joel, Felicity, and Fireflower followed Thornleaf through a short enclosed passage that led to a large open courtyard area resembling an exotic arboretum. Colorful trees and bushes of all shapes and sizes surrounded a lush expanse of soft golden grass, and at the center of the area stood a fountain whose spouts of water appeared to defy gravity as they looped and twirled around each other in midair. A young child sat next to the fountain's base, playing with a small animal that looked like a cross between a squirrel and a monkey.

"Sammy!" Joel shouted.

The animal looked up, blinked, and then ran across the grass toward Joel and the others. Joel knelt down and reached out, but Sammy bypassed Joel's outstretched arms and leaped directly onto his shoulders. Joel laughed as his little friend ran in circles around his neck.

"It doesn't get any cheesier than that," Felicity groaned.

"How has he been?" Joel asked as Sammy settled on his left shoulder.

"He has been doing well," Fireflower replied. "In fact, he—"

The child next to the fountain began to wail in a shrill pitch that sounded like guitar feedback. The surrounding vegetation shifted colors several times while the fountain sprayed water around the courtyard like an out-of-control lawn sprinkler. Joel ducked and covered his ears with his hands.

"Can someone turn that thing off?" Felicity shrieked, also covering her ears.

At that moment, an elderly female came rushing into the courtyard from the opposite end. She shouted, "Starpollen, no!", dashed toward the child, grabbed him, and then held him tightly in an awkward embrace. After a few seconds of struggling, he appeared to settle down;

the wailing stopped, and the colors and fountain returned to their original states.

"That child is Starpollen," Fireflower said to Joel and Felicity, wiping fountain water from her brow. "He is Auravine's younger brother."

"Is he a Wavemaker too?" Joel asked as he stood up. Sammy hopped to the ground and shook himself off.

"Not exactly," Thornleaf sighed. "He and Auravine were orphans—when we took her in, he came along. He can barely speak and shows no interest in wavebow training, but he does exhibit some unique and unusual abilities, as you just witnessed."

The elderly native walked up, holding Starpollen's hand and wearing a distraught look on her face. "Please forgive me. I should not have left him alone like that."

"It is fine, Mother," Fireflower said. Then, turning to Joel and Felicity, she added, "You remember my mother, Yellowpetal. She is helping us take care of things here."

"Um, hello," Joel said. Like Fireflower, Yellowpetal looked quite a bit older than he remembered.

"Hey," Felicity said.

Yellowpetal's eyes widened with recognition. "Oh—offworlders! Welcome back! I am sorry; I thought that you were some other villagers."

"We're wearing Halloween costumes," Joel explained.

"How...nice," Yellowpetal replied, a confused expression on her face. "At any rate, I am glad that you are able to join us for tonight's ceremony."

"Okay, yeah, that's the second time someone's said something about a ceremony," Felicity said, turning to Fireflower. "Is that why you needed us to come back?"

"Partially," Fireflower replied. "You see, I—"

"Is everything all right?" Auravine asked as she entered the courtyard with a white wavebow hanging at her waist. "Did something happen to Starpollen?"

"He was upset that the silvertail ran away from him," Thornleaf replied. "Everything is under control now."

At the mention of the word *silvertail,* Starpollen began to make a low whining noise. Yellowpetal knelt down next to him as the Aura in the air started to buzz.

"Oh boy," Felicity muttered, covering her ears again.

Joel looked down at Sammy. "Sammy, go play with Starpollen."

Sammy looked up at Joel.

"It's okay," Joel nodded, kneeling and motioning toward Starpollen. "Go on."

Sammy cocked his head and looked at Joel for another second before he turned and scampered up Starpollen's left leg. The young boy—whom Joel thought resembled one of his sister's fifth-grade classmates—stopped whining and began laughing instead. The buzzing sound ceased.

"That was close," Felicity exhaled.

"Thank you. You are very kind," Auravine said to Joel with a small smile.

"Um, okay."

"I can tell that you are very compassionate and understanding."

Joel merely stood up and looked at the ground, unsure of how to respond.

"Now," Auravine said, pulling a small white jar from her tunic, "your hand, please."

"For what?" Joel said, suddenly feeling flustered.

"Your fingers."

"Oh, right."

Joel held out his right hand.

"Forgive me—I meant your other hand," Auravine said.

"What? Why?"

"Trust me." Auravine smiled.

Joel reached out with his undamaged left hand. Auravine seized it and dunked his fingers into the jar, which contained a cold, pudding-like substance. Joel jerked his hand away, splattering some of the substance onto Auravine's tunic.

"Oops, sorry," Joel mumbled.

"My fault," Auravine said, wiping herself off. "I should have warned you. Since you are not from this world, some of your own essence is required to regrow your fingers."

"Essence?"

"Skin, hair—something like that," Fireflower explained. "In this case, a sampling from your intact fingers. Correct, Auravine?"

"Yes, that is correct," Auravine replied. "Now please, your other hand."

Joel slowly extended his right hand, giving Auravine a wary glance. She carefully poured the remainder of the jar's contents onto the stumps of Joel's fingers. As the substance dripped down his hand and fell to the ground, she began to play an intricate minor-key melody on her wavebow. "You may feel some slight discomfort," she warned.

Joel gulped and set his jaw. Over the course of his life, he had learned that whenever someone said something like that, they usually meant "you will feel a lot of intense pain." *Why can't people just say what they mean?* He complained silently as Auravine's instrument took on a bright yellow glow. After another two seconds, the glow turned into a crackling wave of golden light that shot out and struck Joel's right hand. Joel winced as his fingers became very hot, although, true to Auravine's word, the feeling was more uncomfortable than painful.

The gold lightwave turned a brilliant, pure white, then red, then purple before shifting back to gold and repeating the cycle once more. Auravine's eyes were screwed tightly shut, and her body was shaking; Joel wondered if she was actually in more discomfort than he was. Just as he was about to suggest that they take a break, he felt a stretching sensation in his finger-stumps, as if someone were pulling on them. His eyes grew wide with amazement as all of his missing fingers then slowly regenerated. One knuckle...two knuckles...the music grew louder...a fingernail...

Finally, the tips of his fingers appeared and the music abruptly stopped. Auravine fell to one knee, gasping.

"Whoa—are you okay?" Joel asked, looking from his freshly regrown fingers to Auravine and then back again.

"Yes," Auravine exhaled as Fireflower helped her up. "That incantation just requires a lot of energy."

"Healing has been Auravine's special interest ever since she started training with us," Fireflower said with a hint of pride. "She has an extraordinary gift, one that has not been seen for generations."

"How convenient for you," Felicity mumbled, looking at Joel out of the corner of her eye. Thornleaf stood next to her, a nonchalant expression on his face, while Yellowpetal followed Starpollen and Sammy—who had both apparently ignored the proceedings—behind a small group of trees.

"Your fingers—how are they?" Auravine inquired, still catching her breath.

Joel wiggled his new digits. "They're—they're great. Thanks."

"Okay, so that's settled." Felicity said. "*Now* can someone tell us the big reason why we needed to come back here?"

CHAPTER 4: LEARN TO FLY

Joel examined his fingers once more, marveling at how absolutely normal they looked and felt. No scar lines. No discoloration. No sign that anything was ever wrong with them. He wanted to ask Auravine how she'd done it, but the young female shaman was already stumbling past him, holding a hand to her head.

"Please excuse me," she murmured. "I will be in the main hall."

"Will she be all right?" Joel asked Fireflower.

"Yes," Fireflower said. "She just needs to rest and regain her energy."

Felicity loudly cleared her throat. "Hello? Anyone gonna answer my question?"

"Not only spirited but demanding and impatient as well," Thornleaf said with a roguish grin.

"That's not an answer," Felicity shot back. "What's all this about a ceremony?"

Fireflower turned to Felicity. "Tonight we are holding a ceremony to celebrate the nineteenth anniversary of Marshall Byle's defeat," she replied. "And you will be our guests of honor."

"Oh," Felicity said, seemingly taken aback. "Okay, well, that sounds cool and all, but...not really what I was expecting. I thought you said you needed our help."

"There is a bit more to the story," Thornleaf said.

"Wait," Joel said, glancing at Fireflower. "Did you say, 'nineteenth anniversary'?"

Fireflower nodded. "I did."

"It's been nineteen years since we were here?"

Fireflower nodded again. "It has."

Joel blinked. "Whoa—seriously? But it's only been about six months since..."

"If you recall, time moves differently here."

Joel was about to say *no wonder you look so old,* but then he remembered what Mrs. Wilson had told him in his social communication class ("That's not a polite thing to say, Joel."). He settled on "wow" instead.

"Forgive me," Fireflower said, sounding contrite. "I meant to invite you back sooner, but so much has been going on since you left."

"She has her hands full just trying to keep all of us young ones in line." Thornleaf smirked.

"My daughter cannot even take credit for this celebration," Yellowpetal said with a smile as she rejoined them. "It was Auravine's idea. That girl has always been good at marking special occasions."

"As well as being tearfully sentimental," Thornleaf remarked, drawing a chuckle from Felicity.

Fireflower gave the tall shaman an annoyed glance before turning her attention back to Joel. "The main ceremony will take place in a few hours, after the moons are out. Guests from all over the island will be arriving, including the chiefs from all four villages."

"I am here! Let the celebration begin!" a jovial voice called out from the courtyard entrance. Joel turned and saw a short, thin male native with a blue-tinted wavebow approaching them.

"You are late," Thornleaf said.

"I told you I would be late," the newcomer said with a grin. "*You* should try harvesting sunseeds with the kind of crazy weather we've been having. Speaking of which, did Riverhand find Redstem yet?"

"Not yet," Thornleaf replied.

"Well, I am sure she is fine. That girl can take care of herself. What about Auravine—is she all right? I saw her in the main hall, meditating. She looked very tired."

"Yes, she is all right," Fireflower answered.

The newcomer pulled a pouch out of his supply pack and handed it to Yellowpetal, glancing at Joel and Felicity as he did so. "And who might these two be?"

"They are Joel and Felicity," Fireflower said. "Joel, Felicity—this is Windblade, another member of our order."

"Ah, the legendary offworlders!" Windblade exclaimed, his eyes lighting up. "Back at last! I am so sorry that I did not recognize you."

"We're wearing Halloween costumes," Joel explained once again.

"I am not sure what you just said, but I am honored to finally be in your presence," Windblade gushed. He grabbed his blue-tinted wavebow and started to strum a few chords. "I even composed a special wavecast just for—"

"Please, Windblade," Fireflower interrupted, holding up her hand, "save it for the ceremony." She turned to Joel and Felicity. "Pardon his enthusiasm. He is a great admirer of your accomplishments."

"A fan, huh?" Felicity said. "Cool."

"So, is that all of the other Wavemakers?" Joel asked.

"There are actually two others—Riverhand and Redstem," Fireflower replied. "Which leads us to the reason I need your help."

"Finally," Felicity muttered.

"Windblade, please set up the guest hut for Joel and Felicity," Fireflower said. "In the meantime, Thornleaf and I will show them around the temple, and I will explain everything along the way."

"Of course," Windblade said. "One sleeping mat or two?"

"Two," Felicity quickly replied.

Windblade nodded and left, along with Yellowpetal. Then Joel, Felicity, and Thornleaf followed Fireflower as she headed to the far end of the courtyard and up a sloping ramp that resembled a giant celery stalk.

"It all began about a month ago," Fireflower said. "One evening as I was flying back to the temple I noticed some strange shifts in the Aura that were unlike anything I had ever seen. Then, afterward, a most unusual storm occurred—heavy sheets of ice-cold rain, along with gusts of powerful, swirling winds."

Felicity sniffed. "Hey, during the winter back home, that happens, like, every single day," she commented. "The storm, I mean—not the Aura stuff."

"Well, as you know, such weather is not normal for Spectraland," Fireflower said. "But it began to happen every night. Then, last week, Redstem went missing during one of these storms while she was at her home village of Bluecrest. Riverhand has been out trying to find her, but he has been unsuccessful so far."

"I still believe that she has been abducted," Thornleaf said.

"By who?" Joel asked.

"The Silencers," Thornleaf replied.

"Who are the Silencers?" Joel asked.

"A misguided group of villagers, led by one very stubborn old man, who are opposed to the existence of the Wavemaker Order," was the tall shaman's scornful response. "They are jealous of our powers and would do anything to stop us from using them."

"Thornleaf, we already discussed this," Fireflower said. "Although the Silencers may indeed be responsible, we cannot come out and accuse them until we have definite proof."

"Why not?" Felicity asked. "They already sound like a bunch of jerks to me."

"Right now, the tension between our groups is higher than it has been in quite some time," Fireflower explained, "partially due to my recent perfection of the flight cast, which the Silencers strongly disapprove of."

Thornleaf snorted. "They are even blaming it for the strange Aura and weather conditions, if you can believe that."

"Their leader, Stoneroot, has managed to convince two of the four chiefs to support his position," Fireflower continued, "and more villagers than ever before are now sympathizing with them. To accuse the Silencers without evidence could spark a civil war."

"Wait, I still don't understand," Joel said as they arrived at a lily-pad platform overlooking a large grassy field behind the temple's main structure. "Why would people support them? I thought that everybody in Spectraland loved the Wavemakers."

"It is a rather...complex situation," Fireflower replied, stopping near the edge of the platform.

"If you ask me," Thornleaf muttered under his breath, "I think that Stoneroot is secretly using an illegal mind-control potion."

"Now, Thornleaf," Fireflower said in a patient-but-firm tone of voice that reminded Joel of his mother, "you know that such a thing is not possible."

"But you have heard the rumors, just as I have."

"Those rumors are only idle gossip—completely unfounded."

"It would make sense, though, would it not? With an elixir to control people's thoughts and actions, Stoneroot could easily gain power over—"

"That is enough," Fireflower interrupted. "Now, please do not mention this again. Especially at tonight's ceremony, in front of the chiefs."

"Even the chiefs who support the Silencers will be there?" Felicity said. "Won't that be kind of, I dunno...awkward?"

"Perhaps," Fireflower replied, "but that is precisely why it is so important that this ceremony takes place, not only in spite of, but also in light of the recent events. It will be a way to remind everyone of all the good the Wavemaker Order has done for Spectraland."

"So that's it?" Felicity said. "We came all the way here just to be the special guests at this party?"

"No, there is more," Fireflower said. "After the ceremony is over, I would like the two of you to help us search for Redstem, as well as solve the mystery of who, or what, is behind these unusual occurrences. I believe that Joel's Sight power will be very useful in that regard."

"Um, okay," Joel said. The power that Fireflower referred to as the Sight was his ability to notice tiny details that no one else seemed able to see. It was generally just a novelty back home, useful for video games, egg hunts, and the like, but here in Spectraland, it was what enabled him to locate the Songshell and eventually defeat Marshall Byle, among other things.

"All right, so we're gonna be like private detectives, or whatever," Felicity said. "That's cool with me. But why wait until after the ceremony? Since we have a few hours, shouldn't we get started now?"

Thornleaf sniffed. "After the storms began, the chiefs imposed a ban on flying," he said. "And without flying, there is not much we can do in just a few hours."

"I am confident that the ceremony will sway people's opinions about flying, and about our order in general," Fireflower explained. "At least enough so that we can then fly out in the open once again, which will make our investigation much more efficient."

"But we flew out in the open on our way here," Joel pointed out.

"I took a risk in doing that," Fireflower admitted. "But it was a relatively short flight, so hopefully no one saw us. No one who would have a problem with it, anyway."

"Okay, so until then, I guess we're just gonna continue with the big tour?" Felicity said.

"Actually, I have a better idea," Fireflower replied. "How would you like to learn how to fly—on your own?"

Felicity's face lit up. "Oh, heck yeah."

"But...doesn't that mean we'd be flying out in the open before the ceremony?" Joel said, feeling confused.

Fireflower smiled. "We have a secret location."

♪♪♪

Trotting along a rough dirt trail at a moderately quick pace with Joel on her back, Destiny seemed pleased to once again be serving as a mount. Felicity's former mount Dreamer, on the other hand, appeared to miss her retirement, occasionally slowing down and making petulant grunting noises.

"Hey, believe me," Felicity said, patting Dreamer on the neck while she rode, "this isn't the way I wanted to travel either."

"We are almost there," Fireflower said. "She will be able to rest soon."

Joel looked around. He could see nothing but flat, barren land for miles. "Are you sure? This doesn't seem like a very secret location to me."

"It is, trust me."

"Yeah, well, I don't know if you've noticed, but we're totally out in the open here," Felicity remarked. "People will see those flying streaks in the air from all over the island."

"No, they will not," Fireflower said with a faint smile. She urged her large green mount forward until they were both suddenly swallowed up by a sinkhole in the ground.

"Whoa!" Joel exclaimed in alarm.

"Follow her!" Felicity said.

Joel did so. When he and Destiny reached the spot where Fireflower and her mount had disappeared, he was shocked to discover that instead of falling into a hole, they had started down a path that led into an enormous underground cavern. Tiny patches of glowmoss growing on the cavern's ceiling gave the impression of a starry sky overhead, while its floor was covered in a layer of orange grass that looked like fuzzy shag carpet.

"This is where we have been practicing," Fireflower announced. "The grass is soft and thick, so it helps to cushion the impact of any unintended landings."

Joel gulped as Destiny trotted down the path. While knowing how to fly sounded cool in theory, the thought of doing it on his own for real made him feel more than a little nervous, especially after that bit about "unintended landings."

Once they reached the bottom of the path, Fireflower dismounted and walked into the middle of the cavern. Joel and Felicity did the same. While the grass was indeed soft and thick, Joel imagined that falling onto it from the top of the cavern would still be quite painful.

"A flying cast is similar to levitation," the Wavemaker leader said, moving her wavebow into playing position. "Only, you envision your own body, rather than another object, rising into the air."

Joel nodded. "Okay, um, sounds simple enough."

"The only challenging part," Fireflower continued, "is that once the flying Aura is conjured, you must remain focused on maintaining it. In other words, you need to keep the image of yourself flying at the forefront of your mind."

"Spoke too soon," Felicity said, shooting Joel a mischievous glance.

Joel grimaced. Maintaining focus was one of the original challenges he had run into when he was learning how to wavecast.

"So, if you are ready, follow along with me," Fireflower said as she began to perform the same striking melody that she had played on Crownrock earlier that day.

Joel placed his fingers—regenerated ones included—on the silky but resilient strings of his custom-made wavebow, which Fireflower had been holding for him all of these years. After a few seconds of listening, he joined in with her, and a green stream of light began to emerge from his instrument's headstock.

Fireflower nodded. "Very good. Now, envision yourself rising into the air."

Okay, he thought, *imagine yourself taking off...*

The green light stream spiraled around his body until it completely enclosed him in a cocoon of Aura energy. His feet lifted a few inches off the ground. While floating in place, he glanced at Felicity and saw that she had also successfully created the flying cast with her own wave-bow.

"Perfect," Fireflower said. "You can stop playing now. The cast will stay in place as long as you maintain the image in your mind."

"Hey, Joel," Felicity said, "this feels just like floating in water, except—oops, I forgot—you don't know to swim." She snickered.

Joel tried to think of some witty retort. As he did so, his flying Aura dimmed and his feet hit the ground.

"Remember—maintain the image," Fireflower said as she hovered in place, several feet in the air.

"Right." Joel exhaled and closed his eyes. He took another deep breath and felt his body rising up once more.

"Now, simply move yourself in the direction you want to go."

Joel opened his eyes and urged himself forward and up at a cautious angle. Before he knew it, he was five feet above the carpet-like surface below.

This is actually kind of easy! Maybe I can try going a little higher—

"C'mon, slowpoke!" Felicity grinned right before she rocketed straight up into the air.

Relax, he firmly reminded himself. *Ignore her. Go at your own pace.*

After another minute of gradual ascension, Joel felt comfortable enough to begin changing direction in midair. He tried his best to disregard what Felicity was doing, but it was hard to avoid seeing her looping and zooming around like some kind of crazed hummingbird—especially when every so often, she would send a verbal gibe his way, like: "Dude, try to keep up!" or "This can't be that hard!" or "What's the matter, afraid of heights? Oh right—you are!"

Finally, seventeen minutes later, Joel tried to come up with something to say to her in response. He recalled how she and Trevor would occasionally trade barbs back and forth.

Is this considered flirting?

"Oh yeah?" he shouted as Felicity buzzed past his head. "Well, I—um, you don't, uh—"

Felicity simply laughed as she darted away, doing an aerial corkscrew. Joel's stress level began to rise at the same time his body started to descend.

Relax, he told himself again.

At that moment, a shrill melody rang out. With his concentration broken by the sudden sound, Joel's flying Aura vanished altogether.

"Help!" he screamed as he began to fall. A green stream of energy zipped past his face, just missing him by inches. He hit the ground on his back and lifted his head up just in time to see Felicity doing an Iron Man-style landing several feet in front of him.

"Sorry, dude," she said as she straightened up, "I tried to catch you there, but I guess my aim is still a little off. Haven't done this wavecasting thing in a while."

"Um, that's okay," Joel said, getting to his feet. To his surprise, nothing hurt. "What was that sound?"

Felicity nodded in Fireflower's direction. Joel turned and saw the Wavemaker leader speaking into her wavebow as if it were a large phone.

Cool, Joel thought. *I didn't know wavebows could do that.*

"Looks like she got a call." Felicity chuckled. "Pretty annoying ringtone, I gotta say."

"Who is she talking to?"

"Beats me."

A few seconds later, Fireflower returned her wavebow to her side and trotted over to Joel and Felicity. "Joel, are you all right?" she asked. "I saw you fall."

"Huh? Oh, uh, yeah, I'm fine. Thanks. This grass actually *is* pretty soft, like you said."

"Good. I apologize for the distraction. Unfortunately, we must leave, at once."

"Why?" Felicity said. "I was having fun."

"Some uninvited guests have arrived at the temple."

"Who?" Joel asked.

"The Silencers."

CHAPTER 5: THE CEREMONY

Joel, Felicity, and Fireflower rushed back to the temple as fast as they could via slimeback. As they approached the clearing in front of the main entrance, Joel saw a group of sixteen natives lined up in a semicircle around the base of the stairs, while Thornleaf stood near the top of the stairway with his arms crossed. A herd of slimebacks rested near the river that bisected the clearing.

"Fireflower!" one of the natives called out as the trio drew closer. "Glad to see that you are traveling in the way that nature intended!"

"I will handle this," Fireflower said to Joel and Felicity as she slowed her slimeback to a trot. "No need to say anything."

"I wasn't planning on it." Felicity shrugged.

They crossed the river. Then Fireflower stopped in front of the gathering and said in an even tone of voice, "So, I have been told that you are protesting tonight's ceremony. Is that correct?"

"That is correct," another member of the group, an older male, responded. "We will not allow anyone who supports your order to pass through our ranks. We will even defy the chiefs if necessary!"

Thornleaf came walking down the stairs. "You people are a bunch of stubborn fools," he growled. "Especially you, Roundbark. You should know that defying the chiefs will only make things worse for yourselves."

"*You* are the stubborn fool, Thornleaf! You and your fellow deviants who insist on defiling the Aura, even when the damage you are causing is so very obvious!"

"*We* are not causing anything," Thornleaf retorted while angry mutters rose up from other members of the group. "In fact, it is—"

Fireflower struck a single, forceful chord on her wavebow, quieting everyone. "Where is Stoneroot?" she asked after the chord faded away. "Does he know that you are here?"

"Stoneroot is busy," Roundbark replied evasively. "We are here on his behalf."

Fireflower took a deep breath, as if collecting herself before she spoke. "Unless he has had a sudden change of heart," she said, "I do not believe that he wants to start a large-scale conflict any more than we do. If you attempt to stop people from attending this ceremony, you run the risk of doing just that."

"We will do what we must, to protect the Aura and our island."

Fireflower nodded. "All right, I have a proposal," she said. "Instead of protesting out here, what if we allow you to protest inside, while the ceremony is taking place?"

"What?" Thornleaf exclaimed. "Fireflower, I do not think that is a good idea."

"I actually agree with Thornleaf, for once," Roundbark said. "What do we have to gain by being a part of your little self-love festival?"

"For starters, you will not incur the anger of the chiefs and the other villagers who are traveling a very long way to be here. Moreover, you will have an opportunity to present your point of view to a large audience all at once."

Roundbark paused and looked around at several members of his group. "Give us a minute," he said before they began to huddle together.

Fireflower nodded. "Take your time."

Thornleaf walked up to his leader. "Are you sure about this?" he hissed. "Letting them inside the temple? What if they sabotage something? This is probably what they planned all along!"

"I do not think we have much choice," Fireflower said, dismounting. "We cannot force them to leave, but we also cannot allow them to prevent guests from entering."

"I do not trust them. This is exactly the kind of devious plan that Stoneroot would come up with."

"Calm yourself, Thornleaf. I will make sure that someone keeps an eye on them at all times."

Roundbark turned away from his group and stepped forward. "Very well. We accept your proposal," he announced.

"Wonderful," Fireflower said. "If you will follow me, please, I will help you and your party get settled in. Thornleaf, please round up all of their mounts and escort them to the stable."

"I still think this is a bad idea," Thornleaf muttered under his breath as he stalked away.

Joel and Felicity dismounted and followed Fireflower as she headed up the stairs, with Roundbark and his group right behind them.

"Who are these two with you, Fireflower?" Roundbark asked once they had reached the top of the stairway. "Not new apprentices, I hope. You know that would be in violation of the council's orders."

Fireflower opened the double doors with her forearm tattoo. "Actually," she said, turning around, "they are the legendary offworlders, Joel and Felicity."

"Ah yes, of course," Roundbark said, narrowing his eyes. "Dressed up for the occasion, I see."

"These are Halloween costumes," Joel said.

"Costumes, eh? Well, you may want to be careful," Roundbark said, a slight edge creeping into his voice. "Some people may consider your so-called 'costumes' a bit...disrespectful."

"Um...why would do they do that?" Joel asked.

Fireflower stepped in front of Joel. "The offworlders are quite tired, having arrived just a short while ago," she said. "Please excuse them while they rest up before the ceremony."

"What?" Joel said. "I don't—"

Felicity grabbed Joel by the arm. "C'mon, dude, let's go," she said. "I could use a nap."

"Someone will fetch you before the ceremony starts," Fireflower said as Felicity dragged Joel through the double doors and into the main hall.

"Are you really feeling tired?" Joel asked. "I mean, I was, a little, after the flying lesson, but then I felt better on the way back after—"

"I think Fireflower just wanted us to get away from those guys," Felicity interrupted.

"What? Why?"

"Probably before some kind of argument broke out, or whatever. I dunno, that's what it seemed like to me."

"How could you tell?"

"I've been practicing."

"Huh?"

"Like, you know how we have a hard time reading that kind of thing—all those nonverbal cues and tone and stuff?"

"Yeah."

"Well, I've been working on recognizing patterns in what people say and how they react. It's not exact, and I haven't really gotten it all down yet, but I'm getting better."

I've been trying to work on that too, especially when it comes to talking to girls is what Joel wanted to say, but instead he went with: "Oh—cool."

The two of them made their way to the guest hut that Windblade had set up for them. Once they were inside, Felicity set her wavebow down and flopped onto her raised sleeping mat.

"To tell you the truth, I actually am kinda tired," she said, closing her eyes. "You should be too. We've been up for a while, if you think about it."

"I guess," Joel responded. "I still don't really feel tired, though."

"You're probably just amped up from everything that's been going on. Anyway, I'm gonna doze off for a bit. You can do whatever."

"Okay, but, what do you think about this whole Silencer thing? Do you think maybe they're the ones causing the bad weather and stuff? Or do you think that the flying is really what's causing it? 'Cause if it were, I'd feel kinda guilty, since I was the one who introduced Fireflower to flying in the first place."

Felicity didn't reply. Joel wasn't sure if she was really sleeping or simply ignoring him, but in either case, he decided not to continue bugging her. He lay down on his sleeping mat and stared at the roof of the hut.

I'll just close my eyes for a few seconds, he thought. *Then maybe I'll go find Thornleaf or Auravine or someone and ask them more about what's been going on.*

A few seconds passed by. Then Joel opened his eyes and gasped. The quiet surroundings of the guest hut were gone, replaced by bright, flashing lights and a jumble of loud sounds. The sleeping mat underneath him now felt like a vibrating massage chair. When his senses finally adjusted, Joel realized that he was at a rock concert, and that the vibrating massage chair was actually the hands of many people, passing him around as he surfed a large, packed-in crowd that was screaming and cheering and singing along to a song he instantly recognized.

That's "I Am Immortal," the second song on Biledriver's third album. Is that the werewolf band playing it? No, the singer sounds too much like...

Joel raised his head and got a look at the stage.

That's Marshall!

Startled, Joel tried to sit up. The people below him reacted by dropping him onto the ground, where he landed hard on his bottom. Brushing off the pain, he got to his feet and jumped up and down several times, trying to get a good look at the band that was performing.

Holy cow—that's the real Biledriver! What the heck is happening? How did I get here?

Joel looked around to see if Felicity was with him, but there was no one familiar nearby. Not knowing what else to do, he decided to try to move closer to the band. After pushing and elbowing his way through the dense crowd, he finally managed to secure a position in front of the stage barrier. He examined the face of the lead singer.

That's Marshall, all right. But how could that be? He's supposed to be dead.

At that moment, just as the song was finishing up, Marshall caught Joel's eye.

Uh oh, Joel thought, looking away.

"Thank you very much!" Marshall shouted into his microphone. "You really are a lovely audience!"

Whew...maybe he didn't see me after all.

"Now," Marshall said, tuning the sixth string on his guitar to a low D, "before we play our next song, I'd like to take a moment to recognize a good friend of mine—and a budding rock star in his own right—who has taken the time to join us here tonight. Everyone, please welcome...Joel Suzuki!"

All of the stage lights focused on Joel.

Crud.

"Let's hear it!" Marshall shouted.

The crowd erupted into raucous cheers.

"I can't hear you!"

The crowd got even louder.

"Yeah!" Marshall exclaimed as he started up the next song, a particularly heavy and atonal number off of Biledriver's first album. "Now, that's what I'm talking about! You all know this next one, don't you?"

The crowd roared.

"Excellent! You people up front—now is the time to get *crrrrrazy,*" Marshall growled. "I want to see you running headfirst into each other, all right? I want to see the biggest, bloodiest, most violent mosh pit in all of rock and roll history!"

The rest of the band joined in, creating a sound that resembled a fleet of jets taking off all at once.

I've gotta get out of here, Joel told himself.

Unfortunately, before he could identify a plausible escape route through the mass of swirling bodies, a concertgoer built like a professional football linebacker slammed into Joel, crushing him up against the stage barrier. Joel grimaced in pain as he slumped to the ground and more and more bodies began to close in on him.

"Stop!" Joel yelled as loud as he could, but it was useless—barely able to hear himself, there was no way he could expect anyone else to notice his cries.

"Help!" he shouted anyway.

Then a hand grabbed his arm.

"Joel!" a voice called out.

Felicity?

"Joel, wake up!"

The scene abruptly swirled and shifted. The next thing Joel knew, he was back in the guest hut, looking up at several familiar faces: Felicity, Thornleaf, and Windblade.

"It is time for the ceremony!" Windblade announced, grinning.

"Man, you were really out," Felicity said. "I knew you were tired."

"Were you having some sort of vision?" Thornleaf asked.

"Just—just a nightmare," Joel replied, still trying to orient himself.

"About what?" Felicity asked.

"Um...getting stuck in a mosh pit."

Felicity snickered. "That's not a nightmare, that's fun."

"We should hurry," Windblade urged. "We are already late."

"Relax," Thornleaf said. "We will make a showier entrance this way."

Everyone exited the hut. Joel looked up and saw that it was night. The twin moons were out, both of them looking a bit smaller than he remembered. He followed the two native shamans away from the guest hut and across a series of vine pathways that led toward the back of the temple. As they walked, Thornleaf positioned himself next to Felicity and engaged her in conversation, leaving Joel to answer Windblade's many enthusiastic questions about his Songshell adventure.

"Did you really use a sleep cast on the guardian of the Caves of Wrath?"

"Yes," Joel replied.

"Did you enjoy being in Prism Valley?"

"No."

"What does using the Sight feel like?"

"Um..."

After several more minutes, just as Joel felt like asking Windblade to stop, they arrived at a door that had the locking symbol etched into it.

"Are you ready?" Thornleaf asked.

"Nah, I think I want to go back and take another nap," Felicity quipped.

Smirking, Thornleaf pressed his forearm to the door, which swung open with a *whoomp* sound. "There will be no sleeping tonight," the tall shaman said as he passed through the doorway.

Following after Thornleaf, Joel stepped out into a scene that made him do a double take. The large grassy field that he had observed earlier from the lily-pad platform was now filled with hundreds of Spectraland natives, all of them milling about and buzzing with conversation. A big open-air pavilion, complete with a stage area, had been erected in the center of the field, and flanking the pavilion were a pair of twenty-foot-tall statues of some very familiar-looking people.

"Now this is a party!" Felicity exclaimed without a hint of sarcasm.

"Are those statues...of us?" Joel asked, squinting at the giant stone effigies.

"They are!" Windblade said. "Do you like them? I did most of the carving myself."

"Uh, yeah," Joel said, feeling uncomfortably self-conscious. "They're...they're great."

"I knew you would!" Windblade smiled. The thin shaman then played a fanfare-like riff on his wavebow, silencing the crowd. "Everyone!" he shouted, his voice sounding like it was being amplified. "They are here!"

After a pause the crowd erupted into loud cheers. With Thornleaf and Windblade clearing the path before them like a couple of security guards, Joel and Felicity made their way through the mob of appreciative locals.

"Isn't this awesome?" Felicity crowed to Joel.

"Um, yeah, sure," he replied, trying his best to keep looking straight ahead.

They reached the pavilion, which was a classy-looking structure with an arched roof held up by thick, spiraling tree trunks. Pole-mounted torches with blue flames lined the pavilion's rectangular perimeter, and a wooden ramp on one side led up to a platform area that supported a long, surfboard-shaped table. At the table sat a group of natives: Fireflower, a familiar portly male with an upside-down wooden bowl on his head, and three others that Joel did not recognize.

"Okay, I gotta say, this is pretty cool," Felicity said after walking up the ramp.

Fireflower smiled as she got to her feet. "I am glad you like it."

"Offworlders! Welcome back!" the portly male exclaimed. "It has been a very long time."

"Joel, Felicity—you remember Chief Raintree, of Spearwind?" Fireflower asked.

"Yeah, uh, hello," Joel said.

"Sure, why not," Felicity said.

Fireflower motioned in the direction of one of the other natives, a youthful-looking female wearing a crown of flowers. "We also have with us Chief Silverfern, of Headsmouth."

"It is an honor to meet you," Chief Silverfern said in a prim, crisp tone.

"Chief Twotrunk, of Bluecrest," Fireflower continued, turning toward a bulky male whose head was adorned with something resembling a fez made out of leaves.

"Welcome, legendary offworlders," Chief Twotrunk said.

"And Chief Scarskin, of Nightshore," the Wavemaker leader concluded, nodding at a wiry native with a rough complexion and an oversized horned headdress.

"Greetings," Chief Scarskin grunted.

"Yeah, you know, I gotta be honest," Felicity said, taking a seat at the middle of the table, "it's gonna take me awhile to remember all of your names."

"Ah, yes, as I have told you, my chiefs," Fireflower said with a nervous chuckle as she sat back down, "she is very spirited. That quality saved us many times during our mission to stop Marshall Byle, you know."

Feeling even more uncomfortable now, Joel occupied a stone stool near the end of the table, opposite from where Felicity, Thornleaf, and Windblade had all sat down. Two other natives that he didn't recognize entered the pavilion, both of them carrying big stone vessels shaped like hourglasses with handles. Large dishes and bowls filled with bizarre meat and vegetable-like substances covered the table's surface. Joel's stomach rumbled. He did feel rather hungry, not having eaten since before his concert back home, but nothing in front of him looked particularly appetizing.

"So, how have you been, my friend?" Chief Raintree asked Joel around a mouthful of food.

"Um...good."

Raintree looked at Joel expectantly. *Why is he staring at me like that?* Joel thought before he turned his focus to a wooden mug that one of the unidentified natives had placed in front of him.

"Good? Is that all?" Raintree broke the awkward silence. "Surely you must have some stories of your adventures after you returned home."

Adventures? Joel's mind raced. *Well, I don't know if you would call them adventures. Let's see, after I got back, I went to Art's store and apologized, he said that it was okay, and then he suggested that we listen to the song, and then I realized that I'd lost the CD, and then...*

"I know—you must have so many wonderful tales that you do not even know where to begin, am I correct?" Raintree said.

"Uh, yeah," Joel replied.

"I knew it," Raintree chuckled before taking a long draw from his mug.

Joel exhaled, relieved to have that particular conversation over with. "So, um," he said, glancing at Fireflower, "where's Auravine?"

"Out amongst the crowd," Fireflower answered, "escorting our other guests from earlier."

"Oh—you mean the Silencers," Joel said.

Chief Raintree nearly did a spit take. "What? There are Silencers here?"

"Yes, forgive me, my chiefs," Fireflower said, "I was going to tell you—several members of Stoneroot's group are in attendance tonight."

"Why? Were they invited?" Chief Silverfern asked.

"They simply wanted to stage a peaceful protest, so they were allowed in," Fireflower replied. "I assure you, there will be no disturbances."

"Are you positive about that?" Chief Scarskin said, sipping from a small stone cup. "I know that tensions between your groups are rather high at the moment. We would not want a repeat of the tragic events from ten years ago."

"Trust me, nothing of the sort will happen," Fireflower assured the Nightshore chief.

"What happened ten years ago?" Joel asked.

"A skirmish broke out in my village between supporters of the Wavemaker Order and the Silencers," Scarskin rasped. "While the conflicts between the two camps have been mostly contained to the political arena over the years, this particular one turned violent...and deadly."

"With all due respect, my chiefs, I do not think we should be talking about such matters tonight," Fireflower said.

Chief Twotrunk leaned forward and tented his thick, meaty fingers. "Actually, Fireflower, I believe we should.

It sounds as if you have not fully briefed our legendary guests on what has transpired here during their absence." He turned to face Joel. "Are you familiar with how the Silencers began?"

Joel glanced at Fireflower, hoping for some kind of cue as to how to respond, but the Wavemaker leader simply pursed her lips and looked down at the table. Not knowing if she meant anything by that or not, he decided to go with the basic truth. "No."

"You recall how Chief Byle had nearly everyone on the island placed under his mind-control cast?"

"Yes."

"Well, shortly after you left, Fireflower created an incantation that would protect the inhabitants of Spectraland from any similar casts in the future."

"Thus making good on her pledge to prevent a repeat of what had happened," Windblade added, in a manner similar to a student answering a question in history class.

"Everyone was appreciative," Twotrunk went on, "except for one villager who felt that she was doing the very same thing that Byle did: using the Aura to alter people's bodies in an unnatural manner."

"Who felt that way?" Felicity asked. "That Stoneroot guy?"

"Correct. And over time he was able to convince a growing number of villagers that the Wavemakers were not only unnecessary, but dangerous as well."

Joel glanced around the table at the native shamans. He couldn't tell exactly what they were thinking, but he assumed it probably wasn't good; all three of them wore solemn expressions, and Thornleaf was busily ripping what appeared to be a loaf of bread into little pieces.

"That seems dumb to me," Felicity said. "I thought the Wavemakers helped people."

Twotrunk took a sip from his mug. "Well, you see, it is known that all throughout our island's history, from the time when the Songshell was first discovered to the near-disaster wrought by Chief Byle, that the path of the Wavemakers follows the same cycle: they perform good deeds in the name of honor and humility, until one day one of their members becomes consumed by his or her power and decides to abuse it."

"But then they are always contained and defeated by the other, uncorrupted members of the order," Thornleaf blurted out, a defiant edge to his voice.

"Not until many ordinary villagers have already paid the price," was Twotrunk's stern reply.

"Yes," Chief Silverfern agreed, "and now many believe that this latest development—this flying cast, or whatever you call it—is yet another example of the cycle repeating itself, as evidenced by these recent storms and unusual Aura occurrences that have been playing havoc with the lives of our people."

"I understand your concerns, my chiefs," Fireflower addressed all four village heads in a diplomatic tone, "but I assure you, all the members of the current order, myself included, adhere to a strict moral code. We would never consider using our abilities for unethical purposes.

"As for the storms and Aura occurrences, that is another reason why Joel and Felicity are here—I have asked them to assist us in determining exactly what is causing these disturbances, so that we may return things to normal."

"What else could be causing them besides your flying cast, Fireflower?" Twotrunk asked in a somewhat accusatory manner.

"Well, there are—"

"The Silencers themselves," Thornleaf interrupted. "As you know, they have been developing new technologies over many years now. Surely, you must all see that they could have easily gained the capability to do something like this."

"Do you have any proof?" Silverfern asked.

"Not yet, but—"

"Then we must not discuss this now," Fireflower snapped as she shot Thornleaf a disapproving look. "Forgive me, my chiefs," she said, softening her tone, "but if at all possible, I would prefer to focus on happier matters, at least for tonight."

"I agree," Raintree said, gnawing on a big green bone that was shaped like the capital letter *A*. "This is not the time for politics. This is a celebration, after all!"

"A celebration that would be unnecessary, had a Wavemaker not brought Marshall Byle over to Spectraland in the first place." Twotrunk sniffed.

Joel frowned as he recalled what Fireflower had told them the last time he was here, which was that Marshall Byle was brought over to Spectraland by a Wavemaker looking for an advantage in the civil conflict known as the Fourfoot War.

"Oh, come now, Twotrunk," Raintree chuckled. "Stop being such a killjoy and try some of this stripeclaw steak. It is delicious."

Just then, a shrill melody sounded from Fireflower's wavebow—the same melody that Joel had heard when they were at the secret flying-practice site.

"Man, you have *got* to change that ringtone," Felicity said to Fireflower.

"Please excuse me, everyone," the Wavemaker leader said as she picked up her instrument, whose strings were now giving off a faint yellow glow. "Riverhand, is that you?"

"Yes, Fireflower," a male voice said. "Please pardon my interruption."

"What is it? Have you found Redstem?"

"Not yet, I am afraid. But I believe that I know where she might be. The evidence seems to indicate that she was taken by razorbears."

"Razorbears? Are you sure?"

"I know that it seems unlikely, but I was finally able to locate a witness, and he said that he saw Redstem confronting a razorbear stampede single-handedly. After I investigated further, my tracking cast led in the direction of their master den. I was about to go there myself, but I thought that I should check with you first."

"No, do not go there on your own—that is too risky. Are you at Bluecrest right now?"

"I am."

"Wait there. Windblade and I will join you shortly."

"Yes, Fireflower."

"Windblade," the Wavemaker leader said as the strings on her wavebow dimmed, "please start making preparations for the two of us to travel to Bluecrest. Thornleaf, I will leave the chiefs and the offworlders in your care tonight. Make sure that the ceremony proceeds as planned."

"Yes, Fireflower," Windblade and Thornleaf said in unison.

"If I am not mistaken, Fireflower," Chief Twotrunk said as Windblade departed down the ramp, "I heard you say that you will join your colleague *shortly*. Is it your intent to *fly* to Bluecrest?"

"Please, Chief Twotrunk, it is an emergency. A member of our order—and your village—has gone missing. If she has been abducted by razorbears, it is critical that we find her as soon as possible."

Twotrunk held his beefy hand up to his chin. "Redstem is a respected and well-liked member of my community. But if we were to lift the ban on flying now, it could very well stir up some unrest."

"I think, under these circumstances, a temporary reprieve would be in order," Scarskin said.

"But they would be flying to save one of their own," Twotrunk countered.

Scarskin turned to Fireflower. "Nothing less than they would do for any villager, am I correct?"

"Of course, my chief."

"Hmm. Very well," Twotrunk said. "If Raintree and Silverfern concur, then you may be allowed to fly to Bluecrest tonight. Raintree?"

"I was never in favor of that ban to begin with," Raintree said in between bites of a large purple root-like object.

"Silverfern?" Twotrunk said.

Chief Silverfern simply sat there, saying nothing.

"Silverfern?"

"Very well," Silverfern sighed. "I concur. But only for tonight."

"Thank you, my chiefs." Fireflower nodded. "I will depart right after I open the ceremony." She stood, walked to the edge of the platform, and played a brief note on her wavebow. Then she spoke, her voice amplified.

"Thank you all for joining us here tonight. As you know, nineteen years ago our island's existence was threatened by the duplicitous one known as Marshall Byle."

A loud round of boos and catcalls rose up from the crowd.

"But thanks to the valiant and heroic efforts of two brave offworlders, we were able to thwart his evil plans before it was too late."

Felicity leaned toward Joel. "This is cool and all, but it's like she downloaded this speech from generic-speeches-dot-com."

"Is that really a website?" Joel asked.

"Dude, I'm kidding."

"Oh."

"I hope that we can treat tonight's festivities as a reminder of all the important services that the Wavemaker Order has provided to the people of Spectraland, and that we shall continue to provide for many more years to come."

"We do not need your services!" someone in the crowd shouted. "We would be better off without you!"

From his seat Joel looked out into the mass of natives surrounding the pavilion. He spotted Roundbark and several other Silencer members standing near the base of the ramp, but there was no sign of Auravine.

"Please help yourselves to food and drinks," Fireflower went on, ignoring the outburst, "and we will begin the ceremony shortly. Again, I thank you for coming, and—"

At that moment, the entire scene was suddenly bathed in a pallid orange glow that reminded Joel of the sodium streetlights outside of his apartment building back home. Agitated gasps and murmurs rippled through the crowd.

"The moons are on fire!" someone yelled.

Wavemakers and chiefs alike all rushed to the side of the pavilion to look up at the sky. Indeed, the shining silver light of the twin moons had been replaced by an undulating haze of dark-orange waves, making the heavenly satellites appear as if they were engulfed in flames. Fragments of Aura darted back and forth through the air like angry bees, and a stiff, chilly wind began to blow.

"Fireflower, what is hap—" Silverfern started to say, but then the rest of her sentence disintegrated into bursts of static.

A harsh ringing noise sounded in Joel's ears, and he suddenly felt very dizzy. His eyesight became blurred, and a sharp pain shot through his head, forcing him to his knees. Clenching his teeth, he tried to look around to see what was happening, but to no avail; the entire scene around him was hazy, and the act of turning his neck, even slightly, brought on waves of intense agony. As large drops of very cold rain began to fly sideways into his face, the blurriness before him turned darker and darker until finally, he mercifully passed out.

CHAPTER 6: RAZORBEARS

Joel, a static-drenched voice said. *Wake up.*

Abruptly, Joel sat bolt upright, as if startled out of a deep sleep by an obnoxious alarm clock. Breathing heavily, he spun around to take in his surroundings. The rain and winds were still present, but the orange light was gone, along with his headache, and his vision was clear. He saw that he was on the platform of the pavilion, surrounded by unmoving bodies—including that of his fellow offworlder.

"Felicity!" he shouted, scrambling over to her. Her eyes were closed, and she was very still, as if she had stopped breathing. "Felicity?" he repeated, shaking her shoulder. He wanted to check her pulse, but he wasn't sure how to go about doing that. While he fumbled with her wrist, he heard someone running up the platform's ramp. "I need some help—" he started to say as he turned his head. For a panic-filled moment, he thought that the person coming up the ramp was Marshall Byle, but then he realized that it was Auravine, wearing a dark, hooded shawl.

"Joel?" Auravine said, pulling back her hood. "Are—are you all right?"

“Yeah, um, I think so, but everyone else—”

Auravine knelt down next to Felicity. “I believe she is just stunned,” the healer said. She played a few short notes on her wavebow, and a couple of seconds later, the female offworlder’s eyes fluttered open.

“Thank goodness,” Joel exhaled.

“Whoa,” Felicity said, slowly sitting up. “That was pretty intense. What happened?”

“I, uh, I’m not sure,” Joel answered as Auravine moved over to Chief Silverfern, who was lying on the ground a few feet away. “I was knocked out too. I think everyone was.”

Felicity got to her feet and looked around. “Yeah, I can see that.”

“Auravine, do you know what has happened here?” Chief Silverfern asked after she had fully regained consciousness.

“Some kind of disruption in the Aura,” Auravine replied as she worked to revive Thornleaf. “Similar to the other occurrences that we have been seeing, only much stronger.”

“The Silencers!” Thornleaf exclaimed the instant he woke up. “Where are they?”

“Down in front of the stage,” Auravine responded. “They passed out as well.”

“Are they still unconscious?”

“I believe so. After I woke up, I immediately came up here.”

“Did you see Windblade?”

“I did not. I thought that he was with you.”

“Fireflower sent him inside, but he could not have gone far. I will look for him,” Thornleaf said, and then he hurried down the ramp.

Auravine turned her attention to Fireflower and the other three chiefs, reviving each of them in turn. After she was done, Chief Twotrunk stood up.

"Well, I believe that what we have just experienced is evidence that the Aura is offended by this celebration," the Bluecrest leader declared as he straightened his fez-like headdress. "It is a direct response to the return of the one who introduced the flying curse to our island."

Joel gulped, suddenly feeling very guilty.

"Yes," Chief Silverfern said, "it appears that the cycle is repeating itself after all."

"Hey, in case you forgot, Joel did that to help *save* this place," Felicity snapped. "There's no cycle, or whatever—he wasn't abusing his power or anything like that."

"Nevertheless," Twotrunk said, glowering, "the Aura is displeased, and once again, we all had to suffer her wrath as a result."

"Please, everyone," Fireflower mumbled, apparently still a bit disoriented, "let us not engage in—"

"The Silencers are still out cold, and I found no sign of Windblade," Thornleaf announced breathlessly as he came back up the ramp.

"What?" Fireflower exclaimed. "Windblade is missing?"

"Yes, and I believe I know what has happened to him."

Everyone looked at Thornleaf expectantly.

"This is a scheme devised by Stoneroot," the tall shaman declared. "After his people got themselves invited onto the temple grounds, they used their Aura disruption technology to bring down our shield, and then he himself snuck in and kidnapped Windblade."

"There's a shield?" Joel asked.

"That golden energy dome that surrounds the Temple," Auravine explained. "There is one at Crownrock as well. I am sure you saw it when you arrived."

"Oh—yeah."

"But why would Stoneroot want to kidnap Wavemakers?" Chief Silverfern asked.

"Probably to hold them as hostages," Thornleaf replied. "I expect that he will demand we renounce our abilities in exchange for their release."

Twotrunk waved his hand dismissively. "That is ridiculous. Stoneroot would never resort to such a measure."

"Then where else would the young shaman have disappeared to, Twotrunk?" Chief Scarskin asked. "Are you saying that the Aura caused him to vanish into thin air?"

"We all know that the Aura is capable of many things that seem beyond belief," Twotrunk responded. "Especially when angered, as she has been."

"With all due respect," Fireflower said, having fully regained her bearings, "I must insist that we refrain from speculation until we can gather more information."

"What about those razorbear thingies you were talking about?" Felicity asked.

"It seems unlikely that they are responsible for Windblade's disappearance as well as Redstem's," Fireflower said, "but perhaps there is some sort of a connection."

Thornleaf turned to Fireflower. "I will question the Silencers while you meet Riverhand at Bluecrest."

"No." The Wavemaker leader shook her head. "In light of this new turn of events, I think it is better that I stay here while you go to Bluecrest instead. Contact Riverhand and let him know what is happening."

Thornleaf paused and frowned before replying. "Very well," he exhaled.

"With your permission, Fireflower," Auravine said, "I will go and check on the rest of the guests."

"Yes, of course," Fireflower replied. "Thank you, Auravine."

As Auravine exited down the ramp, Thornleaf made to follow her. "I will depart now," he said.

"Wait," Fireflower said, assuming a thinking pose. "With Windblade missing, you will need someone else to help you if you are to confront the razorbears. Perhaps after Auravine is done..."

"It will take her a while to check on all of the guests." Thornleaf sniffed. "Plus, she is not very useful in a fight."

"That is not true." Fireflower frowned.

"Hey, I'll go," Felicity volunteered.

Joel glanced at Felicity. "Yeah, um, me too," he said.

Fireflower furrowed her brow. "I am not sure that is a good idea. Razorbears are among the more dangerous creatures on this island."

"C'mon, isn't this what you brought us over for?" Felicity said. "Plus, Joel can use his Sight to help search for Redstem. Right, Joel?"

"Uh, right."

Fireflower regarded Joel and Felicity with a contemplative eye for a few moments. "All right," she finally said. "I will investigate matters here while the two of you accompany Thornleaf. Please be careful."

"Hey, remember, this is us you're talking to." Felicity smirked. "We're not called *the legendary offworlders* for nothing."

Twotrunk cleared his throat. "Fireflower, I hope you are not planning on continuing with this ceremony," he said. "Surely we do not want to anger the Aura any further."

"The ceremony will be postponed," Fireflower said with a reluctant nod. "After we make sure that everyone is well, they can be on their way, if they wish. I only ask that Thornleaf and the offworlders still be allowed to fly to Bluecrest, if possible."

"I agreed to that, so I will stand by my word. Silverfern?"

"I will as well," Silverfern said, although she didn't sound very pleased.

"Thank you, my chiefs."

♪♪♪

Yellowpetal helped Joel pack some supplies and pick out a traveling cloak ("With all of the strange weather, you are going to need it," she insisted, sounding every bit like a worried mother). A few minutes later, he found himself in front of the Wavemaker Temple, floating tentatively six feet above the ground inside a cloud of dark-green Aura energy.

"Are you sure you can do this?" Thornleaf asked.

"Um, yeah, sure." *I hope,* Joel added silently.

"Then here we go," the tall shaman said before he launched himself toward the sky, with Felicity quickly following suit.

Joel took a deep breath.

C'mon, Suzuki, you can do this.

He endured an initial series of sputtering lurches before he was finally able to smooth out his ascent and catch up with the other two. Then, as they soared across the landscape, he managed to settle down and maintain his concentration, even as he recognized familiar areas below: the Coast of Fang, which was the long stretch of beach where Felicity got stung by a man-sized jellyfish creature; the Flaming Fields, a canyon that was home to a guardian entity called the Heatwraith; and even the Colorbridge, a tunnel made up entirely of Aura waves that served as a passageway to the Caves of Wrath, where they had originally located the Songshell.

Eventually, they crossed over into territory that Joel didn't recognize. Bluecrest was the one main village he hadn't visited yet, so he felt a small measure of excitement over seeing a new part of Spectraland, even if the circumstances that were taking him there were less than ideal. After passing over a high ridge, Joel observed a secluded stretch of shore that, at first glance, seemed to be covered by a large sheet of tinted glass, but he soon realized that it was actually a beach made up of shiny blue sand. On the far side of the shore stood a single, tall hill with a cluster of huts and tree houses nestled into its side.

"Is that where we're going?" he yelled into the wind. No one replied. Thornleaf began to make a beeline descent toward the hillside settlement.

Okay, I guess it is, Joel reasoned.

As they got closer, he spotted a stout male native standing just beyond a rock wall that lined one end of the village. The native waved at them, with a right hand that appeared to consist of only two large fingers. Just then, a thought popped into Joel's head.

How do I land?

By the time he started to verbalize his question, he was already a mere fifteen feet above the ground. While Thornleaf and Felicity slowed down, Joel found himself plummeting straight toward the two-fingered native, whose eyes widened as he tried to get out of the way.

"Look out!" Joel yelled, but it was too late; he crashed into the native, and the two of them fell to the ground and rolled over several times before coming to a stop up against the rock wall.

"Sorry! I'm sorry!" Joel exclaimed as he untangled himself. "Are you okay?"

"Yes—yes, I believe so," the native grunted.

"Riverhand has endured much worse collisions before." Thornleaf chuckled as he made a smooth two-footed landing.

Felicity touched down next to Joel and gave him a brief once-over. "Nice job. That was even better than a stage dive, I bet."

Gee, thanks for asking if I'm all right is what Joel wanted to say, but instead he settled on: "Um—I don't know. I've never done a stage dive before."

Felicity rolled her eyes.

"So," the two-fingered native said as he stood up and dusted himself off, "you are the legendary offworlders, I presume?"

"Uh, yeah," Joel answered, also getting to his feet. "I'm Joel, and that's Felicity."

"An honor. I am Riverhand, one of Fireflower's Wavemakers."

"Nice to meet you," Joel said.

"Yo," Felicity said.

"Thank you for helping me with the search for Redstem," Riverhand said, taking out a small piece of parchment that had a remarkably well-drawn portrait of the missing Wavemaker on it. He handed it to Joel. "This is what she looks like, in case you were not aware."

"Why were you waiting for us out here?" Thornleaf asked.

"Most of the villagers who are sympathetic to our order are at the ceremony," Riverhand replied. "The few who are still here are...not very hospitable, shall we say."

"Idiots," Thornleaf muttered. "Well, let us head up to the razorbear den."

"So...we're not gonna get to see the village?" Joel asked, tucking the portrait away.

"You heard the man," Felicity said. "Sounds like we're not exactly welcome here at the moment."

Disappointed, Joel followed as Riverhand led them away from the village and into a nearby forest of trees that resembled giant sea anemones.

"So, Riverhand, what exactly did your witness see?" Thornleaf asked as he played a short, shimmering note on his wavebow, causing its headstock to light up with a faint white glow.

Using his clawlike fingers, Riverhand plucked out the same note on his own instrument, illuminating it as well. "He described the same things that happened to you at the temple: wind, cold rains, and the moons appearing as if they were in flames."

"Interesting. I had not seen that effect on the moons until the ceremony."

"Also, all of the village's slimebacks and livestock appeared to be ill."

"Hmm. What about Redstem?"

"The witness said that while Redstem was investigating, she was attacked by the razorbears."

"Did he see them carry her off?"

"No—at that moment, he blacked out. By the time he came to, she and the razorbears were gone."

"So, um, what are razorbears, anyway?" Joel asked as they walked together through the forest.

"Bears with razors, I'd guess," Felicity remarked.

"They are vicious, intelligent creatures that often prey on the people of Bluecrest," Riverhand answered.

"They probably noticed the odd weather and Aura disruptions and saw it as a good time to strike." Thornleaf sniffed.

"Possibly," Riverhand said, "although the witness said that they seemed more distressed than anything else."

"If those things live nearby, why would anyone want to start up a village here?" Felicity asked.

"The village actually came first," Riverhand replied. "It was not until many years later that the razorbears migrated into this area, probably attracted by the fertile farmlands. By then, the villagers were unwilling to relocate."

"Besides that," Thornleaf added, "the view of Bluesand Beach from the village plateau is spectacular."

"You've gotta be kidding," Felicity scoffed. "A *view*? Are you serious?"

"The people of this island take their aesthetics very seriously," Thornleaf responded. "This view, in particular, is beyond extraordinary. You have to see it for yourself to understand."

"C'mon, how can it be better than flying over the beach, or whatever?"

"That does not provide the same perspective. The lighting and Aura angles from the village plateau are unique. I will show it to you sometime."

"Meh, I dunno...is it really worth it?"

"I promise you will not regret it. In fact, you may even feel motivated to compose new pieces of music afterward."

"Yeah, right—a *view* is gonna make me feel like writing a song."

"Visual beauty is very inspirational—especially for creative types like us."

"Oh it is, is it?"

"Indeed."

"Hey, uh, so...are we almost there?" Joel asked, feeling a strange need to change the subject.

"A few more minutes," Riverhand responded. "We should probably keep our voices down as we get closer."

Sure enough, after four more minutes of hiking, they arrived at a row of bushes, beyond which Joel could see a gaping cave-like hole in the side of the hill.

"Wait," Felicity whispered, "if they took Redstem a week ago, wouldn't they have, like...eaten her by now?"

"Razorbears do not eat their victims," Riverhand replied. "They are vegetarians."

"Oh. Then what—"

"They use their victims as toys, playing with them until they eventually die of their injuries."

"Ugh." Felicity grimaced. "That actually sounds worse."

"It means that she could still be alive, though, if they do, in fact, have her."

"Good point."

"Well," Thornleaf said, stepping through the bushes, "let us find out, shall we?"

With the tall shaman in the lead, the group walked single-file into the mouth of the cave, which turned out to be a tunnel that had been dug directly into the dirt like a rabbit's burrow. Once they were a few feet in, Joel was almost overcome by a wave of rotten-leaf stench.

"Ugh, what is that smell?" Felicity said.

"Quiet," Thornleaf snapped.

Felicity made a little grunting noise but otherwise did not respond.

Wow, no comeback, Joel thought. *Weird.*

They continued down the tunnel, ducking under the occasional overhanging tree root as the path took several twists and turns along the way. Finally, they rounded a corner, and Thornleaf held up his hand. Everyone stopped. The tall native glanced back while pointing at something up ahead.

Looking past Thornleaf, Joel saw, in a chamber about ten feet away, a large pile of spiky brown fur on the ground. Upon further inspection, he realized that it was not one but several—possibly six or seven—creatures huddled together in a big sleeping mass, their heads apparently tucked underneath one another.

Thornleaf raised his wavebow and fired a broad stream of red light at the pile. He held the wave steady, the hum of his instrument sounding very loud in the enclosed space, until he abruptly cut it off five seconds later. "Fortune is with us—we caught them all sleeping," he said. "It should be safe to perform a tracking cast now. Riverhand?"

Riverhand nodded. He played a few short notes on his wavebow, causing the dim white glow of his illumination cast to shift into a light shade of green. "The tracking cast is sensing something in the chamber up ahead," he announced.

"Is it Redstem?" Joel asked.

"It would appear to be," Riverhand replied, sounding puzzled, "but the signal is very weak."

"Let us have a look," Thornleaf said, moving toward the chamber.

"You're sure you stunned all of those things, right?" Felicity asked.

Thornleaf looked over his shoulder. "Of course."

"All right, just checking. Don't want any nasty surprises."

The four Wavemakers entered the chamber as Riverhand's instrument began to emit a soft but steady buzzing sound. The area was a dome-shaped space nearly eight feet high and fifteen feet in diameter, with walls made up of dirt and rocks packed around thick tree roots. The razorbear pile lay in the middle, and scattered on the ground around it was a mixture of branches and bones, along with foul-smelling clumps of what Joel assumed were the creatures' droppings.

"*So* gross," Felicity exclaimed, shaking her head. "Seriously, you'd think they'd dig out a separate place for their bathroom."

"Razorbears may be intelligent," Thornleaf said, "but they are not known for their cleanliness." He turned to Riverhand. "Anything?"

"Well, the signal is getting slightly stronger," Riverhand replied as he moved his wavebow around like a metal detector. "It seems to be coming from the far end of the chamber."

"There's nothing there," Felicity said, carefully making her way past the razorbear pile.

Joel followed after her and scanned the far end of the space. After a couple of seconds, he noticed something. "No, wait—over there," he said, pointing.

"What do you see?" Riverhand asked.

Joel ran over to the wall of the chamber and crouched down. The corner of what looked like a piece of red fabric was sticking out of the dirt. Joel pulled it out, shook it off, and showed it to the others.

"That is a piece of her tunic," Riverhand said as the buzzing from his wavebow grew louder and more urgent sounding. "That must be what the tracking cast has been sensing."

"Are you sure?" Thornleaf said. "Nothing else?"

Riverhand waved his instrument back and forth, up and down. "Nothing," he replied. "This is it."

"What if there's, like, a hidden chamber, or something?" Felicity asked.

"If there was, and she was in it, the tracking cast would have picked it up," Riverhand replied.

"So she is not here, as I suspected," Thornleaf declared. "That piece must have been all the razorbears were able to make off with after the real culprits appeared on the scene."

Riverhand turned to him. "Real culprits? Who would that be?"

"The Silencers."

Felicity covered her nose. "Whatever. Can we get out of this stinky hole now?" she said. "I don't think I can stand being down here another second."

Riverhand played a few short notes on his wavebow, changing his tracking cast back into a light cast. "So, Thornleaf," he said as he headed back toward the tunnel, "you really believe that the—"

He was interrupted by a loud growling sound.

"What the heck is that?" Felicity said.

Before anyone could answer her question, a large razorbear—which, now that Joel could see one of their faces, looked more like a vulture than a bear—burst into the chamber, screeching and roaring with furious rage as it swiped its long claws at them. One swipe connected with Riverhand, and his blood went flying through the air as he fell to the ground.

"The mother!" Thornleaf shouted.

Panicking, Joel grabbed his wavebow, but before he was able to lift it into playing position, the razorbear turned on him. Out of the corner of his eye, he saw Thornleaf, wavebow raised, aiming in his general direction. Then, just as the razorbear reared back to strike, the tall Wavemaker fired out a bolt of red light that missed its mark and hit Joel square in the forehead instead.

CHAPTER 7: BLUECREST

"You're joking, right? Come now Joel, I've seen you fight. You're pathetic," a voice sneered in an English accent.

Joel opened his eyes. He was on top of Crownrock, standing in front of none other than Marshall Byle.

What the—how did I get here?

"Right, then, I'll fight you," Marshall snickered, placing his wavebow on the ground. "Should be worth a good laugh or two."

Marshall threw a punch. Almost unconsciously, Joel's hand went up, knocking Marshall's arm aside. Marshall threw a second punch. Feeling as if some other force were controlling his actions, Joel ducked out of the way and lunged forward. He wrapped his arms around Marshall's waist and wrestled the larger man to the ground. With a loud, frustrated yell, Marshall pushed Joel off of him and threw him to the side. Joel rolled several feet before he came to a stop.

"All right, you little git, it's on," Marshall growled as he got to his feet.

Joel tried to stand as well but, overcome by a sudden burst of dizziness, he slumped back down on the ground.

What the heck is going on? This is like déjà vu or something...

"Joel! The shell!" an unfamiliar voice called out.

Still woozy, Joel barely managed to turn his head in the direction of the voice. Instead of a person, though, what he saw was the Songshell, lying on the ground a foot away from his face. He reached out for the powerful artifact, but just as his fingers grazed its glowing purple surface, another hand swooped in and picked it up.

"Ha-*ha*!" Marshall exclaimed. "I was wondering where that had got to!"

What the—Marshall has the Songshell? This isn't how it happened before...

"Don't fret, mate, I won't kill you," Marshall laughed. "I still want you to watch as I go through the Rift and leave this little pond behind. It's quite a sight, believe me. Think of it as, I don't know, my final show for you."

As Joel struggled to get up, Marshall's laughter grew louder and louder until it sounded like a stadium full of movie villains all cackling at once. Joel covered his ears, but the laughter continued to reverberate inside of his head as the world started to spin. He squeezed his eyes shut.

When he opened them again a few seconds later, the scene had abruptly shifted. The laughter was still there, but it was quieter and lacked the same level of malice. Sitting up, Joel saw that he was in a hut, on a sleeping mat, while Felicity and Thornleaf sat at a round stone table nearby. Riverhand lay on a raised mat on the opposite end of the hut with his head facing the wall.

"—quite an amazing coincidence," Thornleaf was saying with a subdued chuckle.

"Yeah, and—oh, hey, Joel!" Felicity exclaimed, turning toward him.

"What...what happened?" Joel said, blinking.

"Mister Bad Aim here hit you with a stunning cast by mistake." Felicity grinned.

"Saved your life, though," Thornleaf said. "When you fell, the razorbear missed you and I was able to stun it with my next shot."

Although if you'd hit it with your first shot, it wouldn't have been able to take a swipe at me in the first place is what Joel wanted to say, but instead, he asked: "Riverhand—is he okay?"

"He was badly injured, but he is alive," Thornleaf answered, looking at the figure on the raised sleeping mat. "I healed him to the best of my ability, though I admit, healing is not one of my strengths."

"Wow, a little modesty," Felicity said with mock surprise. "Didn't know you had it in you."

"Perfection is uninteresting." Thornleaf smirked. "Near-perfection, on the other hand..."

"Um, so where are we?" Joel asked as he got to his feet.

"Bluecrest," Thornleaf replied. "In Redstem's hut."

"Why didn't you guys get me up earlier?"

Felicity glanced at Thornleaf before she replied. "We tried, actually. Would've been easier than carrying you back here. But for some reason, you wouldn't wake up."

"It appeared as if you were having a vision," Thornleaf added, his expression turning serious. "Were you?"

"Just another nightmare, I think," Joel replied.

"Again?" Felicity said. "What was this one about—stage diving?"

"Actually, it was about Marshall. We were back on Crownrock, but this time, he got the Songshell, and it didn't explode."

"Okay." Felicity nodded. "That can't be a vision, 'cause the shell *did* explode, and Marshall is dead."

"Yeah, I guess. The thing is...my other nightmare about the mosh pit? Marshall was in that too. He was alive, back on Earth, playing a big concert."

"Hmm," Felicity said, making a face that reflected skepticism, concern, or a mixture of both. "Eh, you're probably just having some post-traumatic stress about the guy, or whatever."

"Maybe," Joel said as he looked out one of the hut's windows, squinting at the broad daylight. "But I don't think that—wait, it's daytime? How long was I out?"

"Just overnight," Felicity answered.

"Did—did you guys sleep?"

"Well..."

"I used an antifatigue cast so that we could stay up and monitor you and Riverhand," Thornleaf replied.

"Oh." A vision suddenly flashed in front of Joel's eyes, one of Felicity and Thornleaf standing on a ledge near the village outskirts overlooking the beach with the blue sand. He blinked hard, feeling that what he just saw seemed too real to chalk up to his usual paranoid imagination. For a moment, he considered asking the two of them more about what they were up to last night, but instead, he decided to change the subject. "So...did you let Fireflower know what happened with the razorbears?"

"Yes," Thornleaf replied. "I reported everything to her, including what the witness had told Riverhand about the flaming moons and such. She and Auravine are on their way here now."

"Are they flying?"

"Yes. Twotrunk and Silverfern consented to that. They also gave us permission to do something else, which I insisted on."

"We're gonna go see that Stoneroot guy," Felicity elaborated.

"Oh—so Fireflower didn't find Windblade?" Joel asked.

"Nope," Felicity replied.

"Did she talk to Roundbark?"

"Yes," Thornleaf answered, "but he denies everything. Fireflower wanted to use a lie-detection cast on him, but unfortunately, that request was turned down."

"By who?"

"The chiefs."

"Why?"

"You certainly are a persistent questioner."

"Um, thanks."

"I did not mean that as a compliment."

"Oh."

Thornleaf sighed. "Stoneroot managed to convince the chiefs a few years ago that the lie-detection cast was an abuse of our power. Similar to what he is trying to do now with our flying cast."

There was a knock on the door of the hut. "Thornleaf?" a voice said.

"Yes?"

"Your colleagues have arrived."

"Enter."

The door opened. A middle-aged female native that Joel didn't recognize stepped in, followed by Fireflower and Auravine.

"How is he?" Fireflower asked as Auravine rushed over to Riverhand's side.

"Stable," Thornleaf responded.

"You should have been more careful," the Wavemaker leader scolded her second-in-command.

"When I stunned the sleeping pile, I assumed that was all of them," Thornleaf retorted while Auravine began to play a soft melody on her wavebow. "Everyone knows that a mother razorbear and her pups always stick together."

"Not this time," the middle-aged female said. "The pups were sick, and the mother was out gathering food for them."

"Be serious, Skyleg." Thornleaf sniffed. "Razorbears never get sick."

"I believe that the strange Aura event may have affected them," Fireflower said.

"Why do you think that?" Thornleaf asked.

"The witness said that Bluecrest's slimebacks and livestock were ill, did he not?"

"According to Riverhand, yes."

"Well, now the animals at the temple are also ailing."

That got Joel's attention. "You mean Sammy?"

"Yes."

"And the slimebacks too?"

Fireflower nodded. "Yes—it appears that any animals directly exposed to the flaming moons become stricken by some form of ailment. As a consequence, anyone who came to the temple on slimeback is still there, as their mounts are unable to travel. That was a big reason why I was able to convince Twotrunk and Silverfern to let us continue flying."

"The well-being of Wavemakers should have been reason enough," Thornleaf muttered under his breath.

"Speaking of which, you simply *must* find my daughter as soon as possible," the native called Skyleg said.

"We are doing everything we can," Fireflower said.

Skyleg shook her head. "I knew her involvement with your order would come back to haunt her one day. I should never have let her go."

"That is a ridiculous thing to say," Thornleaf snapped as he stood up from his seat.

"Is it really, Thornleaf?" Skyleg said, holding her ground. "Is it so hard to imagine that a parent wants only what is best for their child?"

"Redstem *wanted* to be a Wavemaker. She is proud of what she has accomplished. You should be too!"

"Thornleaf, that is enough," Fireflower said. "Skyleg, I respect your opinions, but now is not the time for this particular argument. We will be visiting Stoneroot shortly."

"As I have said," Skyleg sighed, "I find it hard to believe that Stoneroot would be responsible for any of these strange happenings."

"Then maybe he will at least have some useful information for us. Auravine—how is Riverhand?"

"I have finished healing all of his injuries," Auravine replied. "But he will need a bit more rest. I would like to remain here with him awhile longer—if Skyleg consents, of course."

"Do whatever it is you need to do," Skyleg said. "Just...just find my daughter and return her safely." She turned and rushed out the door.

"Nice lady," Felicity said with a humorless chuckle. "Didn't even say hi to us."

"Maybe she didn't recognize us because of the Halloween costumes," Joel suggested.

"Yeah, I'm thinking that's probably not it."

"She is just upset, understandably," Fireflower said. She turned to Auravine. "I will be going with Thornleaf and the offworlders to the Silencer Stronghold now.

Notify me when Riverhand is well enough to travel on his own."

"Yes, Fireflower."

"Finally, we will get some answers," Thornleaf said with an ominous edge as he exited the hut.

Joel strapped on his wavebow and supply pack and then exited the hut as well, feeling glad that he would get to see a bit of Bluecrest after all. That feeling quickly turned sour once he got outside, however, as he was greeted by a much different reaction than the one he had received last night at the celebration.

"There he is!" a villager standing near the hut yelled. "The offworlder who brought the curse to Spectraland!"

"Go home!" another villager shouted. "Leave our world! Never come back!"

"This is all your fault! You are worse than Chief Byle!"

Feeling shocked and guilty, Joel's initial impulse was to turn around and duck back into Redstem's hut. Before he was able to do so, though, Fireflower grabbed his arm.

"Ignore them," she said. "You are not to blame for anything that has happened. We must keep going."

As Fireflower pulled him along, Joel examined his surroundings. Behind the scattered handfuls of protesters, he saw a village that was technologically more advanced than the others he had visited before (whether that was a feature unique to Bluecrest or merely a natural result of the nineteen years that had elapsed, he wasn't sure), but also in a state of serious disarray and disrepair. The damaged structures included collapsed multilevel treehouses, entire huts that had been completely flipped over, and a system of long wooden flumes—apparently designed to carry water throughout the village—that had been broken in at least six different places.

"Did you see this?" Joel said to Felicity.

"Well, yeah...last night. I guess the storms really did a number on this place."

"Why didn't you guys help fix it?"

Felicity's eyes widened. "Hey," she hissed, "I asked Thornleaf if we should help, but he said no! Something about causing more problems than it would solve."

Joel turned around to face the protesters that had been following them. "Um—we can help you repair the village!"

"Joel," Fireflower said, "please, do not engage them."

"We do not want your help!" one of the villagers shouted. "When the others return from your so-called celebration, we want them to see exactly what your violations have led to!"

"Can't we just fly out of here now?" Felicity asked Fireflower.

"No—it would be considered disrespectful. We must wait until we are well away from the village."

"Really, Fireflower," Thornleaf said, "I do not think it would matter much at this point." He raised his wave-bow.

"Thornleaf, no!"

A protester pointed at the tall shaman. "He is turning his weapon on us!"

At that, some of the other protesters began throwing rocks or other pieces of debris at Joel and the others. Thornleaf played a quick note on his instrument, creating a yellow Aura shield that deflected the incoming projectiles.

"You people are idiots!" he yelled, taking down the shield and firing a red bolt of light over the heads of the protesters.

"Thornleaf, stop!" Fireflower shouted. "Everybody run—we need to get out of here, now!"

Joel took off running, following Fireflower and Felicity as they sprinted toward the edge of the village. Looking over his shoulder, he saw Thornleaf bringing up the rear and shooting down the occasional rock or piece of wood that was being hurled in their direction. Even after the four Wavemakers had exited the village proper, the protestors continued to chase after them, shouting not-so-nice epithets along the way.

"Can we fly *now*?" Felicity demanded.

"Yes!" Fireflower replied, raising her wavebow.

Still running, Joel grabbed his own instrument and played the flying cast melody. Just as he took off, he stumbled and spun around in midair like a propeller, kicking Felicity in the head in the process.

"Ow! Dude, what the—"

Unnerved, Joel lost his focus, and his flying Aura dimmed. Just as he was about to fall, Felicity grabbed him by the wrist, and some of her flying Aura seeped onto him as a rock went whizzing past his face.

"Hang on!" she shouted. For a moment, he wondered why she would say that when she was the one holding on to him, but he decided to shrug it off as they rose up into the air and soared away.

CHAPTER 8: STONEROOT

The four Wavemakers flew across the island at their fastest possible speed. Eventually, they landed in a small valley that was dominated by a massive, pyramid-like structure that rivaled the grandeur of the restored Wavemaker Temple; constructed entirely of stone and surrounded by trees and a moat, it resembled a cross between a Mayan temple and a Roman fortress.

"Well, that's another point for me," Felicity said, releasing Joel from the cocoon of her flying cast.

Joel stood up and dusted himself off. "What are you talking about?"

"Each time one of us—"

"Why did we have to flee?" Thornleaf snapped at Fireflower. "Those fools are no match for us!"

"Because now is not the time for us to get involved in a confrontation like that," Fireflower replied in a calm but steely tone. "I hope that when we see Stoneroot, you will control yourself a little better."

"Do not treat me like a child, Fireflower."

"I would not, if you would stop acting like one," the Wavemaker leader said as she walked away.

Joel glanced at Felicity, who returned his glance with a *Yeah-I'm-staying-out-of-that-one* look.

No one said another word until they all arrived in front of the structure, which was even more impressive up close. The large bricks that made up the Silencer Stronghold's walls were covered with intricate carvings of faces, animals, and symbols, while well-cropped patches of glowmoss arranged along the ridges of the building gave it an elegant, fancy feel. Across the surrounding moat, about twenty feet away, a large rectangular landing area jutted out into the clear water, and from that area, a steep stairway led up to a stone door in the middle of the structure.

"So, what do we do, ring the doorbell?" Felicity asked.

As if in response, Fireflower played a single, loud note on her wavebow, nearly causing Joel to jump.

"Little warning next time?" Felicity remarked, cleaning out her ear.

"Stoneroot!" Fireflower called out, her voice amplified. "This is Fireflower! We are here to talk to you, by order of the chiefs!"

A minute passed, and nothing happened.

"Maybe he's not home," Joel said.

"Or pretending not to be," Thornleaf grunted.

Fireflower frowned. "Roundbark said that he should be here," she said at normal volume.

"Can't we just fly across?" Felicity suggested.

"No," Fireflower said. "Because that would be considered—"

"Disrespectful, right." Felicity took a step forward and peered down into the clear water. "Well then, why don't we just walk across? This seems pretty shallow."

Thornleaf reached out, grabbed Felicity by the arm, and pulled her back.

"Hey, watch it!" she snapped, yanking her arm away.

Thornleaf took a lifepod out of one of his belt pouches and tossed it in the water, which then churned voraciously as something—or some things—swiftly tore apart the little fruit.

Felicity exhaled. "What the—"

Looking into the water, Joel spotted the movements of tiny creatures that were apparently devouring the lifepod's remaining pieces. "Um, there's stuff swimming around in there."

"Crystalfish," Thornleaf explained. "Practically invisible in clear water, and extremely deadly."

"Okay, fine, forget it," Felicity said. "Anybody else have an idea?"

"Well," Joel said without really having an idea, "we could, uh..."

He was interrupted by a loud sound, like stone grinding on stone. He looked across the moat and saw that a narrow plank was slowly emerging out of the landing area's edge.

"So he is here, after all," Thornleaf said. "Probably was busy preparing his defenses."

The plank continued to inch toward Joel and the others until, finally, it spanned the entire length of the moat, stopping at the edge in front of them.

"Everyone, follow my lead," Fireflower said. "And be careful."

"Like we were planning on doing anything else," Felicity muttered.

They walked across the plank and up to the top of the stairs. Once they arrived there, the stone door raised up like a stage curtain, revealing three sturdy-looking natives who each held a long spear in their hands.

"What is your business here, Wavemakers?" the native in the middle, a broad-shouldered male with an oddly pale nose, demanded.

"Whitenose?" Thornleaf exclaimed with genuine surprise. "You have joined the Silencers?"

"Indeed I have, Thornleaf." Whitenose nodded.

The tall shaman took a step forward. "I always suspected that you were secretly jealous of me, but I never thought you would stoop to this."

"After the storms laid waste to my family's farm last week, I realized that what Stoneroot has been saying all these years actually does make quite a bit of sense."

"I told you, we are not to blame for the storms! It is—"

"We have come to see Stoneroot," Fireflower loudly interrupted, "by order of the Chieftain Council."

"Do you have a decree?" Whitenose asked.

Fireflower pulled out a piece of parchment, unrolled it, and held it out. Whitenose took the parchment, even as he shot Thornleaf a cautious glance. The broad-shouldered native looked the parchment over for a couple of seconds and then said, "Very well. Follow me, please."

With Whitenose in the lead and the other two Silencer guards behind them, the four Wavemakers entered the structure, the immediate interior of which reminded Joel of a throne room. It was a large, open hall with a tall ceiling, not unlike the main hall at the Wavemaker Temple, but instead of a dais at the front, there was a low platform supporting a chair made out of some kind of crystalline material. Irregularly shaped fragments of reflective glass covered the walls, as if someone had broken a giant mirror and tried to glue it back together in a random, haphazard manner.

"Wait here," Whitenose said once they had reached the front of the hall. His voice was oddly dead in a place where Joel would have expected to hear lots of echo. "I will let Stoneroot know that you are here to see him." He disappeared through an opening behind the crystalline chair.

"So, how do you know that guy?" Felicity asked Thornleaf.

"He *was* my best friend," Thornleaf scoffed. "One of the last people I would have expected to join this misguided group."

One of the other guards cleared his throat, as if to remind Thornleaf that he could hear everything the tall shaman was saying.

After what felt like a very long time (but was, in reality, only thirty seconds), Whitenose came back out through the opening behind the chair, followed by an older native who was just as tall as Thornleaf and probably about twenty pounds heavier.

"Greetings, Wavemakers," the native said in a low, breathy voice as he cast a wary glance at Joel and Felicity. "I understand the chiefs have approved of this little get-together. What can I do for you?"

Fireflower gave a respectful nod. "Hello, Stoneroot. We just wanted to ask you a few questions."

"Very well," Stoneroot said. He sat down on the crystalline chair as Whitenose stood off to the side. "You may proceed."

"I assume you are aware of the recent storms and the unusual Aura shifts that the island has been experiencing?"

"I am."

"Well, last week, during a storm at Bluecrest, a member of my order disappeared. We thought that perhaps razorbears were to blame, but as it turned out, that was not the case."

"I see."

"Then last night, at our ceremony, the temple was struck by a similar storm, after which another Wavemaker was found to be missing. Members of your group were there, but you were not among them. When I asked them where you were, they avoided answering me."

Stoneroot raised an eyebrow. "Are you here to suggest that I had something to do with all of this?"

"I am not suggesting anything," Fireflower responded. "I am merely investigating all of the possibilities."

"Then let me save you some time," Stoneroot said, standing up. "I was not with Roundbark and the others because I was on my way back from the Sacred Site."

"What were you doing there?" Thornleaf demanded.

Stoneroot paused before responding. "Conducting a ceremony of my own. You see, you are not the only ones looking into these strange occurrences. I too have been searching for reasons as to why the Aura appears to be punishing us, so I thought that if I prayed and meditated there, some answers would be revealed to me."

"So, did you discover anything?" Fireflower asked.

"In fact, I did."

"What was it?" Thornleaf asked.

Felicity turned to Joel. "This is like pulling teeth," she whispered in his ear.

"Huh?"

"Forget it."

Stoneroot began to pace around his chair. "I discovered, to my shock and surprise, that the Aura there was waning...dying, almost. There were even moments when it would fade and disappear altogether before it returned at a mere fraction of its usual strength. It was like nothing I had ever witnessed before. That was disturbing enough, but then, after each of those moments, I heard something—something that, although distressing, gave me the answers I was looking for."

"Oh, c'mon, just spit it out already," Felicity spoke up. "This whole dragging-it-out-for-dramatic-effect thing is *so* corny."

Fireflower turned to her. "Felicity, please—"

"It is quite all right," Stoneroot said with a smirk. "This is one of the legendary offworlders, is it not?"

"That's right, man. And this dude here is the other one," Felicity said, pointing a thumb at Joel.

"Um, hello," Joel said with a little wave.

Stoneroot chuckled. "Here to assist Fireflower in unraveling this mystery, I assume. Well, you will be glad to know that your work is already done. For you see, I am not responsible for any of these strange occurrences. No, in fact, the ones responsible for angering the Aura are none other than the Wavemakers themselves."

"We have already heard that from Roundbark and your other weak-minded followers, old man," Thornleaf fumed. "But the fact is, you have no proof."

"And that, my boy, is what I was trying to tell you," Stoneroot retorted. "Each time the Aura at the Sacred Site vanished, I heard a melody—a strange song reminiscent of those that Wavemakers play when they willfully manipulate the Aura in an unnatural fashion."

"That is not possible," Fireflower asserted. "None of us would have been up there, and even if we were, none of our wavecasts would have had such an effect."

"Oh, I am well aware of that," Stoneroot said, sitting back down on his chair. "What I am saying is that it was a sign, a cry for help, telling me that your latest deviance—that action you call flying—is destroying the Aura."

"That is ridiculous." Thornleaf snorted.

"Is it? Think about it, Thornleaf. I have been saying for years now that taking advantage of the Aura as you do can only lead to disaster. That is why the cycle of the Wavemakers always ends in the near-destruction of your order—it is the Aura protecting and defending herself, asserting her power over everyone who would dare to defile her."

Joel frowned; he had to admit that, in a way, what Stoneroot was saying did have a certain logic.

"And now," the Silencer leader went on, "by flying, you are forcing the Aura to help you do something that no creature in the history of Spectraland has ever been able to do. She has tried to fight back by creating these storms, to warn you and to stop you. But you continue to persist. So, just like when your order was wiped out at the end of the Fourfoot War, now the Aura is seeing to it that you are eliminated once again, this time directly, by causing your members to disappear, one by one. Unfortunately for the rest of us, we have to suffer the collateral damage, as always.

"Now do you understand why I do what I do? Why I want the Wavemaker Order abolished, once and for all? It is to protect *all* the inhabitants of Spectraland—yourselves included."

"Yes, Stoneroot, I have heard these arguments before," Fireflower said evenly. "But as always, I must respectfully disagree. As I have told you in the past, those other events had nothing to do with our use of the Aura. They were simply the unfortunate results of some very poor decisions."

"But if that is the case, how do you explain what I experienced at the Sacred Site? And where have your fellow shamans gone?"

"Simple," Thornleaf said. "You are lying, and you are keeping them captive somewhere."

Stoneroot laughed. "Is that what you think? Ah, my boy, you always did have such a good sense of humor. Unfortunately for you, though, I do not know where they are, and I am telling the truth about what happened at the Sacred Site."

"Do you swear that you are being honest with us?" Fireflower asked.

"If you do not believe me, perhaps you should go up there and see for yourselves."

"We may do just that. However, that still does not—"

"Yes, yes, I know," Stoneroot said, waving his hand. "You think that I have your precious colleagues. I assure you that I do not."

Neither Fireflower nor Thornleaf said anything in response.

"How about this?" Stoneroot sighed, closing his eyes. "I will allow you, just this once, to perform one of your wavecasts on me, to confirm that what I am telling you is the truth."

Fireflower and Thornleaf glanced at each other. Then the Wavemaker leader raised her wavebow and played a soft but eerie-sounding melody. A dark-blue stream of light flowed out of her instrument's headstock and swirled around Stoneroot for ten long seconds before it finally dissipated.

"So, what did you learn?" Stoneroot said, slowly opening his eyes.

Fireflower paused for a second before replying. "That you are indeed telling the truth."

Thornleaf turned to her. "He must be deceiving us somehow," he said. "He has probably developed some way to beat the truth cast."

Stoneroot laughed once more. "Trust me, Thornleaf, if I knew how to do something like that, we would not even be having this discussion right now."

"Enough with the denials," Thornleaf said with an exasperated sigh. "I know what you are capable of. I know how you have managed to sway so many people to your side."

"All right, tell me," Stoneroot said as he leaned forward in his chair, his expression turning serious. "How?"

"Thornleaf," Fireflower hissed, "do not—"

"You have secretly developed a forbidden mind-control potion."

Stoneroot stood up. "How dare you accuse me of such a criminal act?" he barked.

"Admit it, old man," Thornleaf snarled, stepping onto the platform. "You may have everyone else fooled, but I know better."

"Thornleaf, get down," Whitenose warned, raising his spear.

"You know nothing," Stoneroot scoffed, coming face-to-face with Thornleaf. "Is this what the Wavemaker Order has taught you? How to be an ignorant, insolent child who goes around making ridiculous allegations?"

Joel glanced at Felicity as the two guards behind them raised their spears. She returned his look with an expression that seemed to say *I don't know what to do about this, do you?*

"The Wavemaker Order has taught me more than you ever could have," Thornleaf shot back. "I do not need to resort to illegal, underhanded schemes to achieve my goals."

"Thornleaf, stop this at once!" Fireflower snapped.

"Hear that, Thornleaf?" Stoneroot said. "Your babysitter is ordering you to stop. Are you going to listen?"

"I will give you something to listen to," Thornleaf growled, jamming the headstock of his wavebow into Stoneroot's chest.

Just then, Joel noticed a number of tubelike objects emerging from small holes in the surrounding walls. They all seemed to be pointing straight at Thornleaf. "Um—what are those things?"

"Blowguns!" Fireflower exclaimed.

Thornleaf turned his head. A split second later, a volley of darts zipped out of the blowguns, all of them flying in Thornleaf's direction. At the same time, Fireflower played a note on her wavebow with a quick upstroke, creating a yellow dome of Aura around Thornleaf and Stoneroot that deflected the projectiles at the very last moment. Taking advantage of Thornleaf's distraction, Stoneroot swatted the younger man's instrument away, knocking it to the ground. Thornleaf responded by throwing a punch, which Stoneroot blocked with a raised forearm. As the tussle continued, Whitenose stood next to the Aura-dome, apparently undecided about what course of action to take.

"What should we do?" Felicity shouted.

"Stay calm," Fireflower replied. "I will—"

One of the guards dropped his spear and yanked Fireflower's wavebow out of her grasp.

"Return that immediately!" she said.

Joel whirled around. It appeared as if several of the larger mirrors on the walls were now slowly moving in his direction. For a moment, he thought that the mirrors were floating, but then he realized that they were being wielded like shields by natives who were hiding behind them.

"You Wavemakers cause nothing but trouble for everyone!" the guard with Fireflower's wavebow said. He raised a knee, as if preparing to snap the instrument's neck over it.

"No!" the Wavemaker leader protested.

Before the guard was able to break Fireflower's wavebow, Felicity fired a stunning cast that struck him square in the forehead. As he slumped to the ground, the other guard leveled his spear at Felicity. Seeing that, Joel launched a stunning cast of his own, rendering that guard unconscious as well. Then the natives with the mirror-shields charged, yelling and waving assorted weapons above their heads. The two offworlders strummed their instruments again, sending out waves of Aura energy that crashed into the mirror-shields and then dissipated into harmless puffs of red sparks. The natives were about to close in when—

"Stop!" Stoneroot bellowed.

Everyone froze. Joel slowly looked over at the Silencer leader, who now had Thornleaf in a headlock.

"That is enough," Stoneroot said. He released Thornleaf, and the tall shaman dropped to his knees, gasping for breath. "Fireflower—take this shield down."

Fireflower played a brief note, and the Aura-dome vanished.

"This meeting is over," Stoneroot declared. "While I could inform the chiefs about how you have unjustly accused and attacked me in my own home, I will agree to forget about this little incident, on one condition."

No one said anything.

"You will agree to visit the Sacred Site and witness the damage that your actions have caused. Maybe then you will finally make the right decision and abandon your blasphemous ways before it is too late—for all of us."

♪♪♪

Once they were back outside, Joel was surprised to see that heavy cloud cover had rolled in, darkening the skies in a way that seemed to reflect everyone's dour mood after the disastrous meeting with Stoneroot.

"Do you see now that he is right, Thornleaf?" Whitenose asked as he escorted the four Wavemakers across the moat.

Thornleaf gave Whitenose a side-eyed glare. "The only thing I see is a traitor I used to consider a friend," he grunted, rubbing the back of his neck. "I assure you, we will get to the bottom of this. And when we do, you will regret taking the side of that crazy old fool."

Whitenose shook his head. "It still amazes me that you think of him that way. He only wants what is best for Spectraland."

"So do we, Whitenose," Fireflower said, "and if it turns out that Stoneroot *is* right, then we will have some hard decisions to make."

Thornleaf stopped in his tracks abruptly, almost causing Joel to fall off the plank. "You cannot be serious, Fireflower! I cannot believe you are even considering that possibility!"

"We must remain open to all the possibilities, even the ones we do not like," Fireflower responded as she continued walking.

Everyone followed her until they all reached the other side of the moat. Then Whitenose turned to Joel and Felicity. "I want you to know that I do appreciate you ridding us of that other offworlder. He was directly responsible for many tragedies in my village."

Joel furrowed his brow. "Other offworlder?"

"He means Marshall," Felicity said.

"Oh—right."

"Still, though, it would be best if you returned home," Whitenose said. "Not everyone feels the same way I do."

"Yeah, we noticed," Felicity remarked. "Thanks for the tip."

"All right, enough of this," Thornleaf growled. "Leave us, Whitenose. We have work to do."

"I am sorry, Thornleaf," Whitenose said as he turned around. "I know this is all very disappointing to you."

"*You* are the only disappointment!" Thornleaf called after the departing guard.

"I realize that you are upset, Thornleaf, but shouting at your friend will not help us solve this mystery," Fireflower said once Whitenose was out of earshot.

"He is no longer my friend," Thornleaf muttered through clenched teeth.

"That is enough," the Wavemaker leader said, her tone hardening just a bit. "You need to settle down. Your temper just nearly started a war back there."

"They were the ones who fired sleepdarts at me," Thornleaf protested.

"Because you aimed your wavebow at Stoneroot. Now, I will not tolerate any more—"

A shrill melody sounded as Fireflower's wavebow lit up.

"Seriously, that ringtone is just the *worst*," Felicity groaned.

"Auravine?" Fireflower said into her instrument. "How is Riverhand?"

"Still not completely recovered," Auravine's voice said through crackling static. "But I would like to fly him back to the temple, if that is all right with you."

"Why? What is happening?"

"The villagers here are becoming a bit...restless with our presence. Especially after these dark clouds suddenly appeared."

"Very well. Just be careful. And keep me apprised of his condition."

"I will. Thank you, Fireflower."

"Okay, so what now?" Felicity asked as the strings on Fireflower's wavebow dimmed. "Are we going to that place...what was it called?"

"The Sacred Site?" Joel said.

"Yeah, that. What is it, anyway?"

"It is an area with a high concentration of positively charged Aura," Fireflower replied. "Villagers will sometimes travel there to gain enlightenment or pray for favorable outcomes in their endeavors."

"Oh, so, like a good-luck spot, or something," Felicity said. "Wouldn't a place like that be overrun with visitors?"

"It probably would be, if it were not so difficult to get to," Thornleaf answered. "It is at the top of Sunpeak Mountain, the highest point on the island."

"Of course it is," Felicity chuckled. "But hey, we can just fly there, right?"

"Actually, we try not to visit the site ourselves, because we want to avoid the perception that we are abusing our abilities," Fireflower said. "But in this case, it appears that we have no other choice. If the flying cast has in fact harmed the Aura like Stoneroot claims, I should be able to find out for sure once we are there."

"Honestly, I think that would be a waste of time," Thornleaf mumbled.

"Thornleaf, we need to find Redstem and Windblade, and the Sacred Site is our only lead at this point," Fireflower said. "Besides, we agreed to Stoneroot's condition."

"I am sure that he is just baiting us into going there." The tall shaman sniffed. "It may even be a trap of some sort."

Fireflower cocked her head. "A trap? I highly doubt that."

"You continue to underestimate him," Thornleaf said, defiance creeping back into his voice. "He probably has some other devious plan in mind. No, I think that instead of going to the Sacred Site, we should break into his stronghold and look for Redstem and Windblade before Roundbark and the others return."

"That is something we are definitely *not* going to do," Fireflower snapped, her patience apparently wearing thin. "Now, no more debate—we are going to the Sacred Site."

CHAPTER 9: SPIRAL LANDING

The four Wavemakers managed to fly for several miles before a heavy rain started to come down. Joel squinted as drops of water hit him in the face and his cloak became soaked.

"Should we keep going?" he shouted.

"Yes!" Fireflower shouted back.

Easy for her to say, she's had more practice doing this, Joel grumbled to himself. *Too bad we're not like birds, with their oily, waterproof feathers and stuff.*

Five minutes later, however, the rain grew even heavier. Lightning flashed in the distance, causing the Aura to shift, and a round of thunder rumbled a few seconds later. A strong gust suddenly blew, forcing everyone off course.

"Whoa!" Joel exclaimed, struggling to regain control.

"This is not cool!" Felicity yelled to anyone who could hear her.

Fireflower looked back at them. "*Now* we should stop!"

The Wavemaker leader went into a nosedive, heading for a clear patch in between clusters of seaweed palm trees. Joel followed her green Aura stream until they were about thirty feet off the ground, at which point he remembered something important.

"Hey—wait!" he shouted. "I don't know how to land!"

"What?" someone—probably Felicity, although with the wind and rain whipping past his face, Joel wasn't completely sure—shouted back.

"I don't know how—" he started to repeat before he realized it was probably no use. In his mind, he pictured how the others had landed before, and tried to imagine himself doing the same.

Oh man, he thought, *I don't know if I can do this...*

Through the downpour, he observed the other three going through a series of steps: bending their knees, tilting back, and then raising their arms while extending their legs out again.

Wait, what? Bend knees, tilt back, and then—whoaaaaohhhnoooo...

Tilting back too far, Joel flipped over backward several times as if he were in a carnival ride car, only without the car. He closed his eyes, clenched his teeth, and thought desperately about slowing way, way down. Seconds passed. No impact.

Did I do it?

Opening his eyes, he saw that he was hovering a foot above the ground, surrounded by a burrito-like blanket of green light. The blanket then set him down on a small patch of white grass before it faded away.

"Gotcha that time." Felicity grinned, walking up to him and blowing a wisp of green Aura from her wavebow like it was a smoking gun. "Man, I'm really winning now."

"Um, thanks," Joel said as he got to his feet. "But what do you mean by—"

"Are you all right?" Fireflower asked.

"Yeah, but, uh...before we fly again, can someone teach me how to land? I never got that far during our lesson."

Thornleaf played a short tune on his wavebow, creating a dome of Aura over the foursome that shielded them from the downpour. "Landing is simply a matter of confidence," the tall shaman said. "You cannot be tentative. You just have to do it."

"Yeah, dude, just don't think about it too much," Felicity added, squeezing rainwater out of her braids.

"Um, okay," Joel said.

"What they are telling you is correct," Fireflower said as another flash of lightning went off overhead. "It is just like setting down any levitating object."

"Do you think I should, you know, practice, or something?"

"Perhaps later. It would be dangerous to fly in these conditions. We should wait here until this storm eases up."

"Not that I'm anxious to fly in the rain," Felicity said, "but shouldn't we try to make it up to that sacred place before, like, nightfall? In case that moons-on-fire thing happens again?"

"That would be best," Fireflower agreed, "but at the moment, it would be far too risky. Hopefully, the storm will pass soon."

"Okay, well, why can't we just fly above the clouds?"

"Unfortunately, the flying cast is not yet advanced enough to allow us to do that."

"Of course it isn't," Felicity sighed.

"No matter," Thornleaf said as he played another, more complex tune, "seeing as how there are no Silencers around to create that moonfire effect anyway." He finished up his melody, and the Aura-dome expanded into a full-blown energy tent. Then the tall shaman sat down and pulled a lifepod out of one of his belt pouches.

"Moonfire—that's a World of Warcraft spell," Felicity said, mostly to herself.

Joel shot her a surprised look.

"Which...I know because some friends of mine in high school used to play that game," she quickly added.

"I thought you said you didn't really have any friends in high school," Joel recalled.

Felicity abruptly turned away and sat down next to Thornleaf. "Hey, uh...so how many of those things you got there?" she asked with a smirk.

"Why, are you hungry?" he said, offering her his partially eaten fruit. "You can have some of this one if you like."

"Yeah, sure, why not." She shrugged, accepting the lifepod and taking a bite out of it.

Joel frowned as he remembered the time, back during their first go-round in Spectraland, when he'd offered Felicity some of his leftover lifepod and she'd turned him down. *Maybe that was because she was still mad at me*, he rationalized.

An hour passed by. While Fireflower spent the time meditating, Thornleaf and Felicity remained engaged in idle small talk, leaving Joel to occupy himself with random thoughts about baseball statistics, video game side quests, and how cool it was that his supply pack appeared to be completely waterproof. But after yet another hour, neither the rain nor Felicity and Thornleaf's ongoing banter had stopped, so Joel—tired of feeling invisible—decided to try and inject himself into the conversation.

"So, um, what do you guys think really happened to Redstem and Windblade?"

"You have already heard my opinion on that matter." Thornleaf grunted.

"Who knows?" Felicity said. "I mean, that's why we're going up to the Sacred Site, right? To find out."

"Yeah, I guess. But I was thinking...what about the Lightsnakes?" Joel suggested, recalling the reptilian creatures that used to inhabit a parallel plane of existence called Prism Valley. "They used to kidnap villagers before, right?"

"That is a possibility," Fireflower said, breaking out of her trance, "although an unlikely one. The portal to Prism Valley is gone, and no one has seen a Lightsnake since we defeated their queen nineteen years ago."

Felicity clicked her tongue. "You mean since *I* defeated their queen."

"The legend tells it somewhat differently," Thornleaf chuckled.

"Well, then you better get your history books fixed."

"Okay, well, what about Darkeye?" Joel asked. "He was interested in how Wavemakers could do the things we do, remember? Maybe he kidnapped Redstem and Windblade, and now he's experimenting on them or something."

"Yeah, now *there's* a nice thought," Felicity said.

"Fortunately, that one is not a possibility," Fireflower replied. "I captured him shortly after you left. He has been rotting away in the Pit of Ashes ever since."

"Pit of Ashes?" Felicity said. "Is that some sort of jail?"

"Yes," Thornleaf answered. "It is a highly secure prison in a remote area of the island, used only for the most serious offenders."

Hmm, Joel thought. *Let's see...where else could Redstem and Windblade have gone? Could Stoneroot really be right—could the Aura have actually made them disappear? Or is Thornleaf right, and Stoneroot is holding them captive somewhere? But Stoneroot passed that lie-detector test, so that can't be it...funny how Thornleaf still suspects him, though. It's almost as if he wants a reason to...*

Joel cut off his own train of thought as a flicker of movement from off in the distance caught his eye. He was immediately reminded of the time he first saw Sammy during a similar storm, but this time, whatever was making the movement seemed to be quite a bit larger.

"Hey, uh, guys," he whispered, "I think there's something coming toward us."

"What? Where?" Felicity said, her head whirling around.

"Over there, behind all those trees."

"I do not see anything," Thornleaf said. "Are you sure? Maybe that ability of yours is defective."

"Well, um, maybe, but actually, I didn't really activate it, so—"

The sounds of snuffling and footfalls could now be heard amidst the pounding of the rain. Everyone stood up and got their wavebows ready. A burst of thunder roared.

"Okay, yeah, there's totally something coming," Felicity hissed.

A few moments later, a creature that looked like a cross between an armadillo and a kangaroo emerged out of the trees. Atop the creature sat a native wielding a spiral-shaped bow.

"It's one of those vagabond dudes!" Felicity shouted as she took aim with her wavebow.

"No, do not fire on him," Thornleaf said, placing a hand on Felicity's instrument.

"Wavemakers!" the native with the spiral bow exclaimed as three others appeared behind him, all similarly mounted on the kangaroo-like animals known as scaletops. "I thought we would never find you!"

"Hello, Cloudpalm," Fireflower exhaled. "You took us by surprise there."

"Apologies." Cloudpalm nodded. "We did not mean to startle you."

"Wait," Felicity said, "you're *friends* with these guys now?"

"Yes, for quite some time," Thornleaf replied. "So remain calm."

"I—I was just—ugh, forget it," Felicity sputtered.

"How did you know we were here?" Fireflower asked.

Cloudpalm faced upward, despite the rain that continued to pour down. "We saw your trails in the sky. Then, after the storm began, we saw those trails head downward in this direction. We thought that you might be in need of help, so some of us ventured out to look for you."

"We appreciate your concern," Fireflower said as more lightning flashed overhead. "We were actually on our way to the Sacred Site when we were forced to land."

"The Sacred Site?" Cloudpalm said with a tilt of his head. "Could this have something to do with the recent oddities that we have been observing in the Aura?"

"Yes, you could say that."

"I see. Well, it is getting rather late in the day, and the rain shows no sign of letting up. We would be pleased and honored if you would join us as our guests, at least until the conditions are once again favorable for your preferred method of travel."

Felicity turned to Fireflower. "I thought we wanted to get to that place before the moons came out," she said in a low voice.

"Yes, but the storm is now even worse than before," Fireflower replied. "This may actually be our safest option."

"All right, fine, whatever. You're the boss."

"What do you say, Fireflower?" Cloudpalm asked.

The Wavemaker leader turned and nodded. "Thank you, Cloudpalm. I believe we will accept your offer."

♪♪♪

The newly expanded party traveled through the rain toward the Dragonspine range. Each Wavemaker rode tandem with one of the vagabond natives while maintaining an umbrella-like Aura shield over their heads along the way. As they rode, Cloudpalm filled Joel and Felicity in on his people's history.

"We are known as the Roughrock Tribe, named after the pass that leads up to where we reside," he said. "After the two of you left, Fireflower established a relationship with us, and over the years, she and her apprentices helped us build a permanent home for ourselves, so that we would no longer be vagabonds."

Joel looked up at the mountain range and saw, at a point where nothing used to be, a cone-shaped structure that resembled a giant pine tree. "Is that it?" he asked, pointing over his front rider's shoulder.

"It is," Cloudpalm answered, turning his head. "We call it Spiral Landing."

"We are very grateful for everything that the Wavemaker Order has done for us," Joel's front rider said.

"Were you guys at the ceremony last night?" Felicity asked.

"We were not," Cloudpalm replied. "Despite our gratitude, we choose not to get involved in the politics of the other villages."

"So I guess that hasn't changed," Felicity muttered.

"It is a position that we accept and respect," Fireflower said. "Our groups support each other in different ways." Just as she finished speaking, her wavebow came alive with the now-familiar sound of someone trying to contact her. Joel gave Felicity an expectant look.

"What?" she said.

"I thought you were gonna complain about her ringtone."

"Nah, I'm done with that."

"Riverhand is doing better," Auravine's voice sounded through Fireflower's instrument. "By tomorrow morning, he should be at full strength."

"Wonderful," Fireflower said. "What of the guests that were still there?"

"I was finally able to turn my attention to their mounts, so they have all departed."

"Well done."

Joel leaned toward Fireflower's wavebow. "Is Sammy all right?" he asked. "And Destiny?"

"Joel?" Auravine said. "Is that you?"

"Yeah."

"It took longer than I expected, but yes, I was able to cure them. Where are you now?"

"Um—we're on a dirt trail, in the middle of some seaweed palm trees, next to—"

"We were on our way to check out the Sacred Site when a storm forced us to land," Fireflower said.

"Oh no—are you all right?" Auravine asked.

"Yes, some members of the Roughrock Tribe found us," Fireflower replied. "We will be staying at Spiral Landing until the weather clears up."

"Do you want me to join you?"

"No, it is too dangerous to fly in this storm. Stay inside the temple with Riverhand and double the Aura protections. Contact me if anything unusual happens."

"I will."

They continued to travel until they arrived at the base of Roughrock Pass. From there, Joel could make out additional details of the Spiral Landing structure: constructed primarily of interconnected slabs of wood, it was covered in thick, leafy vines, and the small, circular windows that dotted its surface made it look like a cross between a huge Christmas tree and an apartment building.

"Hang on," Cloudpalm warned before the scaletops began to bound their way up the rocky trail.

"Couldn't we—have flown—the rest—of the way?" Felicity shouted as she and her front rider's mount hopped over a series of small ridges and boulders.

Finally, after an excruciating nine-mile journey, they made it to the top of the pass, at which point the scaletops continued to bounce around as if they had just gotten warmed up.

"This is why we use scaletops instead of slimebacks," Cloudpalm said, dismounting. "They are slower but have more stamina."

"How come they aren't sick?" Joel asked.

Cloudpalm adopted a quizzical expression. "Why would they be?"

"Well, because...have you noticed anything weird about the moons lately?"

"They are smaller than usual," Cloudpalm replied, "but that is due to the Zenith Phase—an infrequent but perfectly normal occurrence."

Hmm, Joel thought. *So he hasn't seen the Moonfire yet. It's starting to sound like maybe it's not an island-wide thing....*

Cloudpalm turned to face everyone. "If you will all follow me, please," he said. Then, together with his scaletop, he entered the cone tower through a wide arched entryway that was draped in thick vine-ropes. The Wavemakers all took down their Aura-umbrellas and went inside as well. Once there, the other three natives led the scaletops away while Joel looked around. A giant spiraling walkway that resembled a coiled snake extended up from the ground all the way to the top of the structure. Bridges that branched out from the walkway at regular intervals led to pods that were attached to the structure's walls. A number of natives—Joel counted thirty-two that he could see—moved about, some on the ground, some on the walkway.

"Fireflower and her Wavemakers are here!" Cloudpalm announced. A ripple of murmured greetings followed, with some natives peering over the side of the walkway at their visitors. "You must excuse us," he said, turning to Joel and Felicity. "Even after all these years, social niceties are something that we are still getting used to."

"No problem," Joel said, still gawking at the hive-like interior of the structure. "I, uh, I know how you feel."

Cloudpalm turned back to Fireflower. "It is almost time for me and the other tribal advisors to have our evening meal. Would you care to join us?"

"We would be happy to," Fireflower replied. "Although we must be on our way once the weather clears up."

"Of course."

"Is Chief Sandthroat here?" Thornleaf asked.

"He is currently on a fishing expedition, as he normally is these days."

"In this storm?" Felicity said.

Cloudpalm smiled. "Chief Sandthroat does not mind a little rain. And unlike you, he does not need to fly to go about his business, so he is quite safe out there."

"Still sounds crazy to me," Felicity muttered.

"I will show you to the eating area now."

Joel and the others followed Cloudpalm up the spiral walkway, which was constructed out of wooden planks that were lashed together with vine and rope. It swayed and made ominous creaking noises as they walked on it, causing Joel to feel a bit nervous. "So, uh...how come we can understand you a lot better now?" he asked, trying to distract himself from the unstable footing. "Your voices aren't all distorted anymore."

Cloudpalm chuckled. "You will have to ask your fellow shamans about that one."

"We modified the translation cast so that we would have an easier time communicating with each other," Fireflower explained.

Hmm...wonder if I could come up with a talking-to-girls translation cast, Joel mused.

While contemplating how such a cast would work, Joel looked down and was surprised to find that he and the others were now nearly thirty feet above the ground. Before he had a chance to get nervous again, they exited onto one of the side bridges and headed for a large pod that resembled an overgrown potato.

"Here we are," Cloudpalm said, parting the vines that covered the giant potato's doorway. "You may wait here, and I will return with the others shortly."

"Thank you, Cloudpalm," Fireflower said with a nod.

After Cloudpalm turned to leave, the Wavemakers followed Fireflower as she headed into the pod. Once inside, Joel looked around and saw that there was no furnishing other than a wide straw mat on the ground.

"This is the eating area?" Felicity sniffed. "There isn't even a table or anything."

"Their tribe leads a simple life," Fireflower said, sitting down on the mat. "They actually prefer it that way."

"Just to have a domicile like this was quite a big step for them," Thornleaf added.

As Felicity and Thornleaf sat down, Joel walked over to a round hole in the far wall and looked through it. If the moons were out, he couldn't tell, as the sky was blanketed in heavy cloud cover. The only thing he could make out through the driving sheets of rain was the Wavemaker Temple's golden dome of Aura off in the distance, shining like a tiny beacon.

"Well, I'm not even hungry, anyway," Felicity said around a loud yawn. "That lifepod was pretty filling."

"Regardless, you should try to eat some of their food," Thornleaf advised. "It would be considered rude not to."

"Ugh, are you serious?"

"I know rudeness is part of your nature, but it would be best not to offend our hosts."

"Hey, shut up. You're offending me with your face."

"That is not possible. My face is a vision of flawlessness."

"Wow, get over yourself already, will ya?"

Joel glanced over at them, expecting to see angry expressions, but instead, both Thornleaf and Felicity were smirking, and the Aura in the space between them appeared to flare and flicker.

Is this considered flirting?

Confused (and a little annoyed), Joel turned his attention back to the window. At that moment, he saw a small glowing spot hovering just above the Wavemaker Temple like a UFO. It resembled ball lightning, only it was orange in color. Then, a heartbeat later, the Aura-dome surrounding the Temple vanished.

"Hey, uh—check this out," he said.

"Check what out?" Felicity said in an irritated tone, as if Joel had interrupted something important.

"There was a—" He blinked, and the Aura-dome was back, brighter than before, with no sign of the orange spot. *Hmm...must've just been Auravine doubling the protections or something*. "Um, never mind."

"Dinner is served," Cloudpalm announced as he entered the pod. He was followed by two other Roughrock natives, one of whom was carrying a wooden tray with seven small bowls on it. All three of them sat down, and the native with the tray began handing out the bowls to everyone.

"Joel, if you would join us, please," Fireflower said.

"Oh, uh, yeah," Joel said, sitting down next to the Wavemaker leader.

"As always, we begin our meal with a brief chant," Cloudpalm said, "to give thanks to everything that life and the Aura has blessed us with."

The Roughrock native began to make a repeated series of guttural sounds that didn't translate into any words that Joel could recognize. As the chant droned on, Joel peered into his bowl. It was filled with a black liquid that smelled like old milk, and various pieces of unidentifiable solids bobbed up and down in it like little buoys. He gave Felicity a side-eyed glance. She looked back at him with an expression that seemed to say either *this chant is not brief at all* or *there's no way I'm eating any of this stuff*, or perhaps both. Finally, after what seemed like a very long time, Cloudpalm stopped chanting and took a sip from his bowl. All of the other natives followed suit, so Joel lifted the bowl to his lips and pretended to take a sip, holding his breath as he did so.

"So, Fireflower," Cloudpalm said, setting his bowl down, "I am curious—what did you hope to learn at the Sacred Site?"

"Well, as you know, there have been some unusual shifts in the Aura recently," Fireflower replied. "At Bluecrest and the Wavemaker Temple, two of these shifts caused the moons to appear as if they were in flames. Have you witnessed that up here?"

"We have not," Cloudpalm replied.

"Interesting," Fireflower said. "Anyway, after each of these occurrences, a member of my order was found to be missing."

"That is alarming," one of the other Roughrock natives said. "But what does the Sacred Site have to do with it?"

"We had reason to suspect that Stoneroot was somehow involved. But after we spoke with him, we determined that he was not."

Thornleaf coughed. Everyone glanced at him. "Swallowed the wrong way," the tall shaman explained, pointing at his bowl.

Fireflower gave Thornleaf a sidelong glance. "Stoneroot did, however," she went on, "tell us of some strange events that he witnessed at the Sacred Site. According to his account, the Aura was so weak up there that at times it would fade out completely."

"That is even more alarming," Cloudpalm said. "Did he have a theory as to why it was doing that?"

"In short, he blames it on us," Thornleaf scoffed.

"He believes that our flying cast is destroying the Aura," Fireflower said in a neutral tone, "and that the Aura is now protecting itself by somehow causing Wavemakers to disappear."

"I still believe that *he* is actually responsible for all of this," Thornleaf insisted. "He is using his technology to manipulate the Aura as well as the weather, so that he can then convince the chiefs that we are the ones at fault."

"But remember," Fireflower said, "our truth cast confirmed that he was not lying when he denied his involvement."

"Again, he must have beaten it somehow," Thornleaf grumbled. "You and I both know that despite his growing madness, he is still highly intelligent—as much as I hate to admit it."

Cloudpalm took another sip from his bowl and wiped his mouth. "It sounds to me as if you are considering only two possibilities—that it is either yourselves or the Silencers who are behind these events. Which is understandable, given your history of conflict with one another. But have you stopped to consider that there may be another possibility?"

Fireflower cocked her head. "What are you suggesting?"

"From the top of our tower, we have seen, on occasion, a strange, almost wraith-like apparition hovering out over the ocean, near the area of the Forbidden Tides. Some of our older tribe members, including Chief

Sandthroat, believe that this apparition strongly resembles someone that you are quite familiar with."

"Who?"

"Chief Byle."

CHAPTER 10: AURAVINE'S STORY

"Wait," Felicity said, "you're telling us that Marshall Byle is alive, and that's *he's* the one doing all of this stuff?"

"I am not saying either of those things," was Cloudpalm's calm response. "I am merely suggesting that, perhaps, since you and the Silencers have been so busy blaming each other, you both have forgotten to think about who else may be responsible."

Joel gulped. Could this be what his nightmares were trying to tell him? That Marshall Byle really did survive the explosion of the Songshell? It didn't seem possible—in the time right after the explosion, Joel somehow knew for sure that Marshall's Aura energy had left the Biledriver singer's body completely. But then again, Joel had felt the same thing about Sammy, and the little silvertail came back to life shortly thereafter...

"Um, did anyone ever go back to look for Marshall's, uh, you know...remains?" he asked.

Fireflower and Thornleaf exchanged wide-eyed glances. "Yes, I did," was the Wavemaker leader's stiff reply. "Shortly after you returned home."

"And what did you do with them?" Felicity asked.

"I buried them...at the Sacred Site."

Felicity rolled her eyes. "Ugh, seriously? I guess you guys have never seen a zombie movie before. Why didn't you burn them or something?"

"That practice is reserved for individuals of honor," Thornleaf answered. "Not murderous demons like him."

"But then you buried him at a place called the Sacred Site? That doesn't seem to make any sense."

"That is where all evildoers are buried," Fireflower explained. "Our belief is that the powerful pure energy of the Sacred Site cleanses their remains of corruption and protects the island from their continued influence."

"Okay, whatever."

"This is all just idle speculation," Thornleaf said with a skeptical air. "I doubt very much that Byle has returned. There is no way that his Aura energy could have reinhabited what is now merely a set of dusty and broken bones."

Joel was suddenly struck by a sinking feeling in the pit of his stomach. "But, uh...maybe he's not a zombie, or whatever. Maybe the Songshell explosion turned him into a wraith, and now he's part of the Aura—just like his made-up story about Fourfoot, remember?"

"I suppose that is possible." Fireflower furrowed her brow. "But if that is true, he should have been able to terrorize us much sooner."

"Yes," Thornleaf agreed. "There would have been no reason for him to wait nineteen years."

Felicity shrugged. "Who knows—maybe he was weak, and it just took him that long to rebuild enough strength," she suggested. "Seriously, you guys need to watch a lot more movies. You could learn a thing or two."

"Well," Fireflower said, "if he is truly part of the Aura, I should be able to confirm that at the Sacred Site as well."

"Hey, uh, could I go up to the top of the tower?" Joel asked Cloudpalm. "I wanna see if I can see the same thing you guys have been seeing."

"Of course," Cloudpalm replied. "But would you like to finish your meal first?"

Joel looked at his bowl, which was still full. He could have sworn that one of the solid pieces in it was now moving around on its own. "Oh, well, I..."

"Being offworlders, they are not yet used to some of our native cuisine," Fireflower said. "If you could please excuse them, it would be greatly appreciated."

"Understood." Cloudpalm nodded.

Felicity set her partially consumed bowl down on the mat and shot Thornleaf a dirty look. "Could've said something earlier," she muttered under her breath. Thornleaf merely smirked in response.

Joel glanced at the tall shaman and thought *I'm gonna have to practice that facial expression.*

♪♪♪

The four Wavemakers followed Cloudpalm up the spiral walkway, which creaked louder and louder the higher up they went. Even though Joel didn't look down at any point, he estimated that they were nearly one hundred and twenty-five feet above the ground by the time they got to the top, where a vine ladder led up to what looked like the entrance to an attic.

"After you," Cloudpalm said to Joel.

Joel exhaled and climbed up the ladder. He emerged into a cone-shaped area that he assumed was the very tip of the Spiral Landing structure. A portion of the cone's surface was cut away, creating a large curved triangle opening that provided a magnificent view of the ocean below.

"We often come up here to relax, or to see if conditions are favorable for fishing," Cloudpalm explained after everyone had entered the space. "Chief Sandthroat was actually the first one to witness the apparition."

Joel walked up to the opening and scanned the surrounding area. The rain was still coming down in heavy sheets, and there was nothing out there that resembled Marshall Byle in the slightest.

"See anything?" Felicity asked.

"Um, not yet—hold on," he said. He took a deep breath and went through the standard routine that served to activate the Sight: relaxing, clearing his mind, and then thinking of a list of random miscellaneous details.

Let's see, how about...Adventure Time season two episodes in reverse alphabetical order: Video Makers; To Cut a Woman's Hair; The Silent King; The Real You; The Pods...

The Aura outside shifted and swirled a bit, but still, nothing that looked like Marshall appeared. Joel did, however, notice some strange undulations in the water out near the horizon.

"I don't see Marshall, but...there's something weird in the ocean, far away, like, way over there," he said, pointing.

"I believe you are seeing the area of the Forbidden Tides," Cloudpalm said.

"You mentioned those earlier," Felicity said. "What are they, anyway?"

"They are walls of waves, hundreds of feet tall, that surround the entire island. Many have tried to go through them before. Only a few were fortunate enough to be washed back toward the shore. The rest were never heard from again."

"I don't see any big waves," Joel noted.

"They only appear if you cross a certain line, known as the Far Edge. But once triggered, they take but a few seconds to rise up to their full height. No boat is fast enough to escape their grasp. That is why no one knows what, if anything, lies beyond."

"But wait," Felicity said, turning to Fireflower and Thornleaf, "now that Wavemakers can fly, can't you just, you know, fly over them?"

Fireflower smiled. "Believe me, that was one of the first things I attempted after I perfected the flying cast," she said. "Unfortunately, I discovered that the closer you get to the Tides, the more the Aura seems to dissipate. I ended up falling into the ocean and was fortunate to make it back alive."

"A problem that could easily be solved if you would just let me continue my research," Thornleaf said.

Fireflower's expression hardened. "You know my feelings about that subject, Thornleaf."

"What subject?" Felicity asked.

"I have been looking into a way to store and transport Aura energy, similar to what the Songshell was able to do," Thornleaf answered. "We would be able to accomplish so much more—including flying over the Tides. It would be revolutionary."

"We have enough trouble with the Silencers as it is," Fireflower scolded. "We do not need to introduce yet another thing for them to rail against and rally around. Especially something like that."

"But if we can prove that Stoneroot is behind these recent Aura disruptions, all of the chiefs will fully support us, and then we can end his resistance for good."

"Even if the Silencers did not exist, I still would not approve," Fireflower said, shaking her head.

"But Fireflower, think about it—think about what it could mean not only for the order, but for all of Spectraland's inhabitants as well! And since each of us would have one, there would be no opportunity for abuse!"

"Enough," Fireflower snapped. "I have heard these justifications before, Thornleaf. My answer is still no."

During the uncomfortable pause that followed, Joel thought about what Thornleaf had just said. The original Songshell was a powerful artifact—so powerful that a previous generation of Wavemakers had tried to destroy it, after one of their members had used it for evil purposes. After their attempts proved unsuccessful, they hid it instead, and it lay dormant for many years, until Marshall tricked Joel and Felicity into helping him recover it. Marshall's own evil plan eventually backfired on him when he tried to absorb too much power with the shell, leading to its—and his—supposed destruction.

Now, nineteen years later, it sounded as if a new generation of Wavemakers—namely Thornleaf—wanted to recreate the potential of the Songshell. Joel understood Thornleaf's reasoning; the shell's power could have many practical and beneficial applications, and if each Wavemaker had their own, it would be no more or less dangerous than, say, a wavebow.

On the other hand, he understood why Fireflower would be so opposed to it. The original shell had been the cause of much grief and tragedy on the island; grief and tragedy that she had vivid memories of—unlike Thornleaf, who was a mere toddler at the time—and so, she would naturally not be pleased about anything that would serve as a reminder of that experience. And on top of that, like she said, the Silencers and their supporters would view it as yet another example of Wavemaker hubris.

At that moment, Joel heard the sounds of someone coming up the vine ladder. A Roughrock native who Joel hadn't seen before poked his head up, like a gopher emerging from its hole. "Pardon the interruption," the native said, "but another Wavemaker is here, apparently with urgent news."

Fireflower turned around. "Another Wavemaker?"

"Send them up." Cloudpalm nodded.

The native climbed up into the space, and after him came Auravine, out of breath and soaking wet.

"Auravine?" Fireflower exclaimed. "What happened? Why are you here?"

"I—uh..." Auravine managed to say before her eyes rolled back in her head and she began to fall forward.

"Auravine!" Fireflower said, rushing over and catching the young healer. Everyone else gathered around.

"Apologies," the Roughrock native said, sounding surprised. "She did not appear injured when she arrived."

Fireflower laid Auravine on the ground facedown. There was a large burn hole in the girl's tunic that exposed a nasty-looking red welt on her back.

"Eww." Felicity winced. "What happened to her?"

"She must have been struck by lightning," Fireflower said, quickly playing a short progression of lush, complex chords on her wavebow. "It looks like she tried to heal herself but did not have enough energy to complete the job."

A pulsating golden spot of energy appeared on Auravine's back. Several seconds later, the welt disappeared, and Auravine moaned softly.

"Auravine," Fireflower said, turning the young healer over, "how do you feel?"

"Better, thank you."

"Why did you fly through the storm?" Thornleaf asked. "Is everything all right?"

"No," Auravine replied softly. "Riverhand and Starpollen...they...they are gone."

"Gone?" Fireflower echoed. "Did the same thing happen?"

Auravine nodded. "Yes. The moons burst into flames, and then the Aura protections vanished, even though I had strengthened them. I could not see—everything was dark and blurry, and when it was finally over, they were missing," she said.

Oh no, Joel thought. *So that thing I saw earlier* was *the Moonfire! Dangit, I should have said something. But Felicity seemed annoyed, and then we had to eat...*

"Why I was spared, I do not know," Auravine went on, "but I was too afraid to remain there, so that is why I came straight here without contacting you first. I am sorry, I—I should have—"

"Auravine, please, relax, I understand," Fireflower said in a maternal tone. "What about my mother? Did she see anything?"

"No, she—she was in the dining hut, preparing dinner...apparently, Starpollen had wandered outside for a moment. Then, after it happened, she rushed to find him and tripped...she hurt herself quite badly and was unable to move. I was able to heal her afterward, but it was much too late by then."

"Was there anyone else there?" Thornleaf demanded. "Roundbark, or any of the Silencers?"

Auravine shook her head. "No, I did not see anyone."

"They must have been in hiding," the tall shaman mused.

"Why do you think that?" Cloudpalm asked.

"You said that you have not witnessed the Moonfire up here, correct?"

"That is correct."

"Then I am now convinced that the Moonfire is a localized event, created by some kind of Aura-disruption technology."

"What, like fireworks that knock out the Aura or something?" Felicity asked.

Thornleaf raised an eyebrow. "Fireworks?"

"Yeah, they're these...ah, never mind."

Joel considered saying something about the orange spot that he had seen, but, anticipating that someone would get mad at him for not reporting it earlier, he decided to bite his tongue.

"What about the Aura shifts and bad weather that have been affecting the entire island?" Cloudpalm said.

"Probably a side effect purposely manufactured by Stoneroot," Thornleaf growled.

"Enough of this speculation," Fireflower said. "All we know for sure is that Riverhand and Starpollen are gone as well now, and that this situation is becoming worse by the moment. We need to head for the Sacred Site the moment the storm passes. In the meantime, Auravine can get some rest."

"I could use a little nap myself," Felicity said, stretching. "That antifatigue cast is starting to wear off big time."

"You are all welcome to stay here for as long as you need to," Cloudpalm said.

"That is much appreciated, Cloudpalm." Fireflower nodded. "Could you please have one of your evening guards wake me if the storm happens to let up?"

"Of course. I will escort you to the guest quarters now."

"Thank you."

♪♪♪

Several hours later, Joel lay awake, staring at the roof of the giant potato-like pod that was Spiral Landing's guest quarters, while Felicity, Fireflower, Auravine, and Thornleaf all slept nearby. His mind whirled with thoughts as the storm continued to rage outside.

Could Marshall really be alive? It would be bad if he somehow managed to get back into his body, like Sammy did, but even worse if he turned into a wraith and merged with the Aura...which, if he did, could totally explain the whole Moonfire thing, and the Wavemakers disappearing, and the weather...

Unable to sleep, he got up and decided to head for the top of the structure once more to see if he could spot the Byle-like apparition. Spiral Landing was mostly quiet; a few Roughrock natives passed him as he went up the walkway, but none of them said anything to him. After reaching the top, he climbed up the vine ladder and into the cone-shaped lookout area. The wind was blowing some of the rain through the opening in the wall, so he waited until it changed direction before he moved forward.

Okay, time to turn on the Sight, he thought as he stared out at the ocean. *Hmm, let's go with...players taken in the first round of the 1987 Major League Baseball first-year player draft: Ken Griffey, Jr.; Mark Merchant; Willie Banks; Mike Harkey; Jack McDowell—*

"Joel?"

"Huh?" he said, whirling around. Auravine was standing there, a few feet away. "Whoa, you scared me—" *Wait, that's not a confident thing to say.* "I mean, hey, Auravine. You're, uh, you're awake."

"Yes," Auravine said, walking up to him. "I got up and noticed that you were gone, so I went to look for you, and one of the tribe members told me they saw you headed up here. Is everything all right?"

Joel tried to put his hands in his pants pockets before he remembered that his faux-Spectraland leggings didn't have pockets. "Yeah, uh, totally. I just couldn't sleep, that's all. What—how about you? How are you feeling?"

"Much better, thank you." She smiled. "Fortunately, Fireflower is an excellent healer."

"Well, I...I thought you were supposed to be even better than her," Joel said. *Uh oh—did that come out right? That was supposed to be a compliment, but then it sounded like maybe I was insulting her or something.*

Auravine chuckled softly, much to Joel's relief. "I may be able to do certain things that she cannot, like regeneration, but I still have much to learn. I have this unfortunate tendency to run out of energy rather quickly."

"Oh," Joel said. He was just about to launch into a monologue about the different kinds of magical healers he was familiar with from video games, books, and movies when he remembered that showing interest in the other person's life was usually a better way to keep a conversation going. "So, um...how did you decide to become a healer, anyway?"

"Well, healing has been my special interest ever since I started training as a Wavemaker. You see, I—" She paused for a moment as her expression turned sorrowful. "When I was six years old, my parents were hurt in a conflict that took place in our village. The regular doctor was unable to help them. Fireflower arrived soon after, but by then it was already too late—they had passed away from their injuries."

"Oh, that's...that's terrible." *I hope that was the right thing to say.*

"It was then that Fireflower discovered me, so to speak," Auravine continued, looking out the opening. "She found that I had the potential to become a Wavemaker, so she took me in, along with Starpollen, who was just an infant at the time. When I began my training, I swore to learn all I could about healing, so that no other child would have to suffer a similar fate."

"That makes sense." Joel nodded. "What was the conflict about, anyway?"

Auravine narrowed her eyes. "It was a fight between supporters of the Wavemaker Order and some of Stoneroot's followers," she said, her tone turning dark. "It started out as a simple argument, but it quickly escalated into violence. My parents were just innocent bystanders, but they were the ones to pay the highest price."

"Oh—sorry." *Ugh, stupid—shouldn't have asked her that question. Now she's upset. Stupid, stupid, stupid.*

An awkward silence ensued, during which Joel thought about excusing himself and returning to the guest quarters, or, perhaps jumping out of the opening in order to escape the uneasiness. Before he was able to do either, however, Auravine spoke up again.

"It is such a beautiful view from up here, even with all of the rain."

"Um, yeah."

Auravine turned to him. "Can I ask you a question?"

Joel gulped. "Sure."

"Have you ever made a big decision in your life that you were not totally certain about?"

"I'm not sure what you mean."

"Say you were faced with a choice...a choice between two paths."

"Okay."

"And even though you did not know which path was correct, you still had to choose one and follow it through."

Joel took a couple of seconds to process what she'd said before he replied. "Oh, well, yeah," he said. "I do that all the time, actually."

"Can you give me an example?"

Joel's mind raced. There were so many examples to choose from. *Just pick one, Suzuki,* he told himself. "Okay, like...earlier this year I decided to try and ask this girl, Suzi, to the prom."

Auravine furrowed her brow. "According to the translation cast, a prom is...some sort of formal gathering at which boys and girls stand at opposite sides of a large room?"

"Uh, yeah, something like that. Anyway, I wasn't really sure about it at all—I was freaking out, telling myself I couldn't do it, even looking for a way to escape."

"Sounds very frightening. How did you eventually complete this mission?"

"Well, I had promised my sister that I would do it, so..."

"Interesting." Auravine nodded. "So the promise to your sibling gave you the courage and confidence to go through with this deed, even though you were not sure it was the right thing to do."

"Well, I dunno about that last part, but—"

"Did this girl accept your invitation?"

"Actually, I never got a chance to ask her. But I tried. I talked to her, at least, which was the scariest part."

"I see. She must have been very intimidating—you do not seem to have the same problem speaking to your other fellow offworlder."

Joel cocked his head. "Hmm, I guess. And that's weird, 'cause actually, Felicity is *way* more intimidating than Suzi."

Auravine smiled. In the moonlight, at that moment, she resembled Suzi so much that Joel had to blink several times to make sure he was still looking at a Spectraland native. "Maybe you are braver than you realize," she said.

Joel felt his face getting hot. "Ah, well, I dunno about that."

"I think you are. It takes a lot of courage to do what you did, because once you have chosen a certain path, there is no turning back."

I don't know about that either is what Joel wanted to say, but, reluctant to disagree with her, he simply muttered, "Um, thanks."

"I aspire to that same level of courage," she sighed.

"Is...is that because there's some kind of big decision you have to make?"

"You could say that."

"What is it?"

"I would rather not discuss it," she replied curtly.

Oops, Joel thought, cringing. *Did I say something wrong? Did I make her mad? Did I—*

"Joel? Auravine?"

Joel turned to see Fireflower climbing up into the lookout space.

"What are you two doing up here?" the Wavemaker leader asked.

"I was just, uh, trying to see if I could see the, you know, the—" Joel stammered.

"We were just talking," Auravine said. "Neither of us could sleep, given everything that has been going on."

"Well, it must have been quite an engrossing conversation," Fireflower said with a grin, "if you have not noticed that the storm has started to abate."

"Ah, so it has," Auravine said, looking back out. "I suppose we shall be on our way, then?"

"Indeed," Fireflower said. "We need to get to the Sacred Site as soon as possible."

"But...what if the Moonfire happens again?" Joel asked. "Like, while we're in midair or something?"

Fireflower gave him a sideways head motion that was the Spectraland equivalent of a shrug. "Let us hope that it does not," she replied before she disappeared back down the vine ladder.

That's not very reassuring, Joel thought.

"Thank you, Joel," Auravine said.

"For what?"

"Your wisdom."

"Um, okay." *Not exactly sure what she's talking about, but whatever...*

CHAPTER 11: SUNPEAK

Joel was still thinking about his conversation with Auravine as he and the other Wavemakers soared through the night sky toward a large ramp-shaped mountain that rose high above everything else in the island's landscape.

I wonder what kind of decision she has to make...maybe she's doubting her choice to become a healer, since that's what we were talking about right before that. Or maybe she's thinking about quitting the order, because of all the stuff that's been going on?

And I totally should've given her a different example, Joel chastised himself. *Why'd I have to tell her about the time I tried to ask Suzi to the prom? That was dumb. I should've picked something better, like when I decided to go with Marshall to Spectraland, even though I wasn't sure it was the right thing to do.*

They neared the mountain. It was very ridged and rocky, and the cliffs that lined its summit were covered in patches of white and topped off by thick stands of trees.

Speaking of Marshall...he can't be back. He just can't be. But if it's not him, and it's not Stoneroot, then what is it? Could it really be that the Aura is punishing Wavemakers? Or is it someone else? Before the Roughrock natives found us, I was thinking about how Thornleaf kept insisting that Stoneroot was guilty...I hate to say this, but—what if it's Thornleaf? Maybe he's trying to frame the Silencers so he can turn the chiefs against them, or worse...

Suddenly, Joel felt his Aura energy drop off.

Uh oh—focus! he reminded himself as his body began to drift downward. But even after he reestablished the image of flying in his mind, he noticed that his cocoon of green Aura energy was still slowly fading away. Starting to panic, he looked around to ask someone for help. Unfortunately, everyone else appeared to be in a similar predicament.

"Land—now!" Fireflower yelled.

Stretching her arms out, the Wavemaker leader began to head down toward a point near the middle of the mountain.

"We can make it!" Thornleaf shouted, continuing on his current upward trajectory.

"Thornleaf, no!" Fireflower shouted back. She tried to reverse course, but doing so only caused her flying Aura to shed several additional layers of sparks. Struggling to right herself, she fell like a wounded bird toward an area of flat land in between two slopes.

Oh no—Fireflower! Joel thought, pressing his arms against his sides in an effort to speed up as he followed after her. His flying Aura was flickering now, and the ground was coming up quick, but he took a deep breath and steeled his nerves.

Relax...be confident, he told himself. *You can do this. You can do this.*

With only spotty fragments of Aura energy left around him, he set his jaw and zoomed toward Fireflower like a guided missile as the last of her flying Aura vanished. Then, moments before impact, he grabbed hold of the diminutive shaman and squeezed his eyes shut.

Soft landing, soft landing, soft landing, soft—

They struck the ground. Grunting, Joel lost his grip on Fireflower as he rolled over nine times before finally coming to a stop.

Whew. He exhaled, opening his eyes. *I did it.* He started to push himself up. *I hope Fireflower is—*

"Look out!" Auravine screamed.

Joel turned toward her voice. Just a few yards away on the ground, the young healer was tripping over herself and stumbling in his direction as the remains of her flying Aura trailed off. "Whoa!" he shouted, trying to scramble out of the way; before he was able to do so, however, Auravine's momentum carried her forward, and she crashed right into him, like a tackler piling on top of another player who was already down.

"Joel—I am so sorry!" she said, their faces a mere three inches apart. "Are you all right?"

"Yeah, um, I think so," he replied, blinking fast. "Are—are you?"

"I believe I am," she said with a slight grimace as she got off of Joel and back on her feet. "What happened to Fireflower?"

"She's over here," Felicity called out.

Joel got up and saw, about twenty-five feet away, Felicity helping Fireflower into a sitting position. He and Auravine ran over to them.

"I am fine," Fireflower said, "just some minor scrapes. Thank you, Joel, for catching me."

"You're welcome."

"You did an excellent job there."

"Um, okay."

"Two forced landings in one day," Felicity said. "I'm starting to think that this flying cast still needs a little work."

"This one was unusual," Fireflower said, slowly standing up. "Our Aura energy should not have suddenly run out like that."

"Maybe it's related to what Stoneroot was saying about the Aura disappearing at the Sacred Site," Joel suggested.

Fireflower nodded. "That is possible." She turned to Auravine. "Auravine, are you injured?"

Joel turned to Auravine as well. She pulled the left strap of her sleeveless tunic off, apparently in order to inspect a red spot on her skin near her shoulder. Joel froze for a second before abruptly looking back at Fireflower.

"Nothing serious," Auravine replied. "Just a bad bruise."

"Let me see if I can take care of that," Fireflower said, playing a few short chords on her wavebow. A brief flash of golden light burst out of the instrument's headstock, but nothing else happened. "Hmm. Interesting."

"Great," Felicity huffed. "So let me guess—now we have to hoof it up the rest of the way, right?"

"At least until our energy returns." Fireflower nodded.

"*If* it returns," Felicity muttered.

Fireflower glanced around. "Did any of you happen to see Thornleaf?"

"Last I saw, he was still heading upward," Felicity answered. "I was gonna follow him, but then you started to fall, so I figured I should, you know, try to help out, or whatever."

"Then we need to search for him," Fireflower said. "Hopefully, he is not hurt."

"Why don't we just use a tracking cast?" Joel asked.

"Dude," Felicity said, plucking a couple of notes on her wavebow to no effect, "no Aura. Remember?"

"Oh, right. Well, uh, maybe I can use the Sight to help look for his trail, or something."

"That is a good idea," Fireflower said.

Joel tried to clear his mind and think of a random list, an exercise that was made a bit more difficult by the lingering image of Auravine's bare shoulder.

Okay, let's see, something easy...how about...oh, I know, Doctor Who *companions: Susan Foreman, Barbara Wright, Ian Chesterton, Vicki Pallister—although that last name is not really official—Steven Taylor...*

He looked up at the mountain and saw some residual specks of green Aura leading to a point about a hundred or so feet above them.

"Over there." He pointed. "I think that's where Thornleaf landed."

"Should we just yell out his name?" Felicity asked.

"Not a good idea," Fireflower replied. "This mountain is home to wild creatures known as swordcats."

"There's always something," Felicity mumbled.

"They are usually not hostile, but loud sounds could startle them into defending their territory. We are fortunate that our landing did not lead to such an incident. Be careful as we proceed—swordcats have an uncanny ability to appear suddenly, as if out of nowhere."

"Sounds like my old cat," Felicity remarked.

They walked until they reached a rocky trail that zigzagged its way up the mountain. Not having slept earlier,

Joel was starting to feel quite tired, but without any Aura energy with which to perform an antifatigue cast, there was not much he could do about it. As they slogged along, he decided to try to distract himself from his growing exhaustion by sharing his suspicions about who was responsible for everything that had been happening.

"Hey, um, Felicity," he said softly, slowing his pace.

She stopped and turned around. "What?"

"I...I think I know who might be behind all of this," he said, walking up to her.

She paused for a couple of seconds and then said, "Okay, who?"

"Thornleaf."

"Pfft—are you serious?"

"Yeah," he said as they resumed walking, "I mean, haven't you noticed—he's trying really hard to blame the Silencers, even after Stoneroot passed that lie-detection cast."

"Yeah, sure. So?"

"So, I think that maybe he created a wavecast that makes the Moonfire happen, and then when everyone is unconscious, he kidnaps the Wavemakers and hides them somewhere. And afterward, he tells everyone that the Silencers did it, so that people will turn against them."

"Okay, normally I would think that maybe you were on to something, but dude, that theory just sounds crazy."

"What? Why?"

"I don't even know where to begin." Felicity shook her head. "Okay, first of all, at the party, he got knocked out too, remember?"

"Maybe he was faking it."

"Okay, well, when those last two disappeared—what were their names again?"

"Riverhand and Starpollen?"

"Yeah, them. When they disappeared, Thornleaf was with us at that Spiral Landing place."

"Um...maybe he has an accomplice?"

"Like who?"

Joel frowned. *Could Thornleaf possibly be working with...*"Marshall?"

"Are you serious?" Felicity laughed. "Even if Marshall *is* somehow alive, why would anyone on this island want to work with him? Why would they trust him?"

"Well, we did."

"Hey, at the time, we didn't know that he was a total sociopath. These people do."

"I guess."

"Look, there's just no way it's Thornleaf, okay?"

Joel saw Fireflower glance over her shoulder at them. "How do you know?" he said, lowering his voice to just above a whisper.

"I just do. Can we drop this for now?"

"No, wait, I have more ideas about this. I—"

"You know what I think?" she interjected with a half smirk. "I think you're just jealous."

Joel stopped in his tracks. "Jealous of what?"

"Jealous of...oh, never mind," she said, her smirk shifting into a frown. "Why don't you go tell Fireflower about your crazy theory?"

"Well, because I'm not totally sure yet—plus, I'm afraid she'll freak out," he replied, but Felicity had turned away, shaking her head, which Joel recognized as a cue that she wasn't listening to him any more.

Confused by her reaction, Joel trudged along in silence as the group continued to make its way up the path. He contemplated his theory some more, but after about ten more minutes of doing so, he started to develop a headache, so he decided to give it a rest. He shifted his thoughts to episode names from season three of *SpongeBob SquarePants* and got as far as "Krusty Krab Training Video" before he suddenly noticed an Aura trail that he recognized as Thornleaf's in the middle of the path. Before he could say anything, Fireflower stopped and inspected the ground.

"I believe this is where Thornleaf landed," she announced.

"Wait—what?" Joel said. "You can see his Aura trail too?"

Fireflower gave Joel a puzzled look. "Aura trail? No. There are tracks in the dirt."

"Oh."

Felicity chuckled. "The old-fashioned way."

They followed the tracks (and the Aura trail) until the path took a hard right turn and veered upward. Right after the turn, Joel spotted a figure lying on its back in the middle of the path.

"Thornleaf!" Fireflower shouted in alarm. Everyone rushed toward the fallen shaman. He was conscious but obviously in a great deal of pain. "What happened?" Fireflower said, kneeling by his side.

"Swordcat attack," Thornleaf grunted through clenched teeth. "They were crazed and vicious, but I managed to fight them off with my bare hands."

"Are you wounded?" Auravine asked, looking Thornleaf over. "Where are you hurt?"

"I believe my ankle may be broken, but that is all."

"No lacerations?" Auravine said, sounding incredulous. "You are very fortunate."

Felicity snickered. Everyone turned to look at her. "You hurt yourself when you landed, didn't you?"

"How did you know?" Thornleaf said, managing a small smirk.

"Psychic powers." She shrugged.

"You have psychic powers?" Joel asked.

Felicity knelt down and hoisted Thornleaf's arm over her shoulders. "Dude, seriously? Just help me carry him."

With the two offworlders assisting Thornleaf, the group moved over to a flat area nearby where there were a number of large rocks suitable for sitting on and leaning against.

"The rest of you should go on without me," Thornleaf insisted, grimacing as Joel and Felicity placed him on the ground next to a tall, flat rock.

"We will not leave you here alone in this condition," Fireflower said.

Auravine knelt down by Thornleaf and inspected his ankle. "This does look rather swollen," she said, "and in my haste to leave the temple, I did not bring any traditional remedies." She turned to Fireflower. "What are we going to do? Should we carry him up?"

Fireflower paused for a moment before responding. "No." She shook her head. "There is still too far to go. Stoneroot said that the Aura at the Sacred Site would fade away but then it would return. Hopefully, if we wait, some energy will come back—at least enough to heal Thornleaf."

"And if it doesn't?" Felicity asked.

"I am trying not to think about that possibility."

"Great."

"Let us give it until morning, and then we will decide from there."

"What are we gonna do until then?" Joel asked, sitting down against a headstone-shaped rock.

"It is only a few more hours," Fireflower replied. "We can rest for now. You, especially, must be quite tired."

"Nah, not really," Joel said, yawning.

Felicity sat down and moved her wavebow into playing position.

"What are you doing?" Fireflower asked her.

"Warding off boredom."

"What do you mean?"

"Since we have some time to kill, and these things aren't working anyway, I'm just gonna play some tunes on it."

"I will join you," Thornleaf said.

"Dude, chill. Your ankle's broken."

"I do not need my ankle to play a wavebow."

"Fine, whatever."

Felicity strummed the introductory chords to "Gloria" by Second Player Score. After a few seconds, Thornleaf joined in, playing the progression a couple of times through before launching into an impressive-sounding solo.

"Hey, not bad," Felicity said. "You catch on pretty quick."

"Do not doubt my skills, offworlder," Thornleaf said.

"Wow. Brag much?"

"Are you jealous of my talent?"

"Did I say that?"

As Joel looked back and forth between Felicity and Thornleaf, trying to figure out whether their conversation was a real argument or not, he noticed some small sparks start to drift out of their wavebows. At first he thought it was a result of their ongoing banter, like what had happened back at Spiral Landing, but then he realized that they were beginning to create actual wavecasts with their music.

"Hey, uh—guys?"

Felicity turned to him. "What?"

"I think the Aura might be coming back."

"Oh yeah, you're right," she said, looking around. "I guess we should—"

Before Felicity could finish her sentence, the sparks of Aura suddenly bloomed into large, hazy clouds of orange-tinted energy that obscured everything in Joel's line of sight.

"Felicity?" he exclaimed as he quickly stood up. "What's going on?"

"Hello, Joel." A voice that was definitely not Felicity's echoed around him.

"What—Marshall?"

"Grab your wavebow, mate, it's time for us to jam."

"Jam? What are you talking about?"

The surrounding clouds of Aura receded, and Joel found himself at one end of what looked like a giant laser tag arena at the bottom of an open-air sports stadium. Instead of dividing walls and poles, however, the arena was partitioned by stacks of amplifiers and speaker cabinets. Bright neon lights flashed everywhere, and the large crowd in attendance buzzed with anticipation.

"We're going to have a wavebow fight!" Marshall's voice reverberated throughout the stadium. "The rules are simple—first person with three hits is the winner, and gets to move on to the next round!"

Joel looked up at the scoreboard. On it there was a picture of Marshall and a picture of himself. Next to Marshall's picture was the word *HOME*, and below the word was a large number two. Next to Joel's picture was the word *VISITOR*, with a big number zero underneath it.

I'm already behind. Of course. "Um, what happens to the loser?"

"Do you really have to ask? He dies a horrible, gruesome death, naturally."

"Well...I know this is only a vision—a nightmare!" Joel yelled. "If you kill me here, I'll just wake up back on Sunpeak!"

"Believe what you want, my boy," Marshall snickered. "But if I were you, I wouldn't take that chance. Are you ready?"

"I—um—"

"Begin!"

The lights dimmed. The crowd roared. The Biledriver song "At All Costs" came blaring through the stadium's sound system.

That's an interesting song choice for this situation, Joel thought. *Sure, it's pretty rockin', but I would have thought that a more appropriate one would have been "Let's Go" from their second album, because that's more like—*

A stream of red Aura streaked over Joel's head.

Whoa! Okay, gotta focus here, he told himself, moving behind a nearby amp stack.

"Comin' to getcha!" Marshall said.

Joel took a deep breath as he clutched his wavebow to his chest. *All right, relax, stay calm, you can do this. Besides, this is just a nightmare—it's not even real. Right?*

"Come out, come out, wherever you are!" Marshall called.

Joel peered around the amp stack. He caught a quick flash of movement some forty yards away.

That must be him.

Joel raised his wavebow and fired out a quick stunning cast that struck a speaker cabinet. The crowd jeered.

"Missed me!" Marshall cackled. "Didn't think it was going to be that easy, did you?"

Joel frowned. *No, I didn't,* he grumbled. *But seriously, this is stupid. I know that this is just a lousy nightmare and I'll wake up any moment now.*

Emboldened by that thought, Joel stepped out from behind the stack and ran toward where he saw the movement. As he did so, he noticed, out of the corner of his eye, an amp head surrounded by a green cloud of Aura flying through the air toward him. He ducked just in time, and the amp head crashed to the ground. The crowd gasped and groaned, as if their favorite player had just missed a game-winning layup.

"Oh, did I forget to tell you?" Marshall said. "Hitting each other with levitated objects counts as a point!"

Joel whirled around, looking for where Marshall could possibly be. "Where are you? Stop hiding!"

Marshall laughed. "Blimey, aren't we brave all of a sudden? Very well, your wish is my command."

A figure in a gray hooded sweatshirt and a long black trench coat emerged from behind a row of cabinets twenty yards away. Wavebow in hand, the figure took several slow, measured steps in Joel's direction as the background music faded into silence.

"Marshall?" Joel said, aiming his own wavebow at the figure. "Is that you?"

"Of course it's me," Marshall said, pulling off his hood. "Who else would it be?"

"Well, um, it didn't necessarily have to be you. I mean, it could've been—"

"Enough talk!" Marshall snapped. He raised his instrument and grinned. "It's time for a good old-fashioned duel."

"A duel? Wait, but I—"

Marshall played a lick on his wavebow, generating a broad stream of orange light that shot out directly at Joel. With no room to dodge, Joel conjured up a golden Aura shield that deflected the orange stream, sending it into a nearby amp stack that then quickly dissolved into a smoking heap. The crowd booed.

"Not bad," Marshall said. "But see if you can block this."

Marshall played a fast Mixolydian arpeggio, causing six separate streaks of energy to snake out of his instrument's headstock. They whipped back and forth in the air several times like a set of twitchy tentacles. Then they all reached out for Joel at once. Tracking them independently, Joel fired short blasts of Aura at each tentacle, causing them to explode into small showers of sparks before any of them could touch him. The crowd booed again, but this time there was some scattered applause mixed in.

"Hey, this is kinda fun," Joel said.

"Ah yes, I forgot that you have 'the Sight'," Marshall sneered, unperturbed. "But you can't stop what you can't see, now, can you?"

"What do you—?"

Marshall played a heavy riff, and all of the lights went out, plunging the whole arena into an inky darkness. The crowd gasped. Joel blinked and squinted, hoping his eyesight would adjust, but before it had a chance to do so, he felt his entire body freeze up.

"Now it's time to put an end to this little game," Marshall said.

Joel began to feel tingly and cold, like everything was going numb. "I—I'm not afraid!" he shouted, trying to muster as much defiance in his tone as he could. "I know this is only a nightmare!"

"You know what?" Marshall chuckled. "I have a confession to make: you're right."

"Um—I am?"

"Yes. It is a nightmare that I have created for you. And not in the figurative, 'welcome-to-your-worst-nightmare-I'm-going-to-kill-you' kind of way. No, this is an actual, honest-to-goodness bad dream, something that is totally, completely in your own head."

"What? I don't understand..."

"I am alive, Joel," Marshall purred, his voice sounding closer and closer with every word. "And I have control over your subconscious thoughts. I can invade your mind and make you see whatever I want you to see. What do you think of that?"

"You're—you're lying!" Joel said, his head spinning. "Or this is still a nightmare, and I'm just imagining you saying those things! I'm still not afraid!"

A moment later, Marshall's face appeared out of the darkness just a few inches away from Joel's. He tried to look away, but he couldn't move his head. The crowd roared.

"Well, then," Marshall said, raising an eyebrow, "I guess I'll just have to make the next nightmare a lot more frightening."

The background music came back on at full force, along with the lights. As the song churned on and the crowd continued to cheer, Joel felt dizzier and dizzier until finally, the entire scene around him swirled together and disappeared, like water going down a drain.

CHAPTER 12: THE SACRED SITE

"Hey, wake up."

Joel blinked several times, trying to bring the world into focus. When he did, Felicity was looking down at him.

"We're heading out in a minute," she said.

"Huh? What?" he said, still feeling a bit disoriented.

"Our energy's back. Auravine's fixing up Thornleaf now. After that, we're going to the Sacred Site."

"Oh—okay."

Joel stood up and looked around. It was nearly dawn, and he was back on Sunpeak, in the same flat area with all of the rocks. Behind Felicity, he saw Auravine playing a healing cast next to Thornleaf as Fireflower stood beside them.

"Another bad dream?" Felicity asked.

"Kind of."

"About Marshall?"

"Yeah."

"Did it tell you anything, like whether he's actually alive or not?"

"Sort of, I guess."

Felicity furrowed her brow. "What do you mean?"

"Well, he said he was alive, but the whole dream was kind of unreal—it was like laser tag, but with wavebows."

"That sounds kind of cool, actually," she chuckled.

"It sort of was, at first. But then he said he'd actually created the dream, and that he's able to invade my mind and make me see stuff. That part freaked me out."

"Hmm. Okay, well, hopefully we'll find out some answers real soon here."

Several minutes later the five Wavemakers launched themselves into the air and toward the top of the ramp-shaped mountain. As they neared their destination, Joel realized how Sunpeak probably got its name; the trees on the summit bore large golden spheres that reflected and magnified the sun's emerging rays in such a way that it looked like it was rising out of the top of the mountain itself. It was such an amazing sight that several moments passed by before Joel realized that he had become unfocused and was beginning to lose altitude.

"You all right?" Felicity called out.

"Um—yeah, I got it."

They started to descend, heading for an open meadow near the summit that looked like it was covered in tin foil.

Okay, Joel thought, *if I can do an emergency landing with the Aura running out, then I should be able to make a regular, normal landing. Right?*

The ground approached. Joel saw the others moving into position, so he did the same.

Don't be tentative. Try not to think too much. Just do it.

Three seconds later, he touched down on both feet next to the others on what turned out to be soft, shiny, silver grass.

I did it!

"Hey, you did it," Felicity said, echoing his thoughts. "Finally."

"Well done," Fireflower congratulated him.

"Thanks." Joel grinned, stepping in place to make sure that he really was on solid footing.

"So, is this the Sacred Site?" Felicity asked Fireflower. "Seems kinda empty."

"No, it is over there," Fireflower replied, pointing to a plateau about four hundred yards away that was topped by a tall rock formation.

Felicity rolled her eyes. "Are you serious? Why didn't we just fly directly to it?"

"If our flying is, in fact, what is angering the Aura, I did not want to take that chance," Fireflower explained.

"Okay, again with the respectfulness thing." Felicity sighed. "I gotcha."

"You could probably benefit from a little exercise anyway," Thornleaf quipped.

"Geez, you're such a jerk," she muttered, slapping the tall shaman on the arm.

"Shall we get going?" Fireflower interrupted, much to Joel's relief.

As they walked out of the meadow and toward the plateau, Joel looked around. The wide, grassy pathway they were traversing was lined with dozens of the golden-fruited trees that he'd seen earlier, reminding him of a golf course fairway, albeit one that had been festively decorated for the holidays.

"What kinds of trees are these?" he asked.

"They are called goldenorb trees," Fireflower replied.

"Are the fruits edible?"

"You can eat them," Thornleaf said, "if you want to die a slow, painful death."

"Oh."

"Does anyone mind if I use a gentle heat cast?" Auravine asked as she tightened her shawl around herself. "It is rather chilly."

Joel hadn't really noticed up until this point, but now that she had mentioned it, he realized that the air was thinner and colder up here, reminding him of a brisk mid-April day in Seattle.

"Go ahead," Fireflower responded.

After no one else objected, Auravine played a brief chord on her wavebow, surrounding herself with a faint red glow. Thornleaf and Felicity moved ahead of the others, talking and occasionally laughing, so Joel—spurred on by a feeling that might have been jealousy—decided to try to engage Auravine in conversation.

"Hey, uh...nice heat cast."

"Thank you," Auravine said. "You are not cold?"

"What?"

"I noticed that you have not generated a heat cast of your own."

"Oh—well, yeah, I'm actually kinda used to this temperature."

"Your home is like this all the time?"

"No, just during certain times of the year."

"Interesting. Most of Spectraland is around the same temperature all year round."

"Yeah, I grew up in a place like that. It's an island called O'ahu, which is part of the Hawaiian island chain. It's the third largest by size, but it has the most people out of all the islands, and—" Joel paused, realizing that he was starting to ramble. He glanced at Auravine, concerned that he had lost her, but to his surprise, she seemed to be paying rapt attention to him. "And, um, anyway," he continued, clearing his throat, "I lived there until a few years ago, when I moved to the mainland."

"Why did you move?"

"My, uh, my parents split up."

"I am sorry to hear that. That must have been a difficult experience."

"Yeah, I guess. I got over it after a while, though. Mostly, anyway."

"How did you accomplish that?"

"I dunno...I guess I just sort of focused on stuff that I liked, stuff that I was interested in. I tried to distract myself as much as I could, so that I wouldn't think about what happened. Sometimes I would even make up imaginary worlds where my parents were still together. It was like I wanted to run away from the memory or something."

"I understand. I did something similar after my parents died—although it was a bit more literal."

"You did? What did you do?"

"Well, a few days after they passed, to get away from everything that reminded me of them, I ran away from the village," she said with a faint smile. "I got lost and accidentally wandered into the Jungle of Darkness, which, as you know, is a very dangerous place."

"Yeah. I wandered off once when I was a kid, but that was at the mall. Not exactly the same thing."

Auravine chuckled.

Cool—she thought that was funny. "So, uh, how did you get out of there?"

"I was saved by a wraith, who scared off the beasts and directed me out of the jungle."

"The Jungle Wraith? The same one that helped us fly to Crownrock to stop Marshall?"

"Yes."

Joel frowned. From what he could recall, the Jungle Wraith dissolved after it had helped him, Felicity, and

Fireflower reach Crownrock in time, and they hadn't encountered it at all on their return trip to locate the slimebacks, who they had been forced to abandon in the jungle earlier.

I wonder if that was actually Marshall, Joel wondered. *Based on what Cloudpalm was saying, it just might have been. Should I tell her that? But what if she gets upset? Hmm...guess I'll keep my mouth shut. I mean, who knows, the original wraith could have regenerated or something...*

"So, after that," Auravine continued, "I would occasionally go back there to visit it, and we became friends. It counseled me and helped me get over my loss. It even suggested that I train as a healer. It told me that I was destined to save many lives."

"Wow, that's pretty cool. The Jungle Wraith didn't seem that friendly when I met it."

"Perhaps it took pity on a sad and lonely little girl."

Joel wasn't quite sure how to respond to that, so instead of saying something potentially inappropriate or offensive, he decided to keep his mouth shut. Auravine remained quiet as well until they reached the Sacred Site, which, with its various rock formations, pillars, and walls, resembled a cross between Stonehenge and some of the Hawaiian heiaus that Joel remembered learning about in grade school. Wisps of silver and gold Aura energy floated around listlessly, and Joel could hear a faint droning noise, like the hum of a worn-down guitar amplifier on standby.

"It seems that the Aura here is much weaker than it should be," Auravine said, breaking her silence. She turned to Fireflower. "I neglected to ask before, but is that why you wanted to investigate this place?"

"Yes, it is," the Wavemaker leader replied, a concerned look on her face. "Stoneroot told us about this. I will go to the main altar and attempt to commune with the Aura to see if I can learn some answers. In the meantime, Thornleaf—run a tracking cast for the missing Wavemakers. The rest of you look around and see if you can find anything unusual."

"Aye, Captain," Felicity said.

"Um...where's the graveyard?" Joel asked.

"Over there," Thornleaf said, pointing to a spot at the far end of the site that was sectioned off by a low rock wall.

"You're gonna go see if Marshall did the zombie thing and crawled out of the ground?" Felicity asked.

"Yeah. Did you...did you want to come with me?"

"Nah, I'm gonna go help Thornleaf look for the others."

"Oh—okay."

"I will accompany you, Joel," Auravine said.

"Have fun." Felicity sniffed. She started up a tracking cast on her wavebow and walked away.

Joel turned and headed toward the far end of the site. As he did so, tiny white flakes began to fall from the sky.

"Hey, it's snowing," he said.

"Amazing," Auravine said, looking up. At first Joel thought that she was being sarcastic, but based on her tone and expression, she seemed to be genuinely surprised by the sudden onset of frozen precipitation.

"Does it always do this up here?" he asked.

"I do not know for sure," she replied. "I have heard stories, but this is actually my first visit to the Sacred Site."

"Oh."

They reached the burial area, which was a square plot of land about ten feet by ten feet in size. Six stones, each about the size of a bowling ball, were arranged on the grassy surface in two rows of three. All of the stones had inscriptions on them, and a faint layer of yellow Aura energy hovered just above the ground, like some kind of translucent picnic blanket.

Joel stopped at the edge of the area, not wanting to step in the wrong spot. "Which one is Marshall's?" he asked.

"I believe it is...that one," Auravine answered, pointing at the stone closest to them on the right.

Joel looked at the stone. The inscription on it was written in the Spectraland language, but the more he stared at it, the more the writing seemed to form the word *Byle*. The ground around the stone appeared intact and undisturbed. "I guess everything's okay here," he said, almost to himself.

"Yes, it does appear that way."

"Who are the other five stones for?"

"The worst criminals in Spectraland history," Auravine replied, her voice shaking slightly. "The one next to Chief Byle is Chief Fourfoot. And behind him is Graymold, the Wavemaker who first discovered the Songshell. For many years, it has been Spectraland's tradition to inter these types of offenders here, to seal off their negative energy from the rest of the island and preserve peace and balance among our people."

"Oh, yeah—Fireflower mentioned something about that."

"Unfortunately, it does not seem to work," Auravine continued, her tone turning bitter and melancholy. "Somehow, strife and violence always manage to return, stronger than ever."

Joel looked away, unnerved by Auravine's sudden mood swing and unsure of what to say in response. The snow began to come down a little heavier, and the humming noise in the background grew a bit louder. "Well, um, yeah, I guess," he stammered, "but, you know, I think there's always going to be conflict, and people who do bad stuff...I mean, that's just part of life, unfortunately."

Auravine turned to face him. "In your world, perhaps. But it does not have to be that way here."

"How's it look over there?" Felicity called out. Joel turned and saw his fellow offworlder approaching with Thornleaf. "Any evidence that jerk-face came back from the dead?"

"What? Jerk-face?" Joel said.

Felicity sighed. "I mean Marshall."

"Oh—uh, no. Did you guys find anything?"

"Nope. This whole private investigator thing is harder than I thought it would be."

"I knew that coming up here would be a waste of time," Thornleaf grumbled.

"Where is Fireflower?" Auravine asked.

"Still at the main altar, I believe," Thornleaf replied. "We should go and—"

The humming noise in the background suddenly crescendoed into a sound that resembled squealing feedback. Auravine's heat cast vanished, along with all of the wisps of Aura that were in the air.

"What the heck?" Felicity exclaimed.

"The Aura's gone," Joel said, looking around. The yellow layer of Aura that had covered the gravesites was now absent as well.

"Yeah, I noticed."

Then, as a stiff breeze began to blow, the feedback morphed into an atonal melody that Joel found very familiar.

Hey, that sounds just like—

"No need to be alarmed," Thornleaf said.

—Marshall's guitar solo from Biledriver's first live EP—

"I am sure there is a simple explanation for what is happening here."

—the one that they recorded in Seattle—

"One that has nothing to do with angering the Aura, or any of that nonsense."

—and released in between their third and fourth studio albums.

"Uh oh," Felicity said, taking a step back. "Is that simple enough for you?"

Joel turned to follow her gaze. Out from behind every rock and pillar within view, several large slithering creatures with glowing red scales and gator-like heads had emerged. "Are those...Lightsnakes?" he said.

"They cannot be," Thornleaf answered with uncharacteristic alarm. "They no longer exist!"

"Well, these seem pretty real to me," Felicity said, urgency creeping into her voice. "Any suggestions?"

"Stun them!" Thornleaf barked, raising his wavebow. The tall shaman gave his instrument a good strum, but nothing happened other than the sound of a slightly out-of-tune A chord.

"No Aura, remember?" Felicity said.

The Lightsnakes swarmed their way toward Joel and the others, looking like a river of red as their numbers grew with each passing second.

"Run!" Thornleaf yelled.

The group turned to run, but they found themselves cut off by another group of Lightsnakes that had appeared, seemingly out of nowhere.

"Doesn't anybody have, like, a knife, or something?" Felicity shrieked.

No one replied. The Lightsnakes closed in. Frantic, Joel whirled around, searching for a possible avenue of escape, but he and the others were now surrounded on all sides by the writhing eel-like creatures.

"Fireflower!" Thornleaf shouted. "Where are you? We need help!"

Several Lightsnakes right in front of Joel were coiling up, as if tensing to strike. Anticipating what they were going to do, he turned his wavebow around and grabbed it by the neck with both hands. "Look out—they're gonna—"

A Lightsnake leaped up at him. He swung his instrument like a baseball bat, knocking the creature away.

"Nice shot!" Felicity exclaimed as she turned her wavebow around as well.

Joel gave her a quick grin before he took a backhanded swipe at another leaping Lightsnake, knocking that one away.

"Wavebows should not be used in that fashion!" Thornleaf snapped as he ducked under a Lightsnake's attack.

Felicity swatted away two Lightsnakes in quick succession. "Shut up and swing!" she yelled.

A Lightsnake coiled around Joel's right leg. He struck it on the head, causing it to loosen its grip, and then kicked at another one that was attempting to wrap itself around his left leg. He glanced at Felicity and saw that she was busy flailing away with her wavebow, repelling the creatures that were coming at her from every direction. Auravine, however, did not seem to be doing as well.

"No—get off of me!" the young healer screamed.

Auravine was being dragged to the ground by several Lightsnakes that had her firmly in their grasp. Joel swung his wavebow and hit one of them that had wrapped itself around her waist.

"Ah!" Auravine cried, buckling over.

"Oops—sorry!" Joel said. Holding his wavebow in his right hand, he grabbed at the Lightsnake with his other hand and tried to pry it off of her. As he did so, though, another Lightsnake bit his right wrist, causing him to drop his instrument. Wincing in pain, he bent over to try to retrieve his wavebow, but then he was knocked down from behind. Within a matter of seconds, he was overcome by a mass of Lightsnakes.

CHAPTER 13: AN UNEXPECTED ENEMY

With a Lightsnake coiled around his head, Joel couldn't see a thing. But judging from the odd, bumping sensation, he assumed that he was being carried along on the backs of several Lightsnakes while several more remained tightly wrapped around his body. Remembering what had happened the last time he was constrained by the grotesque gator-eel creatures, he tried to startle them by faking a sneeze, but this time, they reacted only by tightening their grip on him.

Okay, he thought, *so that didn't work.*

After what felt like a very long time (but was, in reality, only twelve minutes), the Lightsnake around Joel's head uncoiled itself and slithered away. Then, a moment later, all of the other Lightsnakes released him as well, dropping him to the ground. His first instinct was to jump to his feet, but to his dismay, he found that he was stuck on his back in a thick layer of sticky, viscous fluid. He was in some kind of dark cave, with Felicity on one side of him and Thornleaf on the other.

"So this is what a roach trap must feel like," Felicity remarked.

"Felicity?" Fireflower's voice sounded. "Is that you?"

"No, it's—" Felicity started to say before catching herself. "Yeah, it's me. Fireflower?"

"Yes. Where are the others?"

"I am here," Thornleaf said.

"Um, me too," Joel replied.

There was a pause. Then Fireflower asked: "What about Auravine?"

No response.

"I saw her getting captured by the Lightsnakes," Joel said.

"That's a big help," Felicity muttered.

"I hope she is all right," Fireflower said. "What about the rest of you—is anyone hurt?"

"Nope," Felicity answered.

"I am fine," Thornleaf declared.

"Me too," Joel said, trying to ignore the pain in his right wrist where the Lightsnake had bit him. "Just—just a little stuck."

"As are we all, it seems," Fireflower said. "I must apologize—I did not expect us to be attacked by Lightsnakes."

"I don't think any of us did," Felicity said.

"Those accursed creatures are supposed to be extinct," Thornleaf groused. "Were you able to commune with the Aura?" he asked Fireflower.

"I am afraid not," she replied. "They captured me before I was able to do so."

"Of course they did," Felicity muttered. "Not that it matters, I guess, since now we know who's behind the kidnappings."

"We do? Who?" Joel said.

"Hello? The Lightsnakes?"

"Oh, right."

"Something about this situation still does not add up, though," Fireflower said. "The other Wavemakers are not here, and they all disappeared in conjunction with the Moonfire. We were simply ambushed. This could just be an unrelated incident."

"I do not believe that it is," Thornleaf said. "I think that the Lightsnakes are working with Stoneroot."

"Seriously?" Felicity scoffed.

"Think about it—he knew that we were coming up here. It was all a trap, just like I said earlier. That is why the truth cast confirmed what he was saying—he *himself* does not have the missing Wavemakers, the Lightsnakes do! They must have made some kind of deal to eliminate us."

"Then where are the others?" Felicity said.

"I fear the worst," was the tall shaman's grim reply.

A few moments passed, during which nothing could be heard but a howling wind outside the cave.

"Um...there is something else, though," Joel spoke up.

"What?" Felicity said.

"Remember that feedback sound we heard when the Aura disappeared?"

"Yeah, what about it? You know, you can just continue with what you're saying without me prompting you all the time."

"What do you mean?"

"Never mind. Go on."

"Well, the sound...it wasn't just a random sound. It was Marshall's guitar solo from Biledriver's first live EP. Like, exactly, note-for-note."

"Dude, that solo didn't even *have* notes. It was just a wall of noise."

"I know it sounded like that, but trust me, it had notes."

"Okay, fine, I believe you. But so what?"

"I dunno, I'm just saying...maybe he actually does have something to do with all of this. Maybe he created those Moonfires. Maybe he's the one destroying the Aura."

"I think that my theory is a bit more believable," Thornleaf said as a clap of thunder sounded. "If Marshall Byle, as a wraith or not, had enough power to do those things, then why did he not just kill us right away? Why hide in the shadows and bother with all of these petty little machinations?"

"Well, he doesn't like to be bored, I know that," Joel responded, starting to feel a little irritated.

"I think that your fearful memories of him are influencing your feelings on this matter."

"I'm serious, though. I know what I heard."

"Hey, you wanna know what I think?" Felicity interjected. "I think that, right now, it doesn't matter who's responsible. What *does* matter is: how the heck are we gonna get out of here?"

"Felicity is right," Fireflower said. "Rather than debating amongst ourselves, we need to be thinking of a way to escape."

"Uh, well...can you do that hands-free wavebow thing?" Joel suggested, recalling how Fireflower had the ability to perform a wavecast without touching her instrument.

"No Aura, remember?" Felicity said.

"Oh—right."

"I don't know why you guys keep forgetting about that."

"Even if the Aura were available," Fireflower said, "I am afraid that particular technique only works if the wavebow is within my line of sight."

"Figures." Felicity sniffed.

"With enough effort, I should be able to free myself from this substance." Thornleaf grunted. The sounds of the tall shaman struggling against his bonds went on for another full minute or so before they stopped.

"Any luck?" Felicity asked.

"Not yet," Thornleaf exhaled. "But I believe that if I—"

Joel heard the slithering of a Lightsnake. Out of the corner of his eye, he watched as the creature slithered over Thornleaf's face and then over his torso, leaving its back half over the tall shaman's mouth.

"What happened?" Felicity said.

"The Lightsnakes are back," Joel replied. "And, uh, I think they heard us talking."

"Great," she sighed.

A moment later, a different Lightsnake covered Joel's body and mouth in a similar fashion. He rolled his eyes to the left and saw that Felicity had also received the same treatment. She tried numerous times to bite the Lightsnake, but it merely avoided her attempts until she finally gave up.

"You probably taste bad, anyway," she mumbled before the creature covered her mouth once more.

As the sounds of a thunderstorm raged on outside, Joel continued to try to think of another way to escape.

If I remember correctly, Lightsnakes can't stay on the island's surface for too long because of their unstable Aura presences. So they're going to have to let us up eventually, in order to take us back to wherever their new lair is. Then, when they do, we can make a break for it. So for now, we just have to wait.

As he waited, Joel occupied his mind with random lists, song lyrics, and thoughts about how he couldn't wait for Fireflower or Auravine to heal the lingering pain in his wrist. Several hours passed by, but still, the Lightsnakes did not move.

What the heck are they doing? Or, I mean, not doing? I mean, why aren't they moving? Don't they care that they're basically killing themselves by just staying here?

Several more hours passed by. Even though Joel couldn't raise his head to see outside, he knew that nighttime had arrived.

Weird—the Lightsnakes have been here all day. Well, maybe they'll wither up soon, or whatever, and then we can just walk out of here. I guess that—

Hello, Joel, a faint, familiar voice interrupted.

Joel frantically searched the cave for a second before he realized that the voice was coming from inside of his head. *Nineteen?*

I do not have much time, so I need to make this brief.

Where are you? Can you help us? Joel said in his mind before he remembered that the powerful and mysterious tiger-ram entity known as Nineteen could only speak to him telepathically, not hear him.

The other Wavemakers are being held captive, Nineteen said in his calm, silky voice. *You need to rescue them before it is too late.*

Held captive? Where? By who? Oh, right—he can't hear me. Dangit.

I will send help for you. After that, you must—

Nineteen's voice abruptly broke up into static, as if the connection had been lost.

Nineteen? What happened? I must what?

Suddenly, Joel developed a splitting headache. A moment later, a man-sized creature with an alligator head, three arms, and three legs came marching into Joel's field of vision, followed by several more just like it. One of the creatures stopped next to Joel, and the Lightsnake that was on top of him slithered away.

"What's happening?" Felicity said. "Who are these guys?"

"I think we're being rescued," Joel said, even though talking made his headache worse.

"But these are *full-grown* Lightsnakes," Fireflower said, sounding like she was in pain as well.

"I know, but Nineteen—he said—"

The full-grown Lightsnake that was standing next to Joel reached down and grabbed his arms with two of its large pincer claws. Then it pulled him up, ripping him off of the sticky surface in the process.

"Are you rescuing us?" Joel asked. "Did Nineteen send you?"

The full-grown Lightsnake made a noise that sounded like a snicker. Its comrades grabbed Felicity, Fireflower, and Thornleaf and pulled them up off the ground as well.

"Hey, not so rough," Felicity complained.

The drone Lightsnakes all skittered out of the way as their upright counterparts began to drag the four Wavemakers along the ground toward the cave entrance. Now feeling faint and woozy, Joel saw that outside the cave, it was snowing heavily and everything was bathed in a sickly orange light.

It's another Moonfire, he realized. *The drone Lightsnakes were waiting for nightfall. They were holding us until the big ones could get here.*

"I'm not sure...this is a rescue," Felicity said in a voice barely above a whisper.

"I think...you're right," Joel responded.

"Joel...you said you...spoke to Nineteen?" Fireflower rasped.

"Yeah...he said that he was sending help...and that we need to...save the other Wavemakers," Joel managed to croak before his ears started to ring and his vision became blurry.

The Lightsnakes dragged Joel and the others out of the cave and into a full-blown snowstorm. Squinting, Joel could make out two orange spots in the sky that he assumed were the moons, and a dark blob standing on the ground about ten feet in front of him that he assumed was someone in a hooded cloak, holding a big bag.

Who is that? Joel wondered. *Stoneroot? No, too thin. Marshall? No, too short.*

The hooded figure approached. Joel blinked furiously as he fought to focus. Then, for a brief moment, he caught a good glimpse of the figure's face.

Wait—that's...that's Auravine!

Auravine returned his stare. She had a vacant, faraway look in her eyes.

"Auravine," Joel said with all the strength he could muster, "help...help us."

The young healer appeared to say something in response, but all Joel could hear amidst the loud ringing in his ears was crackling static. She looked at the Lightsnake that was holding Fireflower and then pointed at the orange spots in the sky.

Auravine—what are you doing?

The Lightsnake took a few steps forward before it launched itself into the air and flew through the swirling snow toward the moons. It grew smaller and smaller until finally it vanished.

What the heck? Joel thought as he struggled to remain conscious. *It just took Fireflower! And Auravine was directing it!* Suddenly, he felt nauseous; he wasn't sure if it was a symptom caused by the Moonfire or by his shock at seeing someone he trusted—and liked, perhaps?—turning out to be the one who was behind the kidnappings all along.

Auravine said something else that also came out as static, and the Lightsnake holding Thornleaf took a few steps forward as well. Instead of becoming airborne, however, it turned and made a screeching noise. The Lightsnake carrying Joel also turned. Several blurry shapes that looked vaguely like oversized lions were moving toward them.

What are those things? Joel wondered as everything around him became a few shades darker.

Auravine shouted out a stream of static while the three remaining Lightsnakes screeched like crazed monkeys. Then the lionlike shapes charged. The Lightsnake holding Thornleaf took off, but before it could get too high, one of the lionlike shapes leaped forward and seized the Lightsnake's right leg in its mouth, pulling both Lightsnake and Thornleaf back down to the ground. Joel's Lightsnake dropped him facedown in the snow and swung its pincers at another lion-shape, which dodged the blow. Joel tried to crawl back toward the cave, but he barely had enough strength to keep his eyes open at this point. The last thing he felt before he passed out was the sensation of something big and soft burrowing underneath him, lifting him up, and carrying him away.

CHAPTER 14: SWORDCATS

Joel awoke to the sound of loud purring. His headache was gone and his eyesight was clear. He was lying on his side with his left arm under his head and his right arm out in front of him. As the purring continued, he saw the Lightsnake's bite mark on his right wrist slowly heal up and disappear.

"Whoa," he whispered.

Looking up, Joel saw that the source of the purring noise was an animal the size of a large lion with an appropriately catlike face, a corona of spiky horns, and a shaggy silver-gray coat that seemed to be made out of long, serrated knives. Startled, Joel sat up and scrambled back a few paces.

"What the—who are you?"

The creature cocked its head even as it continued to purr.

Joel looked around. It was still dark out, but the moons were normal. He and the animal were in the middle of a thick copse of goldenorb trees, along with Felicity and Thornleaf, who were both lying on the ground, unconscious. Four more of the lionlike creatures were also there, all of them sitting and purring.

"So I guess you were the ones who saved us, huh?" Joel said. "Did, um...did Nineteen send you?"

The creature stopped purring and made a little growling sound that seemed more like a response than a threat.

"I guess that's a yes? Anyway, thanks."

Joel carefully reached out to try to pet the animal when suddenly—

"Agh!" Thornleaf exclaimed. "Swordcats!"

Joel pulled his hand back. Thornleaf had awoken and was scrambling to back away from the animals.

"Don't worry," Joel said, "they're friendly."

Thornleaf shot Joel an incredulous look. "Friendly? Swordcats are wild, dangerous beasts. Travelers to the Sacred Site know to avoid them at all costs!"

"They don't seem dangerous to me. In fact, I think they saved us from the Lightsnakes."

"Saved us for their own consumption, perhaps! Where are our wavebows?"

"Um...I dunno."

"What's all the ruckus?" a faint voice said. It was Felicity.

"Oh, hey, you're awake," Joel said.

"Yeah, no kidding, genius." she coughed.

"Quiet," Thornleaf hissed, getting to his feet. "These are swordcats. We need to slowly walk away from them and hope that they do not pounce."

"I really don't think they're gonna attack us," Joel insisted.

One of the swordcats walked behind a goldenorb tree and returned with something that looked like a six-legged, three-tailed fish in its jaws.

"What the heck is that?" Felicity said as she sat up.

The swordcat trotted over and dropped the bizarre fish thing in front of her. Then it looked up at her expectantly and resumed purring.

"I think it wants you to have that," Joel said.

Felicity wrinkled her nose. "Uh—no thanks," she said to the swordcat. "You...you eat it. It's yours."

"See?" Once again, Joel reached out to pet the swordcat in front of him. This time the animal leaned forward, allowing Joel to stroke the side of its face.

"How are you doing that?" Thornleaf asked in amazement.

"Weird, right?" Felicity said. "It's like he's some kind of animal whisperer or something."

"It's not me," Joel said, still petting the swordcat. "I think Nineteen sent them to help us."

Thornleaf raised an eyebrow. "Nineteen? You mean that indigenous creature you met in Prism Valley?"

"Yeah."

"Not to sound ungrateful or anything, but if he's around, why isn't he helping us out more?" Felicity asked. "Or, you know, at least tell us who's kidnapping all the Wavemakers."

"I dunno...it seems like he can only talk to me when I'm around that Moonfire thing," Joel answered.

"Figures."

"He did say that the other Wavemakers are being held captive," Joel continued, "and that we need to rescue them before it's too late."

"Held captive?" Thornleaf echoed. "Where? By who?"

"I think he was about to tell me when he got cut off and the Lightsnakes showed up."

"Of course," Felicity muttered. "Did they take Fireflower? I couldn't see too well, but it looked like they did."

Joel nodded. "Yeah. One of them flew up into the sky with her, and then they disappeared."

"Hmm," Thornleaf mused. "Probably some sort of illusion manufactured by Stoneroot. Did you see that hooded figure standing in front of us?"

"Um...yeah."

"I am quite sure that was him. One of the mature Lightsnakes must have flown him back up to the Sacred Site while the drones kept us trapped in that cave."

"Actually, I got a pretty good look at the figure, and...I don't think it was him."

A pause ensued. The swordcat that Joel was petting raised a paw to its mouth and began to lick it.

"Just tell us who you think it was," Felicity sighed.

"What? Oh, well..." Joel hedged, reluctant to say what he thought. He didn't even want to believe it himself. "I...I think it was Auravine."

"That is crazy," Thornleaf scoffed. "You must be mistaken. I do not blame you, though, given the effect that the Moonfire had on all of us."

"I'm pretty sure it was her. I could make out the shapes of her facial features and stuff."

Felicity gave Thornleaf a side-eyed glance. "Not sure I'd want to argue with Mister Sight Guy here. Besides, you gotta admit—she wasn't with us in that cave, and we don't know where she was all those other times someone got taken."

Thornleaf snorted. "But why would Auravine be kidnapping Wavemakers?" he said. "And why would she be working with Lightsnakes? What motivation could she possibly have?"

Joel frowned, recalling the fact that Auravine did not want to tell him about the big decision she was facing. *Could this be what she had been talking about? Could she really have chosen to betray the Wavemaker Order?* "I dunno. It doesn't make a whole lot of sense."

"No, it does not," Thornleaf agreed.

Felicity clicked her tongue. "But you just said that it was her. Are you changing your story now?"

"No, but there must be a good explanation," Joel replied. "She did look a little weird—especially her eyes. They were kinda blank, like how all the villagers looked the last time we were here. I dunno, maybe...maybe she wasn't doing it willingly. Maybe she was under some kind of mind control."

"Mind control..." Thornleaf echoed, furrowing his brow. Then his eyes flashed, and he exclaimed, "Of course!"

"Wait," Joel said. "Are you being sarcastic?"

"Remember what I said when we were on the look-out platform at the temple?" Thornleaf went on, ignoring Joel's question. "About how Stoneroot possessed an illegal mind-control potion?"

"Yeah," Felicity said, "although I think the fight you had with him about that subject is a little more memorable."

"His potion—that is what you are referring to, is it not?" Thornleaf said to Joel, ignoring Felicity's remark.

"Um, sure." *Actually, I was just reaching for a reason as to why Auravine would do something bad, but whatever...*

"This explains so much," Thornleaf said, nodding.

"Hold on," Felicity said. "I thought Stoneroot told us that he *didn't* have a mind-control potion."

"Actually," Joel said, "come to think of it, he never denied it. He just said 'how dare you accuse me of such a criminal act'."

"Okay, fine." Felicity sniffed. "But even if he does, I thought that everyone on the island is protected from mind control."

"Mind-control *wavecasts*," Thornleaf said. "But Stoneroot is an expert in traditional medicines. Fireflower thought he would not have the knowledge to create such a thing, but she constantly underestimates him."

"Man, for a guy who hates him as much as you do, you sure seem to know a lot about him," Felicity said.

Thornleaf paused before responding. "It is always good to be familiar with one's adversaries."

"Did you train with him when you were younger or something?" Joel asked.

"Why would you think that?" Thornleaf said, somewhat defensively.

"I dunno. Back at the Silencer Stronghold, you said something about the Wavemaker Order teaching you more than Stoneroot ever could have."

"I did not say that."

"Yeah, you did," Felicity nodded. "I remember that part, at least."

"I—that is just a common Spectraland expression. The translation cast probably did not communicate it to you properly. Anyway, we are getting off track. We need to focus on the situation at hand."

"Okay, sheesh," Felicity huffed.

"Um...what were we talking about again?" Joel asked.

"Stoneroot's mind-control potion," Thornleaf replied.

"Oh, right."

"I have another question about that," Felicity said. "Say Stoneroot really does have a mind-control potion. Why did he only use it on Auravine? Why not on all the Wavemakers?"

"She is young and impressionable, while the rest of us are more strong willed," Thornleaf answered. "But once he has everyone else in captivity, he will be able to break us down over time. Then he can administer the potion and make us all publicly renounce our abilities. That must be his plan!"

"Either that or he's just letting the Lightsnakes kill everyone while he blames it on the Aura," Felicity said. "Isn't that what you were worried about earlier?"

Thornleaf shook his head. "That was before this revelation about the mind-control potion came to light. I realize now that we will be of more use to him alive than dead."

"Okay, um, wait," Joel said, trying to keep up. "So, we're thinking that Stoneroot has Auravine under mind control, and he's using her and some Lightsnakes to kidnap Wavemakers so he can brainwash us?"

"Pretty much, yeah." Felicity shrugged.

"It is all so clear now," Thornleaf said under his breath, as if he were talking to himself. "He has become just as bad as Byle. He will use us to end our own order forever. He will take over the whole island. He may even use the two of you to..."

"To what?" Joel asked.

Thornleaf exhaled. "To perform misguided missions for him back on your homeworld."

"Misguided missions?" Felicity said, furrowing her brow. "Like what?"

"Like capturing—or eliminating—others with your abilities, to make sure that no more Wavemakers cross over into Spectraland."

Joel swallowed. *Okay, yeah, that doesn't sound good.*

"All right, fine. Obviously, we've gotta stop the guy," Felicity said as she got to her feet. "So what's our next move?"

"The first thing we should do is locate our wavebows," Thornleaf said, looking around. "I do not suppose these creatures know where they are, do they?"

Joel turned his attention to the assembled swordcats. One of them turned its head and licked its shoulder, but other than that, there was no response. "I don't think they do."

"Auravine or the Lightsnakes probably rounded them up, don't you think?" Felicity said. "I mean, we were stuck in that cave for, like, forever, so they had a lot of time to scrounge around."

"We should probably check the Sacred Site anyway," Thornleaf said.

"Isn't that gonna be a major hike to get back up there?" Felicity said. "I'm not really in the mood for—"

The swordcat next to Felicity walked behind her and pushed its head into the back of her legs. She shrieked as she fell to her knees.

"They are attacking!" Thornleaf yelled. "Run!"

Shocked, Joel moved to help Felicity, but as he did so, the swordcat stuck its head between her legs and propped her up on its back.

"What...what just happened?" she exclaimed, brushing her hair out of her eyes.

"Um, I think it wants to give you a ride," Joel said.

"You can't be serious."

"I am."

"There is no way I am going to trust one of these beasts to serve as a mount," Thornleaf scoffed.

"Hey, I say we give it a shot," Felicity said as the swordcat she was sitting on made a little gurgling noise. "They actually do seem pretty cool."

"Um...is it okay if I ride you?" Joel asked the swordcat in front of him. It replied with a short, affirmative-sounding growl, so he carefully climbed onto the creature's back. "See?" he said to Thornleaf. "They want to do this."

"C'mon, man," Felicity said. "If they wanted to eat us, they would've done it already."

Thornleaf flashed a skeptical expression at the other swordcats. One of them, the largest of the group, sauntered up to him and began rubbing its cheek against his leg. "Very well," the tall shaman sighed as he clambered aboard the animal. "But even so, it will still take us a long time to get back to the Sacred Site."

"Beats walking." Felicity shrugged. "Besides, maybe they're faster than you think."

A few moments passed by. The swordcats made no effort to move.

"Or, maybe not." Thornleaf smirked.

Felicity shot him an unamused look. "So, like, how do we do this?" she said, turning to Joel. "Do we say 'giddyup' or something?"

"Um...I'm not sure."

"Why don't you ask your guy there?"

Joel looked down at his swordcat. "Are...are you going to go?"

"I knew this was foolish." Thornleaf sniffed.

"We're ready," Joel said to his swordcat. "You can go now."

Rather than going anywhere, the three swordcats that were carrying the Wavemakers crouched down and closed their eyes.

"All right, that is enough," Thornleaf said, "I am getting off of this—"

Then, without warning, the swordcats leaped up and took off.

"Whoa!" Joel yelled, grabbing the animal's horns to keep himself from falling. After a few seconds of racing through the goldenorb trees, Joel let go of the swordcat's horns, leaned forward, and wrapped his arms around the animal's shoulders. He turned and saw that Felicity and Thornleaf were right behind him.

"Yeah!" Felicity shouted, laughing. "Now, that's what I'm talking about!"

Joel grinned. When he turned back around, however, his grin vanished. They were headed, at full speed, straight toward a giant boulder beside a particularly dense cluster of trees.

How do I steer this thing? he wondered urgently.

The swordcat tensed its muscles.

Whoa—is it gonna try to jump over?

The boulder was coming up fast. Just as Joel was about to bail out, the swordcat leaped. There was a brief flash of light, and Joel felt a strange sensation, as if a giant hand was grabbing his insides and pulling them forward. After blinking several times, he saw that they were now in a completely different area; the goldenorb trees were few and far between, and there was a small, grassy clearing up ahead. He looked back and saw Felicity, Thornleaf, and their respective swordcats, but no sign of the boulder he thought they were all going to crash into.

What the heck?

His swordcat tensed once more. Then it leaped again, leading to another flash of light and another tugging sensation. The next thing Joel knew, they were bounding up a rocky trail similar to the one he and the other Wavemakers had taken before they found Thornleaf. Joel looked up and saw that they were now very close to the mountain's peak. His swordcat ran for a few more seconds before it slowed to a trot.

"Okay, now, *that* was seriously awesome," Felicity said as she and her swordcat caught up to Joel.

"Yeah," Joel agreed. "It's like they can teleport or something. Short-range teleportation."

Thornleaf and his swordcat trotted up on the other side of Joel. "So that must be how they are able to appear out of nowhere," the tall shaman remarked.

"Yup," Felicity chuckled. "Just like regular cats back home."

♪♪♪

Soon after, the three Wavemakers and the swordcats arrived back at the Sacred Site. The snow had stopped, but the Aura seemed even weaker than before, and the droning sound could still be heard, loud and clear.

"If the Lightsnakes show up again, these things can take 'em, right?" Felicity asked Joel as they rode their new mounts through the various rock formations.

"What things?"

"The swordcats."

"I hope so."

Joel's swordcat growled, as if to concur with Joel's opinion.

"I wonder why they didn't get sick," Felicity went on. "Like the other animals who were exposed to the Moonfire."

"I think they have healing powers," Joel guessed. "My wrist got bitten by a Lightsnake, but after the swordcats rescued us, it healed up, like, instantly."

"Ah, maybe that's what all the purring was about," Felicity said. "I've heard that the vibration of a regular cat's purr can promote healing, or something like that."

"I've heard of that too!" Joel exclaimed. "Like, the frequency of a purr is somewhere around twenty-five hertz, which is supposed to improve bone density, and because cats sleep so much, they—"

"This is all very fascinating," Thornleaf interrupted, "but we should stay focused on finding our wavebows."

"Fine, whatever," Felicity said. "Just don't suggest that we split up. I've seen enough horror flicks to know that that's a bad idea."

The trio began searching around. To look for Fireflower's wavebow, they went to the main altar, a circular stone platform surrounded by carved wooden columns that resembled totem poles.

"Hey, I don't suppose *you* can do that communing-with-the-Aura thing," Felicity said to Thornleaf.

"If I could, I would have mentioned that already," Thornleaf groused.

"All right, just checking."

They found nothing at the main altar. So they decided to head for the other place where the rest of them last had their instruments in hand: in front of the burial area. As they trotted along, Joel noticed that—apart from the whole teleportation thing—riding a swordcat was quite similar to riding a slimeback; both animals did mostly whatever he asked them to do, as long as they were capable of doing it. As for Felicity, she seemed much more at ease with her swordcat than with her slimeback, Dreamer, and even Thornleaf's swordcat appeared to respond well to his commands, despite the tall shaman's continued misgivings about riding such a creature.

"We should name these guys," Felicity said, stroking her swordcat's shiny yellow coat as they approached the gravesite. "I'm calling mine Goldie."

"Okay," Joel agreed, "I'll go with...Platinum."

"Seriously?"

"Yeah, 'cause he's kind of that color, and, you know, gold and platinum, like albums, and stuff."

"All right, sounds good. What about you, Thornleaf?"

"I am not naming this beast," Thornleaf scoffed. "I can still hardly believe that I am using one as a mount."

"You're no fun all of a sudden."

"If it is fun you are looking for, I—"

"Hey, uh—guys?" Joel said, noticing a hole in the ground where there wasn't one before. "I think we have a problem."

"Let me guess," Felicity said. "That's Marshall's grave."

"Yeah," Joel confirmed.

"Did he crawl out?"

Joel got off of Platinum and crouched down in front of the exhumed plot. "I don't think so. It looks like somebody dug it up."

Felicity made a gagging noise. "Gross. Who would wanna do that?"

"Stoneroot would," Thornleaf said, his voice grim.

"What? Why?"

"I do not know, but I can only assume that it would be for some sort of terrible experiment."

"Then why wouldn't he have just dug it up the first time he was here?"

"Because he wanted Auravine and the Lightsnakes to do it, so that he can remain blameless. Just like with everything else."

"I guess that makes sense, but still—gross."

Returning to their wavebow hunt, they looked around for several more minutes but came up empty.

"So, are you guys ready to admit I was right?" Felicity said.

"About what?" Joel asked.

"That the wavebows wouldn't be up here."

"You didn't say that. You said that Auravine or the Lightsnakes probably rounded them up."

"Dude, same thing."

"This is a very unfortunate situation," Thornleaf grumbled. "Without our wavebows, breaking into the Silencer Stronghold to rescue the others would be an act of sheer folly."

"Don't you guys keep spares or backups at the temple?" Felicity asked.

"Unfortunately, no. The Luthier only makes one instrument per Wavemaker."

"We could go see her," Joel suggested. "She made me a new one before."

"That was part of a special deal that Fireflower struck with her."

"Ugh," Felicity said, "of course it was."

"Should we go tell the chiefs about our theory?" Joel asked. "Maybe they can help us."

"Not yet," Thornleaf replied. "We have no proof of Stoneroot's guilt, and knowing Twotrunk and Silverfern, they would probably blame the reappearance of the Lightsnakes on us."

"Okay, so now what?" Felicity asked.

Her question was greeted by nothing but the droning noise in the background. One of the swordcats let out a huge yawn.

C'mon, think, Suzuki, Joel prodded himself. *Let's see, in all of the movies and TV shows that I've seen, any time someone is under mind control, there's almost always a way to snap them out of it. So, if we can find out what that way is, we can get Auravine back to normal, and then she can lead us to the others.*

But what would that way be? If it was a potion that Stoneroot used, then there must be an antidote...would he have the antidote? Even if he did, though, he obviously wouldn't just give it to us, and like Thornleaf said, we can't just go breaking into his place without our wavebows. So, who else might have an antidote to a mind-control potion? Hmm...oh, wait—

"I have an idea," he announced.

"Just spit it out, man," Felicity sighed.

"Oh—uh, right. Where's the Pit of Ashes?"

CHAPTER 15: PIT OF ASHES

With the swordcats alternating between occasional bursts of teleportation and a more standard form of movement (running), Joel, Felicity, and Thornleaf made it across the island in relatively short order. Eventually, as yet another set of dark clouds rolled in, they arrived at a dusty, desertlike plain that was completely barren except for a small, square hut that sat right in the middle of the area. In contrast to other huts on the island, which were mostly made out of wood and other plant-based materials, this one looked to be composed of stone and hardened clay, and it had thick, black vertical lines painted on its sides.

"I think the swordcats are getting tired," Joel noted as Platinum slowly trudged along the gravelly surface.

"They can rest soon," Thornleaf replied. "We are almost there."

"I don't see a pit anywhere," Felicity said, squinting.

"It is underneath that hut."

"Are you kidding? Doesn't seem very secure to me."

"Just wait," Thornleaf said.

As they continued across the plain, a light rain began to fall.

"Hey, so, tell me your plan again," Felicity said to Joel as they drew closer to their destination.

"Again? It was pretty simple."

"Yeah, well, I wasn't really paying attention the first time."

"Um, okay. So, I figured that first, we should get some kind of antidote for mind-control. Then tonight, after the moons are out again, Auravine and the Lightsnakes will probably try to come and get us, right?"

"Sure, yeah, why not."

"All right, so before nightfall, each of us takes our swordcat and goes to a different location."

"Split up, in other words."

"Um, yeah."

"I don't like it already. But go on."

"Okay, so, since Auravine can only cast the Moonfire in one place at a time, after we split up, she'll be forced to try to kidnap only one of us."

"Wait—tell me again how you know that."

"Know what?"

"That she can only cast it in one place at a time."

"Well, Cloudpalm said that he never saw the Moonfire at Spiral Landing. Plus, if she could, then she and the Lightsnakes probably would've tried to kidnap Wavemakers from different locations at the same time."

"I guess..."

"Also, I actually saw the Moonfire from a distance," Joel confessed.

"You did? When? Where?"

"The night Riverhand and Starpollen got taken. When we were at Spiral Landing." Joel said with a flinch, expecting either Felicity or Thornleaf to scold him for not saying something about it sooner.

"What did it look like?" Felicity asked.

"Kinda like ball lightning, but orange. It appeared over the temple for a few seconds, and then it was gone."

"Hmm. All right, continue."

Whew, Joel thought. *No one got mad.* "Okay, so then, when Auravine and the Lightsnakes show up to kidnap one of us, that person's swordcat will hold them off. While that's happening, the other two will spot the Moonfire off in the distance, and their swordcats will teleport over to that location."

"I'm getting a headache already."

"Just bear with me here. So then, one swordcat will grab Auravine, one will grab the person who's there, and the other will continue holding off the Lightsnakes until they all have a chance to teleport back to where another one of us is, and then that person will give her the antidote."

"Man, that plan is so complicated, it's ridiculous. No wonder I tuned out before."

"Actually," Thornleaf said, "I think it is rather simple. I am not sure why you are having trouble grasping it."

"Oh, shut up," Felicity said.

Joel grinned. *Cool—Thornleaf likes my plan.*

"In fact," the tall shaman went on, "it is so basic, even a scaletop would be able to comprehend it."

"You're really annoying sometimes, you know that?" Felicity said.

Wait, Joel thought, *is he actually insulting my plan, and flirting with Felicity at the same time? Man, this is so confusing...*

Moments later, the trio arrived at the hut and dismounted. Thornleaf rapped on one of the structure's stone walls, which had a small hole in the middle of it.

"Hello," he said. "This is Thornleaf. Who is on guard duty?"

There was a pause. Then a voice behind the wall replied, "What is your business here?"

"We need to see the prisoner."

"Who are the other two with you?"

"They are Joel and Felicity, the offworlders."

Another, longer pause ensued. Then, the stone wall slowly moved a couple of feet to the side, and a female native armed with a long spear emerged.

"You know that unannounced visits to the Pit of Ashes are highly irregular," she said, pointing the spear-tip at Thornleaf's face.

"Good to see you too, Amberweed," Thornleaf chuckled, pushing the spear aside.

"You are terrible," Amberweed said with a smirk as she lowered her spear and took a step back. She glanced in Joel and Felicity's direction. "So, the legendary offworlders?"

"Yes," Thornleaf replied, turning to them. "Joel and Felicity, this is Amberweed, a good friend of mine from Headsmouth village."

"Um, hello," Joel said.

"'Sup," Felicity grunted.

"An honor." Amberweed nodded. "And what are these creatures with you?"

"They're swordcats," Joel answered.

Amberweed's jaw dropped. "Swordcats? From Sunpeak? How did you manage to tame them?"

"A long story," Thornleaf said. "I will tell you all about it later. Can we see the prisoner now?"

"Yes—yes, of course. Please, follow me."

Amberweed walked back into the hut, and Joel and the others followed. Inside, it was rather dark, with the only light provided by a small patch of glowmoss on one of the walls next to a wooden chair and a table. The swordcats curled up next to each other on the floor by the table and closed their eyes.

"So, are you enjoying your shift out here?" Thornleaf asked. He walked over to the opposite wall, where a black rectangular block about the size of a treasure chest lay on the ground.

"Oh, this duty is the *worst*," Amberweed groaned, walking over to stand beside the tall shaman. "I just arrived here last night, so there are still six more days before I am relieved. It will be pure agony."

"When is Chief Silverfern finally going to promote you to full-time personal guard service?"

"Be quiet," Amberweed said, hitting Thornleaf on the arm. "You know that she only considers the most senior guards for that assignment."

Felicity cleared her throat. "Hey, aren't we in sort of a rush here?"

"Forgive me," Amberweed said. "Thornleaf, I thought you were going to levitate the block aside—where is your wavebow?"

"Gone. You will have to push the block manually."

Amberweed raised an eyebrow. "Is this another one of your jokes?"

"I am afraid not."

"Hmm. What happened to your wavebow, may I ask?"

"Another long story," Thornleaf replied.

"You are being very evasive today," Amberweed said as she crouched down next to the block. "More so than usual."

"Suffice it to say that we think Stoneroot is involved."

"Speaking of Stoneroot—" Amberweed grunted as she pushed the block, which was apparently very heavy. "Did you hear about what happened?"

"No," Thornleaf said. "We have been out of touch for a couple of days. Was it something unfortunate?"

"Not for him. The Chieftain Council voted to make him one of their members."

"What?" Thornleaf exclaimed. "Oh, wait, I see—you are making that up. Not bad, Amberweed, you almost had me fooled there."

"I am not making that up," Amberweed exhaled as she stood up. The block had been moved far enough to reveal a hole with a vine-rope ladder leading down. "After what happened at your ceremony, there was enough public sentiment in his favor that the Silencer Stronghold was granted full village status."

"I cannot believe this." Thornleaf shook his head, uncharacteristically aghast. "Did even Chief Raintree vote in Stoneroot's favor?"

"I am not sure, but he was probably under a lot of pressure to do so," Amberweed replied. "The storm that followed the ceremony only served to worsen the unrest."

"Then our mission just became a little more urgent," Thornleaf said as he climbed into the hole. "You may wait here. The offworlders and I only need a few minutes."

"I have not fed the prisoner yet, so he may be a bit cranky," Amberweed warned.

Joel and Felicity followed Thornleaf down the vine-rope ladder. They descended for nearly twenty feet and then landed at the top of a corkscrew staircase that was coiled around a thick stone column. Looking around, Joel saw that the column extended down the middle of a giant gourd-shaped chasm that had only a blanket of steam as its floor some two hundred feet or so below. Little flakes of ash swirled around in the air, along with faint wisps of dark-purple Aura.

"Okay, I guess this *is* a pretty serious jail," Felicity said.

As they walked down the staircase, Joel saw, affixed to the walls of the chasm at various different points, large square cages that were made up of thorny vines twisted around wooden planks. The first three that they passed were empty.

"So, he's in one of these?" Joel asked.

"Yes, the lowest one," Thornleaf replied.

After passing two more empty cages, they approached the final one, which was attached to the wall at the chasm's widest point, just above the blanket of steam.

"Feels like a sauna in here," Felicity remarked, wiping her brow.

"Is someone—*hic*—there?" a voice said as they got close.

"Hello, Darkeye," Thornleaf said once they were level with the cage, which was a good thirty feet away.

"Ah, Thornleaf," Darkeye purred. "Has the lovely Amberweed been—*hic*—relieved of duty so soon?"

"I am not here to guard you," Thornleaf responded. "I am here to ask you a question."

"You and two—*hic*—others, apparently. Who are they, may I—*hic*—ask? I cannot see as well as—*hic*—I used to," Darkeye said with a raspy chuckle.

"They are the offworlders, Joel and Felicity."

Joel squinted at Darkeye. The wizened old native's empty eye socket seemed even larger and deeper than before, but other than that, the rest of him didn't seem to have changed at all—including his distinct lack of a personal Aura presence.

"What a—*hic*—pleasant surprise!" Darkeye exclaimed. "It certainly has been a—*hic*—very long time. So what—*hic*—can I do for you?"

"Are you able to create an antidote for mind control?" Thornleaf demanded.

Darkeye's one good eye widened. "Well, now, that—*hic*—depends."

"On what?"

"Well, first...what kind of—*hic*—mind control?"

"All kinds."

"Hmm, that would require a very—*hic*—powerful antidote indeed. If I created such an elixir for you, what would I—*hic*—get in return?"

Thornleaf pulled a lifepod from one of his belt pouches. "How about a meal," he said, sounding impatient and annoyed. "I heard that you may be hungry."

Darkeye snickered. "Come now, Thornleaf, you know that Spectraland law—*hic*—requires that I be fed no matter what," he wheezed. "Surely, you have something—*hic*—better to offer."

"What is it you want?" Thornleaf asked, taking a bite from the lifepod.

"I think that I would prefer something a little more—*hic*—permanent. Something like...my freedom."

"There is no way I will agree to that," Thornleaf scoffed.

"Then good luck with—*hic*—your mind-control victim, whoever they—*hic*—may be."

Thornleaf gave Joel and Felicity a scowling glance.

"Hey, don't look at me." Felicity shrugged.

Thornleaf turned back to Darkeye. Several long seconds passed by while the two of them simply stared at each other, saying nothing. Then the tall shaman took another bite from the lifepod and tossed the remainder of it into the blanket of steam below. “Very well,” he sighed. “Your freedom it is.”

Joel glanced at Thornleaf, unsure if that was a good idea or not.

“Excellent,” Darkeye said, flashing his toothless grin. “Now, the particular antidote that you—*hic*—require has three main ingredients that will need to be—*hic*—combined with the proper catalyst fluid generated by my—*hic*—internal organs.”

“Yuck,” Felicity muttered.

“So,” Darkeye continued, “after you—*hic*—release me, I will accompany you to the places where these—*hic*—ingredients can be found, and afterward, I will—*hic*—provide you with the catalyst.”

Joel narrowed his eyes. He was about to say something about how Darkeye would probably try to run away from them before the antidote was complete, but before he was able to do so, Thornleaf spoke up.

“How about this,” the tall shaman said, “you tell us what the ingredients are and where to find them and give us the catalyst fluid now. Then, if the antidote works, I will arrange for your release.”

“What assurances do I have that—*hic*—you will stand by your word?”

“Forget it,” Thornleaf grumbled, turning around. “We are wasting our time here. We will figure something else out.” He started to walk up the staircase.

“Um—but—” Joel glanced at Felicity, who merely shrugged and turned to follow the tall shaman. While Joel wasn’t too keen on the idea of freeing Darkeye, he knew that they really needed that antidote. He glanced back at the imprisoned old native before he turned and started up the staircase as well, wondering what they were going to do now. They had almost reached the level of the next cage when—

"No—wait," Darkeye called out.

Thornleaf stopped and looked over his shoulder but said nothing.

"Fine," Darkeye hissed. "I agree to—*hic*—your terms."

Joel let out a little sigh of relief.

"Excellent," Thornleaf said, pulling an object that resembled a wooden saltshaker from another, different pouch on his belt. He walked back down and underhanded the object at Darkeye, who caught it with one hand after it passed through the planks of his cage.

Pretty good depth perception for someone with just one eye, Joel thought.

"Throwing things instead of—*hic*—levitating them, Thornleaf?" Darkeye asked as he inspected the vial-like object. "What happened to your—*hic*—precious wavebows?"

"The steam down here is bad for their strings," Thornleaf replied dismissively. "Now hurry up with that fluid."

Darkeye opened the top of the vial and held it in front of his face. His pale single eye rolled upward in its socket, and a horrible gurgling noise could be heard from his throat. After thirteen seconds of gradual crescendo, the gurgling noise escalated into a loud hum, and then, with a sudden snap like a single firecracker going off, Darkeye opened his mouth, and a thick, purple liquid began to pour out, rolling off of his tongue and into the vial.

"That is just *so* disgusting." Felicity shuddered.

Darkeye finished up and closed the vial. Then he threw it back over to Thornleaf with a surprising amount of zip for someone who looked so frail.

"Perfect," Thornleaf said, putting the vial away. "Now, the ingredients."

Darkeye did not respond.

"Well?"

"Give me a moment to—*hic*—remember exactly what they are."

"Are you sure you really want your freedom?" Thornleaf snapped.

"Ah, yes, the first—*hic*—ingredient is...the golden sap from the trunk of a—*hic*—yellowbranch tree."

"Go on."

"The juice of a bloodseed from—*hic*—the heart of Red Gulch."

Felicity turned to Joel. "You're gonna remember all of this, right?"

"Uh, yeah, sure."

"Finally, you will need the—*hic*—venom of a bloomfish, which I believe the offworlders are—*hic*—already somewhat familiar with."

"Ugh, seriously?" Felicity groaned. "I hate those things."

"Does it matter how much we have of each, in relation to each other?" Thornleaf asked.

"No, the quantities do not—*hic*—matter. This is not a recipe for soup."

"Very well. Once we combine all the ingredients, how can we confirm that we have prepared the antidote correctly?"

"It will give off a—*hic*—wisp of light-blue smoke, turn as clear as water, and then smell like—*hic*—slimeback droppings."

"Gross," Felicity muttered. "Glad *I* don't have to drink it."

"All right, Darkeye," Thornleaf said, "we will be back."

"Soon, I—*hic*—hope."

The three Wavemakers turned and walked up the corkscrew staircase.

"Hey, you know, that was some decent bargaining there," Felicity said to Thornleaf as they neared the top. "I'm gonna have to take you used-car shopping with me."

"So, are we really gonna release Darkeye if the antidote works?" Joel asked. "I mean, he *was* Marshall's accomplice when Spectraland was almost destroyed."

"That is the deal we just made," Thornleaf replied.

"Besides," Felicity said, "coming to him was your idea, remember?"

"Well, yeah, but..."

They climbed up the vine-rope ladder and emerged back into the guard hut.

"Your swordcats are quite the sound sleepers," Amberweed said, absently inspecting the tip of her spear by the light of the glowmoss. "Did you get what you needed?"

"We did, thank you," Thornleaf said.

"I do not suppose you want to tell me what it was."

"Maybe later. We do need a few more things from you, however."

Amberweed raised an eyebrow. "Oh?"

"We need to borrow some weapons from your cache."

"There is not much here, you know that," Amberweed protested, placing her hands on her hips. "And whatever little there is, I cannot let go of. If a senior guard were to arrive for a surprise inspection—"

"Then I will take full responsibility," Thornleaf interrupted. "Please, Amberweed, this is an emergency situation."

"That you want to tell me nothing about."

"For now."

Amberweed paused and narrowed her eyes at the tall shaman.

"Please," Thornleaf repeated.

"Very well," the guard sighed. "This must be for something extremely important. I have never heard you say the word *please* twice in the same day before."

"Well, it is a special occasion."

Amberweed walked over to the table and pulled a small basket out from underneath it. As she did so, the swordcats got up, stretched, and sauntered aside.

"I hope they are ready for some extensive travel," Thornleaf said to Joel.

"Um, okay."

"This is all I have," Amberweed said, opening the basket. "Two short clubs, a few knives, a couple of blowguns..."

"The knives and a blowgun will do," Thornleaf said. "I assume you have some sleepdarts as well?"

"Of course. I can only give you a couple, though. I need the rest to shoot at the occasional fangworm that wanders by outside."

"Fair enough," Thornleaf chuckled. "How many doses does each dart have?"

"Three," she replied, handing over the weapons.

"That will suffice. Do you have leg sheaths for the knives?"

"Somewhere in here...yes, here you go."

"Perfect. Oh, and we also need some glowmoss stones, just in case."

"So demanding," Amberweed sighed. "Anything else?"

"No, that is it. I appreciate your assistance, Amberweed."

"You will owe me a big favor for this."

"Maybe I will say *please* three times the next time I see you."

Joel was about to point out that Thornleaf had just said *please* three times already when Felicity brushed past him, heading for the stone door.

"All right, let's get going," she grunted. "How the heck do you open this thing?"

"Before you go," Amberweed said, "I just want to remind you that many people are on Stoneroot's side now. So whatever you may be planning to do, you should probably be cautious."

"At this point," Thornleaf said, "I am not sure caution is a luxury we can afford."

CHAPTER 16: YELLOWBRANCH

Joel had to admit that traveling by swordcat, while both fun and efficient, could also be a bit disorienting at times. On some occasions, it would appear as if the animal's teleportation ability had flashed them forward only a dozen yards or so, while on other occasions it seemed as if they had skipped over miles of terrain in the blink of an eye. And apparently, it wasn't only space that the creatures were able to warp but time as well; in one instance, Joel could've sworn that after what felt like a good thirty-five minutes' worth of traveling, the position of the sun and the clouds in the sky had not changed at all. And so it was following an indeterminable amount of time that the three Wavemakers and their mounts found themselves approaching a large cluster of yellow palm trees that looked quite familiar.

"Hey," Joel said to Felicity, "isn't this that jungle we went through before?"

"What? When?"

"You know, when we were trying to catch up to Marshall at Crownrock."

"I guess." She shrugged. "I dunno, dude, that was awhile ago."

"You mean six months? Or nineteen years?"

"Whichever. So, what were we supposed to get from this place again?"

"Golden sap from the trunk of a yellowbranch tree," Joel answered.

"Sounds easy enough," she said, "but I'll bet you anything it's not."

"You are right—it is not," Thornleaf said. "Only about one in a hundred yellowbranch trees produce sap at any one time."

"And let me guess—no one remembers to mark the right tree."

"Well, they change with each passing day."

"Of course they do."

"If I had my wavebow," Thornleaf continued, "I could use a wavecast to locate one of them, but without it, we will have to check each tree by hand."

"Awesome," Felicity sighed. "And how many trees are there?"

Joel squinted at the upcoming jungle. "Looks like...thousands, maybe?"

"You gotta be kidding me."

"Let us just hope that fortune is with us today," Thornleaf said.

They entered the jungle and dismounted. Joel walked up to one of the trees and inspected it. While it was similar to many of the other palm-type trees he had seen in Spectraland, he noticed that up close the bark of this particular variety formed a unique pattern that resembled a bunch of backgammon boards all lined up next to and on top of each other.

"So, uh, how are we supposed to check for the sap?" he asked.

"Like this." Thornleaf unsheathed his knife and stuck it into the tree in front of him.

"Did you hit the jackpot?" Felicity asked.

Thornleaf withdrew the knife and looked it over. "No." He pointed at Felicity's leg where she had strapped on one of the sheaths that Amberweed had lent them. "Do you know how to use a knife?"

"What's there to know?" She sniffed.

"What about you?" the tall shaman asked Joel.

Joel looked down at the knife that was in his own leg sheath. "Um, I guess."

"Then both of you—start checking as well. The sap should be a thick, golden fluid that hangs on your blade as you draw it out."

"Sure thing, boss," Felicity said. As she started to stab away with alarming gusto, Joel prodded the tree next to him with his knife.

There must be a faster way of doing this, he thought. *Otherwise, this could take forever—and we don't have that kind of time.*

"You need to thrust the knife into the tree as far as you can," Thornleaf told him.

"Huh? Oh—right."

Joel steadied himself and pushed the knife into the trunk of the tree. After a couple of seconds, he tried to pull it back out, but he found that it was stuck.

"Pull harder," Felicity said, noticing his predicament.

Grunting, he gave it a second, and then a third try.

"Dude," Felicity chuckled, "we're gonna have to get you an athletic-ability potion or something."

Ignoring her remark, Joel tried again, and again. On his sixth try, he used both hands to pull, and finally, the knife slid out.

I hope that's a good sign.

He inspected both sides of the blade. No sap.

Dangit.

They continued in this fashion for what seemed like forever (but was, in reality, only half an hour) until they were nearly forty yards deep into the jungle and Thornleaf held up his hand, signaling them to stop.

"Hold on," the tall shaman said quietly. "Did either of you hear that?"

"Hear what?" Felicity asked.

"The sounds of conversation. There must be others nearby."

"Should we look for them?" Joel asked as the swordcats took a few steps back and crouched low to the ground. "Maybe they know the right tree."

"No," Thornleaf said, taking out the blowgun he had borrowed from Amberweed. "They may be members of Stoneroot's group."

"Why would those guys be here?" Felicity said.

"If the yellowbranch sap is used for the antidote, it may very well be a part of the original mind-control potion as well."

"Oh—kinda like a vaccine," Joel said.

"I don't think that's exactly how vaccines work," Felicity said.

"I know, that's why I said 'kinda'."

"Quiet," Thornleaf hissed.

"Can you see them?" Joel asked.

"No."

"Hey, Joel," Felicity whispered, "maybe you can spot them with the Sight."

"Good idea."

Hmm...let's go with...songs from The Dambuilders' Encendedor *album, from last to first: Fur, Delaware, Shrine, Collective, Colin's Heroes...*

Joel's surroundings appeared to swirl for just a second. Then he noticed a flash of movement in between a group of trees some twenty yards away. More than that, though, he also observed something interesting about the backgammon-board-like patterns on the trees themselves: while most of them were exactly the same, one particular tree had a pattern that was just slightly different.

"I think whoever it is, they're over there," he whispered, pointing. "And they're coming closer. But I also saw—"

"Coming closer?" Thornleaf echoed. "Quick, hide."

The trio ducked behind a nearby bush while the swordcats silently slunk away. A few heartbeats later, a pair of natives came into view; one of them was Whitenose, the guard from the Silencer Stronghold.

"—am telling you, I swear that I heard something," Thornleaf's former friend was saying.

"You are probably just losing your mind," his companion responded, plunging what looked like a short spear into one of the yellowbranch trees. "I know *I* am, having to check all of these trees for sap."

Out of the corner of his eye, Joel saw Felicity pointing at the blowgun in Thornleaf's hand. The tall shaman glanced back at her and shook his head, as if to say *no, not yet.*

"But if there really are daggermoles around here," Whitenose said, "perhaps we should cut this expedition short."

Whitenose's companion pulled out his spear, looked at its tip, and frowned. "And risk incurring Stoneroot's wrath again? We are already on his bad side, Whitenose. Why do you think we drew this miserable sap-harvesting job in the first place?"

"It is just that...well, to tell you the truth, I have some reservations about this whole endeavor."

"What endeavor? Are you referring to the mind-control project?"

Joel, Thornleaf, and Felicity all glanced at each other in turn.

"Yes," Whitenose replied, absently twirling his own short spear as if it were a giant drum stick. "It all just seems rather...misguided. I think that Stoneroot should be able to accomplish all of his goals without having to resort to such unethical measures. I am not sure this is what I signed up for anymore."

"Well, with all of the power he seems to be accumulating, it would probably be unwise to leave his service at this point."

"You may be right, but—" Whitenose froze and turned his head. "There is definitely something nearby," he said, looking in the direction of the swordcats.

"Where?" the other Silencer guard said, craning his neck. "I do not see anything."

Whitenose raised his spear and took a few cautious steps forward. "Over there," he said in a lowered voice. "Some large creatures...watching us."

The swordcats began to let out a low, rumbling growl. Grimacing, Joel looked back at them and made a frantic downward motion with his hand.

Be quiet! he shouted in his head, hoping that the animals would get the message.

"What—what are they?" Whitenose's companion mumbled, his tone growing increasingly nervous with every word.

"I do not know," Whitenose replied. "But they appear to be rather ferocious. Stand your ground."

"We—we were not trained for this."

"What are you saying, Woodstalk? Just a moment ago, you were unafraid of daggermoles!"

"I do not even know what daggermoles are! I have never been more than a few miles outside of my own village before!"

"What? Well, just—just try to stay calm," Whitenose groused, shaking his head. "Perhaps we can scare them off."

As the two Silencer guards drew closer, the swordcats' growls became louder. Thornleaf looked over at Joel and Felicity and made a number of cryptic gestures with his hands. Felicity nodded in response.

I have no idea what you're trying to say, Joel thought, giving the tall shaman a sheepish shrug.

"I have never seen beasts like these before, Whitenose," the guard named Woodstalk whimpered. "I think we should return to the slimebacks before—"

At that moment, all three swordcats leaped forward at once, roaring viciously. Both Silencer guards screamed and recoiled. Woodstalk tried to turn and run, but he lost his footing and fell to the ground. While Goldie and Platinum circled around Whitenose with their teeth bared, the other swordcat jumped in front of Woodstalk and let out a long, menacing growl.

"No—don't hurt them!" Joel exclaimed, stepping out from behind the bush.

Whitenose turned to Joel with a shocked expression. "The offworlder?"

"Yeah, um, hi."

"So," Thornleaf said, stepping out as well, "Stoneroot has a secret mind-control project, does he?"

"Thornleaf?" Whitenose said, incredulous. "What are you doing here?"

"*I* will be the one asking the questions," the tall shaman snapped. "Tell me what you know about this project!"

"I swear, Thornleaf, I know none of the details. I was just sent out here to look for yellowbranch sap. That is all."

"Do not lie to me! Tell me everything, or else these beasts"—he pointed at the swordcats, who were all still growling ominously—"will make life very miserable for you."

"I, uh, I don't think—" Joel started to say before Felicity grabbed his arm and pulled him aside.

"Just go with it, dude," she whispered into his ear.

"I don't want the swordcats to hurt them," he whispered back.

"They won't. He's just bluffing."

"Who is?"

"Thornleaf."

"Are you sure?"

"Pretty sure. Now what was the other thing you said you saw?"

"Oh, uh—over here," Joel said, walking over to the yellowbranch tree that had a pattern different from the others.

"What is it?" Felicity asked, following after him.

Joel took out his knife. "I'm not sure, but I think that..." He plunged the knife into the tree.

"You think this is the right one?"

Joel waited a couple of seconds before he pulled the knife back out. A gleaming, golden substance slowly dripped off the tip of his blade, like very thick syrup.

"Yup." He grinned.

"Not bad." Felicity smirked. "All right, let's get that into the vial and get out of here."

The two offworlders walked back to where Thornleaf and the swordcats still had the Silencer guards at bay.

"We got it," Joel announced, holding up his knife.

"Good." Thornleaf nodded. He took out the wooden vial and handed it to Joel.

"What are we gonna do with these two?" Felicity asked.

"I have not decided yet," Thornleaf replied. "They both continue to deny that they have any knowledge of Stoneroot's plans."

"I told you, that is because we do not!" Woodstalk, still laid out on the ground, declared. "You see, Thornleaf, this is why I joined the Silencers—because you are nothing but a bully who uses his advantages over others to get what he wants!"

Joel frowned as he finished dripping as much sap as he could into the wooden vial. *Is that what people think of the Wavemakers—that we're bullies?* "Well, um, we got the sap," he said, closing the vial. "So maybe we should just let them go."

Before Thornleaf could respond, the swordcats stopped growling and looked up, their ears alert.

"What's the matter?" Joel asked the animals. "Do you hear something?"

A few moments later, there was a rumbling, gurgling sound that seemed to come from everywhere at once.

"Okay, even I can hear that," Felicity remarked.

"What's making that noise?" Joel asked Thornleaf as he tried to give the vial back to the tall shaman.

"Quiet," Thornleaf hissed, holding up his hand.

"Sorry," Joel whispered. Not wanting to disturb Thornleaf's concentration any further, he put the vial into his own supply pack.

"Daggermoles," Whitenose muttered.

Thornleaf's eyes darted around. "We should leave," he said, "before they have a chance to—"

At that moment, the ground around them erupted in a shower of dirt and leaves and a group of man-sized porcupine-like creatures jumped out, grunting and screeching. The swordcats stood up on their hind legs and extended their claws, which turned out to be long, bony appendages that reminded Joel of a preadamantium Wolverine from the X-Men.

"Call the swordcats off!" Thornleaf shouted to Joel. "We need to get out of here!"

"Okay, uh—"

But then, moving very quickly for their size, the daggermoles formed a tight circle around the group.

"We are surrounded!" Whitenose yelled.

"Yeah, obviously!" Felicity yelled back, holding out her knife.

The daggermoles started to close in. Hissing and growling, each of the swordcats engaged one of the creatures, but there were still five more left to deal with. Joel looked around as he brandished his knife, unsure of what, exactly, he should do.

"Woodstalk, help us!" Whitenose called out.

Outside the ring of daggermoles, Woodstalk scrambled to his feet. For a moment, Joel thought that the Silencer guard would use his short spear to attack one of the creatures from behind, but instead, he turned and ran away.

"You coward!" Whitenose shouted.

One of the daggermoles noticed the fleeing native and began to chase after him. Joel considered trying to escape through the gap that it left, but two daggermoles simply moved over to fill it.

"What should we do?" Felicity shrieked as the creatures took a step closer.

"No sudden movements," Thornleaf said, slowly raising the blowgun to his mouth. "I will shoot a sleep-dart at the one in front of me. After he falls, the rest of them should back off."

Just as Thornleaf pressed the blowgun to his lips, however, the daggermole took a swipe at him. The tall shaman ducked under the blow, but for some reason, he crumpled to the ground a moment later. Swearing, Felicity knelt down to check on him.

"We have no choice!" Whitenose declared, sounding very agitated. "We need to fight our way out!"

"Wait," Joel said as he glanced at Felicity, who was still crouched over Thornleaf. "She's not ready to—"

Shouting some kind of bizarre battle cry, Whitenose thrust his spear at a daggermole, and all-out chaos ensued. Amidst the roaring of the swordcats and the wild screeching of the daggermoles, Joel slashed his knife around in a random, desperate fashion, trying his best to fend off the flailing limbs of the giant porcupine-like beasts that seemed to be coming at him from all directions. After several long seconds, he turned to see Felicity lying facedown on the ground with a large, bloody gash across her back where a daggermole had apparently torn through her tunic.

"Felicity!" he cried. He tried to go to her, but a daggermole stepped forward, blocking his way. An angry fog rolled into his head. "Move!" he screamed, savagely lunging and slashing at the creature with his knife. In the heat of the moment, he wasn't quite sure what he had done; all he knew was that the daggermole staggered away, and that his path was now clear. He rushed over and knelt beside Felicity's prone figure.

"Felicity," he said, not wanting to touch her for fear that he might injure her further. "Are you okay?"

There was no response.

Joel looked around for the swordcats, hoping for some help. All three of them were busy fighting the remaining daggermoles, of which there were four still standing. Off to the side, Whitenose, who had apparently lost his spear, was lifting Thornleaf up onto his shoulders.

"Come with me!" the Silencer guard shouted to Joel. "I have slimebacks waiting nearby!"

"Felicity is hurt!" Joel yelled.

"Just bring her!"

For a moment, Joel considered doing as Whitenose had suggested, but he didn't want to leave the swordcats, who looked like they were starting to wear down.

"Platinum!" he called out. "Let's go!"

Platinum turned and dashed over to Joel, and the other two swordcats followed. While the apparently injured daggermoles stumbled toward them like a group of giant zombie porcupines, Joel picked Felicity up and draped her over Goldie's back. Then he jumped onto Platinum, nearly buckling the animal's legs in the process. As Platinum looked back at him with a classic annoyed-cat expression, Joel pointed at Whitenose, who started racing off in the opposite direction.

"Follow him!" Joel exclaimed.

The swordcats did, but instead of running, they leaped forward, and Joel saw nothing but a flash of bright light.

CHAPTER 17: RED GULCH

The next thing Joel knew, he was in a ravine fifty feet deep and twenty feet wide. A shallow-looking stream, its water reflecting the deep scarlet hue of the surrounding rock walls, snaked through the middle of the ravine floor. Small bushes with silvery leaves and spiky red flowers were scattered sporadically throughout the area.

"Where...where are we?" he asked, blinking fast.

The swordcats did not answer. Instead, they hobbled over to a nearby recess in the wall, assumed sphinxlike positions, and began purring. Joel got off of Platinum and, as carefully as he could, lifted Felicity off of Goldie.

"Felicity?" he said. "Can you hear me?"

No response.

"Oh man—please don't be dead, please don't be dead," he fretted as he gingerly placed her facedown on the ground. Her wound didn't look quite as serious as he had originally feared, but she was still bleeding rather profusely nonetheless.

"Can you guys heal her?" he pleaded to the sword-cats. While Goldie and Platinum ignored him, choosing instead to lick various sections of each other's bodies,

Thornleaf's unnamed swordcat stood up and walked over, purring loudly as it did so.

"You can heal her, right?" Joel asked, trying his best not to sound too demanding. "C'mon, I know you can."

The swordcat stopped purring, sniffed at Felicity's wound, and then gave it a few good, long licks. After it was done, it resumed purring and looked at Joel with a nonchalant expression.

"Did...did you do it?" Joel said. He looked back at Felicity and saw that her injury, while now cleansed of blood, was still there. He put his hands on his head. "Aw, man—now what am I gonna do?"

Feeling panic start to set in, he started rummaging through his supply pack to see if, by some miracle, there would be anything in there that could help him in this situation. While doing so, he glanced back at Felicity and noticed that her wound appeared to be just a tiny bit smaller.

"Whoa," he said, looking at the swordcat next to her. "Are you...?"

As the swordcat continued purring, Felicity's wound became smaller and smaller, until finally, after another minute or so, it had vanished altogether, leaving just a small pink scar in its place.

"Wow," Joel exhaled. "That was awesome. Thanks, uh...I think I'll call you...Doc."

The swordcat made a little grunting noise then laid down and closed its eyes. A few moments later, Felicity began to stir.

"Felicity?" Joel said.

She made a soft groaning sound in response.

"How are you feeling?"

Her eyes fluttered open.

"Are you awake?"

"No, I always sleep with my eyes open," she muttered.

Joel grinned as he helped her sit up.

"We always seem to pass out a lot whenever we're on this island," she remarked, rubbing her temples. "What happened, anyway?"

"We were looking for yellowbranch sap, and then Whitenose and that other guy showed up, and then—"

"No, no, I know all that. I mean, the last thing I remember was pulling that sleepdart thingy out of Thornleaf's leg. Stupid guy shot himself while he was ducking. Anyway, next thing I know, I'm here."

"Well, you got kinda...hurt, I guess, by the daggermoles."

"Like, badly?"

"Um, sorta. But Doc was able to heal you."

"Who the heck is Doc?"

"Thornleaf's swordcat," Joel replied, nodding at the now-sleeping Doc. "I gave him that name just now. He did a really good job."

Felicity turned to the swordcat. "Well, thanks, Doc, I owe you." She looked around. "But where's Thornleaf? And where are we?"

"Uh," Joel said, taking a moment to process her two-part question, "Whitenose took Thornleaf, and...I'm not sure."

"Wait, what do you mean, 'Whitenose took Thornleaf'?"

"He rescued him from the daggermoles. Or, at least, I'm pretty sure he did. I was trying to follow them when the swordcats teleported and we ended up here."

"Well, then, shouldn't we go look for him?"

"Um, well, the plan will still work without him."

"What plan?"

"To give Auravine the antidote. I mean, we didn't actually need the third person, really. The swordcats can just teleport to wherever the second person is, and—"

"Never mind the plan, what about Thornleaf?" Felicity interrupted as she got to her feet. "What if he's in trouble?"

"I, uh, I guess that could be a problem, but..."

"But what?"

Joel glanced at the swordcats. Goldie and Platinum paused from licking each other and returned his glance with what he could have sworn were shrugs. "But...I don't think the swordcats know where to find him. We could be searching for a long time, and we have to go through with the plan tonight."

Felicity let out a long, heavy sigh. "Okay, fine. We'll finish the plan first." She stepped out of the recess and looked around. "I guess the good news is that we're already in Red Gulch."

"Wait, what? You mean, where the second ingredient is?"

"Yeah."

"How do you know?"

"Well, I'm not a hundred percent sure, but we're in a gulch, and it's red. So, if I had to guess, I'd say the swordcats knew that this was the next place we needed to get to."

Joel looked at Goldie and Platinum as the two of them lay down next to Doc and closed their eyes. "You guys are awesome," he said.

♪♪♪

After the swordcats woke from their brief nap, Joel and Felicity walked with them alongside the clear, flowing stream as they searched for what Darkeye had called "the heart of Red Gulch." Occasionally, tiny, furry creatures resembling gophers with roaches' antennae would pop their heads out of holes in the ground, only to vanish a fraction of a second later.

"Okay, I still don't see this 'heart' place, or whatever it is," Felicity said as Goldie circled around a gopher-roach hole. "Do you think he was using some kind of metaphor?"

"Um...I was never really clear on what a metaphor is, exactly," Joel admitted.

"It's a figure of speech. Like, 'time is an illusion, and so is death.'"

"Oh, hey, that's a quote from *Avatar: The Last Airbender*!" Joel said, excited. "Book Two, Episode Four, 'The Swamp.'"

"Huh? Oh, I guess. I don't know, I thought I was making that up."

As Doc made a futile lunge at a gopher-roach, Joel started to think about all of the episode names from *The Last Airbender* television series, starting with the very first one.

Book One, Episode One: "The Boy In The Iceberg." Oh, wait, there was the pilot episode before that, which, technically, was the first one. Okay, so anyway, moving on, Book One, Episode Two: "The Avatar Returns." Book One, Episode Three: "The Southern Air Temple." Book One, Episode Four: "The Warriors of—"

At that moment, he spotted something unusual up ahead.

"Oh—hey, check that out," he said.

"Check what out?" Felicity replied.

Joel squinted as he moved from side to side. About thirty feet away, at the base of the rock wall where the ravine made an abrupt ninety-degree turn, there appeared to be an open archway that led to a new path. Beyond the archway, the cliffside that lay off in the distance blended in perfectly with the closer wall, creating the illusion that there was no opening at all, regardless of which angle you looked at it from. "There's an opening," he said, jogging toward it.

"What? Where?" Felicity called after him. "Like, a crack in the wall, or something?"

"No, no, a big opening," he replied as he picked up speed, not looking back out of fear that he would lose track of where the archway was.

"Dude," she yelled, "you're gonna run into the—"

Joel passed through the archway. From where he stood, a curved land bridge sloped downward into a bowl-shaped valley that was filled from side to side with thick, intertwining crimson vines, like a giant neuron forest. A slab of earth stretched over the area like the retractable roof of a sports stadium, and slim rays of sunlight streamed through the narrow space between the slab and the upper rim of the valley.

"Okay, I gotta admit, that's pretty cool," Felicity said after she had caught up to Joel. "It's like that scene at the end of *Last Crusade*."

"What, this valley?" he asked, wondering what she was talking about. *Does she mean* Indiana Jones and The Last Crusade*? Because there were no red vine valleys in that movie...*

"No, no, that hidden opening. You know, how it was all naturally camouflaged, like that bridge Indy had to cross to get to the Grail."

"Oh yeah! So, which one of those movies is your favorite?" he asked. "I actually liked that one the best, and then the first one second, and then the second one third, and then the fourth one fourth."

"You liked the third one the best?" she said, shooting Joel an incredulous glance. "Dude, c'mon, everyone knows you can't beat the first one. Especially with all that gross face-melting action at the end."

"Um, wait, uh...did I say the third one? I meant the first one," Joel fibbed.

"Yeah, right."

"No, really."

"So the first one is your favorite."

"Yup, the first one. Really good. The best."

"Okay, whatever you say," Felicity chuckled. "Anyway, you think this is the place we need to go?"

Joel glanced at the swordcats and asked, "Is this the right place?"

Platinum let out a little gurgling growl.

"I think it is," Joel said.

Felicity raised an eyebrow. "Seriously?"

"Well, they knew to come to this gulch, so I just figured..."

"All right, fair enough," she sighed. "Let's check it out, I guess."

They walked down the land bridge and into the interwoven cluster of vines. Upon closer examination, Joel noticed that the vines' red hue was due to a complex network of veins that covered each vine's surface, making them appear a little like giant, stretchy arms. The vines themselves also blocked out a good portion of whatever light the valley's "roof" let in, and although Joel expected the temperature down here to be a bit cooler due to the shade, it was actually uncomfortably warm and humid, as if heat were being trapped and recirculated.

"Man, what a creepy place," Felicity said. "So, what were we supposed to find here again?"

"Um...Darkeye said it was called a bloodseed. 'A bloodseed from—*hic*—the heart of Red Gulch', he said."

"Nice impersonation," Felicity remarked. "I don't suppose the swordcats know what one of those things looks like, do they?"

Joel looked at the swordcats. None of them made a sound. "I, uh, I don't think so."

"Great."

"Oh, but remember—Thornleaf said that they look like slabs of raw meat."

"He did? When did he say that?"

"Right after we left the prison."

"Are you sure?"

"Yeah, he said that sometimes you can find them at the village markets, but that they're not in season right now, so we have to go to where they grow."

"I don't remember any of that."

"Well, you did seem kinda distracted there for a little while. Like you were bothered by something."

"No, I wasn't," she said defensively. "I just wasn't paying attention, that's all."

"Um, okay."

Feeling somewhat confused by Felicity's response, Joel pulled out a glowmoss stone as they traversed deeper into the valley and the area became darker. Felicity followed suit. They continued walking at a careful pace, holding out the stones like flashlights as they stepped over, ducked under, and squeezed in between the vines. Then, after about nine minutes had passed, they came to a stop.

"Hey—check that out," Felicity said, aiming her glowmoss stone at what looked like a clearing some fifteen feet up ahead.

Joel pointed his stone at the same spot. Indeed, there was a room-sized clearing where a number of the vines terminated in flowers that resembled giant red daisies, forming a sort of floral canopy around the area. "Do you think that's the 'heart' that Darkeye was talking about?"

"I was just about to ask you that. Guess we should take a look."

They entered the clearing. As Joel looked around, he spotted something.

"Oh, uh—I think I found them," he said.

"The bloodseeds? Where?"

Joel lifted up his glowmoss stone. About ten feet above the ground, a dozen thick red slabs hung from the flowers' faces like raw steaks on meat hooks.

"Eww, gross," Felicity said. "You call that a seed?"

"I guess."

"All right, whatever. Let's just grab one and bail."

"Um...how are we gonna do that?"

"I dunno. Why don't you ask the swordcats to jump?"

"Okay." Joel looked at Platinum and pointed up at the red slabs. "Can you get one of those for us?"

Platinum looked up at the bloodseeds, hissed, and backed away a few steps. Goldie and Doc followed his lead and did the same.

"I don't think they like those things," Joel said.

"Yeah, I can see that," Felicity grumbled. She turned to face the swordcats. "C'mon, you guys," she said encouragingly, "it's meat! Cats love meat!"

"Well, it probably just looks like meat, but it's not."

Felicity rolled her eyes. "You didn't have to say that out loud."

"Sorry."

"Forget it," she sighed. "So, now what? Can *you* jump that high?"

"Um—"

"Never mind. I don't even know why I asked."

"I know," Joel said, trying to think as fast as possible, "why don't...why don't I lift you up? Like, you know, manually."

"Are you serious?"

"Yeah. I mean, what else are we gonna do?"

"All right, good point," she said resignedly. "Okay, so, like, how are we gonna do this? Do I step on your hands or something?"

Joel knew what she was talking about. But while he had seen it done in movies and on television, he thought that it would be kind of difficult to pull off in real life, and on top of that, the thought of having her dirty footwear on his hands was a bit off-putting. "Um, actually, I was thinking—I'll just hold you by your legs and then lift you up."

She gave him a look that he couldn't immediately decipher. "I dunno..." she said.

"Don't worry, I can do it. I, um, I took a weightlifting class in school a couple of years ago."

"A couple of years ago."

"Yeah."

"All right, fine."

Joel bent at the knees in front of her and wrapped his arms around her legs. "Okay, so I'll just—" He grunted and shifted his weight, trying to maintain his balance.

"Hey, I'm not *that* heavy, you know," she griped.

"No, I know, I'm—hold on," he stammered as he slowly stood up. She was right, she wasn't *that* heavy, but it was an awkward position, and he wasn't sure he'd be able to lift her high enough for her to grab the bloodseed.

"This would be so much easier if Thornleaf was here," she grumbled.

She was right—at nearly six feet tall, Thornleaf probably would have been able to just jump up and grab the bloodseed. But for whatever reason, Joel felt bothered by her comment nonetheless. With a small jolt of angry adrenaline, he set his jaw and lifted.

"Okay, whoa, that's good," she said. "Just a little higher."

With another grunt, he shifted his arms in an effort to boost her up some more.

"Ow!" she exclaimed. "Are you sure you can do this?"

"Yeah—uh, just—just try to relax."

"*You're* telling *me* to relax—that's new."

Feeling a bit steadier now, he attempted to boost her up again. "What?"

"Never mind—a little more, I almost got it."

Joel flexed his knees, preparing to boost her up one last time.

"Hello?" an unfamiliar voice called out. "Is someone there?"

CHAPTER 18: SPARKLEBLOCK

Startled, Joel stood up straight, a bit faster than he had intended to. Feeling Felicity's weight fall forward, he lost his footing, and she shrieked as his knees buckled and she came crashing down on top of him. Landing hard on his side, his elbow stung, but he felt otherwise uninjured.

"Are you okay?" he asked Felicity after she had rolled off of him.

"Yeah—got it," she puffed, holding the bloodseed up.

Just then, an elderly female native emerged out of the darkness carrying a glowmoss-covered stone in one hand and something that looked like a shepherd's crook in the other. The swordcats cautiously stepped forward and sniffed at her ankles.

"Oh, my," the native said, petting Platinum in between his horns. "You certainly are a big boy."

"Um, hello," Joel said as he stood up.

"Greetings, young ones," the native said. "Are you here to find bloodseeds?"

"Maybe," Felicity answered, hiding the bloodseed behind her back as she got to her feet. "Who are you?"

"I am Sixhair, the caretaker of this orchard," the native replied.

"Caretaker?" Felicity said. "You mean, like, you work here?"

"I am the owner."

Felicity turned to Joel. "Okay, no one said anything about a flippin' *owner*," she hissed under her breath.

"Um...maybe we can offer to pay her for it."

"With what? Lifepods?"

"By the way," the native said, "you probably do not want to keep the particular bloodseed that you are holding, as it will not be ripe for several more weeks. Here, I can take that from you."

"How do we know you're telling us the truth?" Felicity demanded. "For all we know, you just want this for yourself."

Sixhair smiled. "You are welcome to keep it, if that is what you prefer. It will not be good for whatever purpose you have in mind, though, be it food or medicine. Are you in need of just one?"

"Um, yeah, pretty much," Joel replied.

"Then, if you would like to come with me, I would be happy to provide you with a more suitable specimen."

"Give us a sec," Felicity said, pulling Joel aside. "What do you think?" she whispered into his ear. "Should we trust her?"

Joel glanced over at the swordcats, who were busy rubbing up against the native's legs. "Well, they seem to like her."

"Maybe she just smells like swordcat-nip, or whatever."

"Maybe, but if she says that this bloodseed is no good, then it's probably better to make sure. And if something goes wrong, the swordcats can always, you know, help bail us out of trouble."

"All right, fine."

Joel turned to Sixhair. "Okay, we'll come."

"Wonderful. If you will follow me, please."

Joel, Felicity, and the swordcats followed Sixhair as she navigated her way through a twisted maze of red vines, occasionally pulling some aside with her shepherd's crook.

"We hardly get visitors here," Sixhair said, ducking under a low vine. "Of course, that is mostly due to the hidden location of our orchard."

"Yeah, um, sorry about that," Joel said. "We didn't mean to trespass or anything. We didn't even know someone actually lived here."

"That is quite all right," Sixhair chuckled. "Were you the one to spot the entrance?"

"Uh...yes."

"Hmm. Very interesting."

As Joel pondered what she meant by that remark, they arrived at a clearing dominated by an enormous wedge-shaped hut. Joel noticed that the hut's construction was a lot more sophisticated than any other Spectraland hut he had seen, including chieftains' residences; utilizing more wood and stone than plant material, it could almost pass for a modern Earth house, especially if you replaced the stand-alone torch next to its front door with a mailbox.

Felicity whistled. "Pretty fancy digs."

"Bloodseeds are quite a valuable commodity in Spectraland," Sixhair explained as they approached the hut. "So we are able to trade them for many nice things."

"You keep saying 'we'," Felicity noted. "Is there anyone else here?"

"Yes," Sixhair replied, opening the door to the hut. "Oh, Rocktoe!" she called out. "We have guests!"

"Guests?" a voice said from inside the hut. "Well, please, come inside!"

Joel's eyes grew wide as they entered the hut. Sixhair wasn't exaggerating when she had said 'nice things'; the interior looked more like a high-class tropical hotel lobby than a semiprimitive domicile. Most of the furniture—chairs, tables, and stools—was made of carved, polished wood, and the floor was covered by a soft, fuzzy carpet that probably had been culled from animal fur. Elaborate paintings and carvings hung from the walls, and a number of glowmoss stones lined the ceiling in a manner similar to track lighting. A wooden spiral staircase in the middle of the floor led up to the hut's second level.

"Man, if we weren't in a rush, I'd wanna hang out here for a few days," Felicity said.

"Welcome!" an elderly male native with a Fu Manchu mustache said as he came walking down the staircase. "What a nice-looking young couple—oh, and animal friends as well!"

"This is my spouse, Rocktoe," Sixhair said to Joel and Felicity. "Rocktoe, this is—actually, I never did get your names, did I?"

"Oh, uh, yeah, sorry, I'm Joel—Joel Suzuki."

"Felicity."

Rocktoe's jaw dropped. "Joel and Felicity? The legendary offworlders?"

"Ah, no wonder you were able to find the entrance to the orchard!" Sixhair laughed. "I must apologize—I thought that you were ordinary villagers. My eyesight is not what it used to be."

Joel looked down at himself; even though he had lost a few arm-leaves and his body paint had washed off in spots, his Spectraland getup was still relatively—and impressively—convincing. "We're wearing Halloween costumes," he said.

"I see. On some sort of stealth mission, eh?" Rocktoe said. Then, lowering his voice to a conspiratorial tone, he added, "Can you tell me what it is about? Has the war begun?"

"Uh, well..."

"Rocktoe, stop it," Sixhair scolded. "Please forgive him," she said to Joel. "He can be quite nosy at times. You do not have to answer his questions. Besides, I am sure there is no war."

"I am telling you, Sixhair, if it has not started yet, it will soon!" Rocktoe insisted. "That must be why the offworlders are here—to assist Fireflower with her fight against Stoneroot and his followers!"

"Wait—you guys know about all of that?" Joel asked.

"Why wouldn't they?" Felicity shrugged at him. "It's a small island."

"I hear things all the time during my occasional trips to the village marketplaces," Rocktoe explained. "Sixhair and I have been hoping that it would not come to this, but apparently our hopes were in vain."

"Well, there isn't really an all-out war just yet," Joel said. "But, uh, there have been some strange things going on. That's kinda why we're here, actually."

Rocktoe raised an eyebrow. "Oh? Can you tell me more?"

"It's kind of a long story," Joel replied. "See, first we were playing a show back home, and then during our second song, I saw Fireflower in the audience, and then—"

"We think Stoneroot has one of the Wavemakers under mind control," Felicity interrupted. "And he's using her and some Lightsnakes to kidnap other Wavemakers."

"Lightsnakes? Mind control?" Rocktoe exclaimed. "Why did you not just resist them with your wavebows?"

"Well," Joel said, "the first time a Wavemaker got kidnapped, no one else was really there. This was a week before we got here, Spectraland time, and that's part of why—"

"They created some kind of wavecast that disrupts the Aura and makes us all loopy and stuff," Felicity cut in.

"I see," Rocktoe said, stroking one side of his long mustache. "So, Stoneroot is attempting to win the war before it even begins. He has always been a crafty one."

"Yeah, so, we're here because we need bloodseed juice for the mind-control antidote," Joel said.

"Much better job of summarizing there," Felicity remarked.

"Um, thanks."

"We will be happy to help you." Sixhair nodded. "We support the Wavemakers in this conflict. Even though we think Stoneroot has some valid ideas, we do not approve of his methods."

Rocktoe held up his hand. "Before we do so, however, we must make sure that you are who you say you are."

"Rocktoe, they found the entrance to the orchard," Sixhair said. "Who else could have done such a thing?"

"It may have been a lucky accident. Where are their wavebows?"

"We lost them," Joel said.

"We think the Lightsnakes took them," Felicity added.

Rocktoe folded his arms. "Hmm...or perhaps Stoneroot has figured out our location, and you two are agents of his, pretending to be the offworlders."

Sixhair shook her head. "You can be so paranoid at times," she sighed.

"How can we do this...oh, I know!" Rocktoe exclaimed.

"What are you going to do?" Sixhair asked.

"You will see," he said as he jogged back up the stairs. "Just give me a few minutes."

"Please, have a seat," Sixhair said to Joel and Felicity, motioning toward a couple of wooden chairs. "I will get you something to drink while we wait."

Joel and Felicity sat down on the chairs, while the swordcats spread themselves out on the fuzzy carpet. "So, uh, how long have you and Rocktoe lived here?" Joel asked, recalling what he had learned in his social communication class about how to make small talk.

"I have been here all my life," Sixhair replied as she stepped onto a nearby raised platform. "This orchard has been in the care of my family for generations. Rocktoe was originally from Spearwind, but after we married, he came to live with me."

"It's funny," Felicity said, "I think you guys are, like, the first couple we've met on this island. Everyone else seems to be single."

"Well, love can be a difficult thing to find," Sixhair said, opening a tall cabinet and taking out a large stone jug. "And even more difficult to maintain."

Tell me about it, Joel grumbled to himself.

Sixhair poured liquid from the jug into several wooden cups as loud rummaging sounds could be heard from the upstairs level of the hut. "At least the two of you were as fortunate as Rocktoe and I." She smiled.

"What?" Joel said.

"Oh—no, no," Felicity said, "we're—we're just friends."

Sixhair looked over at them. "Ah, forgive me. I assumed that you were a mated pair."

Felicity shook her head. "Yeah, no, we're not...what you just said."

"A shame—you seem so good together," Sixhair said, handing a cup to Joel.

"How did you and Rocktoe meet, anyway?" Felicity asked in what seemed like a hasty attempt to change the subject. "You know, with you having been stuck down here, or whatever."

Sixhair chuckled as she handed a cup to Felicity. "Well, one day I accompanied my mother on a trading trip to the Spearwind marketplace, and Rocktoe was a young man who was working there. I would like to say that we fell in love the moment we saw each other, but to be honest, I did not even notice him at first."

The rummaging sounds stopped. "Of course you did!" Rocktoe said from upstairs. "All the girls noticed me. They could not help it!"

Sixhair rolled her eyes as the rummaging sounds resumed. "Anyway, he approached me and began talking, and it all started from there."

"What did he say to you?" Joel asked, hoping to come away with some ideas.

"You know, I do not even remember," Sixhair replied with a Spectraland shrug.

Joel frowned, disappointed.

"But the words he said were not as important as how he said them," Sixhair went on, taking a seat on a nearby stool. "He just seemed very bold, poised, and self-assured. I think it was that quality that I found to be the most attractive thing about him. And I still feel that way to this very day."

Joel sniffed at his cup as he digested what Sixhair had just told him. The liquid inside of it smelled good, like fruit punch. He took a small sip. To his surprise, it even tasted like fruit punch.

"So, like, after all this time, don't you guys get bored of each other?" Felicity asked.

"Oh, I am not saying that it is always easy, being together so much," Sixhair replied. "I think that one of the keys—for us, at least—has been that we have a lot of similar interests."

"We both like nice things!" Rocktoe said from upstairs.

"But doesn't that make you more like...I dunno, buddies, or something?" Felicity said.

"Well, there is more to it than that," Sixhair replied. "We continually challenge each other, which helps to keep things fresh. At the same time, we also accept each other for who we are as individuals. It may sound complicated, but when you care for each other as much as we do, you find a way to make it work."

"Hmm," Felicity said, taking a sip from her cup.

"Found it!" Rocktoe declared. A moment later, the native ran down the stairs, holding up a cube-like object.

"I had almost forgotten about that thing," Sixhair said, smiling and shaking her head.

"What is it?" Joel asked.

"It is called a sparkleblock," Rocktoe replied, showing the object to Joel and Felicity. Slightly larger than a Rubik's Cube, it appeared to be made out of a clear, gelatin-like substance. "An old Wavemaker friend of mine gave it to me a long time ago. Said that it might come in handy one day. I never guessed that he might have been referring to this moment."

"All right, so what does it do?" Felicity asked.

Rocktoe shook the sparkleblock, and dozens of tiny, multicolored lights appeared inside of it. The swordcats perked their heads up, their curiosity piqued.

"Whoa, cool," Joel said.

"It is basically just a puzzle," Rocktoe said, "but an extremely difficult one. I have never seen anyone able to solve it, not even the friend who gave it to me." He handed the sparkleblock to Joel. "But if you truly are the offworlder with the power of the Sight, it should be no problem for you."

Joel stared, transfixed, at the sparkleblock. The little specks of light moved around together in different shifting patterns, like schools of fish, changing colors as they did so. "What do I have to do?" he asked.

"You move it around in your hand and try to guide the main light," Rocktoe said, pointing at one of the lights in the corner of the sparkleblock, "through the maze of other lights, until it reaches the opposite corner."

"Sounds easy enough." Felicity sniffed.

"Oh, but believe me, it is not," Rocktoe said. "Give it a try."

Joel gave the sparkleblock an experimental twist. The main light floated downward for a bit before it ran into another light and reappeared back in its original corner.

"See?" Rocktoe cackled.

"Rocktoe, we are wasting their time," Sixhair said. "They need to be on their way."

"Yeah, what she said," Felicity agreed.

"No, no, I can do this," Joel protested, twisting the sparkleblock around again. This time the light got as far as the middle of the cube before it hit another light and reappeared, once more, in its original corner.

"Are you sure?" Felicity said. "Remember, we kinda really need that bloodseed."

Joel took a deep breath and closed his eyes.

Let's see, think about...official Legend of Zelda *titles and their years of release:* The Legend of Zelda*, 1986;* The Adventure of Link*, 1987;* A Link to The Past*, 1991;* Link's Awakening*, 1993...*

Joel opened his eyes. He twisted and turned the sparkleblock around for what felt like an eternity (but was, in reality, only thirty-seven seconds) until finally, the main light slipped through a tiny ring of other lights and settled into the opposite corner of the cube. All the specks of light turned bright gold, and the sparkleblock began to emit a soft, high humming sound.

"Amazing," Rocktoe whispered, awestruck.

"Yeah, good job, dude," Felicity said in a sincere tone of voice that Joel didn't hear her use too often.

Sixhair stood up and smiled. "I will get your blood-seed now."

"You solved that in much less time than I expected," Rocktoe said to Joel. "It appears that the stories I have heard about you were not mere rhetoric."

"Well, I'm usually pretty good at puzzles and stuff," Joel said, starting to feel a little embarrassed.

Sixhair returned with a bloodseed in her hand. It was a much darker shade of red than the ones out in the orchard. "This is the ripest one I have," she said. "After a few more hours, the juice should be ready to add to your antidote. Until then, try to keep the skin of the fruit intact."

"Works for me," Felicity said. She took the bloodseed from Sixhair and held it out to Joel. "Here, stash it in your pack for now."

"What? My pack?"

"Yeah. I have pointy stuff in mine."

"Um, okay," Joel said. To free up his hands, he offered the sparkleblock back to Rocktoe.

"Actually, you keep that," the native said. "I think you will get more enjoyment out of it than I ever have."

"Are—are you sure?" Joel said.

"Just take it, dude," Felicity sighed. "He's offering it to you. Besides, you never know when things like that will come in handy around here."

"Okay, well...thanks."

"You are welcome." Rocktoe nodded. "Think of it as a token of our new friendship."

"And a reminder of some of the things that I have told you," Sixhair added with a knowing smile.

Joel wasn't sure exactly what she meant, but he returned her smile anyway as he opened up his supply pack and placed his new belongings inside of it, next to the wooden vial.

CHAPTER 19: SANDTHROAT

After leaving Red Gulch, it took the swordcats nearly a dozen teleportation jumps before they were able to get Joel and Felicity to their third and final destination: the Coast of Fang.

"So, I'm gonna leave you in charge of getting this one, okay?" Felicity said as she, Joel, and the swordcats trudged along the beach.

"Um, sure," Joel replied. The last item on Darkeye's list was the venom of a bloomfish, the man-sized jellyfish-like creature that had stung Felicity during their previous visit. He understood why she would be reluctant to face one of those creatures again. "Although, I mean, I'll probably need some help."

"No, I'm just gonna stand around watching you."

"What? Why?"

"Dude—sarcasm."

"Oh, right."

"Seriously, how long have you known me now?"

"A little over six months. Well, actually, it's kind of hard to say, exactly, because of the differences in Earth and Spectraland time. I think, first, you have to calculate—"

"Forget it. Do you see any bloomfish yet?"

He scanned the shoreline for any signs of the glowing pink and purple flowers that represented the dormant forms of the bloomfish. "Um, no, not yet."

Felicity patted Goldie on the back. "Well, I guess these guys need to rest for a bit anyway." She walked over to a patch of yellow grass on the high end of the beach and sat down.

"What should we do if the bloomfish don't show up?" Joel asked as he followed after her.

"Can the swordcats teleport over water?" Felicity said.

All three animals started making little growling noises.

"Didn't think so," she chuckled. "Well, we could always swim out there ourselves and look for them."

"I don't know how to swim," Joel said.

"Dude, *I know*. I'm just giving you a hard time."

"Oh—uh, okay."

"You totally need to learn how to recognize sarcasm."

"I already know how to recognize sarcasm. What you just said isn't sarcasm."

"I know—oh, never mind."

Joel frowned, feeling as if he had just lost another prime opportunity for the kind of witty banter that seemed to come so naturally to guys like Trevor or, for that matter, Thornleaf. He knew that, if all went well, this period of time when he and Felicity were alone together would soon be coming to an end, and he wanted to take advantage of it while he could. He thought back to the articles he had read about talking to girls, as well as the general everyday conversation techniques he had learned in his social communication class.

"So, uh," he said, "which show did you like the best?"

"Huh? What are you talking about?"

"Our summer tour—which one of our shows did you like the best?"

"That's a pretty random question."

"Yeah, I guess it is," Joel said, frowning again. *Well, that didn't work,* he groused to himself. He turned his attention to the small waves that were lapping up onto the shore at regular, ten-second intervals.

"I liked the one we did in San Fran," she finally said, pulling a lifepod out of her supply pack and taking a bite. "The crowd was kinda small, but they had a lot of energy, and it seemed like they really knew our songs."

"Oh—uh, yeah," Joel said, somewhat surprised that she had actually responded.

"Didn't you think so?"

"Um, sure, but...to be honest, I thought that you were mad about that one."

"Why did you think that?"

"You know, like, 'cause you threw your guitar across the stage."

"Dude, I was excited," she said. "You know, having fun, getting caught up in the moment. I felt like doing something crazy, so that was it. Probably not the smartest move, I know, but hey—rock 'n' roll, right?"

"Yeah, uh, right."

"Which show did you like?"

"Well...that one, I guess."

"Now you're just saying that. C'mon, seriously. What happened to the guy who disagreed with me about Marshall's first two albums?"

What happened to the girl who seemed to be interested in me as more than a friend? is what Joel wanted to say, but instead, he went with: "Um, I'm still here."

"I know that," she chuckled. "But remember right after that whole deal, when you had so much confidence? You were talking, smirking, telling me about appreciation. Then, I dunno, it was like after we got home, you just sort of went back into your shell, even after the band started to take off."

"I, uh...I guess I was just afraid of turning into a jerk. You know, like Marshall."

"You don't have to be a jerk or a bad guy. You just have to be confident."

There's that word again, Joel thought. "But, like, how?"

"You know, like...like James Bond."

"I'm not really that familiar with James Bond."

"Okay, well, like..."

"Harry Potter?"

"Eh..."

"Luke Skywalker?"

"More like...more like Han Solo. Or, well, maybe Luke in *Return of the Jedi* when he was going to Jabba's palace. That was pretty hot."

"Um, okay."

"Dude, c'mon. You're a rock star. A real one. Just think and act like it. Stand up for yourself, you know?"

"Well, um...I disagreed with you a few minutes ago."

"About what?"

"Sarcasm."

"Hmm, I guess you did."

"So was that being confident?"

"Eh, that was more like...actually, I'm not sure what that was. I dunno, it's complicated."

That's for sure, Joel thought. He looked out again at the waves, which were now arriving every seven seconds.

"Anyway," Felicity said, "what I'm trying to say is—don't be afraid to say what's on your mind, or to say how you feel about stuff. Don't worry about what other people think, or if they agree with you or not."

"You mean, be more like you?"

Unexpectedly, she laughed. "Yeah, right, exactly. Good one."

Joel could feel himself start to blush. "Um, thanks."

"I dunno," she said, "maybe I'm a little extreme. You know, sometimes I can't help myself. I think it's like a defense mechanism, to be honest. So no, don't go that far. Just be yourself, or whatever. Accept and embrace who you are. Be the best version of Joel that you can be."

"Now you're starting to sound like Art."

"Yeah, I think we hang around that guy too much."

They sat in silence for the next two minutes as the waves continued to roll up. Then, during the third minute, Joel spotted something.

"Hey, look," he said, pointing toward the ocean.

Felicity got to her feet. "Are they here?" she asked.

"No, it's something else," he replied, standing up as well. "It's out on the water—kinda far away."

"I don't see anything. What is it?"

"I dunno, but I think it's...it's coming closer."

As the light slowly approached, Joel gazed out at the horizon. A warm breeze began to blow, and the streaks of Aura off in the distance formed a surreal, rainbow-colored cascade that was more amazing than any video of the northern or southern lights that he had ever seen. Suddenly inspired, he was struck by the notion that this moment might be the perfect time to do...something, although he wasn't quite sure what that something was. Reach out and hold her hand, perhaps? No, no, too forward. Ask her how she felt about him? Maybe, although that didn't feel quite right. Admit that he was jealous of Trevor and Thornleaf? That could be a good place to start...

Sometimes, you just gotta say, what the heck.

"Hey, um, so...you know, I, uh..."

"Dude," she said, hitting him on the arm. "It's a boat."

"What?"

"The light—it's coming from a boat. And there's someone on it. Don't tell me you don't see it."

Joel refocused his mind. She was right—a small boat, like an outrigger canoe, was heading toward them with some kind of lantern perched at its bow. It carried a single occupant who paddled at a steady pace, alternating strokes on each side of the vessel.

"Oh—uh, yeah...yeah, I see it."

"Must be one of those Roughrock guys," she said as the swordcats got to their feet. "Maybe they can tell us where to find the bloomfish."

"Yeah, maybe."

"So, what were you gonna say?"

"Um—that—that I saw a boat."

"I knew you wouldn't miss it," she chuckled. "I mean, if *I* noticed it, I'm sure you saw it a lot sooner."

Unsure if that was a compliment or not, Joel remained silent as the boat drew closer and closer. Once it was about twenty feet from the shore, he saw that while the paddler was not anyone he had met earlier at Spiral Landing, it was someone who was still quite familiar to him.

"That's...that's the vagabond who ambushed us the first time we were here," Joel muttered, half to Felicity, half to himself.

"You mean the guy you talked out of killing us?" Felicity asked.

"Yeah."

"Well, he should be cool now, right? I mean, those other guys fed us dinner and everything. Sort of, anyway."

"I guess."

"That's not very reassuring."

"What do you mean?"

"Never mind. Keep your knife handy, just in case."

"Greetings!" the native called to them as he got out of his canoe and pulled it onto the sand. "You are Wavemakers, are you not? Did my people send you down here?"

"No, we're just passing through," Felicity replied.

The native pulled a fishing net out of his canoe that was filled with squirming, slimy creatures. For a hopeful moment, Joel thought that they were bloomfish, but on second glance, they actually looked more like squids with peacock feathers. "Passing through?" the native laughed. "Well, I suppose you can do things like that when you are riders of the sky." He walked up to Joel and Felicity, carrying his bounty over his shoulder like Santa Claus hauling a bag of toys. He was definitely the same vagabond native who had ambushed them on Roughrock Pass all that time ago, although naturally, he now looked quite a bit older. He wore a modest headdress made up of intertwined vines, and a spiral bow hung at his side. "And what fantastic creatures you have with you! Are they swordcats, by any chance?"

"Yes," Joel answered.

"Unbelievable! Leave it to the Wavemakers to tame such wild beasts." The native smiled. "Forgive me—you seem familiar, and yet I do not recall your names. Are you new apprentices, perhaps?"

"Um, no," Joel said. "We're—"

"Wait a minute," the native said, coming closer. "You are...the offworlders, correct? From a long time ago?"

Joel glanced at Felicity, who said nothing.

"You are!" the native laughed. "A valiant attempt at blending in, I must say," he said, wiggling one of Joel's arm-leaves. "But I would recognize your faces anywhere, even after all these years. Your names are Joel and Felicity, correct?"

"Sure," Felicity said, still looking wary.

"My name is Sandthroat," the native said. "I apologize for missing your visit the other day." He held up his net. "I spend most of my time now out on the water, indulging my favorite hobby."

"Wait," Joel said, recalling details of their earlier visit to Spiral Landing. "Sandthroat, as in...Chief Sandthroat?"

"Yes," Sandthroat replied. "I was the leader of our tribe back before we became an actual settlement, so it was only natural that I continue serving in that role. I realize you may remember me as something of a...of a..."

"A bully?" Joel offered.

"A mugger?" Felicity suggested.

Sandthroat chuckled. "Yes, I suppose either of those descriptions would fit. And I apologize for that as well. But you must realize, there were good reasons for our former way of life. Has Fireflower told you the stories?"

"No," the two offworlders said at the same time.

"Well, then you must join me back at the tower for dinner! Trust me, I have some very entertaining tales to share with you. I will have my people cook up these beauties, and then we can—"

"Actually," Joel interrupted, "we're on kind of a mission."

"And we're in a rush," Felicity added.

"I see." Sandthroat nodded. His expression quickly shifted from excitement to disappointment, making Joel feel a bit uneasy. "Wavemaker business—I understand. In fact, Cloudpalm did tell me that you were previously on your way to the Sacred Site. What were you able to discover up there?"

"Eh, I dunno if we wanna get into it," Felicity demurred. "It's a pretty long story."

"Maybe we should tell him," Joel said to her. "'Cause, you know, maybe he can help us."

"Yes, perhaps I can," Sandthroat said, putting his net on the ground. As he did so, one of the peacock-squids wriggled out and flopped around for a moment or two before Goldie swiftly pounced on it. "Please, tell me."

Joel and Felicity glanced at each other, shrugged, and then proceeded to outline everything that had happened to them since they had arrived at the Sacred Site, as well as their plan for breaking Auravine out of her mind-control state.

"Interesting," Sandthroat said after they were done. "I had heard the rumors about Stoneroot, but I never would have guessed that they were true. These are some disturbing developments indeed."

"So, um, can you help us?" Joel asked.

"I would love to, but obtaining bloomfish venom will not be an easy task."

"We figured," Felicity said. "Do you know how to do it?"

"It is not the how that is the problem," Sandthroat answered. "The how is actually rather simple—incapacitate one of them and then drain the venom from their limbs. The problem is that during this time of year, bloomfish are not in season."

"You gotta be kidding me," Felicity grumbled. "First bloodseeds, now bloomfish."

"What does 'not in season' mean, exactly?" Joel asked.

"It means they do not come close to the shore," Sandthroat replied. "They gather to breed by the Far Edge, right next to the Forbidden Tides."

"Man, I knew we were gonna have to go out there sooner or later," Felicity sighed, looking at Joel. "I called it, remember?"

"You did?"

"Or maybe I just thought I did. I dunno, I figure that we always end up having to go to all the most dangerous places around here eventually."

"But wait," Sandthroat said, his expression brightening, "I forgot—it will not be a problem for you. You are riders of the sky! You can simply use your powers to go out there, capture a bloomfish, and then return."

"We already told you, we don't have our wavebows," Felicity said.

"Ah, yes, so you did."

"What if you took us out there on your boat?" Joel asked.

Sandthroat hesitated for a moment before responding. "That is...rather risky, I am afraid. You said that you were aware of how dangerous the Tides are?"

"Sure—something about how they're big waves that no one's been able to cross, blah, blah, blah," Felicity answered. "But we don't need to cross them, we just need to get to the general area, right?"

"That alone is an extremely hazardous undertaking," Sandthroat said with an edge of nervousness creeping into his voice.

"Oh, c'mon," Felicity said, slapping the native on the arm. "You're a strong, brave chief, right? I remember when you ambushed us, you were all, like, 'our tribe takes care of itself!' and 'don't tell us what we don't understand!'" she went on in a faux-macho voice that made Joel concerned about upsetting the former vagabond leader. To his surprise, however, it seemed to have the opposite effect.

"Yes, I did say those things," Sandthroat chuckled. "But time has tempered my bravado, I must admit. I no longer possess the reckless courage of youth."

"Are you kidding?" Felicity said. "You look exactly the same as when we first met you. Like you haven't aged a day. Still all fit and muscly and stuff."

Joel looked at Sandthroat, then at Felicity, and then back at Sandthroat again. True, the native was in good shape, but still, it was rather obvious that he had aged a considerable amount. Joel opened his mouth to make that point. "Um—"

"And wouldn't that be an awesome story?" Felicity continued. "How you helped the Wavemakers save Spectraland by taking them out to the Forbidden Tides to catch a bloomfish? You would be, like, the greatest fisherman ever!"

Sandthroat paused, apparently considering her words. Then, he said, "You know what?"

Joel cringed. *You know what* is what his father used to say before announcing some kind of punishment, as in *You know what? I think you should have no TV for a week.* Perhaps Felicity had gone a little too far after all.

"You are right!" Sandthroat smiled.
Joel exhaled with relief.

CHAPTER 20: BLOOMFISH

Sandthroat gave Joel and Felicity a crash course in paddling before the three of them set out in the Roughrock leader's canoe, leaving the swordcats behind on the beach. Joel was initially excited about the prospect of seeing the Far Edge up close, but a mere twenty minutes into what was supposed to be a three-hour journey, his excitement had been completely replaced by anxiety, exhaustion, and a slight bit of nausea as the vessel made its way over sets of ocean swells that got stronger the farther out they went.

"Looks like your companion could do with a bit more stamina," Sandthroat said to Felicity with a laugh.

"I keep telling him that," she replied, although it looked to Joel like she was starting to struggle as well.

They continued on, with the two offworlders taking occasional breaks while Sandthroat kept paddling non-stop. While doing so, he told them stories about how Fireflower helped his people organize into a more civilized tribe, how they built the tower known as Spiral Landing, his unsuccessful attempts to join the Chieftain Council, and other, more esoteric subjects like spikefin fishing and the various methods for brewing nightwine.

While the native spoke, Joel stared back at the island. From out here he could see that it was blanketed in Aura waves of all colors that swirled around through the air like gigantic rainbow ghosts. Also, right above the island hung a dense pack of dark clouds that spat out the occasional bolt of lightning, causing the Aura below it to shift and flicker each time it did so.

"Hey, um," Joel said after Sandthroat had finished detailing a recipe for something called Burnt Leg of Bullrat in Sunseed Sauce, "do you guys see that?"

"See what?" Felicity said quickly, apparently eager to change the subject.

"The island," Joel replied, pointing. "It looks like everything is concentrated over there—the Aura, the storms...it's like in those cartoons, when the rain clouds just hover over one person's head."

"Except for the storms, that is how it has always been," Sandthroat said.

I guess that's what Fireflower meant when she said that the Aura runs out as you get closer to the Tides, Joel mused to himself. *It's like the Aura is only a part of Spectraland, and nowhere else.*

"Wait," Felicity said, looking at Sandthroat, "if there's no Aura out here, how come we can still understand you?"

"I am not sure," the native replied with a thoughtful look. "The specifics of the translation cast is a subject that you will have to take up with Fireflower. It is fortunate that it does still work out here, though, because now I can tell you about the time I actually went hunting in the Jungle of Darkness! You see, it all began when...."

"Yeah, real fortunate," Felicity muttered.

As the time dragged on, Joel started to feel increasingly seasick. Still facing the stern of the canoe, he hung his head over the hull and stared down at the passing water.

Ugh...I think I'm gonna vomit.

"Hey," Felicity said after a few minutes had passed, "you probably shouldn't do that. You'll feel better if you're looking up."

With a small groan, Joel lifted his head. What he saw at that moment definitely did not make him feel any better, though: from this distance, the storm clouds that were hanging above Spectraland looked almost exactly like Marshall Byle's face.

"Whoa," he muttered. "You guys need to check this out."

"Yeah, yeah, we saw the Aura already," Felicity said over her shoulder as she continued paddling.

"No, no...the storm clouds."

"We saw those too."

"No, it—they—now they look just like Marshall."

"What? No way."

"I'm serious. Look."

Both Felicity and Sandthroat stopped paddling and turned around.

"Well, whaddya know," Felicity exhaled, "it really does look like ol' scar-face."

"I forgot to ask you about that," Joel said to Sandthroat. "The apparition you saw—did it look like that?"

"Not quite," Sandthroat responded, staring at the storm clouds. "The one I saw was an entire figure, drifting out over the ocean. But still, it did strongly resemble Chief Byle, just as those clouds do now."

"What do you think it means?" Joel asked.

"I had previously thought that perhaps his lingering evil influence had something to do with the recent shifts in the Aura and the strange weather we have been experiencing. After you told me your story about Stoneroot, however, I dismissed that notion. But now I am not so sure."

"Well, either way," Felicity said, "since we're already out here, we might as well finish getting what we came for. Agreed?"

"Agreed." Sandthroat nodded.

"Um, yeah, sure," Joel said.

They paddled with a renewed sense of urgency for another hour or so. Then, finally, they arrived at a still patch of water that was covered with the familiar luminescent pink and purple blossoms.

"Sheesh," Felicity said, "there must be, like, hundreds of them."

Joel did a quick scan of the area. "Probably around four hundred and fifty," he said. Then, a moment later, he spotted a long strip of water, right beyond the patch of blossoms, that appeared to be a bit darker than the rest of the ocean. "Is that the Far Edge?" he asked Sandthroat.

"It is," the Roughrock leader replied. "Even the slightest movement within it would awaken the Tides."

"Cool," Joel said. "Kind of like a motion-sensor alarm."

"Okay, enough chitchat," Felicity said. "How do we catch a bloomfish?"

"We will need to carefully pick one from off the edge of the shoal," Sandthroat whispered. "Then we will have a few seconds while it awakens and blooms. The moment it finishes doing so, we will need to disable it before it can sting us, or alert the others."

"Why can't we just—disable it, or whatever—while it's still in flower form?" Felicity said.

"It needs to be in full bloom in order for us to obtain its venom," Sandthroat explained.

"Of course it does," she sighed. "Too bad the sword-cats aren't here."

"We should get moving," Sandthroat warned. "If we wait too long, a group of them might awaken—and then we will be in serious danger."

"All right, all right," Felicity said. "Man, we should have planned this out on the way here instead of wasting time talking about all of that other nonsense."

Sandthroat maneuvered the canoe around to the far left end of the shoal, where the sleeping bloomfish were more sporadic. A couple of blossoms with a decent amount of space around them appeared to be the best targets.

"One of us will pick the blossom," Sandthroat said softly as he positioned the canoe within arm's length of one of the stragglers, "and one of us will stab it with a knife after it blooms. The other will start paddling away once we have the bloomfish securely in hand."

Felicity's hand shot up. "I'll paddle," she volunteered. "There's no way I'm touching one of those things again."

"Then I will pick the blossom," Sandthroat said.

"Wait, um—" Joel stammered, realizing that he had ended up with the most gruesome task. "Shouldn't...shouldn't you stab it?" he said to Sandthroat.

"Picking it is the most hazardous job," Sandthroat replied. "After it wakes up, it will change into its full form. While it does, the picker will need to hold it steady. The bloomfish will try to attack whoever is in contact with it at the time."

"You don't have to remind me of that," Felicity muttered.

"Well, um, that's cool, I can do that," Joel offered.

"That is brave of you, young Wavemaker," Sandthroat said, "but holding the bloomfish steady requires...a certain amount of physical strength, shall we say."

"Uh, okay, but—"

"Dude, just let him do it," Felicity said to Joel. "C'mon, you've stabbed giant fishes before. Remember that angler-mammoth?"

"What? No, I didn't stab that, I cut off its filament. And plus, it was dark, and—"

"We really should get on with this," Sandthroat interrupted.

Conceding, Joel took a deep breath and gripped the handle of his knife. *Okay, Suzuki, you can do this,* he assured himself.

Sandthroat slowly reached out over the side of the canoe as Joel and Felicity watched. Three seconds later, the native yanked his arm back up, a flower cluster in hand. "Prepare yourself," he said to Joel, holding the cluster near his chest.

"Um—where do I stab it?" Joel asked, feeling increasingly frantic.

The cluster began to shake. "In the eye!" Sandthroat replied.

"The eye? What eye?"

Before Sandthroat could respond, the flower cluster burst with a subtle *pop,* and a cloud of tiny spores filled the air. Tentacles began to emerge from the blossom like black snake fireworks. His panic level rising, Joel tried to find a feature on the growing bloomfish that could pass for an eye, to no avail.

"Not yet!" Sandthroat exclaimed. "It must be in full bloom!"

"Okay, I'm getting out of here now!" Felicity declared as she started to paddle.

The bloomfish quickly expanded until it was the size of a small person. Like an expert wrestler, Sandthroat held it tightly, keeping the creature's tentacles in check whenever one of them threatened to lash out. Joel spotted an oval-shaped area of discoloration on the head of the bloomfish that he assumed was the eye.

"Now!" Sandthroat exclaimed.

His knife hand shaking, Joel hesitated. Stabbing this creature without provocation, after having woken it up from its peaceful slumber, just seemed wrong to him. And besides, weren't Wavemakers forbidden from killing?

"Quickly!" Sandthroat said.

Joel aimed his knife at the bloomfish's eye, but he just couldn't bring himself to finish the deed. *There has to be a better way to do this,* he thought. While he wavered, two of the creature's tentacles, having grown even larger, broke loose from Sandthroat's grip.

"Fool!" Sandthroat yelled before he tossed the bloomfish overboard back into the ocean. "That was our chance!"

"Why did you throw it back?" Felicity snapped.

"It was about to sting us!" Sandthroat snapped back as he picked up a paddle. "Now it will wake the others. We need to leave, immediately!"

Joel picked up a paddle as well. As he did so, he saw the escaped bloomfish swim over to the mass of dormant blossoms, which, a moment later, started to erupt in rapid-fire fashion.

"Paddle!" Sandthroat yelled.

Joel dropped his paddle into the water. Unnerved and distracted by Sandthroat's agitated demeanor, he mistakenly stroked it the wrong way, causing the canoe to spin around and face what was now a gigantic mass of full-grown bloomfish. Before he could correct himself, three of the creatures launched themselves at the canoe and landed their tentacles up against the bow, knocking the vessel's lantern into the water. Felicity screamed as she dropped her paddle and covered herself.

Sandthroat stood up and began swinging his paddle at the bloomfish in an attempt to fend them off, but for each one that he repelled, several more came forth. "We are lost!" he declared.

For a moment, Joel thought that the native was right. But then an idea struck him. Pulling out his knife, he reared back like a pitcher getting ready to deliver to home plate. *Now would be a good time for some athletic ability*, he thought as he hurled the knife, end over end, as hard as he possibly could, over the burgeoning mass of bloomfish and into the dark waters of the Far Edge. Sandthroat and Felicity—who had since picked up her paddle to help beat back the creatures—were so busy that they didn't notice what Joel had done.

"Help us!" Felicity screamed.

Instead of picking up his paddle, however, Joel pulled the bloodseed from his supply pack. Then he squeezed his way past Felicity, nearly getting hit by her paddle as he elbowed her aside. "Sorry, excuse me," he said as a rumbling sound started up, like thunder in the distance.

"What are you doing?" she screeched, barely dodging the swipe of a tentacle.

Steeling his nerves, Joel held out the bloodseed with both hands, as if he were making a peace offering to the bloomfish. A tentacle lashed out in his direction, and he caught its blow with the meat-slab-like fruit. Then he dislodged the bloodseed from the tentacle and inspected it. A thin, purple liquid started to leak out of a hole in its surface. *Got it.* He smiled to himself as the rumbling grew progressively louder.

"Look out!" Felicity yelled, blocking another tentacle just before it hit Joel in the leg.

"Thanks—um, get ready," he told her as he started to move toward the back of the canoe. The rumbling now sounded like the anticipatory murmur of a stadium-sized crowd of people right before showtime.

"For what?" Felicity asked. Then her eyes grew wide, as if she were just now noticing the rumbling sound. "Oh boy."

"Is that what I—" Sandthroat started to say, right before a wall of water about a hundred feet wide began to rise up from behind the bloomfish.

Sandthroat and Felicity began shouting, but the noise from the rising wave was now so loud, Joel could no longer hear what they were saying. He pulled the wooden vial from his pack, squeezed the purple liquid from the bloodseed into it, sealed it, and returned both items to his pack. *Guess we'll see how waterproof this thing really is,* he thought.

Then the wave came crashing down. Joel closed his eyes, held his breath, and grabbed onto the side of the canoe with all his might.

CHAPTER 21: THE PROM

Joel thrashed his arms and legs. He kept his eyes and mouth tightly shut as he flailed in panic, trying desperately to find his way to the surface. After what seemed like an eternity (but was, in reality, only sixty-three seconds), he began to feel light-headed, and there was still nothing but ocean water surrounding him.

Oh man, I'm gonna drown, he thought.

Unpleasant memories from his entire life began to flash through his mind: the death of his dog, his parents' divorce, the D grade he got in Language Arts. After that, however, a new, unfamiliar image appeared: a large hotel ballroom, decked out in multicolored balloons and streamers.

Wait—I've never been there before.

Then, he heard a loud *whoosh*, and suddenly, the sensation of floating in water disappeared.

"Joel? Are you okay?" a voice said.

Joel blinked several times, trying to regain his bearings. It took him a few moments to realize that, rather than being submerged in the ocean outside of Spectraland, he was now standing on a carpeted surface, inside the exact same ballroom that he had just witnessed in his head. The lights were dim, and a slow song that he didn't recognize blared out of a pair of large speakers. His Spectraland garb had been replaced by an itchy, uncomfortable tuxedo, and in front of him stood a girl in a strapless red gown who looked amazingly like Auravine, just without the arm-leaves.

What the heck?

"Joel?"

"Um...Suzi?"

"Okay," Suzi chuckled, "just checking. You seemed a little out of it there for a minute."

"What—uh, where...where are we?"

"Prom, silly. Are you just messing with me?"

Joel had no idea what she meant by that. "Uh, sure," he ventured.

Suzi giggled. "You're funny. C'mon, let's keep dancing."

"Keep what?"

Suzi threw her arms around Joel's neck. Terrified and exhilarated at the same time, Joel nearly fell backward before he was able to brace himself by wrapping his arms around Suzi's waist, pulling her in as he regained his balance.

"Whoa! Easy there," Suzi laughed.

"I'm sorry! I'm sorry," Joel blurted out, letting go.

"It's cool, don't worry about it. Now c'mon, hold me again."

Joel glanced at the other dancing couples. Noticing that the arms-around-the-waist thing seemed to be a standard practice, he gingerly placed his hands on the small of Suzi's back, making sure to keep their bodies a good four inches apart.

"Oh, don't be shy," Suzi said, pulling Joel close.

Joel gulped and tilted his head away. He clenched his teeth as he fought to keep his hands from shaking. *Okay, this is even scarier than playing a show. Or fighting strange alien creatures, for that matter.*

"It's okay, you can face me," Suzi said gently. "I won't bite."

Joel forced himself to turn his head back, but he stopped short of making direct eye contact. He focused his gaze a little off to the side of her face, where a video of highlights from the school year was playing on a giant projector screen.

All right, I know what's going on here, he thought. *I passed out in the water, and now I'm having a nightmare.*

Suzi rested her chin on Joel's shoulder. The subtle scent of her perfume wafted over him, making him feel light-headed.

Whoa—okay, now this is getting really *scary. Maybe I should try to wake myself up...wait, at the end of my last nightmare, didn't Marshall say something about how he would make the next one a lot more frightening? Could it be him, creating all of this in my mind?*

"I'm so glad you asked me to the prom, Joel," Suzi said. "I was waiting for you, you know."

"What? Waiting for me? I, um, I thought Mitch was your boyfriend."

"Mitch? No, he's not. I mean, we did go out on a couple of dates and everything, but that was it."

"Oh."

"I thought you knew that? After all, you wouldn't have asked me to the prom if I was his girlfriend, right?"

"Um, yeah, right. I was, uh, I was just kidding."

Suzi chuckled in response. "You have such a cool sense of humor."

"I do? Um...are you being sarcastic?"

"Of course not, silly."

Joel gulped. He could almost feel the sweat coming out of his pores.

"Anyway," Suzi said, "as I was saying before, thank you."

"For...what?"

"Oh, c'mon, you know."

"You're welcome—wait, um, no, I don't."

At that moment, the highlight video abruptly segued from a car-wash fundraiser into a fuzzy, blurry image of none other than Marshall Byle.

What the—I knew it!

"For inviting me here tonight," Suzi said.

"Uh...okay," Joel replied automatically, his attention now fully captured by the projector screen.

Marshall's mouth began moving, but Joel couldn't hear what the former Biledriver singer was saying. Instead, subtitles appeared at the bottom of the screen, like lyrics in a karaoke video.

This is a vision of what could have been, the words read.

"I know that it must've been a little hard, because of, well, you know, your...your shyness," Suzi went on.

You think it was fine, that you did try your best.

"But the way you just walked up to me in the hall and said hello—that was so awesome."

Marshall's lips curled into a twisted sneer. *But if only you had the courage to ask her—*

"So, yeah, I'm having a really great time."

*—the answer she gave you would have been...*yes.

"Wait, what?" Joel said.

So you see, Joel, the words on the screen said, *in the long run, you cannot defeat me.*

"I said, I'm having a really great time."

Because no matter how brave you may think you are, you will always be weak and timid when it matters the most.

"You're lying!" Joel blurted out.

"What?" Suzi said, a shocked expression on her face.

"Huh? Oh—um, no, I—sorry, I wasn't—"

To Joel's relief, Suzi's look of surprise morphed into one of gentle understanding. "You're joking again, aren't you?"

"Um, yeah, joking. Heh, heh. Funny, huh?"

Marshall's image faded away, replaced by scenes from the football team's state title game. Joel shifted his focus back to Suzi, who, at the same time, had taken her chin off of his shoulder to look at him. Their eyes locked for a brief instant. Joel thought he was going to faint.

"That's what I love about you, Joel." Suzi smiled. "You're so...unique."

"Um, thanks, well, I—"

Before he could say another word, she leaned in and planted her lips firmly on his. Joel's eyes stretched wide open with shock. Gross yet glorious, it was the strangest sensation he had ever felt in his life, flying and falling from high cliffs included.

What am I supposed to do? he thought, panicking. *I have no idea how to do this!*

Suzi opened her mouth. Summoning up an extra reserve of courage, Joel closed his eyes and followed her lead. Then, abruptly and without warning, she began to blow air down his windpipe.

Joel recoiled, coughing and gagging. *Okay, I have no idea how to do this, but I'm pretty sure it's not like that!*

"He's breathing!"

Joel coughed and blinked. Suzi's face was gone, replaced by Felicity's. Water dripped off of her hair into his eyes, and he realized that he was lying flat on his back.

"Joel, can you hear me?" she said, her hands resting firmly on his chest.

Joel nodded as he coughed again.

Felicity exhaled in relief. "Okay, he's all right."

"Are you sure?" Sandthroat's voice sounded.

"No, I just stopped saving him 'cause I got tired," Felicity said in her most sarcastic tone. "Yes, he's all right."

Joel coughed several more times as he propped himself up on his elbows. His mouth tasted like saltwater and, oddly enough, lifepods. The vast expanse of the Coast of Fang surrounded him, and a light rain was falling.

"Dude, lie down. You need to rest," Felicity scolded.

"Is this—are you—for real?" Joel asked, ignoring her directive.

"What are you talking about?"

"That was amazing," Sandthroat said. "Your gesture of affection brought him back to life!"

"Gesture of—oh, no, no, that was just CPR," Felicity said to the native. "Artificial respiration."

"Incredible," Sandthroat marveled. "You will need to teach me that someday."

"As long as you practice on someone else."

"What—what happened?" Joel asked.

"You should know," Felicity replied. "It was your plan. And it totally worked, by the way, so—good job. A point for you."

"You mean...the wave?"

"I guess you're still a little loopy," she said, squeezing water out of her now-unbraided hair—which had retained, to Joel's amazement, its dyed green hue. "Yeah, the wave—it carried us away from the bloomfish. We did get dunked a bit, though, so you ended up passing out. Again."

"Rousing the Forbidden Tides—that was a very brave move," Sandthroat said. "I suppose I should have expected no less from you."

Joel looked around. Sandthroat's canoe rested on the shore near the water. "Wow, um, yeah...I guess it really did work. But where are the swordcats?"

"Wish I knew," Felicity muttered. "Maybe the wave scared them off or something."

Now worried, Joel got to his feet. "Platinum?" he called out. "Goldie? Doc?"

"Dude, seriously, you need to rest for a bit," Felicity said. "We can look for them later."

Joel scanned the area for any sign of their feline friends, but to his dismay, he saw nothing.

"By the way, you got the venom, right?" Felicity asked. "I saw you do that thing with the bloodseed."

"Oh—um, yeah," Joel said, checking for his supply pack. To his further amazement, it was still strapped to his back. He opened it and found the wooden vial. "I saw the little thorns on the bloomfishes' tentacles, and I figured that the venom came out from there, so I thought that if I made one of them inject its venom into the bloodseed, I could squeeze both the venom and the bloodseed juice out at the same time, and then that would combine into—"

"Just gimme that thing," Felicity interrupted, holding out her hand. "I'll check it."

Joel handed her the vial. She held it at arm's length and opened it slowly, as if she expected something terrible to jump out of it. Once the cover was off, a wisp of light-blue smoke drifted out, and Joel could immediately detect an aroma that reminded him of a zoo, or perhaps a farm.

"Blech," Felicity said, wrinkling her nose.

"Hmm," Sandthroat said as he sniffed the air. "That is the unmistakable scent of slimeback manure. Is it supposed to smell like that?"

"'Fraid so," Felicity replied. She trickled a few drops of the mixture into her palm. "Looks like water. Okay, I think it's good." She wiped her hand on the ground before hastily closing the vial and handing it back to Joel.

"Well done!" Sandthroat exclaimed. "What a brilliant plan."

"Thanks," Joel said, putting the vial back into his supply pack. "Oh—and, uh, thanks, too, by the way, for—"

"Do not move!" a voice shouted from behind. Joel started to turn around to see who it was.

"I said, do not move!" the voice repeated, sounding like it was coming closer. A projectile of some kind zipped over Joel's head. He could hear the soft croaking and shuffling of slimebacks—a lot of them.

"What is the meaning of this?" Sandthroat barked.

"Quiet, vagrant," the voice ordered.

"Vagrant? How dare you!" Sandthroat spat. "I am Sandthroat, the Chief of Spiral Landing, and this beach is my domain. Who are you?"

Joel glanced at Felicity. She gave him a barely perceptible shrug along with a look of concern, as if to say *I'm not sure what's going on, but I think we may be in trouble.*

"We are guards of the Chieftain Council," the voice declared, "and by order of Chief Stoneroot, the three of you are hereby under arrest."

"Under arrest?" Sandthroat echoed, incredulous. "What for?"

"Conspiring to commit treason against the council."

"That is ridiculous!" Sandthroat protested. "We were simply out fishing!"

"No more talking," the voice snapped. Joel felt the tip of something—probably a spear—press into his back. A rough pair of hands tied his wrists together with binding vine.

"This is an outrage!" Sandthroat shouted.

The pair of hands turned Joel around. He found himself facing seventeen slimebacks, fifteen of whom bore riders who were aiming spears and blowguns in his direction. One of the riders was Whitenose.

"You guys know we saved this place nineteen years ago, right?" Felicity said as the guard bound her wrists together as well.

"One more word, and you will be gagged," the guard warned.

"My Chief? What is going on here?" a different voice called out.

Joel turned. Five scaletops were approaching, each of them carrying a member of the Roughrock Tribe.

"Cloudpalm!" Sandthroat exclaimed. "Thank the Aura you are here."

"Your leader is an accused criminal," one of the guards said to Cloudpalm. "We are taking him in for questioning."

"Accused of what?" Cloudpalm asked.

"Treason."

"With all due respect," Cloudpalm said, "I do not think Chief Sandthroat can commit treason against a governing body that does not accept him as a member."

"In that case, we will consider his deeds to be an act of war."

Cloudpalm looked at Sandthroat. For a few moments, the only sounds that could be heard were the crashing of the waves and the breathing of the slimebacks. Then Sandthroat nodded.

"So be it," Cloudpalm said.

In the blink of an eye, the five Roughrock Tribe members whipped out their spiral bows and fired at the guards. Joel whirled his head around as projectiles whizzed through the air in both directions and bodies fell to the ground.

"Wavemakers! Run!" Sandthroat yelled.

Joel shot a glance at Felicity. She made a motion with her head that he assumed meant *let's go*. He wanted to stay and help Cloudpalm and the others, but there wasn't much he or Felicity could do at the moment with their wrists bound. And on top of that, their immediate priority was to find the swordcats and carry out their plan. So he nodded, and they took off running.

"Do not let them get away!" one of the guards cried.

With Felicity in the lead, the two offworlders ran as fast they could through the sand, up toward the nearby tree line. As they did so, several darts zipped past Joel; one of them missed Felicity by a couple of inches.

"Where should we go?" he yelled.

"Just follow me!" she shouted back.

They dashed into the trees. Amidst the whistling of flying darts, Joel heard a *thunk*, and noticed that one of the darts had struck a tree just off to his side.

That was close.

The pair continued to run, weaving their way through a maze of yellow palms. Joel could hear the sounds of slimebacks behind him, but it seemed that they and their riders were having a harder time following him and Felicity as they all got deeper into the increasingly dense jungle.

"I think we're losing them!" he called out.

"Stop talking!" she replied, not looking back.

Hopefully we can find a good place to hide, Joel thought. *Then, after the guards are gone, we can go back and look for the swordcats. It'll be night soon, so we need to find them and get ready to carry out the plan before the moons—*

His foot got caught in something. He let out a startled yelp as he fell, face-first, to the ground. After rolling over a couple of times, he saw what had tripped him: a tree root that he hadn't noticed, jutting out of the ground.

Ow—that was a bad time to lose focus, he scolded himself.

"Joel!" Felicity exclaimed, stopping and turning. "What happened?"

"I just tripped." He grimaced. "I'm okay. Mostly."

"Good," she said, rushing back to him. "Can you stand up? I think I hear them getting closer."

"Yeah," he replied as he struggled to his feet. "Just give me a few seconds to—"

"Um...I don't think we have any more of those."

Joel whirled around. Half a dozen guards were charging in on foot from all sides, their spears leveled at him and Felicity.

"Guess you guys figured out it was faster to just ditch the slimebacks and run, huh?" she remarked.

"This time you are not getting away," one of the guards said.

"You know, you really don't have to tell us stuff like that."

“Enough talk,” the guard snapped. He turned to one of his comrades. “Gag them.”

CHAPTER 22: THE EXECUTION

Riding for several hours on a slimeback—with a gag over his mouth and his upper body wrapped in binding vines—Joel gained a new sense of appreciation for the more efficient forms of travel he had experienced during this second go-around in Spectraland.

Maybe I should introduce the Silencers to the wheel, he mused. *They may not be able to fly or ride swordcats, but at least with some wheels they could get around a little bit faster, and then maybe they wouldn't be as mad at the Wavemakers as they are now....*

Finally, after they had entered a familiar-looking forest of thin, glowing trees, Whitenose, who had been leading their party, called for a break.

"We can only rest for a few minutes," he announced. As the other guards grumbled, he shot a glance at Joel and Felicity. "The offworlders' escape attempt has put us behind schedule."

The slimebacks halted, and everyone dismounted. The guards riding in front of Joel and Felicity lifted the two of them off their mounts and gruffly placed them on the ground. Joel turned to see Whitenose approaching, carrying a couple of lifepods.

"The offworlders should be afforded a break as well," Whitenose said. "Remove their gags."

"As you wish," the guard who was Joel's lead rider responded.

After Joel and Felicity's gags were removed, Whitenose kneeled down in front of them and held the lifepods to their mouths. "Here, take a bite. You must be hungry," he said.

"Why are you feeding them, Whitenose?" one of the other guards asked. "It will not matter soon anyway."

"What is he talking about?" Felicity said, ignoring the offered fruit.

"And where are we going?" Joel asked, doing the same. "Why are we under arrest?"

Whitenose sighed and sat down. "I suppose you are owed some explanations."

"You bet we are," Felicity said.

"To sum it up, you are headed for your execution."

Joel gulped. *Execution?*

"Whoa, whoa, okay, hold on," Felicity said. "I think the translation cast isn't working here, because I just heard you say 'execution'."

"That is, in fact, what I said."

"You gotta be kidding me!" Felicity exclaimed. "What—why are we being executed?"

"Because, unfortunately, you know too much," Whitenose replied. "You know about Stoneroot's plan to create a mind-control potion."

"Well, yeah, because we heard you talking about it in Yellowbranch Jungle," Joel said.

"Precisely," Whitenose said. "You see, after our incident with the daggermoles, I took Thornleaf back to the

Silencer Stronghold. I thought he was hurt, but it turned out that he had just been hit with a sleepdart."

"Well, I coulda told you that," Felicity muttered.

"Once we had arrived," Whitenose continued, "Stoneroot had me report to him everything that had occurred. He became quite upset, naturally, since if word spread about his plan, his reputation would be destroyed, or worse.

"He revived Thornleaf, who then leveled some bizarre accusations at him: that he had Auravine under his control; that he was working with Lightsnakes; and that together they were conspiring to kidnap the Wavemakers and eventually put you all under his command."

"Because that's exactly what he was doing," Felicity insisted.

"That would be impossible, however," Whitenose said.

"What? Why?" Joel asked.

"Stoneroot has not perfected a mind-control potion yet."

Joel and Felicity exchanged surprised looks. *So it's not Stoneroot after all,* Joel thought. *That must mean...*

"He does, however, have a truth potion at his disposal," Whitenose went on. "So he proceeded to use it on Thornleaf, to verify these unbelievable claims that Auravine and the Lightsnakes are, in fact, responsible for the Wavemakers' disappearances.

"He also needed to know where the two of you might have gone after Yellowbranch Jungle, in order to prevent you from telling anyone else about his plans. After further questioning, he got Thornleaf to confess the details of your mission to assemble a mind-control antidote.

"Then he sent out separate teams of guards to the Pit of Ashes, Red Gulch, and the Coast of Fang to arrest you and anyone you came into contact with."

"Oh, c'mon, don't execute that nice old couple from Red Gulch," Felicity said. "They were super cool."

"They will not be executed," Whitenose replied. "If they disappeared for good, there would be too many questions. No, they will simply be imprisoned, along with Amberweed and the vagabond tribe members, until the mind-control potion is ready and he can erase their memories."

"Wait—then why are just the two us getting the axe?" Felicity protested.

"I am afraid that...it was the best option," Whitenose replied with what sounded like a tinge of regret.

"I don't get it," Joel said. "Why is that the best option?"

"He does not have the ability to send you home, he cannot depend on whatever Auravine and the Lightsnakes are doing, and he feels that you are too clever to stay safely locked up for any length of time."

"Well, he's definitely right about that last part," Felicity said with a humorless chuckle.

"And since Wavemakers have been disappearing anyway," Whitenose continued, "no one would suspect anything if you were gone."

"Um...not that I want him to get executed too," Joel said, "but what about Thornleaf?"

"Thornleaf is imprisoned at the stronghold, along with the others. He is being spared because he is Stoneroot's son."

Oh wow, Joel thought. *No wonder Thornleaf knew a lot about Stoneroot—plus, they do look a lot alike.*

"Seriously? His son?" Felicity chortled. "Oh man, that is *so Star Wars.*"

"That is the real reason why Stoneroot started his campaign against the Wavemaker Order many years ago," Whitenose said. "Soon after the two of you left, Fireflower discovered her first young villager with the Wavemaker potential and took him away from his home to be trained at the temple."

"She did? Who was it?" Joel asked.

"Dude," Felicity sighed, "it was Thornleaf."

"Oh—right."

"Instead of feeling honored, Stoneroot was heartbroken. He became so inconsolable that his spouse left him and moved to a different village."

Aliens get divorces? Joel thought.

"After that, he made it his personal mission to put an end to the Wavemaker Order. Over time, he came up with other reasons—I am sure you have already heard most of them—that resonated with people and gained him a small but loyal following. His main motivation, however, has always been the loss of his son, especially as the years passed and they became more and more estranged from each other."

"Okay," Felicity said, "that sucks and all, but there's gotta be a better way to work this all out, don't you think? You know, instead of secret mind-control projects, killing me and Joel..."

"Yeah," Joel agreed, "especially now that he knows the Aura isn't angry, and that it's been Auravine and the Lightsnakes this whole time. They're the ones we have to go after. Once we stop them, then maybe Fireflower and Stoneroot can sit down with the chiefs and come up with a compromise that makes everyone happy."

"It would be nice to end nearly twenty years of tension and conflict," Whitenose said, "but those ideas have been suggested before, and nothing has come of them. Each side has been too stubborn, and it has only gotten worse over time. Stoneroot's mind-control potion, once perfected, will allow him to gain full control of the council and peacefully abolish the Wavemaker Order without anyone else having to get hurt."

"Hello, there's not gonna be an order to abolish if you don't let us save the other Wavemakers," Felicity said.

"I pledged my loyalty to Stoneroot," Whitenose responded. "I am just following his orders."

"Well, um, you should think about changing your mind before you get hurt by our rescuers," Joel said.

"If you are referring to the swordcats, we captured them while they were waiting for you on the beach. They are being taken back to the stronghold along with the vagabond tribe members."

Joel frowned. He was relieved to know where the swordcats were but concerned about what Stoneroot might do to them.

"C'mon, man, we heard what you were saying before in that jungle," Felicity said to Whitenose. "About how you were having second thoughts, and how this whole mind-control thing was misguided and unethical."

"I, uh, I did not say such things," Whitenose stammered as one of the other guards turned and looked at him. "Stoneroot has my complete and total support."

"Yeah, you know," Joel said, "don't be afraid to say what's on your mind, or to say how you feel about stuff. Don't worry about what other people think, or if they agree with you or not."

"Hey, good one, dude." Felicity smirked. "Isn't that what I told you?"

"Word for word." Joel grinned.

"Replace their gags," Whitenose grunted to the nearby guard. "Break time is over."

♪♪♪

They rode for a while longer under a cloudy nighttime sky until they reached an area that Joel recognized as being right outside the Wavemaker Temple. He was about to ask why they were there when he remembered that he had a gag over his mouth. As they drew closer to the temple—its surrounding Aura glow now reduced to a mere flicker—Joel saw another party of slimeback riders waiting for them in the clearing by the river. One of them was Stoneroot.

"Well done, Whitenose," the Silencer leader said once they were within earshot. "But what happened to the rest of your contingent?"

"We ran into some members of the vagabond tribe," Whitenose replied. "There was a small skirmish, but we prevailed. Some of our guards arrested them and are taking them back to the stronghold."

"Very good." Stoneroot nodded. "You can remove the offworlders' gags, by the way. I will be granting them the privilege of a few final words."

The guards riding in front of Joel and Felicity turned around and took off their gags.

"Oh, I've got some words for you, all right," Felicity said.

"Offworlders!" a female voice shouted. It was Yellowpetal, tied up and sitting behind one of the riders in

Stoneroot's party. "What is happening? Where—where is my daughter?"

"Um, she's—" Joel started to say.

"Take her to the stronghold," Stoneroot ordered.

The rider with Yellowpetal urged his slimeback into a gallop, and two other riders followed him as they rode away.

"Why are you arresting *her*?" Felicity snapped. "We didn't tell her anything about your stupid mind-control deal."

"Ah, so you already know why you are here," Stoneroot said.

"Well, we know we're supposed to get executed," Joel responded, "but we don't know why we're *here*, specifically, at the temple, since it would probably be easier if you—"

"Yellowpetal is being taken into custody for her own safety," Stoneroot interrupted. "For you see, the Wavemaker Temple is about to be destroyed."

"Wait, what?" Joel and Felicity said at the same time.

"Yes, I decided that setting the temple on fire—along with the two of you—would be the best way to go about this. It will appear as if the Aura has defended herself once again, and I can rid the island of both you and this bloated monument at the same time."

"You can't do this!" Felicity protested.

"Oh, I can, and I will," Stoneroot said. "I regret that it has to be this way, but I cannot allow you to ruin everything that I have worked for all of these years."

At that moment, the cloud cover parted, revealing the twin moons.

"Ah—a good omen," Stoneroot continued, glancing up at the sky. "I suppose the Aura is pleased, after all."

He looked at Whitenose. "Place them in front of the doors."

Whitenose dismounted, along with the guard that Felicity had been riding with. Then the slimebacks knelt down, and the two guards lifted Joel and Felicity off.

"I'm telling you, we can figure something out!" Felicity exclaimed.

"I am afraid it is too late," Stoneroot said.

Whitenose and the other guard jabbed spears into Joel's and Felicity's backs.

"Okay, okay, we're going," Felicity grumbled.

Whitenose and the other native forced Joel and Felicity up to the top of the stairs, where they were made to kneel down in front of the double doors, facing outward, with Joel on the left and Felicity on the right. The two guards then rejoined their colleagues, three of whom had blowguns aimed directly at the offworlders.

"As you can see, I am giving you two options," Stoneroot said. "You can try to run, but then we will render you unconscious and burn you while you sleep. That is the cowards' option. The other option is to remain awake and say some final prayers to whatever entity you worship before you die with some measure of honor. I leave the choice to you."

For a moment, Joel thought about going with option one, but he realized that if he was going to die, there were some things he wanted to tell Felicity first. He glanced at her, and she glanced back. He could tell from her expression that she was also choosing option two.

"Very well," Stoneroot said. "Burn it down!"

One of the blowgun-wielding natives dipped a dart in a jar and then shot it out at the temple. The dart burst into flames as it soared through the air. It struck a section of the temple's wall to the right of the main entrance. She repeated the process, aiming for the left side this time. Joel looked back and saw that the walls had caught on fire. Stoneroot began to chant in tones that didn't translate into any kind of English words.

Felicity turned her head. "Got any miracles left?" she asked.

"Um...not that I can think of," Joel replied.

"Well then, dude," she sighed, "I hate to say this 'cause it sounds so cliché, but...I guess this is it."

"Yeah, I guess it is," he replied as he tried to muster up the courage to say what he really wanted to say.

"Too bad we didn't get a chance to see if your Auravine plan would work. I actually figured it out on the way here."

"Oh—uh, cool," Joel muttered, wrinkling his nose as the smoke from the burning temple walls began to waft through the clearing.

"Yeah, you know, Thornleaf was right—it really was kinda simple if you just thought it through long enough."

Joel felt himself getting progressively hotter, although he wasn't sure if it was because of the growing fire or his increasing nervousness. Probably both, he figured. "Hey, um," he said, "so, before we die, I need to tell you something."

"Wait, let me guess: it was *you* that scratched up my *Skyrim* disc, wasn't it? And then hid it under the tour-bus bunk afterward?"

"What? No, I didn't. I don't even know what you're—wait, *Skyrim*? You mean...you like video games?"

"No, I—ugh, all right, fine," she groaned. "I guess we're in confession mode now, so I'll admit it. I do. I love video games."

"But...we had a game console on the bus and you never played with it. You always said it was just for nerds, or whatever."

"Yeah, I know. I would play with it when you guys were asleep. I didn't want to...I dunno," she said, shaking her head and biting her lower lip. "Honestly, I don't know why I said that. I guess I just didn't want to seem like more of a tomboy than I already am."

"What's wrong with being a tomboy?"

"Well...I don't know if I wanna tell you."

"Just tell me," Joel said. "We're gonna die, anyway, right?"

Felicity rolled her eyes. "Okay, it's because of Trevor."

A cold feeling hit the pit of Joel's stomach—which, unfortunately, did nothing to stave off the increasing heat from the surrounding fires. "What—Trevor? Uh...what about him?"

"Well, I don't know if you've noticed, but he only goes for the girly-girl types."

"Um, no, I haven't noticed. What's a girly-girl type?"

"You know—the soft, polite, quiet ones who giggle and cry and wear pink clothes and get makeovers and stuff," Felicity said, her lip curling with contempt. "Kind of like Auravine. The opposite of me, basically."

"Oh. So, um...does that mean that you...like Trevor?"

Felicity sighed again. "I don't know, dude. I mean, I guess it's just nice to be paid attention to once in a while. You know, to feel...wanted, I suppose. Especially after everything I went through when I was growing up. I guess I just didn't want him to stop flirting with me, or whatever you would call that thing he does."

Joel's mind spun. "But, well...you shouldn't have to change for him, or hide who you really are. If he's going to like you, he should like you no matter what, even if you're a tomboy, or whatever. Like Mr. Rogers said, to love someone is to accept that person exactly the way they are, right here and now."

"Who's Mr. Rogers?"

"A wise man who had a long-running show on TV," Joel said with a grin.

At that moment, a bright flash of light went off, accompanied by a harsh, dissonant tone. Joel squeezed his eyes shut. When he opened them a second later, he saw that the entire clearing was now bathed in a pallid orange glow. Stoneroot and his followers were all looking around in shock and confusion.

"It's the Moonfire!" Joel exclaimed.

"I can see that!" Felicity said.

Then a sharp pain shot through Joel's head, and although his vision started to blur, he could just about make out what looked like five or six full-grown Lightsnakes, possibly attacking Stoneroot's contingent. A cold rain began to fall.

"Here's our chance!" Felicity said.

"For what?" Joel managed to say through gritted teeth.

"Make a run for it!"

Summoning up an extra reserve of strength, Joel stood up and rushed down the wooden stairway as fast as he possibly could. To his surprise, he was able to make it all the way down without stumbling or falling. He glanced at the shapes of the Lightsnakes and Stoneroot's forces and saw that one of them—he wasn't quite sure which—was headed their way. He turned and tried to run in the opposite direction, but he was stopped by a hand on his shoulder. The sudden contact made him fall to the ground. The hand rolled him over. A figure was looming over him with a blade in its other hand, which slashed at Joel before he even had a chance to close his eyes.

"Now go!" the figure said in a voice heavily drenched in static.

The figure moved away. Joel squinted at it.

Was that...Whitenose?

It took Joel another two full seconds before he realized that Whitenose had severed his binding vines and left his supply pack lying on his chest.

I guess he changed his mind after all.

Grabbing his pack, Joel struggled to his feet and saw the native freeing Felicity and returning her supply pack to her as well.

"You must escape!" was what Joel thought Whitenose was saying; through the static, it was hard to be completely sure.

"But—the Lightsnakes," Joel mumbled, looking around. Between his blurred eyesight and the now-heavy rain that chilled him to the bone, all he could see were a few hazy shapes, almost like ghosts, moving in his direction. As he turned to flee, he felt something or someone scratching at his right leg. He looked down.

Felicity?

But it wasn't her; in fact, there didn't seem to be anyone there. When he looked back up, one of the hazy shapes reached out, grabbed him, and carried him up into the sky.

CHAPTER 23: SALVADOR DALI'S WORST NIGHTMARE

For a moment, Joel wanted to thank whoever was carrying him. Not only had they saved him from the burning temple, but as they rose higher in the air, his headache disappeared and his eyesight began to clear up, much to his relief. Then, however, he saw exactly who his rescuer was: one of the Lightsnakes that had attacked Stoneroot's forces. He tried to struggle free for a moment before realizing that doing so was probably not a good idea, considering how high off the ground they were.

It was a moot point anyway, as the Lightsnake had a firm, bear-hug-like grasp on him. He looked up and saw that the Moonfire was actually an elliptical orange disruption in the Aura about a hundred feet off the ground that was positioned perfectly in front of the twin moons, producing the illusion that the heavenly satellites were covered in flames.

And the Lightsnake was heading straight toward it.

Oh man, Joel thought. *Here we go.*

He thought about closing his eyes, but instead, he turned his head. Next to them was another Lightsnake, this one carrying Felicity. She was shouting something at the reptilian creature, but Joel couldn't hear what it was, so he looked away.

Out of the frying pan, into the fire, he said to himself. *Almost literally. Because, you know, frying pan...the temple...fire...the Moonfire...*

Pleased at what he considered to be his own wittiness, he allowed himself a small smile as they soared up through the Moonfire. He braced himself to be engulfed in searing heat—which he would have actually welcomed a bit, after the icy rain he had just experienced—but instead, a chilly, tingling sensation reverberated throughout his entire body. It was similar to going through the Rift, but more intense, as if his entire skeleton was one big funny bone that someone had struck.

And as if that weren't shocking enough, what he saw next certainly was. He immediately made up a ranking system in his mind:

Surreal Score, from 1 to 10, with 10 being the most surreal.

Spectraland (surface): standard tropical terrain that changes appearance with each Aura manipulation; hybrid animals; people with plantlike characteristics = 6.14.

Prism Valley: landscape that shifts randomly every minute; blurry abstract images; home to gator-eel creatures and a tiger-ram animal that can change into a bubble = 7.56 (points deducted for the Lightsnake lair, a normal-looking cave).

This place = 9.07.

They landed on a surface that was like an immense, endless chessboard, only with each living-room-sized square made up of something different—one was grass, one was water, one was shiny hardwood, and so on.

Trees with long, feathered wings threatened to uproot themselves and take off into the air. The air itself was filled with flying things of all sorts: giraffes with teapots for heads; one-eyed skulls with horns shaped like guitars; giant flaming fire hydrants. The sky around them morphed from blue to green to black to gray and back to blue again at a dizzying, disorienting rate.

The Lightsnake carrying Joel plodded along, apparently unable to continue flying. Once more, Joel thought about trying to break loose, but the Lightsnake tightened its grip on him at that moment, almost as if it had read his mind. Then it stopped and turned toward a nearby ruckus.

"Let me go!" Felicity was shrieking from about ten feet away. She was making a mighty effort to free herself, while her captor was fighting equally hard to maintain its hold on her. As Joel's Lightsnake began to head over in that direction, he suddenly felt something scurrying up his right leg.

What the heck?

Joel looked down, and then up again. In the blink of an eye, a small and furry animal had darted around him. Then it climbed up the Lightsnake's arms as if they were tree branches.

Sammy?

The furry animal settled on the Lightsnake's head and began to furiously claw at its face. The Lightsnake let out a horrific, ear-splitting scream and immediately dropped Joel to the ground (which, at that particular moment and in that particular location, was made up of purple shag carpet). The Lightsnake grabbed at its own face with all three pincer-topped arms in an apparent effort to catch its tiny tormentor, but the animal was able to leap off just in the nick of time.

"Sammy! It's you!" Joel exclaimed. "You must've still been at the temple and escaped when the Silencers set it on fire! I'll bet you were—"

"Yah!" Felicity screeched.

Startled, Joel whipped around just in time to see the Lightsnake crumple to the ground, while Felicity stood next to it, breathing heavily.

"Whoa," Joel said, "how did you—what about the..." He trailed off, noticing that the Lightsnake who'd captured her was also lying on the ground, motionless.

"Sleepdart." Felicity smirked, holding out her hand to show Joel the weapon that she had just stabbed both Lightsnakes with. "The one I pulled out of Thornleaf's leg. That girl at the Pit of Ashes said that it had three doses, so I figured it would come in handy sooner or later. Point for me."

"Wait...you had that thing the whole time?" Joel said as Sammy scurried up his back and perched on his shoulder.

"Yup. Kept it in my pack."

"Why didn't you use it on the bloomfish?"

"Are you kidding?" she scoffed. "No way I was gonna come close to touching one of those things. Didn't I already tell you that?"

"Um, well...you could've thrown it."

"And risk losing it in the ocean? Yeah, right."

"Uh..."

"And now I bet you're glad I didn't," she said, putting the dart back into her supply pack. "Good job voicing your opinion there, though. You're making progress."

"Um, okay."

"So anyway, where the heck are we?"

"I—I think it's some kind of alternate plane," Joel said as he looked up at a flock of seagulls with jet engines that were flying overhead. "Sort of like Prism Valley, but different."

"Ah, and this is probably where the others are, I would bet."

"Yeah, but where, exactly?"

"Good question. Guess we should start looking before the ugly brothers here wake up."

"Okay."

The pair set off walking through the bizarre chessboard landscape, making sure to avoid any squares where the footing seemed less than sure.

"Man, this place is so weird," Felicity said as she worked her way around a pile of bowling balls with pig snouts and sharp teeth. "It's like Salvador Dali's worst nightmare."

"Yeah," Joel agreed. "And it's filled with things from Earth."

"I can see that."

"No, well, I mean—that's kind of strange, don't you think?"

"Why?"

"Like, how would the Lightsnakes know about all of this stuff?" Joel said, gesturing at a fleet of miniature hot-air balloons that were floating by.

"Maybe they can catch Wi-Fi signals up here," Felicity remarked. "Is there a point you're trying to make?"

"Well, you know, since Whitenose told us that Stoneroot didn't have a mind-control potion yet, I'm thinking that..."

"*Marshall* is the one that has Auravine under mind control," Felicity said, finishing Joel's thought. "And this place is, like, his domain, or something."

"Yeah. Remember those nightmares I was having?"

"No."

"You don't?"

"Again—sarcasm."

"Oh—uh, right. Well, remember the one I had when we were up on Sunpeak? When he said that he could invade my mind and make me see stuff? I'm thinking that he was probably able to take over Auravine's mind that way, since, like Thornleaf said, she's impressionable, or whatever."

"Hmm," Felicity said, stepping over a line of fluorescent ants. "Okay, let's assume that you're correct. But then why would he be using her to kidnap Wavemakers?"

"I dunno. But we should—"

Follow the light, a fuzzy, distant voice sounded in Joel's head.

"Hold on," Joel said, stopping in his tracks. "Did you hear that?"

"Hear what?"

Joel covered his ears with his hands in an effort to better hear the voice.

Follow the light, it said again.

"Nineteen?" Joel said. "Is that you?"

Follow the—the voice repeated once more before it dissolved into static.

"Hello? Nineteen?"

The static faded away. Joel lowered his hands.

"Nineteen was talking to you?" Felicity asked.

"Um, I think so."

"What did he say?"

"I think he said 'follow the light'."

Felicity furrowed her brow. "Follow the light? What does that mean?"

As if in response, a column of white light reaching from the ground all the way up into the sky appeared off in the distance. Sammy chittered excitedly.

"I think it means to follow that light," Joel said, pointing at the column.

"Yeah, okay, I got that."

They headed off in the direction of the light column, occasionally looking over their shoulders to make sure that the Lightsnakes were not following them. Along the way, Joel considered telling Felicity what he wanted to say back at the temple, but the moment just didn't seem right anymore. So, instead, he decided to talk about a different subject that he figured was a bit more important at the moment.

"So, um, I guess we need to come up with a new plan now," he said.

"Yeah, you think?" Felicity chuckled. "Sure wish we still had the swordcats with us." She glanced at Sammy. "No offense, little guy."

"At least we still have the mind-control antidote," Joel said, checking in his supply pack.

"But is that gonna work on her? You know, since, like you said, Marshall's probably invading her mind, not using a potion."

"Sure—Darkeye said that it would work on any kind of mind control."

"I don't know how you remember all that stuff. All right, so how are we gonna give it to her?"

Joel pondered that question as they maneuvered around a migrating herd of giant electric fan-faced caterpillars.

"Well," he finally said, "since she wasn't with the Lightsnakes at the temple, she's probably with Marshall and the other Wavemakers, waiting for them to return with us, right?"

"Sure, yeah, why not."

"But what she doesn't know is, we managed to escape from the Lightsnakes. So now, we have a chance to sneak up on her."

"Go on."

"Then, when we do, we dip the sleepdart into the antidote, and then I can just throw it at her."

Felicity flashed him a skeptical look. "I guess that makes sense. But I can still think of a lot of ways that plan could go wrong."

"It's better than winging it, though, right?" Joel responded, recalling his proposed strategy for taking down Marshall on Crownrock six months—or nineteen years—ago.

"I suppose it is," Felicity sighed. "I know we both hate improvising. All right, fine. But let's dip the dart into the antidote now, so that we'll be ready."

"Okay."

"And *I'll* throw it."

"What? Didn't you see me throwing my knife over the Far Edge? I do have *some* athletic ability, you know."

"That's totally different," she said with a smirk. "But hey—I like how you just stuck up for yourself there. You're really starting to get it."

"Thanks." Joel grinned. He took the vial out of his pack and opened it.

"Man," Felicity said, scrunching up her face, "the smell alone should be enough to snap Auravine out of it."

They dipped the dart into the antidote, and Felicity put it into her pack. Then they resumed walking until they reached the column of light. Once there, they saw that the column was emanating from a section of the chessboard where each square in a four-by-four area was made up of a strange substance that neither of them recognized.

"What is this stuff?" Felicity said, giving the substance a tentative toe-tap.

"No idea," Joel replied as he examined the substance up close. It looked and smelled a little bit like sausage.

"So, what do you think we're supposed to do?"

"Um...walk into the light, I guess?"

"I dunno, man, this surface seems a bit...unstable. Are you sure that it was Nineteen talking to you? Maybe this is a trap."

"Well, I don't know if we have any other choices. And those Lightsnakes will wake up eventually."

"I guess you're right," she said. "Okay, here we go."

They tested the substance a few more times for sturdiness before carefully venturing out onto it. The light column dimmed a little, but other than that, nothing happened. They continued walking until they reached the point where the four squares met. There, they saw something on the ground that looked like a small, dark blister. It pulsed, like it had a heartbeat.

"Gross," Felicity said.

Joel extended his foot at the blister.

"Eww, don't touch it!" Felicity exclaimed.

"But...what else should we do?"

"Okay, fine, whatever. Touch it."

Joel gave the blister a gentle nudge with his foot. Soft and squishy, it jiggled. They both stared at it for a few seconds. Nothing happened.

"Any more ideas?" Felicity asked.

"Not really. You?"

"Hmm. Maybe we could—"

Joel never found out what she was about to suggest, because at that moment, the blister started to shake violently. A couple of seconds later, it burst open, and blobs of red liquid spurted out, like lava erupting from a volcano. Felicity shrieked and jumped back. Joel shielded himself with his hands as Sammy fell off his shoulder. The intermittent blobs quickly escalated into a steady fountain that grew bigger and bigger with every passing heartbeat. Without a word, they all turned to run, but the surface started to cave inward toward the fountain of red liquid, the way space collapses into a black hole. Before they were able to reach the edge of the surface, they had fallen and were unable to prevent themselves from sliding back down toward the now geyser-like column of red liquid, which Joel noticed was thick and warm. He closed his eyes and held his breath.

"I hope this is ketchup!" Felicity somehow managed to scream before they were sucked into the hole where the blister used to be, completely submerged in what, to Joel, seemed more like blood than ketchup.

CHAPTER 24: THE STUDIO

Instead of having to swim their way out of a sea of ketchup (or blood, or whatever it was), Joel felt the sensation of falling, as if he were an ant that just got washed down a drain. After what seemed like forever (but was, in reality, only five seconds), he landed with a splash in another kind of liquid—this one colder and thinner. He scrambled around, waving his arms in an urgent, random fashion until his feet hit ground and he realized that he was in a pool of water only about five feet deep. Breaking the surface, he looked up and saw that he was at the bottom of a gourd-shaped cavern. Thin patches of glowmoss on the cavern's walls gave the place an eerie, haunted-house atmosphere.

"Hey, over here."

Felicity was sitting at the edge of the pool, squeezing water and blood/ketchup out of her hair while Sammy groomed himself nearby. Joel waded his way over to them. Felicity extended her hand and pulled him the rest of the way out.

"Not bad." She smirked. "We'll make a swimmer out of you yet."

Joel glanced at her a few times as he tried to catch his breath. Thrashing about in the water had cleaned most of the red stuff off of him, but she was still largely covered in it, having made a swift exit from the pool.

"I know, I know, I must look like Carrie," she said.

"Who?"

"Forget it," she said, scooping water out of the pool to wash red stuff off of her leg. "Man, I'd give anything for a towel right now."

"The most massively useful thing." Joel grinned, amusing himself with the *Hitchhiker's Guide* reference.

Felicity chuckled. "It has immense psychological value."

"Whoa—you've read those books?"

"Read the books, watched the TV show, saw the movie, listened to the radio series. Well, most of it, anyway."

"Wow, cool," Joel said as Sammy clambered back up onto his shoulder.

An awkward pause ensued. Finally, Felicity got to her feet and said, "So, yeah, I think we're getting close."

"How do you know?"

"Just a hunch. I mean, don't you think so too?"

Joel had to agree. Based on his knowledge of pop culture, as well as his own previous experience in Spectraland, it did feel like they were approaching the endgame. "Yeah, I guess," he said.

"You know, it's funny," Felicity went on, "sometimes I feel like I'm just a character in a story that someone else is writing. Like, I have some control over what I do from day to day, but in the long run, everything in life follows a predetermined path."

"Now you're *really* starting to sound like Art."

"I know, right?" she laughed. "But seriously, don't you ever feel like that?"

"Um, sure. All the time, actually."

"You're just saying that."

"No, honestly. Like, remember when Darkeye had us tied up in Nightshore the last time? I felt like there had to be a way to escape, because that whole deal seemed like a movie to me, and in the movies, the good guys always manage to get out of situations like that, somehow."

"Well, let's just hope whoever is writing this has a happy ending planned for us this time too."

They walked out of the gourd-shaped cavern and into a narrow, twisting passageway that was illuminated by sporadic patches of glowmoss. They followed the passageway for nearly ten minutes before they arrived at a large opening. It was dark except for a few multicolored spheres of light that were floating around in the air like luminescent balloons.

"Looks like a party, or a disco, or something," Felicity said.

"Hey, that sounds like that old Talking Heads song," Joel pointed out.

Felicity smiled. "Oh yeah, I guess that's where I got that from. By the way, that song is the only reason I know what a disco is, just so you know."

"Um, okay."

"Well, guess we should check it out."

"Sounds good. Ladies first?"

"No way, dude."

"But you have the antidote dart."

"How about together."

"Okay."

Just as they passed through the opening together, they were immediately and forcefully whisked into the dark space, like crumbs being sucked up by a vacuum. After they had both finished screaming, Joel realized that they were now freely hovering in space, inside of a giant cube, just like the light spheres were. After making sure that Sammy was still perched securely on his shoulder, Joel moved his arms, and his body gently floated upward in response. It was a different sensation than flying. It was probably more like swimming—or, at least, what Joel assumed swimming would feel like, since he didn't know how to swim. Then the spheres of light changed colors and organized themselves into a twisting, snakelike chain—seemingly in response to his movement. At that moment Joel realized why these surroundings felt familiar to him.

"We're inside of a sparkleblock!" he exclaimed.

"A what?"

"A sparkleblock—the puzzle thing that Rocktoe gave me."

"Oh yeah," Felicity said as she looked around. "But...why the heck would there be a giant sparkleblock here?"

"Maybe Marshall's trying to keep us out, or something. But he doesn't know that I've already seen one of these and solved it."

"Yeah, a small, hand-held one. This is, like, the immersive, virtual-reality version. How can you tell which way we have to go?"

"I'll use the small one as a reference," Joel replied, fishing the sparkleblock out of his supply pack. "C'mon, this shouldn't be too bad."

"All right, you lead the way."

Following the patterns in the hand-held sparkleblock, Joel steered himself around and between the large surrounding light spheres, even as they continued to shift into more and more complicated arrangements. Once he and Felicity were near their goal—that being the far corner of the cube—he found himself curious as to what would happen if he, as the main light, came into contact with one of the other lights. So, stopping in front of a dark-blue sphere, he gingerly reached out a finger to touch it.

"What are you doing?" Felicity asked.

"I'm just checking something."

Zzzzaaapp! A mild electrical jolt coursed through Joel's body, causing him to blink and recoil. The next thing he knew, they were all the way back at the starting point, and the light spheres had returned to their original, random configuration.

"What the—" Felicity said. "Yeah, don't do that again, all right?"

"Sorry."

"Just try again."

And so he did. Unfortunately, though, now that he felt somewhat rattled, he ran into a bit of difficulty controlling his body's movements, and even though he knew exactly where he needed to go, he ended up overshooting his intended path. He encountered a similar result two more times before feelings of frustration and embarrassment set in, clouding his focus and leading to yet another failed attempt.

"C'mon, man, you can do this," Felicity sighed after they had, once again, appeared back at the beginning. "This kind of stuff is your thing, remember?"

"Well, it's different when you have to move your whole body through it."

"Sure, but...look, I know I give you a hard time about your athletic ability, but seriously, you can do a lot more than you give yourself credit for."

"I can?"

"Yeah, of course. I mean, think about it: all the crazy jumping and flying and fighting and running around that we do here? That takes some serious physical skill, dude."

"I guess."

"Ugh," she said, rolling her eyes. "Don't make me resort to clichés."

"Huh?"

Felicity paused, as if gathering her thoughts. "Just believe in yourself. Because, well, I...I believe in you."

Joel almost couldn't believe what he was hearing. "Wait—what?"

"You heard me. Now go."

Wow—she believes in me.

His confidence boosted, Joel tried again. He swam through the air around a string of lights. The pattern changed, and he did it again. And again. And again, as the patterns started to change faster and faster. Finally, after a close call that left him short of breath, he did a midair barrel roll through a spinning circle of spheres and ended up in the far corner of the cube. All of the lights turned gold, and a high, humming sound ensued.

"There you go," Felicity said. "Good job."

"Thanks," Joel exhaled, a smile on his face. "You did a good job too, following along like that."

"Sure, whatever. By the way, never tell anyone what I said."

"About what?"

"Perfect."

Then the light spheres vanished, the room lit up, and Joel and Felicity fell a couple of feet onto hard ground as Sammy let out a startled squeak.

"Ow—that was rude," Felicity said, getting to her feet.

Joel stood up as well, looking around; they were back in a cave-like area. The wall of the cave slid open, like something out of a spy movie, and Joel's eyes grew wide as he took in what lay beyond: an enormous, warehouse-like space with carpeted flooring, wood-paneled walls, and stylish track lighting. Large speakers, guitars on stands, and cables on hooks were positioned at various places throughout the room. Six glass-walled booths lined the space's perimeter, and an elevated platform supporting an enormous mixing console, as well as a desk with a laptop computer and three huge monitors, took up most of the area in the middle.

"Okay, I think this is it," Felicity whispered as she unsheathed her knife and extended it, blade-first, at Joel. "Here, you take this."

"Um, okay," Joel said, reaching out. Not wanting to grab the blade of the knife, he awkwardly picked it out of her grasp by its handle, his fingertips touching the palm of her hand as he did so. He gulped as they made the briefest of eye contact.

"Oh, whoops, I—I should've handed it to you the other way," she stammered uncharacteristically. "Sorry."

"Uh—no...no problem."

Felicity closed her eyes and inhaled, as if to reset herself. Then she took the dart out of her supply pack and gripped it tightly. "All right. You guys ready?"

Joel set his jaw and nodded. Sammy gave a little affirmative chirp.

"Here we go."

They stepped through the opening in the wall. Everything was dead silent, and the room appeared to be uninhabited.

"I don't like this," Felicity murmured as they cautiously moved toward the central platform. "Something's wrong."

"Maybe they went out for lunch," Joel said.

"Hey, try using the Sight," Felicity suggested.

"Oh—um, good idea."

Joel took a deep breath and cleared his mind.

Okay, let's see...how about...

"Ah, you're here. Perfect timing," a voice with an English accent rang out through all of the speakers in the room.

Marshall!

"And, of course, you made it through the life-sized sparkleblock unscathed. I knew that would be the perfect way to make sure only you were able to get in here. Last thing I want is for uninvited guests to be crashing our little party."

Joel's head was spinning, both figuratively and literally, as he tried to locate the source of the voice.

"How do you like the place?" Marshall continued. "I wanted to make it somewhere that I could feel comfortable. A place that reminded me of home, of the environment where I was the most creative and had the most fun. So, naturally, a recording studio was the obvious choice."

"Stop being a chicken and come out here!" Felicity yelled.

"Ah, a different way of saying 'show yourself, you coward!'" Marshall laughed. "Brilliant, my dear! You always did hate clichés."

"Yeah, and that includes you," she shot back.

"Oh, I am insulted!" Marshall gasped with fake indignation. "I do understand where you might get that idea. But, really now, how often does one get a chance to be an actual, real-life 'dark lord'? It's hard to resist the temptation to be a bit, shall we say, over the top."

"Shut up and come out!" Felicity shouted. "We know you have the other Wavemakers!"

"And, let me see, you're going to rescue them with a knife and a dart." Marshall snickered. "What an absolutely *ingenious* plan. How long did it take you to come up with that one?"

Joel started to mentally calculate exactly how long before he realized that Marshall was being sarcastic.

"Tell you what," the former Biledriver singer went on, "since I'm such a sweetheart, I'll be proactive and spare you the embarrassment of watching your amazing plan fail miserably."

At that moment, the knife and the dart flew out of Joel's and Felicity's hands and into a storage closet located at the far side of the room. Then, before Joel even had a chance to react, the guitar and microphone cables that were hanging on the walls leapt off of their hooks and wrapped themselves around him and Felicity, even ensnaring Sammy in the process. Joel struggled to break free, but it was no use. The doors to two of the isolation booths flew open, and the cables dragged Joel, Sammy, and Felicity toward them.

"Now that you've made me self-conscious, I suppose I should skip the obligatory explain-things-before-I-kill-you speech." Marshall chuckled as a droning chord began to sound in the background. "Suffice it to say that this moment is the culmination of a *very* convoluted plan—one that was nearly nineteen years in the making and almost failed a good number of times. But, as you are both aware, convoluted plans are my special interest, so in the end, it all worked out."

"You son of a—" Felicity shouted before the door to her isolation booth slammed shut.

A half a second later, the door to Joel's booth closed up as well. He looked through the glass window at Felicity. He couldn't hear her now, but she was still shouting things while the cables restrained her against the wall of her booth.

"My word," Marshall's voice sounded in Joel's booth, reminding Joel of a recording engineer speaking to him from the control room. "She certainly has become a lot more vulgar."

She hardly swears when I'm around, though, Joel realized. *I guess she knows that it bothers me. Interesting.*

"Anyway, I just can't resist," Marshall said. "I simply *must* share the details of my cleverness with you. And now that Miss Smith cannot interrupt anymore, I am free to ramble on to my heart's content. Which is something I'm sure you can relate to, Joel."

A bright, golden light went on in the isolation booth. A chill ran down Joel's spine.

"So, remember when we were on Crownrock?" Marshall went on. "When you so rudely threw the Songshell at me, knowing full well that it was about to explode?"

A flash of movement on the mixing console got Joel's attention: two more volume faders had begun to slide upward. A couple of new notes mixed in with the four other notes that were already in progress, creating a chord that sounded like F-sharp minor.

"Well, after the shell exploded, I found myself having an out-of-body experience, almost exactly the way they describe it in all of those life-after-death stories. I saw my broken body falling into the ocean while my consciousness floated upward toward a tunnel of bright light. I was sure I was on my way to some sort of an afterlife."

As the volume faders moved up higher, Joel started to feel even colder, as if the isolation booth had suddenly been turned into a refrigerator.

"And sure enough, I was. But it was not at all what I had expected. I merged with the light, and for the longest time, that was it. I was merely a disembodied flash of energy, suspended in limbo, aware of my continued existence but unable to form any coherent thoughts. It was a very lonely period, not unlike my youth."

The volume faders hit ten. Joel's teeth were chattering, and he felt like throwing up. He could feel Sammy, who was pressed up against him, starting to go limp.

"Slowly, however, I noticed myself regaining strength. At first, it was just a fleeting sensation here and there. But eventually, all of my memories returned, and with them, my ability to think and reason and perceive the environment around me. I realized that I was in an alternate plane of existence, similar to Prism Valley, a place that I'm sure you recall."

To get his mind off of the fact that his life force was slowly draining away, Joel stared at the laptop computer on the desk. He saw the six different tracks running on the recording software. He also noticed something odd about the computer—it seemed to be running an operating system that didn't normally run on that particular brand of PC, even with an emulator.

"So now I exist in this strange new place as an Auraghost—a wraith, I suppose, like the ones we encountered during our last, fateful journey together. There is a lot more to the story, but your song is almost over, I'm afraid."

The gears in Joel's mind turned.

That operating system cannot run on that computer. Therefore, this cannot be reality.

It is also not a vision of mine, because even though I've seen some wacky stuff, when it comes to details like that, there is no way I would envision something that was so obviously incorrect.

Marshall said that this place was similar to Prism Valley. Which means that it's an actual place, not an image that he projected into my mind.

So I must be seeing an illusion. An Aura-generated illusion, created by Marshall, who previously admitted that "he's no scientist" and, as such, would be someone who would think that this type of computer could run that particular operating system.

Joel could almost feel the puzzle pieces falling into place in his mind. As they did so, the recording studio began to melt away. Everything started to blur and smear, as if someone were taking a pencil eraser to a crayon drawing. The scene that was revealed was something even more startling than finding a recording studio in the middle of nowhere.

In place of the studio was a cave.

In place of the mixing console was Auravine, her eyes screwed shut with intense concentration as she wove a minor-key melody on her wavebow.

In place of the monitors was Nineteen, trapped in a cage made out of dark-purple Aura energy.

In place of the isolation booths were most of the other Wavemakers: Redstem, Riverhand, Windblade, Fireflower, and, of course, Felicity. Their personal Auras were leaving their bodies in long, glowing streams that all converged on Auravine where she stood on the platform. The microphone and guitar cables that held them all in place were actually drone Lightsnakes, and the speakers were simply piles of rocks—except for one, which was actually Starpollen, asleep or unconscious, tied up with binding vine.

In place of the laptop computer was the body of what looked like a mummified corpse, lying atop a slab of black stone. And although the mummy was hideously disfigured, decomposed, and missing an arm, Joel was pretty sure that it was the remains of Marshall Byle.

CHAPTER 25: FINALE

At that moment, it all made sense. Most of it, anyway.

Auravine is using everyone's energy to regenerate Marshall's body, Joel realized. *Then his spirit—or whatever—will reoccupy it!*

His first impulse was to call out to everyone, to point out what he was seeing. But he stifled that impulse, realizing that Marshall—who, Joel figured, must have had a reason to want to maintain the recording-studio illusion—wasn't aware that he could now perceive the situation for what it really was.

And a moment later, that reason became apparent: there weren't enough drone Lightsnakes to go around. Apparently, most of the ones that had ambushed them back on the Sacred Site were now unavailable; Joel figured that because they had spent so much time on the island's surface, they were now sick or dead, having sacrificed themselves for what they thought was to be the final kidnapping event.

And as for the full-grown Lightsnakes, Felicity had taken two of them out earlier with the sleepdart, and the remainder were probably still occupied on the surface with the Silencers.

So each one of the native Wavemakers, being unconscious, had only a single drone Lightsnake to restrain them. Felicity, still struggling with as much effort as she could muster, was occupying the attention of three drones, all of whom seemed like they could use some help.

Hmm, Joel thought, looking over to where the illusory guitars had been replaced by actual wavebows, *if I pretend that I've passed out, maybe a couple of Lightsnakes will release me.*

Joel let himself go limp. Just as he'd predicted, two of the three drones holding him in place slithered off and went over to assist their companions. As soon as they joined them, Joel broke out of the single drone's hold, freeing both Sammy and himself. While Sammy darted over to Starpollen, Joel raced over to the wavebows and grabbed the one he recognized as his.

"What the—stop him!" Marshall's voice cried out.

Three drone Lightsnakes uncoiled themselves from Felicity and slithered over in Joel's direction. Even though he still felt a bit weak, he managed to fire off a stunning wavecast that immobilized two of them. While the third one and Joel's original remaining captor teamed up to subdue him, Felicity was able to break free from the pair of drones that were still on her. She ran over to the wavebows, shouting, "How did you do that?"

"They're not guitars, they're wavebows!" Joel yelled back before one of the drones coiled itself around his mouth.

Felicity grabbed one of the instruments and gave it a quizzical glance before she raised it and shot two quick bursts of light in Joel's direction. Each burst hit its intended target, and both drone Lightsnakes fell off of Joel. As soon as they did, he noticed two more of them sneaking up behind Felicity. They began to coil up, as if tensing to strike.

"Behind you!" he yelled.

Felicity turned. She aimed her wavebow, but then Joel stunned the pair before she had a chance to play a single note.

"Not bad, Quick Draw!" she said, looking over her shoulder.

Joel grinned.

"Forget the others! Get them!" Marshall shouted.

The drones that had been restraining the other Wavemakers all left their posts and headed in Joel and Felicity's direction. At that moment, their surroundings shimmered. Joel noticed Felicity's head whirling around.

"It's a cave!" she exclaimed.

"I know!" Joel said. "Take care of the Lightsnakes—I'll stop her!"

"What? Stop who?"

Without responding, Joel charged toward Auravine, who appeared oblivious to the proceedings, her concentration still locked on regenerating Marshall's body.

"Look out," Marshall's voice warned in a different, lower tone.

After a moment of apprehension, Joel strummed the note that sent a stunning wave at Auravine. Just as it was about to hit her, however, she broke out of her trance and interrupted her healing melody with a loud, piercing chord. A large golden wall of Aura appeared, shielding her and the pedestal that Marshall's body rested on. Joel's cast deflected off of the Aura-wall and crashed into the ground.

"Do not try to stop me, Joel," Auravine growled, her voice drenched in reverb.

"Um—snap out of it?" Joel responded as he backed up a couple of steps. "Please?"

Auravine narrowed her eyes and resumed her healing cast. Joel glanced in the direction of where the storage closet used to be and saw Felicity there, picking what he hoped was the dart off of the ground.

Okay, he thought to himself, *I'll distract Auravine while Felicity hits her in the back with the dart.*

He let fly with another stunning cast. With a frustrated shriek, Auravine stopped her healing cast once more and reerected the golden shield.

"I said, do not try to stop me!" she screamed.

Joel flinched, but he continued to play. As a constant stream of red light poured out of his wavebow, he looked at Felicity, who was staring at the scene from a distance. Their eyes met, and he nodded. Then, with one quick, fluid motion, Felicity hurled the dart at Auravine.

"Behind you," Marshall's voice said.

Auravine turned her head. She expanded her shield into a dome, but it was too late—Joel could see the dart sticking out of the young healer's shoulder.

"Nice shot!" Joel shouted as he halted his stunning cast.

Felicity flashed him a wary half smile in response. A few tense moments passed. Then Auravine turned her head the other way, plucked the projectile out, and dropped it to the ground.

"Um—Auravine?" Joel said. "Are you...yourself?"

Auravine looked up at him as her shield dissolved in a shower of tiny rainbow-colored sparks. "Yes," she replied.

"Cool," Joel exhaled. "Now we can—"

"As I have always been."

She pointed her wavebow at Joel and strummed. Momentarily shocked, Joel managed to put up a shield cast just in time to deflect the crimson bolt of light that burst forth from Auravine's instrument.

"Hey!" he exclaimed. "What—what are you doing?"

"Following the path that I have chosen."

Felicity fired a stunning cast, but Auravine quickly turned and conjured up a shield that blocked the offworlder's lightwave.

"It didn't work!" Felicity shouted. "She's still under mind control!"

"Uh—maybe it just needs time," Joel said, mostly to himself.

Marshall laughed. "So that's what that dart was for—you thought I had her under mind control! What a foolish notion."

"Um, but—"

"No, the only mind control at work here is...my charm," Marshall purred.

"Stun her!" Felicity yelled, and then shot out another stream of red Aura energy that Auravine met with a stream of her own. "She can't block us both!"

Still shaken with disbelief, Joel hesitated for a second, but then he took aim and strummed. Auravine played a fast riff in response, and her Aura stream split into two: one half continued to hold off Felicity's attack while the other half countered Joel's offensive. Joel glanced at Felicity, who rolled her eyes as if to say *all right, I guess she* can *block us both*.

"You see," Marshall said, "Auravine here is my biggest fan—just like how you once were, Joel. And, as you know, devoted fans will do anything for their idols."

Joel looked back at Auravine as their wavecast deadlock continued. "Why—why do you like him?" he shouted at her over the din. "He almost destroyed Spectraland!"

"And now he is going to save it," Auravine replied, her voice amplified. "Once he is back in his worldly form, he will put an end to the silly and pointless conflict between Wavemakers and Silencers that killed my parents."

"What? But he—I don't—"

"Just as you made a promise to your sister, Joel, I made one to my brother—that somehow, one day, we would achieve everlasting peace on Spectraland. No more fighting, no more disputes, no more wars. And Chief Byle is the only one with enough power to make that dream a reality."

"But he's a criminal! You said so yourself!"

"Oh, come now, Joel," Marshall said in his most seductive tone, "don't you believe in redemption? I did my time in purgatory. I've seen the error of my ways. And now I have a chance to make up for my misdeeds—to repay these poor people for everything I did to them."

"By killing the Wavemakers?"

"We're not *killing* them, per se," Marshall cooed. "We're simply...borrowing their energy. We had to do it this way, because they never would have gone along with this plan willingly. But after I am restored, everyone will see that it was all done in the name of peace and harmony."

"Auravine, he's lying!" Felicity yelled. "He's just using you, like he did us! You can't trust him!"

Joel looked at Auravine. Her expression seemed to change ever so slightly, but with all the glare of the clashing lightwaves, it was hard to be completely sure.

"You really aren't going to let us get on with it, are you?" Marshall sighed. "Very well. In that case, I guess we have no choice. Auravine—kill them."

Auravine wavered for a moment. "But...we need some of their essence to complete the process."

"We already have what we need."

"But—"

"Do it!"

Auravine closed her eyes.

Don't do it, Auravine, Joel thought.

Auravine opened her eyes and took a deep breath. Then she gave her instrument a single aggressive strum, raising the decibel level of her wavecast to ear-splitting levels as the color of her dual lightwaves turned a deep shade of violet.

"No!" Joel shouted. He played a different chord on his wavebow, changing his stunning cast into a shield. Glancing at Felicity, he saw that she had done the same.

"I am sorry, Joel," Auravine said, the sound of her voice echoing in his head as she spoke. "But this is what I have to do."

Joel clenched his teeth and dug in his heels as Auravine's stream of light pushed him backward. She was strong, having absorbed a good deal of energy from the other Wavemakers, and with his and Felicity's own energy levels nearly depleted, he estimated that they had about three and a half minutes left—the duration of a typical pop song—before Auravine's cast would break through their defenses.

"Felicity!" he shouted at the top of his lungs, hoping against hope that she would be able to make out his words through the cacophony. "We're running out of time! We have to do something!"

"She cannot hear you, Joel," Auravine said. "We can only hear each other now. I wanted to tell you that I—I wish things could have been different."

Joel wasn't sure how to respond to that. Feeling frantic, he looked around the cave. Nineteen was still trapped in his Aura-cage, apparently unable to even speak telepathically to Joel. All the other Wavemakers remained unconscious. Sammy was nowhere to be seen.

"You are even braver than I imagined," Auravine continued, "and you are truly an amazing, inspirational individual. All the stories and legends that I heard about you are true. That is why I sincerely regret that it has to end this way."

Joel's life began to flash before his eyes. The scenes he saw were not from his youth, however—they were recent, starting from when he was sitting backstage before the Halloween concert.

Reading the article on his tablet computer.

Thornleaf telling him how to land.

Saving Fireflower from crashing.

Two minutes left...

Talking with Felicity on the beach.

Sixhair telling him about Rocktoe.

Felicity saying that she believed in him.

Tell Auravine what you want to say.

"Auravine," Joel said, forcing himself to look her in the eyes. His voice was steady and clear. "Listen to me."

Just spit it out, man.

"You need to stop what you're doing," he said.

"I cannot," she replied. "This is my destiny, Joel. This is my part to play in history. By restoring Chief Byle, I will have prevented many more senseless deaths, like those of my parents."

"But you're causing senseless deaths right now!"

"Only a few. It is...an unfortunate, but necessary, sacrifice."

"Auravine—I need to tell you something: *Marshall* was the wraith in the jungle who helped and consoled you. He's been planning this out the whole time."

"I know."

"Wait—you do?"

"Yes. I have known that all along. He told me how I could become a hero, just like you. I simply had to be brave enough to make the hard choices that I am making now."

"He's just using you! He only wanted you to become a healer so you could restore his body. Afterward, he won't bring peace—he'll destroy everyone!"

Auravine paused and closed her eyes. For a moment, Joel thought that he was getting through to her. But then she opened her eyes and said, "I trust Chief Byle. I believe in him. He is...he is like family to me, more than anyone else. I owe my life to him."

One minute left...

"I don't know this for sure," Joel said, "but I'll bet anything that he sent those animals in the jungle after you first and then called them off, just to make it seem like he saved you. That's how devious he is."

Auravine's expression turned pensive. She did not say anything, however.

"It doesn't matter," Joel continued, shaking his head. "Look—you don't have to listen to me, but don't listen to him either. Listen to *yourself*, to your own instincts. *You* know—in your heart—what is right and what is wrong. Think it through and then make a choice."

"I—I have already chosen my path. I cannot go back."

"Actually, you can. Everyone makes mistakes. I do it all the time—I even helped Marshall get the Songshell, remember? The important thing is to recognize when you're wrong and then to do something about it. Just like I did."

"But..."

"Marshall wasn't lying about one thing: you *are* destined to save many lives. But it's not by restoring him, it's by helping us stop him."

Thirty seconds left...

"Even if he did bring peace, it would be through fear and intimidation," Joel pressed on. "That's not the way to do it."

Auravine's deadly cast pushed Joel's shield back until it was nearly in his face.

Eighteen seconds...

"The Wavemakers and Silencers need to talk about their differences. They need to say what they want to say and then figure out a solution that everyone can accept."

Seven seconds...

"Stop this now, and be a true hero by helping to bring peace to Spectraland—"

Two...

"—the right way."

One...

Auravine's expression softened. Just as Joel's Aura energy ran out, she stopped playing, and her wavecast dissipated.

"What the—" Marshall's voice exclaimed. "Why did you stop?"

"You are right, Joel," Auravine said, a pained look on her face. "You are right."

Joel nodded. "I'm glad you agree," he exhaled. "Now, if you can help us—"

A quick note sounded, and Auravine slumped to the ground, wavebow in hand. Joel became alarmed for a moment, but then he realized that Felicity had just hit the young healer with a stunning cast.

"What?" Felicity said as a wisp of red Aura trailed off from her instrument's headstock. "Was I not supposed to do that?"

"Well, I was gonna have her help us revive everyone and free Nineteen."

"But she was trying to kill us a minute ago."

"I know. I talked her out of it."

"You did, huh?" Felicity smirked. "Well, hey, look at you. We'll make a Han Solo out of you yet."

"Or a Luke Skywalker when he was going to Jabba's palace."

"Whatever. Anyway, Auravine'll be up soon. I didn't have much gas left, so that stunning cast was pretty weak."

"Okay, no problem. Do you know what happened to Sammy?"

"I, uh, I stunned him by accident," Felicity admitted. "While I was shooting at the Lightsnakes, he kinda got in the way."

"Great," Joel said with what he hoped was a smirk. "You're just stunning everybody left and right now, aren't you?"

"Hey, watch it, or you're next," Felicity chuckled.

Is this considered flirting?

Felicity walked up to the pedestal and grimaced. "So this is Marshall, huh? Gross."

"Yeah, I think we were able to stop Auravine before she got too far in regenerating him."

"I can see that." Felicity shuddered. "Well, I can't stand looking at him for another second. I'm gonna go check on the others to make sure they're okay."

"What, scared of a little mummy?" Joel grinned. "I thought you liked horror movies."

"Ha! Dude, you're on a roll."

As Felicity walked over to where the unconscious Wavemakers lay, Joel turned his gaze to Nineteen. The tiger-ram creature was pawing at the wall of his Aura-cage with more than a fair bit of urgency. Puzzled by Nineteen's uncharacteristically agitated behavior, Joel ran over and kneeled down in front of the cage.

"Don't worry," he said, "we'll get you out soon. Just waiting for Auravine to wake up."

"Everybody seems all right," Felicity called out. "Fireflower's even stirring a little."

"Cool," Joel replied.

"How's tiger-guy doing?" Felicity asked as she headed in Joel's direction.

"He seems okay. Just a little anxious to get out, I think."

"I don't blame him."

"Can you try to free him?"

"I would, but I used up whatever energy I had left to stun Auravine."

"Oh, okay."

"Guess there's nothing else we can do for now. We just have to wait until our energy comes back."

"Sounds good."

"Oh no," Felicity said, her eyes growing wide.

"What's wrong?" Joel asked. "I just said that sounds good."

Felicity nodded in the way that people do when they want to silently let you know that there's something behind you.

"I have an even better idea," Marshall's voice said.

Joel peered over his shoulder.

Uh oh.

Marshall, the mummy, was upright and slowly walking over. Despite the fact that he was still missing his right arm, he appeared a bit more whole than Joel had previously thought; large patches of his skin and most of his hair had been regrown, and none of his bones were showing, with the exception of his lower jaw. He was holding Auravine's wavebow in his left hand. "What say I revive all my little friends," the unsightly figure said, "and we pick up right where we left off? How does that sound?"

"Um...that doesn't sound good," Joel said. "That doesn't sound good at all."

CHAPTER 26: CODA

Marshall chuckled—a grisly sight, since his windpipe was still partially exposed. "That was a rhetorical question," he said. "I'm afraid you don't have a say in the matter."

"Take him down!" Felicity yelled. "He only has one hand!"

Joel hesitated, unsure of what to do or how he wanted to do it—the thought of even touching Marshall's gruesome zombie-like figure was enough to make Joel want to gag. During that moment of indecision, Marshall quickly raised the wavebow to his mouth and plucked off a note. In a flash, two of the drone Lightsnakes snapped awake; one of them launched itself at Joel and wrapped itself around his neck, while the other did the same to Felicity, causing them both to drop their wavebows as they tried to pull the drones off.

"Don't tell me you forgot about Hendrix," Marshall said. "Playing with his teeth? No? Anyone? Come now, children, you disappoint me. I know you're young, but you're students of the instrument, after all."

Joel clawed and pulled with his fingers in a desperate attempt to loosen the Lightsnake's grip, but to no avail.

"I apologize—I don't have enough strength to kill you both with a quick wavecast," Marshall continued, taking a couple of plodding, zombie-like steps toward Joel. "So we'll just have to do it the slow and painful way."

"Um—it won't matter if you kill us," Joel croaked. "Auravine won't finish regenerating you. She's on our side now."

"Oh, I'll figure something out, believe me," Marshall said with a hideous grin. "Once I have you and your bandmate out of the way."

Joel looked down at his wavebow. He had recovered a sliver of Aura energy while Marshall was talking, so he figured that if he could just get to his instrument before the drone Lightsnake choked him to death....

"Thinking of grabbing your wavebow, are you?" Marshall cackled. "Well, I'll just take care of that." He played another note with his teeth, and both Joel and Felicity's wavebows flew out of the cave's entrance.

Dangit.

Just then, a red streak of light came shooting out from off to the side. Marshall ducked, and the streak hit the cave wall and dissipated. Joel looked toward the source of the cast—it was Fireflower.

"Release them!" the Wavemaker leader shouted, looking woozy and disoriented.

"Ah, Fireflower." Marshall smiled. "Thought you could sneak up on me, I suppose? Well, despite my bad eyesight"—he blinked in an exaggerated fashion, drawing attention to his grotesque, half-formed eyeballs—"I saw you coming. And now..." The former Biledriver singer played a short riff with his teeth. Three more of the

Lightsnake drones sprang back to consciousness and wrapped themselves around Fireflower's legs and torso, knocking her to the ground.

As he struggled to breathe, Joel looked over to where Auravine still lay on the ground. Beyond her, the other natives were still unconscious, except for Starpollen, who was now awake but seemingly unaware of what was going on. Sammy, also awake, was crouching next to the boy, apparently trying to determine if he could make a charge at Marshall without getting stunned or killed.

"You know, Joel, you deserve everything that's happening to you right now," Marshall said, taking a few steps closer. "You killed me, and now I'm finally getting my revenge."

Joel fought to remain conscious as the edges of his eyesight started to turn dark.

How are we going to get out of this one?

"You deserve nothing but suffering," Marshall continued, "while I deserve to come back to life."

"Sammy!" Felicity somehow managed to call out through gritted teeth. "Come!"

Sammy's head jerked up. After a fraction of a second, he darted away from Starpollen and toward Felicity.

What the heck?

Marshall turned his head. "Stupid pest," he muttered before he generated a brief stunning cast with his teeth. Joel cringed for a moment, expecting the worst, but since the cast wasn't as precise as it would have been had Marshall been able to use two hands, Sammy was able to dodge it.

"Keep—keep running around!" Felicity said.

"Nice try," Marshall scoffed, gearing up for another attempt. "But this time, I won't let that foul creature ruin my victory."

"Don't worry," Felicity grunted. "He won't. Not directly, anyway."

Marshall gave her a puzzled sneer. Just then, a shrill sound, like guitar feedback, pierced the air. It was Starpollen, who had started to cry when Sammy ran away from him. As Starpollen's wail grew louder and louder, hundreds of Aura energy particles began to dance and weave around the young boy like a massive swarm of fireflies.

"Shut it!" Marshall shouted. He raised the wavebow to his mouth and plucked out another stunning cast. Distorted by Starpollen's unusual ability, the resulting stream of red light streaked and twisted wildly about the cavern, dispersing the agitated Aura particles throughout it. "What the devil?" Marshall exclaimed as he struggled to control the errant stream of energy with one arm. After a few seconds, he stumbled, and the wavebow fell out of his grasp.

Joel and Felicity noticed the opportunity at the same time, and both of them started to rush over to the fallen instrument. The drones around their necks reacted by quickly slithering down to their legs, tripping them. After falling hard to the ground, Joel reached out and tried to drag himself forward. As he did so, he saw Marshall, sans wavebow, moving at a surprisingly fast pace toward Starpollen.

"I—said—shut it!" the former Biledriver singer yelled as he raised his hand to strike the boy.

"Stop!" a voice shouted. Joel looked over his shoulder. It was Auravine, holding one of the rocks from a nearby pile. A fraction of a second later, her arm whipped forward and the rock went flying through the air. It zipped over Joel and struck Marshall square in the back of the head.

Wow, Joel thought, marveling at Auravine's accuracy. *She could be a baseball pitcher—a first-round draft choice, even.*

"How dare you hit me?" Marshall barked, turning around.

"You will not hurt my brother!" Auravine screamed, hurling another rock. "Get away from him!"

"Then tell him to be quiet!" Marshall shot back.

"Sammy—go to Starpollen!" Felicity shouted as both she and Joel continued crawling on their elbows toward the wavebow on the ground.

Sammy did as he was told. Then, while Marshall was busy trying to fend off the near-constant barrage of rocks from Auravine, Starpollen stopped crying once Sammy was back in his arms. After that, the Aura within the cavern started to settle down. As it did so, Felicity stretched out with one hand and grabbed the body of the wavebow on the ground. Before she could place her other hand on its neck, though, the drone Lightsnake around her legs slithered up and restrained her arm. So she slid the instrument over to Joel, who seized it with both hands, lifted it ever so slightly, and fired off a brief stunning cast at Marshall that hit the disfigured offworlder right between the eyes.

"Nice shot," Felicity gasped as Marshall fell, face-first, to the ground.

"Thanks," Joel replied, also breathless. "That was, uh—that was a pretty good plan."

"Honestly, I was just winging it."

"Are the two of you all right?" Auravine asked as she ran up.

"Funny question for you to be asking," Felicity muttered.

"Yeah, we are," Joel replied.

"I am truly sorry for I everything I have done," Auravine said as she retrieved her instrument from Joel. "I hope that you will be able to forgive me." She played several short notes, and the Lightsnakes that were restraining Joel and Felicity went limp.

"We'll see about that," Felicity grumbled, getting to her feet.

Joel stood up as well, and the ground began to shake. "Um...I don't think we're done here yet."

"Of course we're not," Felicity said with a humorless chuckle.

"The plane must be collapsing," Auravine said as she looked around. "Chief Byle kept it stable as long as he was in wraith form, but now..."

"Go and set Nineteen free," Joel instructed her. "He should be able to teleport us out."

Auravine nodded and headed over to Nineteen, who was still trapped in his Aura-cage. At the same time, Joel and Felicity hustled over to Fireflower and pried the drone Lightsnakes off of her.

"Thank you," she said, quickly stunning the drones as they tried to slither away. "I will revive the others."

Nineteen came trotting up, followed by Auravine.

Hello, Joel, the tiger-ram creature's voice sounded in Joel's head.

"Nineteen!" Joel said as the shaking got worse and pieces of the cave's roof began to fall. "Not to be rude, but—can you teleport us out of here? You know, like you did in Prism Valley?"

Nineteen paused for a moment before replying. *Unfortunately, there does not seem to be enough energy available here for me to do that.*

"What did he say?" Felicity demanded.

"There's not enough energy," Joel replied. He turned back to Nineteen. "How long do we have?"

About three minutes and thirty-one seconds. I will be fine here, but you and the others must escape before then.

"Let me guess," Felicity said, "not long, right?"

"Yeah," Joel answered, his head starting to spin. "Um, Nineteen—can you do that bubble trick?"

I am afraid not, Nineteen replied. *After being locked up in that cage for so long, it will be some time before I am able to perform that particular transformation again.*

"I take it by the look on your face that the answer is no," Felicity said to Joel.

"Um...right."

Fireflower came running back over, followed closely by the other Wavemakers. "What is going on?" she asked.

"The place is falling apart," Felicity replied.

"We only have three minutes left to escape," Joel added.

"I can fly us all out," Auravine declared. "I have more than enough energy."

"But how can we trust you?" Redstem snapped. "We were like sisters, Auravine, and then you—you nearly killed us all!"

"I—I know that you—"

"What if she lends her energy to everyone?" Joel suggested, anxious to head off a time-wasting argument.

"That is a great idea," Windblade said.

Fireflower shook her head. "No—that process would take far too long. We have no choice. Auravine—go ahead."

Auravine nodded, closed her eyes, and started to play the flying melody.

"Wait—what about Marshall?" Joel asked.

"I say we leave him here to perish along with his accursed domain," Riverhand said.

"I don't think we should do that," Joel countered. "It wouldn't be right. We should take him back with us and put him in prison."

"Besides," Felicity added, "leaving bad guys unaccounted for is never a good idea, believe me."

"I agree," Fireflower said. "He comes with us."

Riverhand made a little grumbling sound but said nothing else. Auravine resumed playing, and a huge cloud of dark-green Aura energy billowed out of her wavebow. It surrounded everyone: native and offworld Wavemakers, Starpollen, Sammy, Nineteen, and even the stunned drone Lightsnakes.

I regret that I cannot come with you, Nineteen's voice said. *But I would like to say—thank you, Joel. You have done well, once again. We will speak again soon.*

Joel nodded at Nineteen as the Aura cloud passed through the tiger-ram creature and lifted everyone else up into the air. Auravine glanced at Joel, as if to ask *isn't he coming too?* Joel shook his head, and they took off. As they passed through the cave entrance, Joel spotted his and Felicity's wavebows on the ground in the area where the giant sparkleblock had been.

"Our wavebows!" he exclaimed.

Fireflower played a short note, and their instruments zoomed up into their hands.

"You're gonna have to teach us that one," Felicity said.

With Auravine in the lead, they flew through the narrow passageway, past the pool, and back up into the surreal chessboard landscape. Everything around them was fading and flickering, like a spotty television signal. Joel estimated that they had just over two minutes left.

"You know where the exit is, right?" Felicity asked Auravine.

"I—I used to," the young healer replied, "but now it is hard to tell, with everything breaking up like this."

"Hold on," Joel said, noticing two familiar and stable shapes off in the distance. "I see something—I think it's the Lightsnakes that took us."

"They probably just woke up," Felicity said.

"Yeah," Joel agreed. "So if you go that way," he said, pointing, "we should be able to find the exit!"

Auravine nodded. The cloud of flying Aura swirled for a bit, and everyone was rearranged into a *V* formation. Then they turned in the direction that Joel had indicated and tripled the speed at which they were moving.

"I hope you are right," Fireflower said as huge swaths of their surroundings began to light up and disappear, like burning celluloid.

Me too, Joel thought.

They flew for another minute before Joel saw that the shapes were, indeed, the full-grown Lightsnakes that had snatched him and Felicity away from the burning Wavemaker Temple. Standing on a patch of surface that was rapidly dissolving as it switched back and forth between red dirt and linoleum, the two reptilian creatures seemed undecided about which was the greater threat, their vanishing environment or the flock of shamans that was headed straight toward them.

"We shouldn't leave them here either," Joel said. He looked over at Auravine. "Can you pick them up?"

"Yes, but—"

“Okay, I’ll stun them first!”

Joel took aim with his wavebow and fired off two short blasts of red light that hit their marks. Then, as the group zoomed overhead, Auravine extended the flying cloud so that it scooped up the stunned Lightsnakes just as the patch they were standing on disappeared.

“Great, now where’s the exit?” Felicity said.

Joel scanned the area ahead. Mostly everything was white.

“Um—it’s hard to tell,” he replied.

“Use the Sight!” Felicity urged.

Despite the distracting urgency of the situation, Joel forced himself to clear his mind.

Random list...random list...something easy...all right, how about...band names that start with the letter M*, in any order: Metallica, Men At Work, Misfits—*

He looked around. Nothing.

Megadeth, Midnight Oil, Melvins—

Still nothing.

Minor Threat, Ministry, Motorhead, Motley Crue, Modest Mouse—

Finally, he noticed a faint, shimmering spot of orange in the air just off to their right.

“Over there!” he shouted, pointing.

The flying cloud veered toward the spot. Just as the last remaining pieces of scenery around them evaporated, Joel felt a cold, tingling sensation. He squeezed his eyes shut. For a long moment, everything seemed still and quiet. Then there was a loud *whoosh*, and Joel opened his eyes. When he did, he saw that they were soaring through the sky above Spectraland, and that the warm morning sun was shining down on them.

“Just in time, as always,” Felicity quipped.

CHAPTER 27: AFTERMATH

Joel looked around the clearing in front of the Wavemaker Temple once more. He took a deep breath, and the images reappeared before his eyes: ghostly echoes of the struggle between Stoneroot's forces and the full-grown Lightsnakes, playing out like a three-dimensional holographic movie that he was able to rewind and fast-forward at will. He saw that most of the guards had fallen victim to the Lightsnakes' attack, with only a few surviving. Whitenose had fled the scene, while Stoneroot and a couple of others had managed to use their sleepdarts to finally knock out their reptilian assailants. Afterward, they'd piled all of the bodies onto their slimebacks and left.

Okay, got it, Joel thought. He disengaged the Sight and trotted back up the wooden stairs, which were in surprisingly good shape; thanks to the cold rain from the Moonfire, the temple had been spared major damage from the Silencers' flame-darts. In the main hall, Redstem was sitting atop the dais with her eyes closed, deep in meditation as a rainbow-colored halo slowly swirled around her head. Felicity was also there, leaning against one of the pillars and half-heartedly fiddling with the sparkleblock that Rocktoe had given to Joel.

"Where is everyone?" Joel asked.

"Shh," Felicity said. "Redstem's still recharging. And I'm next."

"Oh—sorry," he whispered.

"I think Sammy and the kid are with Riverhand somewhere, and Windblade went to take a nap."

"What about Fireflower?"

"She's up in the lookout. Did you find out what she wanted to know?"

"Yeah."

"You can tell me about it later. I'm too tired for any more stories right now."

"Okay."

As Joel started to leave the hall, he heard a soft, high humming sound. He turned to look back at Felicity. She held up the sparkleblock—which was glowing bright gold—and smirked.

"Not bad, huh?" she said.

"We'll make a puzzle-solver out of you yet." Joel grinned.

He headed into the courtyard, walked up the celery-stalk ramp at the far end, and arrived at the lily-pad platform overlooking the field behind the main structure. Fireflower was standing alone there with her back turned to him.

"Um...are you okay?" he asked as he walked up to her.

"Yes, thank you," she replied without turning her head. "And yourself?"

"I'm good."

"You were gone for quite a while. Were you able to find anything?"

"Yeah, a lot, actually," Joel said. He went on to describe what he had seen a few minutes ago in the clearing.

Fireflower turned to him with a raised eyebrow. "That is much more information than I was expecting."

"I know. I was just looking for trails, like you asked, but then all of a sudden I started seeing all of that other stuff. It was kinda weird."

"It appears as if your Sight power has become somewhat...enhanced."

"I guess so, yeah. Don't ask me how that happened."

"Very interesting," Fireflower said. For a moment, she seemed distracted, as if she were trying to remember something. The moment passed, and she looked back up at Joel. "Well," she continued, "whatever the cause, your new abilities should be helpful when we present evidence to the chiefs about Stoneroot's misdeeds."

"Yeah," Joel agreed. "Just wish I would've been able to do that sooner. Then we might've known that Auravine was working with Marshall from the very beginning, and we wouldn't have wasted all that time getting those stupid antidote ingredients."

"But then you would not have learned about Stoneroot's plot," Fireflower said. "Or had what sounded like some very exciting adventures."

"Not sure I'd consider almost drowning to be an exciting adventure," Joel muttered.

Fireflower chuckled. "Now you are starting to sound like Felicity."

"Hmm, I guess I am."

"Even though those ingredients did not help in the end, I am sure that you gained some valuable insights and experience along the way," Fireflower said in a motherly tone. "I believe that you have a saying like this in your world: oftentimes, the journey is just as important, if not more so, than the destination."

"Well, I did find out that Felicity's favorite Indiana Jones movie is the first one."

"I am not quite sure what you just said." Fireflower smiled. "But it sounds like something that is good for you to know. And besides, that antidote might still come in handy one day."

As Joel mulled that over, he stared out at the wide, grassy field. On the other side of the field near the edge of the temple grounds was a small hut, covered in a dome of golden Aura energy; it was the temporary holding cell for all of the prisoners they'd brought back with them from the alternate plane.

"Do you think it's okay to be keeping Auravine in there?" Joel asked. "You know, with Marshall and the Lightsnakes?"

"Yes, it is," Fireflower replied, her smile fading away. "The security measures that I put in place will prevent them from communicating with each other."

"Well, no, I mean, shouldn't she get to stay in her own room? You could still keep her locked up in there, or whatever."

"She is fortunate that we are not sending her straight to the Pit of Ashes," Fireflower said, an edge of bitterness creeping into her voice. "At least not until after her trial."

"She did change her mind about helping Marshall, though. And she flew us all out of there in the end."

"That does not change what she did prior to that, I am afraid," Fireflower sighed. "You must understand, Joel—she was like a daughter to me. There is nothing I would like more than to forget that all this ever happened. But her actions jeopardized not only our lives but the lives of everyone on this island. And possibly on your homeworld, as well. As a wraith, Marshall was limited in terms of what he could do, but if he had been fully restored to his physical form, who knows what evil deeds he may have been able to accomplish."

"Yeah, you're right," Joel said. "Speaking of Marshall, is he gonna get a trial too?"

"I assume that he will, even though he does not deserve it. But that is up to the Chieftain Council to decide."

Joel paused before asking his next question. "Did—did you hear what he said?"

"About what?"

"About me...killing him. Do you think that's true? That I killed him, and so now I deserve nothing but suffering?"

Fireflower turned to face him. "Oh no, Joel, that is definitely *not* true. You did not kill him. In fact, you gave him exactly what he wanted when you tossed the Songshell to him."

"But I knew that it was gonna blow up."

"You also warned him not to continue holding it. Remember?"

"Yeah...I guess."

"At that point, it was his choice. He could have thrown it away, but he decided not to. His desire for its power was the only thing he could think about."

Joel took a deep breath. She was right, but at the same time, he felt that maybe there was more he could have done to prevent Marshall's death. Provided a better warning, perhaps. But then, if Marshall hadn't died at that moment, what would have happened? Maybe he would have woken up before Joel and the others did. Maybe he would have escaped and caused more havoc.

Joel shook his head. *Remember*, he scolded himself, *you can't change the past, no matter how much you regret something you did or didn't do.*

"Here," Fireflower said, pulling a scroll out of her tunic, "I would like you to have this."

"What is it?"

She handed him the scroll. "It is an incantation that will allow you to travel back and forth through the Rift on your own. I apologize—I should have given this to you sooner."

"Oh—uh, thanks," Joel said, unrolling the parchment. A rather complicated-looking piece of music was written on it, but it was nothing that he couldn't handle. "I wouldn't have left anyway. Not until we were able to find you guys."

"I know you would not have," Fireflower said with a soft chuckle. "But now that we are all safe and the main villains are in captivity, you should return home and finish your performance."

"Wait—what? But I thought you wanted me to help you tell the chiefs about Stoneroot. And don't we need to stay here for Auravine's trial? And Marshall's, if he has one? And also..." he trailed off, recognizing the "I would like to say something" expression on Fireflower's face.

"You need to return tonight, Joel, or else you will not make it in time."

"But—"

"Look at this," she said, pointing to a group of notes on the scroll. "This particular part of the incantation will enable you to come back to Spectraland without a large amount of time passing by. You just need to perform it within three days of returning to your world. Which, I must say, is a very fascinating place. Full of amazing music. I studied that one performer—Sting, I believe he is called—from a distance for quite some time."

"Oh—uh, yeah," Joel said awkwardly. *Does Fireflower have a crush on Sting?* "Anyway, so...what you were saying is that I can go back, finish the show, and then get back here in time for everything?"

"Precisely."

"Cool. But, um...why didn't you give this to us the last time? You know, nineteen years ago?"

"Because it did not exist." Fireflower smiled. "The original version was lost with Marshall, so I had to compose a new one, which I did fairly recently."

"Fireflower!" a voice exclaimed.

Joel turned. Yellowpetal was running toward them, and striding across the lily-pad platform behind her was Chief Silverfern and Thornleaf.

"Mother?" Fireflower said, sounding surprised as Yellowpetal wrapped her up in a tearful embrace. "What are you all doing here? How did you—"

"I am so glad you are all right." Yellowpetal smiled. "We ran into Redstem in the main hall, and she explained everything that had happened." The elderly native looked at Joel. "Thank you, once again."

"Um, okay," Joel said. "But...we thought you and Thornleaf were..."

"Whitenose told me all about Stoneroot," Chief Silverfern said. "About his plans to make a mind-control potion, and how he attempted to kill you and burn down this temple. Once I knew about that, I sent my guards to his stronghold, where they arrested him and released his prisoners."

"Then we rode the swordcats back here to try to rescue all of you," Thornleaf added. "But apparently, that was not necessary."

"Then you know what was causing the Moonfires?" Fireflower said to Silverfern.

"I do now," the Headsmouth chief replied. "And I am relieved that they, and their related effects, will no longer be plaguing us. I told Thornleaf that I will allow the continued use of your flying cast."

"What about Chief Twotrunk?" Joel asked. "He seemed to be the one who was the most against it."

"I am sure that he will agree," Silverfern said. "But if not, he will be outvoted," she added with a slight smile. "Tell them what else, Thornleaf."

"Chief Silverfern has asked that I represent the Wavemaker Order in a new round of mediation talks with Roundbark and the other remaining Silencer members," the tall shaman said.

Silverfern looked at Fireflower. "That is all right with you, I trust?"

"Well—of course," Fireflower said, glancing back and forth between Thornleaf and Silverfern, "but are you sure that..."

"I am confident that Thornleaf will do an excellent job." Silverfern smiled.

"I did a lot of thinking and reflection while I was in Stoneroot's prison," Thornleaf said, "and I realized that a lot of my issues with the Silencers were due to my feelings about Stoneroot as a father. While he must stand trial for his crimes, I know that I need to try to forgive him on a personal level, so that I can see the other point of view a little more clearly."

Hmm, Joel thought. *Forgiving your dad...maybe I need to work on that too.*

Fireflower raised an eyebrow. "Do I sense...a little bit of maturity?"

"Perhaps." Thornleaf smirked.

"Well," Joel said to Fireflower, "since it sounds like we don't need to talk to the chiefs anymore, do you still want us to come back?"

Fireflower nodded. "Yes, please," she replied. "Your testimonies will be needed at the trials for Auravine and, now, Stoneroot."

"Okay."

"Also, if you are willing," Silverfern said, "there is something else that you could help us with as well."

"What's that?"

"Darkeye escaped from the Pit of Ashes," the Headsmouth chief answered. "It seems that after Stoneroot had Amberweed taken away, he neglected to replace her with another guard."

"Darkeye probably noticed that no one was coming down to feed him," Thornleaf added, "so he took advantage of the situation. Apparently, he is a lot stronger than he appears."

"Your Sight ability should make recapturing him a much easier task," Fireflower said.

Joel nodded. "Sounds good."

♪♪♪

"Okay, here's your first aid kit," Julio said as he dashed down the stairs. "Now, hurry up and—what the—what happened to you guys?"

Joel looked down at himself. Their costumes were now basically in shambles, with most of the green body paint having long been washed away and the arm-leaves lost in the many skirmishes they'd just gone through in Spectraland. Trevor's bass solo was booming along upstairs.

"Wardrobe change," Felicity said. "You know, for the encore."

"What? What encore? And where's that little girl? And you—" Julio squinted at Joel's face, making Joel feel very uncomfortable. "Your lip—it's not bleeding!"

"Turns out, that was just ketchup," Felicity said. "Take care of this dude"—she nodded at the still-unconscious zombie-werewolf—"while we finish the show, all right?"

"All right, fine, whatever. Just get back up there!"

Felicity grabbed Joel's hand. Her palm felt soft and warm in his as she led him up the stairway back to the stage. "Another point for me." She smirked, looking back at him.

"Huh? Oh—uh, right."

"You still don't know what I'm talking about."

"Um, yeah, I don't."

"Whenever one of us does something to get us out of a sticky situation, I give that person a point," she explained as they stopped at the top of the stairs just off to the side of the stage. "And so far, I'm winning—seventeen to sixteen."

Joel's mind whirled with excitement. Now he wanted to count too. "Oh, cool! But wait—is it just one point per situation? What about if it's life threatening—are there bonus points for that? Because if so, I—"

"C'mon, dude, let's finish the show," she said, running back out onto the stage.

Joel followed her as the crowd erupted into cheers. He smiled as he thought about Felicity's cool point system. Maybe, like Art said, they did have a lot more in common than he thought. Working on his own point system in his head, Joel picked up his guitar and started up the next song, pleasantly distracted.

www.joelsuzuki.com